LIKE OUR ENEMIES

ALBERON, BOOK ONE

K. M. Evans

Copyright © 2026 K. M. Evans

All rights reserved.

No part of this book may be reproduced, distributed, or transmitted in any form or by any means, including photocopying, recording, or other electronic or mechanical methods, without the prior written permission of the publisher, except in the case of brief quotations embodied in critical reviews and certain other noncommercial uses permitted by copyright law.

This novel is entirely a work of fiction. The names, characters, and incidents portrayed in it are the work of the author's imagination. Any resemblance to actual persons, living or dead, events, or localities is entirely coincidental.

Special thanks to Shadiversity on YouTube, for inspiring the back sheath design

Published by PandaFox Publishing

First edition.

ISBN (Paperback): 978-1-971835-00-6
ISBN (Hardcover): 978-1-971835-02-0
ISBN (eBook): 978-1-971835-01-3

Printed in the United States of America

For Corey,
Another day, another adventure

Table of Contents

I	1
II	12
III	22
IV	32
V	42
VI	54
VII	63
VIII	74
IX	81
X	91
XI	100
XII	118
XIII	128
XIV	138
XV	149
XVI	166
XVII	180
XVIII	190

XIX	198
XX	208
XXI	219
XXII	230
XXIII	240
XXIV	247
XXV	258
XXVI	267
XXVII	278
XXVIII	288
XXIX	299
XXX	309
XXXI	323
XXXII	336
XXXIII	350
XXXIV	364
XXXV	369
XXXVI	387
THE MOUNTAIN SONG	396

I

Over the land of Alberon a stale wind blew. On its back a gray-winged gull rode, feathers gleaming in the hot sun from its morning of splashing in the lake that crowned the mountain. It glided over a lush pine forest. The warm air rose above the trees, doing the work to keep it aloft until, with a twitch of its white head, the bird angled toward a wooden outcropping. The perfect spot for a rest and a preen. Three humans stood below the gull's perch and the bird cocked its eye to watch them for a few breaths before folding its head back to nibble at the itch it had stopped to scratch.

At last. Rest.

❖ ❖ ❖

Abner's brow rose beneath the guard's assessing scowl.

"Where you bound, strangers?" The guard's knuckles tightened around the leather-wrapped hilt of his rusted sword.

"An inn, if there is such a thing in this forsaken hovel of an outpost." Abner pushed his voice louder over the bleat of animals being herded into their pens for the night. It was nearing the last mark of the day and the pounding heat of the sun soured his mood almost as much as his sore feet.

Cantus, at Abner's side, handed the guard a coin from his belt. "Could you direct us?"

The guard pawed at the gold, the pressed image of a crown glinting in the light of the torches behind him, and gave a vigorous nod. "Aye, what you want to do is head straight down the main way, then—"

This bleeding muck! Abner pulled his boots from the squelching mud of the path and knocked them against the wooden wall of the outpost with ringing violence, cursing the clods stubbornly clinging to his soles.

A gull picking through its feathers above squawked at him before taking flight.

He brushed a gray feather from his sleeve before following his companion past the guard.

"Oi, be sure to get there before it gets properly dark. It is Demon's Time after all." The guard had already turned back to watch the empty road running out through the valley of Shiloh.

"What did he say?" Cantus asked, his eyebrows pinching together above his eyes. "The *what* time?"

"Demons," chuckled Abner, swinging his loose arms. "Dragons don't seem that far off anymore, do they?" They took the described left turn at the seamstress shop, bringing into view the inn, little more than a shack, ahead of them.

His companion paused, casting a glance over his shoulder. "Think we should turn back, start making our way to Lydia?"

"What? Cantus, don't tell me the 'ever brave and honorable soldier' is still afraid of some children's nightmare story? Demons! Ha!"

"No," the soldier replied, a little too quickly. "I just think that we shouldn't risk being exposed."

Abner rolled his eyes and swung his thick cloak back from his shoulders as he strode forward. "Five weeks we've traveled the kingdom and no one has recognized us. Not one person. You need to stop worrying and focus on our task."

They reached the rough wooden door of the foremost shack, a sign hanging from a jutting arm off the wall. The lantern swinging in the slight breeze above it cast a pale light to compete with the fading sun, and Abner read:

DRINKS INSIDE

It had a carved image of a frothing mug below the words. Hanging off the door was a smaller sign scrawled by hand and barely distinguishable from the weathered wood, adorned with a gathering of carved circles.

Must Pay

Abner smiled, brushing his hand along his belt still heavy with coins after weeks of travel.

"Wait," Cantus said. "You've proven yourself. Let's go home, while we still can."

"Cantus," Abner spit out the name like a piece of gristle caught in his teeth, "You've been given an honor above your station to accompany me. You should feel blessed! Instead you—"

"A lot of good *his* blessing does me if I am dead and devoured by some dark force." The words came out in a rush of panic unusual for the soldier. He took a shaky breath. A long stretch of tense silence followed as he ran a hand over his jaw and pulled his eyes to the ground. "Forgive me, but haven't we risked enough to please him already?"

"I would choose my next words very carefully."

Cantus swallowed. "Forgive me."

Abner shook his head. "Cantus, forgiveness is the one luxury I cannot afford." He paused, a slow grin working its way across his features. "But you can earn back some of my trust."

"How?" Cantus asked.

Abner tipped his chin. "Spend a night with the demon." He snatched Cantus' pack and strode inside, snapping the wooden barrier closed before Cantus could react. Laughing at his own joke, Abner sat himself purposefully at the bar. His nose stung with the odor of the never-washed as he rapped his knuckles on the wooden counter and took in the scene.

Four tables were spread in no definable pattern across the one room shack. A ladder led up to the ceiling where a second level must have served as the barkeeper's apartment. The man himself was a sallow faced, sickly looking fellow with gray hair hanging past his chin on either side of his heavy cheeks. The other men in the bar looked just as unkempt. Abner's eyes swept over a thin man who raked his parchment skin with long dirty nails and his companion whose wide girth was only matched by his bristling red hair.

The barkeeper stumbled over to Abner, looking by his walk as if he'd had one too many himself. "What'll i' be mis'er?"

"Your best, whatever that is."

"Did yeh see tha' sign outside?"

Abner glanced at the door, muttering to himself, "I have money, obviously. I'm not some filthy peasant." Raising his voice and his eyes to the barkeeper's, he said, in his most commanding tone, "My drink? Shouldn't you be going to get it?"

The old man's eyes narrowed as he shuffled away.

An eternity of waiting passed before Abner's shoulders slumped in a heavy sigh. "Curse every Fate. Snails would swim across the Merdian

Sea faster than you pour a bottle! What do I have to do to just get my drink?"

The barkeeper slid a mug to him.

The snide comment died in Abner's throat as a breeze ruffled his cloak and the room became deathly still. Abner turned as the tavern's side door—opposite the one he had entered by—closed. His body stiffened, his heart beating out a pounding anthem against his ribs. The certainty of greater forces than he had ever known crashed on him like never before as the black-clad specter glided into the room.

"The demon," he whispered. *Maybe I should fetch Cantus after all.*

Abner turned back to the bar, tingling energy coursing from the auburn hairs on his head to his long sun-touched fingers.

The specter sat two seats down and signaled to the old man. Speaking so low that no one could hear the words, the demon gave its orders and the barkeeper lumbered off as quick as he could to fulfill them.

Abner licked his lips, scratched his nose, anything to avoid looking at the terrifying robed figure. But, like a moth drawn to the flame that meant death, his eyes strayed to its hem, slowly creeping up with the fabric until he was staring into the wide gaping hole of the creature's drawn hood. A low growl rattled from its depths and Abner recoiled so suddenly he toppled off the stool. Righting himself with a muttered swear, Abner tried to relax. A hissing laugh trickled through the air.

The bartender returned through the side door with three or four bags strapped together and laid them at the creature's feet. He poured a drink for the demon, who, inclining its hood, reached with a gloved hand toward the counter and set down a few copper bits.

Abner's breath caught. Expecting to see a claw or talon, and instead seeing normal fingers was the worst shock yet.

The bartender shook his head and pushed the money back to the creature. "Yeh don' need to pay here. Yeh know tha'."

"Thank you," rasped a voice from beneath the hood.

Something strange in the quality of it made Abner stare.

It wasn't until the hood turned to stare back that he realized his mistake.

Looking away, Abner gathered his drink and found a table in a far corner. He tried not to notice his movements being tracked the entire way and the attention fixed on him as he took a slow, cautious sip. He didn't even taste his drink but felt it hit his stomach like a spear to his gut as it mixed with the roiling anxiety already making his limbs weak and his hands shake. Abner hazarded a glance at the bar a moment later and saw the creature's attention had shifted away.

Slowly, the murmured conversation of the other patrons resumed as the creature quietly raised the mug to its hood for a long drink.

"As I's sayin', that other king is watchin' the land. He won't be content for long to sit and wait for this tyrant's death and an untimely accident to off the prince." The thin man held a shaking finger above his mug as he spoke, his wide eyes flashing in the lantern light. "An' what'll happen to all us ordinary folks when he makes his move, eh?"

"You worry worse than my wife, Brannon," the red-haired man said, picking at his teeth carelessly with a long, dirty fingernail. He studied the gray bit of old meat pinned beneath his nail before sucking it off and swallowing it down.

Abner's mouth bent in disgust.

"Even if the prince gets gutted, oh well. We've survived one tyrant's takeover in our lifetime, we can do another."

Abner's nails bit into his palms as he listened to these men continue to abuse their leader, discussing the old kingdom as if it were paradise, and describing the new king and his son as usurpers and trespassers. Heat rose in his blood, his skin feeling ready to boil.

"Let 'em burn, I say! The lot of them!"

"I'd drink to that—"

Laughter followed with sounds of scattered approval.

"Apparently," Abner said, not looking at either man but speaking just loud enough for them to hear. "Treason to the king is not considered a crime. Apparently the people of this...hovel of an outpost believe themselves beyond the reach of their king."

Both men looked at Abner with wide eyes. He took a long slow sip of his drink, unfortunately tasting the foul flavor this time, before returning their stare.

"Do you have no fear of your king?"

The barroom grew still as the air thickened.

Abner ignored the needle pricks of fear creeping across the back of his neck as the hood turned toward him. He rose, pulling back his cloak enough for the men to see the ruby-pommeled sword at his hip.

The thin man's mouth fell open and his bristly red-haired companion leaned away from Abner, pulling his eyes down.

"Do you fear now, Peasant?"

His thin head bobbed subserviently.

"Stand."

He did, his knees knocking into the table as his eyes darted, searching for a hole to hide in.

"Do you know what the punishment of such words would be in Lydia?"

His head bobbed again.

"Good, then you'll understand." Abner grabbed a fistful of his greasy tunic in one hand as the other launched into the man's jaw. The *smack* of Abner's fist hitting the traitor's scruff-lined cheek echoed through the shack. He expected the throbbing ache in his knuckles, but was taken by surprise at the answering blow that knocked his head into spiraling pain.

His mind slipped away.

Dreaming of dragons and hooded demons, Abner faded in and out of consciousness so frequently that he wasn't sure which images were real. Was it a nightmare he saw of him being dragged by his ankle through the woods by a gloved hand and a hooded face? Was reality his father's beaming smile as Abner presented his sword to him, successful at last in his mission? The look of glowing approval and pride in his son made Abner sure that this must be a dream. Still, it was with profound regret that he opened his eyes and found himself outside.

His lip was bleeding. This was the first irritation he noticed. It was also difficult to draw a full breath. His hands were bound and stretched behind him, tied around the trunk of an old dead tree. He was sitting on the ground, back pressed into the gray rotting trunk while his feet splayed out before him, stiff and uncomfortable. His back ached, pummeled like a blacksmith's discarded anvil. His ears rang with the silence of the wood.

"I'm in the forest," Abner whispered, terror sharpening his foggy mind. His half-remembered dream took shape again. "I've been taken by the demon." His eyes frantically raked the dense ferns and crowding trees, what little he could see, for the monster coming to devour him.

"My sword," he whispered, stretching against his bonds to stare at the empty sheath on his hip. Of course, it wouldn't still be there. Supernatural did not mean stupid, and he knew he would gladly sacrifice that ghoul's life for his own. He cursed to himself, trying to keep his breathing even, forcing his mind to remember his training.

It did no good.

He was terrified and that was not going to change.

A ripple in the ferns twenty paces ahead stole his breath. His eyelids stretched wide, a vain attempt to better see when death was coming. His shoulders jerked the ropes holding him as the ferns parted, and his jaw grew tight as a black paw stepped out of the greenery. Abner, shocked into stillness, watched the long slender form of a fox appear.

The red face snapped to him in surprise and almost backed out of view again.

"Here boy ... girl? Um, fox?" Even if it was a dirty stray, something so brightly colored and so vibrantly alive made Abner feel braver and even hopeful.

The black tipped ears of the fox pinned on Abner. It crept forward a few steps.

"That's a good fox."

It paused, shining wet nose twitching. Another step closer.

"That's it, just keep coming over. Nice and slow."

Cautiously sniffing the air, the fox paused again. Its ears swiveled in a new direction, pointing to where Abner couldn't see. It gave a loud sharp yip and listened. After a moment, it yipped again.

This time, there was an answering sound of footsteps loud enough for even Abner's ears. He looked at the fox.

"Get out of here," Abner whispered, jerking his head. "There's no telling what that *thing* will do to you. Go, while you still have your skin!"

An ear flicked in Abner's direction, but that was all the notice the fox gave to his plea.

"The only *thing* in this forest is you," rasped a voice just out of sight.

Abner wondered what it would be like when his spark left his body. As the robed figure swept into view, he couldn't move beyond this mire of horror. *How would it feel to die?*

The demon carried a heavy object under its arm, moving clumsily as if not used to the weight. Abner forgot its awkwardness instantly as the hood turned to the red fox.

"Get out of here!" Abner yelled, pulling against the ropes.

The demon paused. A fierce whistle pierced the air.

The fox came trotting forward, sitting comfortably at the dark creature's heel. Its white-tufted tail curled over its black paws. The red face watched Abner warily.

"You've cast a spell on it," Abner said, the bark of the old tree crunching beneath his back as he leaned into it.

A rasping chuckle was the only reply.

"Who are you?" Abner demanded. *What are you?*

The creature turned away and began to gather bits of bracken and sticks off the ground. In the process, it set down the heavy thing it had been carrying.

Abner's eyes jumped wide. "That—that sword is mine."

"Find another," the creature said, as carelessly as a demon could speak. It struck a black rock with a sharp stone. Sparks bounced between the two before landing on the pile of bracken the creature had gathered. A fire soon took.

"That one is special. It was given to me by—" he clasped his mouth shut.

"By?" the demon repeated. The fire sent a curling trail of smoke through the towering trees as the thing strode forward. "Who gave it to you?"

Abner said nothing, his jaw locking as he stared into the hooded darkness. "If you were going to kill me," he said with more confidence than he felt, "you'd have done it already."

"Are you worth killing? Or do you bring more trouble than you're worth? Who are you?" The specter leaned toward Abner.

He thought he saw a darker shape amidst the black of the hood's shadow and moved forward despite himself. Perhaps if the demon had a shape rather than a formless cloak it would be less terrifying.

The creature drew back with a hiss. "Where did you come from?"

"If I answer your questions, will you let me go?"

A flicker of something yellow caught the light, a thin strand trailing from the black of the hood as the demon considered its answer. It cocked its hood to one side before turning away without reply.

"I have information you may find valuable." Abner pressed forward, the ropes biting into the skin on his wrists.

"What information?"

"If I tell you, you'll let me go?" A vein throbbing at his throat sent blood pounding into his ears as he waited.

"Depending on what you say."

"I have a guard who travels with me. If I don't return soon, he will go back and tell them what happened. They'll come looking, and they will kill you, demon or not. He may already be on his way. Lydia's barely two days by foot."

The demon stilled, then kicked the sword with the toe of its boot. "Why is this sword so important?"

Abner hesitated. "A man came to court. He claims the ruby on the pommel is enchanted."

The specter froze and when it spoke again, the rasp was gone from its voice. "And what is this enchanted sword supposed to do?" The voice sounded strange now, high and almost breaking toward the last words, as if trying to keep from laughing.

"It's special. The ruby protects the owner from all harm by fire and—"

Cackling, the creature stomped, burying its gloved hands beneath the hood as it worked to stifle the sound.

Abner continued, voice fading with every syllable, "and it can harness the power of the dragon."

"The power of the dragon?" the hooded creature said, voice strained with holding in its mirth, though Abner began to have a suspicion that things weren't as he had thought before. "How would it do that?"

"A dragon would have to breathe fire onto the blade, and the heat would get stuck in the ruby and once you controlled the dragon's fire it gave you control of the beast, and I'm not really sure how it worked. He explained it all to my father."

"The king?"

"Yes, and he said—"

"That would make you the prince."

"I—what? No, I never said that!"

The fox yipped, as if surprised, and growled at Abner, taking a snap at his booted foot.

Kicking the animal away, Abner tugged at his ropes. He knew the demon would be afraid of him now, and he had seen fear motivate even ordinary men to do dreadful things.

"So, you're the prince," the hooded figure repeated, in a deadly whisper. "If I let you go you might return. If I kill you your father certainly will." The breath rasped low, thoughtful. "I never thought I would live to see the prince of Alberon in my forest."

"If you want to live to see the prince of Alberon leave it, you had better let me go." Abner lifted his chin and narrowed his eyes, trying to evoke the reaction in the specter that had been so easy to garner in his subjects. He waited for its hood to droop toward the ground, its shoulders to tighten and lift as if to protect its neck, or its gloved hands to shake.

Instead, the creature tossed a few twigs into the fire, calm and maddeningly careless.

"Let me go! Help! HELP!" he shouted, his tone caught somewhere between a demand and a plea.

"Shout till you're hoarse. It won't do you any good." The creature looked at him for a long dreadful moment, as if challenging him to shout again.

Abner stared at the dried mud caking his boot. "What do you want to know?"

"What is your father so afraid of that he would send his only heir to hunt dragons? The royal family who ruled here before him are all dead. What has he to fear?"

"He's not ... afraid. At least, not of anyone here, in Alberon. The rumors are true. I'm sure you've heard them."

The hooded figure gestured to the surrounding woods, as if to say "Out here?"

"No, I suppose you haven't."

"Normally Jathan tells me the news going around town. This month he didn't get a chance to." The creature turned away and looked into the forest.

"Well, my uncle must have heard how easily this country was taken."

The gloved hands of the hooded figure curled into tight fists and its frame seemed to fill with a sudden powerful energy.

"The family was slaughtered. It didn't take long. I'm sure you're ancient so you know what happened. My uncle's watched the prosperity his brother by union has enjoyed, the easy conquests and unchallenged rule. Apparently inheriting his birthright as my grandfather's heir is no longer satisfying. He's gathering supplies and craftsmen to build warships. It's been confirmed. He's coming."

The fox growled.

The figure's head snapped to Abner, causing the hood to slip. Hastily rushing to pull it back into place, the 'demon' turned away.

For a long moment, Abner couldn't believe it. Then he laughed. "All this time, I've been afraid of *you*?" he said, hysterically. "You're not a demon, there's nothing special about you. You're just a peasant girl who lives in the woods."

"If I'm just a girl, what does that make you, Prince?" challenged the girl, rounding back on him with her hood securely in place once more. The rasp was gone from her voice. "Future ruler of our kingdom knocked silly and taken captive by a 'peasant girl who lives in the woods.' I'm sure your father would be so proud."

"You came at me from behind. You cheated. In a fair fight I have never been beaten."

A call from a faraway bird made the girl turn to listen. After a moment, she picked up the sword.

The fox yipped in fright and bared its teeth at the blade.

The girl hesitated. Turning to Abner, she walked forward, the sword clenched in her hands.

"What are you going to do to me?"

"You're the prince." She dug the point of the blade into the soil at her feet.

"Abner," he said, staring at the black opening of her hood.

"What?"

"My name is Abner of Lydia."

The gloved hands loosened on the pommel of his sword.

"It's harder to kill with a name, isn't it?"

She tightened her grip. "Well, Abner of Lydia, I have a decision to make. I don't think the royals handle being beaten well. You pampered rich are rather sore losers."

"Again, you cheated."

The bird call rang louder this time.

The girl tensed but stayed with her body pointed toward Abner. "Do you want to die?"

"Never."

"But you'll sit and let it happen? How pathetic. Even a rabbit in a trap fights harder than you do."

Abner looked at the sword tip, still buried in the dirt, then back to the hood. "I'm not dying today."

"And why is that?" asked the girl, leaning forward.

"You cheated before."

The girl rubbed the pommel of the sword with her gloved thumb. "Well life hardly ever gives us a fair fight, so—"

Abner smiled. "I can cheat too." Abner shot his foot out, landing a heavy boot against the girl's knee.

Jumping backward, she dropped the sword.

"Now I just need to—" Abner grunted, struggling to twist out of the ropes binding his wrists. His feet locked around the sword to drag it toward him.

She kicked his ankle aside, drawing a hiss through Abner's teeth, before snatching the blade off the ground.

He struggled more fiercely against his bonds as the black hood leaned over him, sword raised in clenched hands. Abner tried to look away but couldn't. That ridiculous black cloak would be the last thing he ever saw.

"Please," he whispered. The lights of his eyes were extinguished with the first blow.

II

Esther lowered the sword as the prince's chin dropped to his chest.
Is he? Fox whined, standing at her ankle and giving the slumped figure a cautious sniff.

"No." Esther pulled her hood up to scratch a spot on her forehead before moving it back into place. "I just hit him on the head with the flat part. He should be fine." She nudged the figure with the toe of her black boot. "Not that he deserves it. Trying to kick out my legs." She looked around, unease tying her stomach into a knot of indecision.

Fox eyed the long glinting weapon in her hand. He whined again, louder.

"I can't get rid of it right now. We need to move. You know what that bird call meant. Someone new has entered our forest. We need to find them." She cast a wary glance to the bound, unconscious prince. "Quickly."

Tilting its head to one side, the fox watched Esther hurry off through the trees before trotting after her.

The wide clearing at the base of the steep water trail which served as their path from the deeper woods toward the outpost opened before them.

Standing at the top of the hill, looking down it with understandable trepidation, was the old barkeeper from Shiloh. His back was bent beneath several large parcels, carried from the bar.

"Jathan!" the girl called, waving.

His eyes found her and he smiled.

Esther scrambled up the water trail, her hood slipping back from her face. She didn't bother fixing it. Jathan was safe.

"Esther," Jathan said, embracing her against his dirty tunic. "Yeh had me worried. Where is tha' man from the bar?"

Esther cast a glance over her shoulder, as if afraid the prince would come stumbling out of the ferns any moment. "I've dealt with him. Everything will be fine."

Jathan watched her, eyes narrowing over his tightened mouth. He grunted as he dropped the bundles at her feet. "Here. Yeh'll need these supplies for the nex' month."

"Thank you, but it's dangerous for you to come to the woods. Especially during Demon's Time."

"There is no demon here," Jathan said, a hand on her arm.

"The villagers don't know that," Esther reminded him, nodding towards the outpost of Shiloh. *They can't. If they think I'm some supernatural monster, they'll leave me alone. No one would ever think of looking here. I could stay hidden.*

"Ten years," Jathan said, pushing a rock down the steep trail with the toe of his boot. "Ten years I've looked after yeh and I still have no idea where yeh came from, who yeh are."

"And I'm very grateful for your help. I was a nameless orphan who you took in, and that's all you ever need to know. Even that is too much for the others." Esther's eyes turned to the fox who waited at her ankle. She smiled at the white tufted face. "I have everything I need."

"What abou' the Lydian? His sword had jewels on it, and there was an attendan' with him. They'll come lookin'. Should Shiloh worry?"

Esther dug at the dirt with the toe of her boot. "No."

Fox's ears twitched back at the unease in her voice.

"He's nobody. There's nothing to worry about."

"Esther," Jathan said, drawing her eyes up to his. "You don' have to be alone in everythin'."

Esther swatted a grass bug buzzing at her ear. "I've taken care of him. I don't want you or Shiloh involved." She thanked him for the supplies, and made her way down the trail, keeping her eyes to the ground. The parcels thumped against her back as she ran.

"Esther!" Jathan called when she reached level ground, letting the momentum carry her to the deep forest edge. She paused just before passing out of sight through the ferns. "Should I be worryin' about yeh, then?"

She turned back with a grin. "Never!" she called and disappeared onto a narrow path through the thicket.

As soon as she was out of sight of Jathan, her bravado slipped away like morning dew beneath the harsh reality of glaring sunshine.

Fox seemed to feel the change. Fur bristling and teeth bared, he stalked beside her as his honey-gold eyes raked the vicinity for signs of trouble, a steady rumbling growl sounding at her knee. *What is it, Human?*

"Nothing. I—" *Poor Fox, he doesn't understand. I will deal with this. I just need a moment, some space to think.* "How about a swim? I'm sweating out of my skin in this cloak."

Fox yipped happily, fur smoothing at the sight of Esther's smile.

She stowed the packs beneath some low hanging branches, placing the sword on top of the bundle with a half-thought to protect it from rusting. Esther raised her brow at the fox, daring him to run. He bounced on his paws as Esther bounded forward. Together they raced through the trees, feet pounding the ground beneath in a sprint that sent them twisting around towering trunks and crashing through ferns with a wild, reckless spirit. Esther treasured every hammering heartbeat, every flick of the fox's white tufted tail as it raced underfoot, forcing her to veer off course.

If she hadn't spent ten years learning every clearing and path in these woods, she might have been surprised by the sudden opening of the ground where a clear spring flowed to fill a shallow pond. Her refusal to admit defeat by slowing down at the finish almost sent her toppling off the small rock face that rose out of the water, but her boots slid to a stop just in time.

The fox didn't slow but leaped off the ledge with a yipping bark, like a child's squeal, as he fell toward the pooling water.

"I win!" Esther called down, unclasping her cloak as the fox reappeared, sneezing water.

Oh, Human. It was a race to the water, not to the edge.

"That has never been the rule!" Esther tossed her gloves and boots aside. The leaves from last autumn still coated the ground, creating a soft padding for her to slide down toward the pond's edge. "If you can only win by cheating—"

Think what you want. The fox pulled himself up the rocky bank, aiming the spray at Esther as he shook free of the dripping water.

"Ugh, dirty dog! Go over there." She held a hand in front of her face.

I thought you wanted to get wet. He struck the water with his paw.

Esther coughed. "I don't like drinking this water. It always makes me feel funny afterward."

Well, I like it. Fox's tongue lapped the water, its white tail flicking at her.

"Really?" Esther grinned. "Let me help you then." She pushed him with her foot, sending the fox forward with a great splash.

He turned on her, honey eyes stretched wide as large beads dripped from his chin.

Esther laughed.

Fox's eyes narrowed. He gripped the leg of her breeches between his teeth, careful not to nip her ankle, and pulled.

"No!" Esther tried to twist away, but couldn't help her grin. "No, you'll tear it! Jathan just brought these the month before last."

Get. In. The. Water! He growled, shaking her heel.

It felt good, fresh, clean. Invigorating. Esther had always loved the water. She let her head dip back, her hair being pulled by the stream as it emptied to the woods beyond them. The water was also cold and offered clarity. A plan must be made.

"Fox?" Esther said, leaving her head in the water. He paused in his game of catching fish. "Have you ever wondered what was beyond the forest? East I mean."

You've always said there wasn't anything different than where we are now.

"Well, I don't know everything. Maybe there is. Wouldn't it be exciting to explore it?"

His feet stilled, and Esther stared at the sky, hoping he couldn't see the stinging tears collecting at the corners of her eyes. *You want to leave?*

Esther let go of her breath. "No. I couldn't leave Shiloh. But you—you could go. There's a world out there, Fox. Why not—"

You want me to leave you?

She blinked heavily, scrubbing at her face with the water. "No. I don't. But, I'm afraid. Fox, I don't want to die, but more than that I don't want you to get hurt."

The man. The man who brought the sword. You're afraid of him.

Esther nodded. "That man has an army that will kill anyone he says to, and no one can stop him or do anything about it. It would be like if every tree in this forest were a man like him with swords, and arrows, and ... if he decides to kill me, I'm already dead. No matter what I do, I can't think of a way out."

Fox swam toward her, finding the bottom of the pond with his back legs and planting his front paws on her arm. *Then we leave. Together.*

Esther shook her head. "So he takes his fury out on Shiloh? After all my years of protecting them, stopping wolves and bears from taking their livestock, I can't abandon them because of my mistake."

We run together, or we face it together. I won't leave you alone.

His honey eyes hardened. Arguing with him now would be as useful as arguing with a stone.

Esther ran a hand over the wet fur, spare strands clinging to her fingers. "You should go, Fox. But I don't want you to." Her eyes filled. "I'd beg you to stay."

No need.

Esther's head dipped toward the water. *Stop crying.* But she couldn't.

Fox's warm tongue rolled over her cheek, licking away the salt.

"Thank you," she whispered against the water.

❖ ❖ ❖

Abner was in the Lydian arena, the stands stretching impossibly high above him.

His father sat in his normal box, jewel-covered hands flashing as he shouted a proclamation Abner couldn't hear.

Shouldn't he be up with his father? Why was he down in the sand? Dread planted a blow through Abner's gut as the king pointed at him with one heavy finger.

The answering roar of the crowd thumped against his eardrums. "Death! Death! Death! Death!"

Abner turned.

The girl in black stood waiting. Her hood was down and golden hair flowed across her formless face. "It's harder to kill with a name, isn't it?" she said, the sound hissing toward him from the skin stretched where a mouth should be.

Abner stumbled away.

The form changed to Cantus who smiled coolly at him, gripping Abner's sword.

"Please," Abner begged, falling backward and dragging himself through the sand. His breath was shallow, his heart beat frantic.

Cantus strode after him.

The arena rang with the echoes of laughter at his cowardice.

"I can't die. I don't want to die. Please, Cantus! Forgive me."

"Forgive you?" Cantus said, letting his head roll to one side. "Abner … forgiveness is a luxury I can't afford." Cantus raised his sword.

Abner couldn't find his breath.

A flash of red and bared animal teeth engulfed the prince.

"Prince Abner? ABNER!"

Shaking, Abner opened his eyes and pulled in a sharp gasp as Cantus' face filled his vision. "What are you—where am I?" Blood pounded his temples. "A dream, just a dream," he told himself, composing the muscles of his face into a look of indignation. "What are you waiting for? Cut me loose!"

Cantus obeyed quickly, slicing through the rope tying Abner's hands and helping the prince to stand on shaking feet.

"How did you get back so quickly? Lydia is days away."

Cantus glanced over his shoulder. "I thought your life was worth more than revenge. I came looking for you myself."

Abner blinked. "But what about—"

"The demon's gone for the moment. It's never been seen in the daylight according to the villagers. You offered me a chance to earn back your trust and I've seen what happens to people who cease being of value to you." Cantus looked shocked at his own words, and tried to cover them by hastily continuing. "Here, Highness. I found this discarded on the trail beneath some trees. The demon must have stripped you of it on the way to its lair."

Abner took the sword, relief flowing down his back. "Thank you, Cantus. My father would not have forgiven me had I lost the enchanted sword he invested so much in."

"Should we make our way out of this accursed forest, Prince? The demon may come back. And, daylight or not, I'd rather not meet it." His eyes widened as he checked over his shoulder again.

Abner nodded for him to lead the way. "How did you find me?"

"I stayed in the village last night and asked questions about the demon this morning. Apparently it comes to town once a month and the bar gives it supplies. As long as the villagers let it pass through, it's never harmed them. When the story spread that you had been taken, the villagers were afraid to even speak of it, lest speaking draw it to them. I got enough information to know where to start looking. The forest seemed impossibly large to search, but, luckily, just as I was about to give up, I reached the top of a steep hill. From there, I saw a pillar of smoke. What a demon needs fire for, I have no idea, but I followed the smoke and eventually found you." Bending beneath some branches, they broke through the ferns.

A grassy clearing ahead rose to meet a flat topped hill with a scarred vein of dirt running down its side. Bugs buzzed through the grass and around their ears.

Abner stomped up the steep incline with gritted teeth. The sandy ground slipped away beneath him and Abner's cheek scraped against the brittle dirt. His breath hissed. He ignored Cantus' hand extended to help as he pushed himself up with a scowl. *I am not weak.*

"What happened?" Cantus asked, dropping his hand.

The prince hesitated. "The demon took me to her—its lair. I fought back and it clubbed me over the head."

"But it didn't devour you?"

"It didn't dare. I believe it's hoping that I will forgive the kidnapping and torture because it did not kill me. But forgiveness—" Abner stopped, his empty stomach twisting with a memory.

"Abner?" Cantus held out a hand to steady him.

"I'm fine, Cantus!" Abner snapped, slapping his hand away.

"Apologies."

Ripping through the last trees of the forest, Abner studied the mud crusted walls of Shiloh. He scowled at the grimy wood baking in the midday sun. "These people have no fear."

Cantus squinted at the outpost. "I don't know about—"

"They have no fear of their king. No fear of their prince. They think they are untouchable out here on the edge of the wilderness. I believe my father should know how his subjects treat him when he is not around to hear. We go to Lydia. My father must know what has happened."

Cantus' relief was visible.

Abner tossed his eyes to the sky. This decision wasn't guided by compassion for the soldier's terror. He had to do something. He couldn't live with this weakness in him. Abner would make himself strong, like his father, like Dennison, whatever the cost. He began to walk forward, purposeful and sure in the king's power to right this wrong.

"Shiloh will burn," he murmured to himself, as a mother coddles her newborn. He nursed his wounds with images of revenge, allowing them to consume any pity he might feel. This wasn't his fault, they had brought this fate on themselves. Justice would be done.

"And your father?" Cantus strode beside him. "The mission?"

"Dragons are a myth." Abner spat to the side. "My father knows that. The point of this was probably to prove I can fight my battles without an army. To teach me that man has nothing to depend on except himself. Now, go into town and get the packs."

Cantus nodded, trotting toward the gates. Abner leaned against the wall and closed his eyes.

"No beggars!" said a rough voice.

Abner ignored the grizzled old guard.

"I said no beggars!" The man poked at Abner's side with his rusted ax.

Abner pinned the ax to the wall with his hip against the flat of the blade, and wrestled the handle from the guard's twisted old hands. He knocked the old man onto his back before tossing the weapon aside.

The guard raised a hand to ward off the next attack, mumbling weakly to himself.

"I will be your KING!" Abner shouted. "I! Demand! Respect!" With each word, Abner landed a blow, venting frustration on the frail body crumpled beneath him.

"And you will have it," said a voice behind him.

Abner whipped around, ready for a fight. His eyes brightened as recognition broke over his features like first mark on the horizon. "Dennison! What are you doing here?"

Dennison's scarred face wrinkled into a smile as he dismounted from his towering gray horse. He handed the reins to a guard riding on his flank, and strode forward to greet his prince.

The guard who rode on the opposite side sat straighter in his saddle as he watched their exchange.

"Your father sent me."

"My father sent the captain of the royal guard to the edge of the kingdom to—what? Spy on his incompetent son?" The sting of anger singed Abner's empty stomach. "Doesn't he trust me?"

Dennison looked away with a folded brow.

"Well, you can report to my father that I am finished and will be returning to Lydia soon."

"I'm not here for you, Prince."

The crumpled heap on the ground moved at the title, and the old guard's features grew bloated with fear. Shaking hands raised in reverence, the old man crawled forward to bow. Abner treated the submissive posturing with as much notice as he would give a dog begging for a bone.

"Then why are you here?"

Dennison watched the prostrated man with contempt. "Reports of the eastern sickness have reached your father in Lydia. He wants me to investigate them. The last thing we need is a widespread malady."

"The only disease in Shiloh is disrespect for one's betters," Abner said, aiming a kick at the old man.

Dennison raised his brow with a nod. "My job is done then. Would you like accompaniment back to Lydia, Highness? The guards can travel back on foot and you can ride their horses."

Abner nodded. "I've sent Cantus inside for the packs. As soon as he returns, we'll leave."

"Yes, Sire," said Dennison, pulling the old man to his feet.

"Wait," Abner said, before Dennison could release the guard to scamper away. "Take him with us, along with any family he has."

"Sire?"

"My father will want to celebrate. It is only right that our subjects should share in the festivities."

A curious light lit Dennison's eyes as his lips pulled back to smile. "The Event? Very well." Dennison snapped his fingers and the guards dismounted, handing their reins to Abner before binding the man and leaving to gather his family.

Cantus returned a moment later, mounting the remaining horse, and the three men left, riding hastily back toward civilization.

Abner grimaced at the plains of yellowed grass, the dirty herds of sheep, and the hot sun beating above. His anger had cooled a little, so all that was left for him to feel was exhaustion, pain, and hunger. His shoulders ached, and the bright sun baked his eyes until they burned.

"Any news?" Abner asked. His pounding head was not helped by the beast's bouncing trot. He pulled it back into a walk.

Dennison and Cantus matched his pace.

"Nothing of note."

"No news?" Abner stared critically at the older man. "Dennison, I have traveled across this kingdom for weeks, seen every hovel and dirty-faced peasant this world has, and in all that time my uncle has made no move?"

The muscles in Dennison's jaw tightened for a moment before he spoke, but they were quickly smoothed away into a practiced calm. "Ships take time to build, Highness. An army does not gather in a day. And your father would not send you out alone if invasion were only weeks away." Dennison paused, an amused smile tugging at the corner of his mouth. "Did you find the dragons?"

Abner glared at him. "All I found were disrespectful peasants, bad food, and dirt."

Dennison chuckled.

"You knew there were no dragons. You knew my father was sending me out on a fool's mission."

Dennison's smile slipped away. He slowed his mount. "Cantus, go scout ahead."

Only after Cantus' retreating back grew hazy with distance did Dennison turn to face Abner. "Desperation can lead men to make rash decisions. Your father, the king, is desperate. He will sacrifice anything ... anyone, to hold onto his power."

"Careful." Abner pulled the leather reins through his fingers. "Words like that can get a man killed. Even a captain of the royal guard."

Dennison stopped to study Abner. "So can silence, Sire."

The prince's horse pawed at the ground, as anxious as its rider.

"Your father is expecting an attack from the west, from your uncle."

"Yes, but, as you said, they have to cross the sea to get to us."

"And your father will grow more desperate the closer they come. You remember what became of the royal family who ruled before your father? Your uncle will be just as ruthless. We must be prepared."

"Prepared to what? Die? Because you make it sound like that is the only option."

"It is not your uncle I want you to be immediately concerned with. Take care, show no hint of rebellion ... until you are ready."

Abner shook his head.

"Your father will be watching for it, and he will not hesitate to crush it, even if it means crushing his only heir."

"My father needs me."

Dennison fixed him in a deadened stare that sent a chill rippling down Abner's spine. Wordlessly, the captain turned away and pushed his horse into a gallop.

The prince had no choice but to follow.

III

Wilderness at last behind them, the tired horses surged toward the glaring white walls of Lydia with a new zeal. Abner's back still ached from his final night of sleeping on the hard ground.

Alberon's capital shone like a beacon across the land.

The prince's chest swelled as his rightful inheritance grew larger and more defined by the moment. Dennison's warnings swirled through his mind in a discomforting eddy, tugging him down into a current of half-realized fears, but he kept himself afloat by imagining the feasting and celebrations awaiting his return.

Reaching the gate just as morning warmth was transitioning into midmark heat, the men pushed their way through the turbulent crowd with the refined impatience learned from consistent good treatment and easy living.

The begging fingers stretched toward the prince earned a quick strike from his hand. They bowed to the ground, as if thankful for the harsh response, and their eyes slid away to their next victim.

Dennison passed him a square of cloth scented with lavender to combat the cloud of dirt and sweat that hung over the lower streets of the city like a brown fog.

At the end of the lane, past the lavish homes jutting off in spiraling streets, the castle loomed to crown the hilltop the city was built upon. The prince trotted under the white gate of the palace, his mind working over what must be done.

Abner's horse was taken, and the prince was led inside for a bath and to change into suitable attire for his audience with the king. He rushed eagerly through these chores, snapping at the attendants dressing him to move faster. He kicked away the man whose clumsy fingers turned his leather boot straps into a nest of knots coiled tighter than a barmaid's hair. At long last he was bathed, oiled, dressed, and deemed himself presentable. Abner exited the room, his vanity kept secure in the layers of finery he was ensconced in.

Cantus met him en route with a small nod of greeting, his cheeks pink from a hasty wash.

His father's throne room was designed to make the ruler look richer than he was. Gigantic gilded doors welcomed travelers with blinding golden light. The prince and his guard marched down the unnecessarily long aisle leading to the wide space before the throne, fanfare blasting in their ears. This was also made of gold, with red velvet cushions adding to the grandeur.

To someone unused to it, the effect would be striking, and they would expect an old wizened King to sit on that throne surrounded by his beloved subjects.

Instead, King Havor paced before his advisers, gulping down enough wine to drown a dragon, fingernails scratching through his oiled black beard. Coughing at the fanfare and the sight of his son, the king's brow wrinkled above his dark eyes.

"Father!" Abner called, chest rising as he strode eagerly forward.

"Hush, boy!" snapped the king, waving him off. "Now, Nexus, what about this herb?"

An old adviser stepped forward with a bow. "It is said to have soothing effects, Sire. As well as certain additional qualities of stimulation."

"Nonsense," shouted a voice, "I have an apothecary my family has used for years who has a better herb for your needs, Sire."

"Father, are you sick?" Abner cut in, anxiously.

The king's eyes narrowed. "No, Abner. Best not to show how eager you are for me to be gone either, boy. Don't show your hand too early."

A nervous laugh flitted through the room.

"Very well," the king said, sitting down on his throne with a heavy sigh. "You have a report for me, I assume? How did it go? Were the dragons ... friendly?"

Abner's jaw stiffened at the mocking smiles of the king's advisers on his back. He forced a breath through his nose. "I found no dragons. I searched every bit of this kingdom. There is nothing."

"You found nothing?" the king's subtle anger warned Abner to choose his words carefully.

"Nothing except demon-worshiping traitors, Sire."

The king's back straightened, taking a real interest at last. "Demon worshipers, you say? Who are these traitors?"

Abner's lips pulled into a cool smile, tasting the beginnings of revenge with the relish of a man starving for respect. He began to tell his story.

Esther mulled over her own selfishness. It was selfish, she knew, to allow Fox to stay. She bit the inside of her cheek as she tested the sharp end of her hunting knife against her fingertips. Not enough. Her stone scraped along the edge again, her eyes drifting to the little chest rising and falling in sleep.

She couldn't force him to leave, he wasn't her pet.

But she couldn't let him stay either, he was her friend.

"After all this time." She tossed the blade to the needle-strewn ground and rose to rekindle the fire with her fire stone. "I'm still just a child. A selfish child."

She had kept busy all morning, practicing with her sling, checking her traps, puttering around their camp. Yesterday, the endless day of waiting, taught her that idle hands make minds run mad. Doing something physical, while probably futile, kept the restless energy somewhat at bay. The imagination, worn ragged with images of what was coming, quieted in the presence of sore fingers and tasks to complete.

"Won't be long now," Esther whispered, staring at the tree wrapped in empty rope where she had dropped the parcels the night before.

When Fox and she had returned to the camp and found the ropes that had bound the prince empty, she should have been terrified.

Furious.

Her head swam with relief instead. The decision was out of her hands. The prince was gone. "If only he'd hurry up. I hate waiting."

She stared at the flickering tongues of orange, wishing she could somehow get it over with. "What if I went to Lydia?" She gasped at the novel thought. "I go to Lydia, I don't wait for the soldiers to come here. I don't endanger Shiloh and I don't risk Fox." It was the only plan that made sense. *Oh. It's simple.* "I could save him," she rose, driven to pace by the frantic pulse filling her limbs with nervous energy. "I could save them all."

Without warning, the fox's consciousness burst into her mind, angrily ripping at her plan. It only took a few moments for the physical fox to come bounding into view, ears pinned against his skull and eyes wide with rage as he scurried around the fire.

You would sneak off in the middle of the night? You would abandon me to face the end alone after everything we've been through? I stay with you! How dare you take my choice from me, Human!

Esther's mouth hung open. She struggled to think past the wild voice echoing through her mind. Her eyes clenched, pain lancing through her temples as the fox's voice grew louder still.

Not your pet! Not your dog! I am a fox. You have not tamed me! You can try to leave, Human, but I will follow. If you die, I will die with my jaw wrapped around your killer. Not your choice! Mine! Mine! Mine!

"Stop!" Esther begged, slapping her ears shut against the clamor caged in her head, as she sank to the ground.

The fox quieted, fuming at her with bared teeth.

Esther's chest sprang through shallow breaths. "Alright," she said, releasing her ears and letting her eyes crack open. "Alright. I won't leave. I promise." She filled her lungs with a long draft of air. The throbbing in her temples receded as she picked up the small blade. Meeting the still cautious eyes of the fox with a hesitant smile, she said, "If we're going to fight, I probably should have kept the sword."

Fox relaxed, his eyes softening.

The fox's forgiveness washed over Esther, comforting her frayed nerves. It was a wonderful thing to be loved by an animal.

Probably would have just stabbed yourself with it, silly Human.

"Thank you."

The fox put one paw forward, and its golden animal eyes had a wild intensity which weighted his word. *Always.*

It was a promise she knew she could trust.

Abner savored his father's attention.

King Havor was never just his father; there was always a barrier of power and title between them. He rarely acknowledged his son beyond basic courtesy or extreme contempt.

The king listened to Abner's story with blank eyes and a finger to his lips.

Feeling his attention slipping away, Abner rushed past his encounter with the 'demon' to recount in detail the treachery he had witnessed. "Those abominable traitors abused the royal name most grievously. I believe we should—"

"You mentioned a demon?" King Havor said, waving a hand over Abner's words.

Stung, Abner nodded. "The outpost was full of stories of a demon who would come into the village. The peasants were terrified of it. They had more respect for a mystical fraud than their leader." Abner arched a brow, waiting.

"How do you know it was a fraud?" asked the king.

Abner's lips parted but no words came. Speaking now of the girl in black would guarantee her death. He had been avoiding her in his thoughts since he had left that cursed forest, but she now came into full focus. The honorable thing would be to tell his father the truth, showing him respect, but his mind struggled with reconciling the idea of honor to conjured images of what his father would do to her. These thoughts collided with one another, ricocheting again and again within a breath, and behind their battle was the command to *just say something*!

"I went looking for it." Abner cleared his throat into the hush held as the room waited.

Cantus studied the prince's face.

Abner took a few bold steps forward, making sure to smash Cantus' foot on the way, rewriting the confused look staining the soldier's features to one of pain. "I thought," Abner's mind raced, "maybe I could find its lair, subdue it, and we could use it to defend us against the coming invasion."

"And what did you find?"

"Nothing. I found nothing."

The king sat back in disappointment. "Then where did these peasants get the idea? Didn't you say it would visit the village?"

Abner shrugged. "Why bother with it? Father, my name was abused. Doesn't that matter to you?"

"No."

Abner drew back as if he had been struck. "They spoke against you as well and your ability to defend this kingdom from the powers that threaten it. Does that pique your interest?"

"Watch that tone with me boy. Spoken like a jilted girl. Honestly, if you hope to do my job someday you will have to grow a thicker skin. If I led a charge every time someone whispered something I didn't like…"

The assembled advisers chuckled dutifully.

"Now, do you have any other failures to report?"

Abner's expectations began to slip away, and he glimpsed a future where he was left with no outlet for this rolling uneasiness in his chest. "Father, please." *Careful*. "I need satisfaction."

"No, Abner," the king said, turning his eyes from his son. "What you need is someone to teach you how to be a man."

"A man like you?" Abner challenged, his cheeks burning. As the gaze of his father drifted back to him, Abner realized his mistake. He had forgotten, for one reckless moment, the intense power of his father's stare. When the king rose from his throne, Abner drew back.

"Leave us," ordered the king.

Abner held his hands stiff at his side, jaw locking beneath the unrelenting stare, as they waited for the hall to empty.

Only Dennison stayed where he was, and the king did not seem to notice him, or just didn't care that the beating should have a witness.

As the doors clicked to a close behind him, Abner's breath jumped in his chest.

"Now boy," the king spat, striding forward, "you had better have something more than *feelings* which prompted you to undermine me in my own court."

His father's hand closed like a vice on the prince's shoulder, and Abner fought the urge to push him away. The king's ruby-studded ring cut into Abner's lip, but he knew better than to let it show as he turned his stinging eyes back to his father's.

"Those demon-worshipping traitors threatened the life of your son. Your only heir. I thought that might mean something to you ... even if I don't."

"How did they threaten my heir?"

"They came at me from behind and then tied me to a tree in the woods. They held a sword to my throat." Abner paused. "Should that assassination attempt go unpunished?"

The king let go of him. "They tried to end my line?"

Abner nodded.

"They have attacked me." The king's eyes swept the hall. He stumbled back to his throne. His usual iron grip gave way to trembling fingers on the arms of the symbolic chair. "They will be dealt with."

"Thank you, Father," Abner said, dipping into a bow. He walked out from the hall dabbing at his stinging lip, a twisted smile growing on the uncut side of his mouth. He soothed his serrated nerves, replaying the conversation through the vision of himself as master puppeteer, his father moving this way or that at his touch. At last he could look toward some peace from the doubts swirling in his mind.

Cantus matched his step as he rounded a corner, brow bent as he took his time to ponder. "Why did you lie, Prince?" The soldier turned to check that they were alone.

"How dare you accuse me of lying!" Abner grabbed Cantus' tunic and shoved his back against the gray stone wall.

A flash of anger burned through Cantus' eyes before he smoothed it away. "The demon is real." Cantus' voice was more careful. "Why didn't you tell the king about it?"

Abner hesitated for a breath. "He doesn't need to know. The creature will not harm us, and knowing my father, he would try to use it somehow."

"If it would help against the invasion why not? Demons are powerful creatures."

Abner laughed at Cantus' ignorance, releasing his tunic. "They may be, but do you really want us bringing one home to live here? The dungeons aren't that far from the soldier's barracks. Maybe it would pay you a midnight visit."

Cantus shivered, shaking his head.

Abner chuckled, leaving him to ponder that possibility while he escaped to the grounds to fit in a few rounds of training before tonight's inevitable feast.

After the third guard fell back on the grass, tucking a sprained wrist to his chest, Dennison nodded for a pause. "That's match."

Abner tossed down his sword, massaging the muscle in his hand with his thumb. Dennison and he walked together to the castle doors as the last mark of the day waned toward night.

"Quite a tale you spun in the hall. Any of it true?" Dennison's eyes did not meet Abner's, but his stride was long and quick, his jaw stiff.

"Some of it." Abner smiled. "Many years in court have taught me how to move my father."

Dennison did look at Abner then. "Perhaps you should have studied a bit longer. You pushed him almost to breaking. You don't want to see what a man like your father does when he's broken."

Abner rolled his shoulders, forcing a calm he did not feel. "I was publicly disrespected. Weren't you the one who taught me that all rebellion must be crushed? That it is easier to win the war if you fight before it's begun? A civil war would cost us much more than a single village."

"Do you believe that their disrespect would lead to war?" Dennison asked, reading the answer already in Abner's eyes.

Uncertainty flooded him. Dennison was direct and unyielding. A powerful ally, but Abner had no idea how to control him. "Maybe," he said, "given time."

"Then I wish you the eye of a kind Fate on your campaign."

Abner nodded.

"Tell me, Prince, what have you actually seen of war?"

Abner chose not to reply, fighting the feeling of childish hurt filling his chest.

"I have seen decades of it. With your father and before. Justice can be done through it, but the cost is high."

Having reached the Great Hall next to the throne room, Abner hesitated, pulling Dennison away from the doors. "You think I should go on the campaign?"

Dennison straightened his tunic and rested his hand on the ceremonial sword hanging from his hip. "I don't believe you'll have a choice."

Abner had no opportunity to reply as the fanfare blasted the announcement of his presence. Accepting his social duty, Abner put on the persona of Prince of Alberon, brushing his hair into place as he sauntered into the hall. He took little notice of the blushing servant girl who bent to pour him wine in a gem-studded goblet. His father watched him, and Dennison tried to make his surveillance of the prince subtle but failed. Abner forced a smile as his plate was filled.

"Different than your recent fare, I would imagine," remarked a nobleman to Abner.

The prince raised a brow but said nothing. The food was excellent, but before his journey he had never known any different. Now his palate craved the delicacies as never before, having eaten little better than slop for five weeks. Glazed pheasant, steam softened vegetables, and imported fruit soon warmed his belly and Abner ordered another plate eagerly.

"Careful Highness," said a man across from him. "Keep going and you may get too big for your throne."

The good-natured laughter trickling along the table sharpened Abner's overloaded nerves like a whetstone on a cutting blade. Abner laughed with them, shaking his head at the man. "Sharp wit, friend."

The man tipped his chin.

"But if you ever insult my royal person again, I will see that your days are short and your death painful." Abner chuckled into the silence flooding the head table.

"Apologies, Highness. It was only meant as a light—"

"Why? Why are you still speaking?" Abner waved a hand, too sharp to be read as dismissive, his jaw held in a vice-grip. "Take him away. He is bothering my royal self."

The guards hesitantly lifted the man beneath his arms, forcing him to his feet.

His wife shrieked in horror.

"Sire!" exclaimed the prisoner, "I am a lord, a nobleman. I have lands, title. You cannot do this."

Abner's eyes narrowed. "You're also an insatiable talker."

"And you, Abner, are a little girl!" snapped the king. "You think you have power beyond what I give you? Release him."

The guards obeyed at once.

Abner's face burned as the arrogant fool adjusted his tunic and resumed his seat, unchecked and unpunished.

The prince's dark eyes turned to his father's and, though he couldn't speak the words, he swore them thoroughly in his heart. *Someday, Father, justice will be taken for everything that's been done.* Blood could only run so deep.

The feast continued in a predictable fashion. Food was followed by excessive drinking and loud laughter.

At last the king stood.

The room quieted as if they had been waiting for him.

"This is our first and last night of feasting together. Messages will be sent to your rooms when the feast is to resume after the prince's return."

Curious glances flitted to Abner from the many smaller tables arranged through the hall.

King Havor cleared his throat, regathering their attention as he raised his hands to encompass the room.

The nobility raised their palms in offering, bowing their heads for the king's recitation.

"You, O King, are infinite." Abner spoke the prayer with the court, glad for the stooped posture shadowing his scowl. It always felt odd, praying to his father as if the king didn't have a beginning and an end. As if the world wouldn't forget him the moment his spark left his body. "Let your eternal light shine on us for another year of glory, blessing us by your continued reign. Every sacrifice and honor to you, ruler and decider of Fate." He raised his eyes, meeting his father's dark stare lit by torchlight. "May—"

"May our glory never fade." The king's deep voice rumbled through the hall.

Others smiled at the king's declaration of a shared legacy with his son, but Abner could hear the words his father meant, and therefore ignored what he said. That was no vote of confidence, but a challenge.

The king's clap echoed, and the doors burst open to flood the hall with streams of multicolored cloth and dancers swaying to a driving rhythm.

Dark, small, and swathed in scarlet, one dancer caught the prince's eye. Drums beat from the back of the room and the girl's hips rocked with their rushed cadence.

Abner's overladen mind didn't allow oblivious enjoyment to clear his anxious thoughts. The king's branding-iron gaze sat hot on his cheek, the tension popping through a muscle in the prince's jaw. Rising from the table, Abner excused himself to the king and notable guests.

Making his way to his rooms, the prince wondered if he had pushed his father too hard.

Tradition favored the strong. Taking power from one's sire when he became too weak to keep it was a custom for many Keldeeman kings. Abner's grandfather had won his throne by subtle bribes and a well-placed dagger in his great-grandfather's chest. Some kings to protect their power would even turn against their sons, but as his father's only heir Abner was relatively safe from any preemptive move of the king. Abner didn't want the crown, not yet, but his challenging words in the throne room may have woken a beast he was not ready to slay.

Emerging onto the balcony that adjoined his room he drew a breath from the heat-laden air like a bucket from a deep well. Every thought on his mind was heavy, weighted with consequences he didn't want to shoulder. Not yet.

"Father's right though. Without him I have no real power." His muttered complaint was lost to the expanse of stars slowly sparking into view. Leaning his forearms on the stone rail, he closed his eyes. "I'll have to take what I want."

Feeling the presence of someone behind him, Abner stiffened. His hand found the dagger in his belt, worn for ceremonial purposes though he felt certain it was sharp enough to cut.

"My Lord," said a soft voice, a foreign touch to it, beneath the rustle of cloth.

Abner turned.

The dancer's scarlet bodice jumped with each quick breath.

"What is it?" the prince asked, not bothering to address her eyes.

"The king sent me."

Abner found her eyes then, and the truth was written there. Everything outside of his room faded away as the pulse of expectation beat through him. "Why?"

The girl came forward, unwrapping the trailing scarlet fabric which hung across her neck. She held his eyes as she dropped it to the floor. "For your pleasure." She dipped into a slow curtsy.

"My pleasure?" Abner said, closing the distance between them. "And what might that be?"

IV

The next morning greeted Abner with a sore back. He rolled to his feet, taking the bearskin blanket covering his bed with him. The dancer woke at the sudden cold and gasped, wrapping her arms around her knees.

Abner felt better. Lighter. He smiled as he poured water into a basin to scrub at his face. A woman had been just what he needed to work out this aggression he'd been feeling.

The dancer and her shredded clothes scattered around his chamber were dutifully ignored by the five servants who answered Abner's call.

"My lord?" the head manservant said. Abner had forgotten his name years ago. "What is it you require?"

"The Aftvar…" Abner waved his hand and the servant bobbed his head in understanding.

"The ritual, of course, of course." With a meaningful look, he directed his assistant to fetch the Healer. While they waited, the old servant's attention turned to the chest at the foot of Abner's bed. "Any thoughts on your attire today, Sire?"

"The blue and gold tunic will do," Abner said, letting the bearskin fall from his shoulders as he slipped on the undergarments handed to him by his manservant.

"Yes, I believe that would suit very well for the day's activities," replied the older man. "After all, the entire population of Lydia will likely come to see their prince depart. So, the blue and the gold. Were you thinking black for the—"

"What do you mean 'depart'?" Abner interrupted. He took a drink from the glass of wine he was offered.

"The battle against the traitors on the edge of the kingdom, Sire."

The Healer arrived. Gray-haired and stern-featured, his hooked nose hung over his lips as he scowled at the room. He bowed to Abner, then ran his gaze over the girl in a quick assessment.

"Healer, thank you for taking the time. The girl needs—"

"I know." The Healer brushed past the head manservant without a glance, setting his black case on the small table beside Abner's bed. "Come here, girl."

She shivered against the bearskin blanket she had retrieved from the floor as she stood before his cold stare. She tipped her chin to meet his gaze.

He mixed a quick drink in a goblet of old wine, combining some crushed leaves and powder which filled the air with a stinging smell. He held out the cup. "Drink."

She blinked at him. "What is it?"

"You wouldn't understand even if I took the time to explain. Drink."

"Milok provides us with something to take the day after."

The Healer smiled coldly. "Effective enough for your usual patrons, but surprise heirs would disrupt the entire kingdom. The king will not risk it."

Her jaw tightened.

"You *will* drink this."

The dancer took the cup and drained it with a grimace, covering her cough as the concoction slid with obvious discomfort down her throat. She wiped her mouth with the back of her hand, glaring at the healer.

He grabbed her chin, forcing her mouth open. After confirming it was empty, he released her, brushing his fingers together as if he had touched something distasteful. The Healer then strode from the room with a quick bow to the prince.

"I always feel awkward watching that," Abner muttered as he turned away, stepping into his breeches.

"It is necessary, though," the old manservant said, slipping the tunic over Abner's head.

"Yes, I supp—where are you going?" Abner turned suddenly toward the door, ripping the tunic out of the old man's fingers.

The dancer froze, her hand on the door post, the stitched hem of the bearskin blanket trembling against her knees.

His eyes flickered over her curves, half remembered sensations whetting his appetite for more. "Find her something to wear."

Bowing, a servant left.

The dancer turned to Abner in surprise.

"She'll need something she can travel in!" he called after the servant. "She's coming with us."

"But—but sire..." sputtered the old man.

Abner's brow rose. "She's coming with us."

The dancer hugged the bearskin tighter across her shoulders. "That wasn't the deal, little princeling. I would check with your papa, he may not want to pay for my extended services and my transport north after the troupe leaves."

"You were paid?"

The dancer raised a brow.

"If I had known I was paying for it, I'd have—"

"*Your father* paid for it. Unless you have a box of crowns hidden beneath your floorboards, one night is all you get."

Abner shook his head. "You forget who you are speaking to. I doubt my father gave his signet press to a contract which means nothing he promised is binding. I doubt he'll even remember you were asked to stay, so I have you for as many nights as I wish."

Her eyes dropped to the floor. When she raised her gaze to him again, they shone with tears. "I ... please—I can't let Milok leave without me. I have ... she needs me."

Abner brushed a lock of hair like black silk over her shoulder. "She can wait. I order you to come. So you will." Her body stiffened like molded stone; her lips trembling beneath his assaulting kiss. "Good. And my father is not to hear of this," Abner looked pointedly at the head manservant.

"As you wish it, Sire."

"If he does, I know whose head to hunt."

The old man's eyes dropped to the ground.

"I'm sorry Tessa," the dancer whispered, turning from Abner as a single large tear fell to strike her cheek. "I'm so sorry."

Abner had no idea who Tessa was, nor did he care. Relishing the feeling of control and the promise of more pleasure in the future, the prince returned to the dressing stand.

Servants brought the girl an old dress and hastily clothed her before leading her from the room.

Her pleading eyes were forgotten as the buckle of his belt was pulled into place.

"Too tight," he grunted, tugging at the strip of leather.

"Apologies," the attending servant said, working with fumbling fingers to loosen it.

Abner fought the urge to kick the idiot's teeth out. Instead, he mused what it would be like in a few days, when he was finally rid of the weight hanging over him. A stubborn core of doubt wriggled into the light, questioning if this heaviness he felt was because of the disrespect to his name or another cause? What if killing the villagers brought no relief? He shook the thought away as nonsense.

Leaving the servants to pack his supplies, Abner walked to the Great Hall. Plates were beginning to leave the tables, but Abner grabbed a few delicacies in time. He didn't order a special plate, contenting himself with bread and sweet meats while sitting slumped in his seat of honor with his feet splayed out in front of him.

The king's mouth grew noticeably thinner as he watched his son.

Abner grinned at his father. "When do we leave?"

The preparatory counsel with the king, Dennison, and a handful of nobles who did little to help the conversation took up most of his morning. Abner staged a loud, dramatic yawn as Dennison pointed out Shiloh's weakness to fire and the fragility of the wooden gates. Observing his father's tightening mouth with a smirk, Abner accepted Dennison's offer to escort the prince to retire and rest himself.

"Does my prince wish to lose his head?" Dennison asked, quietly.

Abner had practically worshiped Dennison since he was a small boy, so the captain's uncomplimentary tone did not rouse his anger. Instead, Abner shrugged. "The king is making a wise decision by going to Shiloh, but he underestimates the lack of any real defenses these peasants have. The maps and charts of weaponry and supplies," Abner smirked, shaking his head. "We are already taking an army to defeat a village with perhaps three swords and a couple axes between them all. Forgive me if I don't take this threat as seriously as he seems to."

"You should take all threats seriously, Abner. And I don't mean the threat of this battle. Your father loves little more than the continued success of *his* crown."

"What are you saying?" They turned into the corridor that held his rooms.

The captain seemed to wear the years of battle and politics like a weight strapped to his shoulders as he paused at Abner's door. The older man pulled it open for the prince to enter, but Abner refused to move. Dennison shook his head, giving Abner a look that—during training—had always made the prince pick himself up out of the dirt to try again, and turned away.

"I'm his son," Abner challenged. "His only heir. He needs me."

Dennison rounded the corner.

Abner fumed with no outlet for the blood pounding through his ears. He kicked the open door, striking the stone wall, before storming into his room.

The dancer jumped at his sudden appearance. She darted onto the balcony with a large, clumsy bundle hugged to her chest. Abner got to the balcony threshold just as she threw one leg over the edge of the railing. With a scream, she let herself fall.

He lunged for her but caught a roll of fabric in his fist instead. Over the edge he saw her clinging to an ill-fashioned rope made of torn bedding. Abner leaned on his elbows, lingering as the wind swayed her over a three-level drop. *This was your plan? It doesn't even reach half-way.* He began to pull the fabric up over the balcony's edge.

Realizing what he was doing, the dancer frantically began to climb down, despite the fact that the end of the rope now swayed two levels above the ground.

"Don't do that," Abner warned, the fabric between them beginning to tear through the strain.

She heard it too and, looking up at Abner with such cold, hateful eyes, for one dismal moment she seemed about to let go of the rope and fall rather than be recaptured.

His hand grasped her wrist and she lost her chance. Abner pulled her up onto the balcony, gripping her cheek. "Don't ever leave without my permission again." He released her.

She drew up to her full height, still much smaller than Abner, and used the back of her hand to strike his jaw.

Abner saw it coming but let it happen. He even let her storm away as if she had won. He left the balcony and closed the doors behind him, shrouding the room in semi-darkness. He'd been hoping for a fight.

Shoving her back against the wall, Abner forced her chin up until her eyes met his. His words echoed against the stone, making the air between them shake.

The threats hit her face like poison darts on a breastplate of steel, only making her eyes harden.

Red spilled into the corners of Abner's vision as he drew back his clenched fist, fingers desperate to make her listen.

Fear flooded her eyes, her mouth dropping open in a gasp of pain.

Abner's vision began to clear. He hadn't hit her, his fist still clenched back at his ear, but his other hand had found its way to her throat. Her furious pulse beat beneath his fingers. He released his crushing grip, stumbling back, his head reeling.

As soon as she was free, she bolted to a corner of the room, curling into herself to be as minuscule as possible.

He couldn't look at her. He couldn't breathe. He couldn't hear anything beyond the terrified pounding blood in his ears. Abner sat on the chest at the end of his bed, forcing his shoulders to rise and fall with each shaking huff of air. Head swimming, he pushed himself off the chest, tossing the bearskin blanket over the girl, and returned to his seat.

The dancer gathered the blanket across her shoulders, shuddering into it.

A quick tap on the door announced the arrival of the head manservant.

Abner welcomed the distraction.

The servant's eyes darted over the scene with a painted-on smile. "The blue and gold still suit you, my prince? Or should you like to change?"

Abner looked down at his pristine garments and grimaced. He wanted these clothes burned so he never had to see them again. "Something else, anything else to wear. Has my father finished his deliberations?"

"Yes, I believe the army is scheduled to depart after the midmark meal."

"So soon?" Abner asked, surprised. "I have never heard of an army preparing to leave so quickly."

The servant opened the chest and began pulling out clothes. "It is rather quick, but as the palace has been preparing for your return feast since you left the supplies were mostly on hand."

Abner gestured weakly toward his preferred ensemble.

"There are to be several scores of infantry, archers, as well as the king's guard." The man worked as he talked, tightening buckles and adjusting fabrics with the clever hands of someone well-practiced in a life of servitude.

Abner's brow jumped. "The king is coming?"

"No, no," answered the servant hastily, making one final adjustment. "He sends the captain and your royal self in his stead." He stood with a heavy puff of breath, admiring his work. Running a comb through Abner's hair and maneuvering it deftly back into place he nodded in satisfaction. "Your sword, my prince." The servant bowed with unusual formality as he handed Abner a plain pommeled sword.

"What is this ugly hunk of metal for? Get me my sword, the one with the ruby!" Abner tossed the weapon down to clatter against the stone floor.

"Ah," the man said, his eyes darting as he bent to retrieve it, "Your father, the king ... ah—"

"I am aware who my father is, now what about him?"

"I was informed your father felt it would be safer for you to not be adorned as a member of the royal house."

My father cared little for my safety when he sent me away. Is this meant to embarrass me? He allowed the plain sword to be fastened around his waist.

"Now, is there anything else you desire to have packed with you?" the servant's eyes surveyed his work with a satisfied gleam.

Abner half turned toward the girl, still huddled in the corner. "No," he said, before the servant could notice what was drawing his attention. "I have all I need."

"Excellent! Then may I suggest we make our way down to the Great Hall for a quick midmark meal before you embark? The kitchen staff have planned to serve a roasted beef platter with some cheeses brought in from the north of—"

Abner was no longer listening, oblivious to everything except the two dark eyes staring into his back as he left the room.

Esther laid awake all night. It was not something she had done since she was a little girl, new to the forest and its noise as animals crept and hunted in the dark around her. Now it was not fear for herself which kept her eyes pinned open, but for the little ball of red fur tucked into her side beneath the canvas tent they shared.

I promised.

She had to remind herself again and again as the moments crept by.

I can't go to Lydia. I promised. She pushed the stubborn thought away, as if throwing it out the door of her mind.

It slithered under the frame to tempt her again. *Don't be a coward. Fix this. Go to Lydia. Save the fox.*

The thought refused to leave the following morning as well.

Go to Lydia.

I promised…

Go to Lydia. Save the fox. What good is your word to the dead?

Enough! Esther threw down her sling, dropping the satchel of river stones hanging at her side. *I'd rather be a liar than let my friends die for my mistake.*

The bundle of fur shifted in sleep, sounds of quiet breathing resuming their unbothered cadence.

I go to Lydia. Alone. She hesitated, feet slowing. *And after I'm gone … what if the prince's anger isn't satisfied with me?* Esther shook her head remembering his threats while tied to a tree, his hatred of her obvious in every word he spat. *If he comes for Shiloh, I couldn't stop him anyway. At least this way ... there's a chance.*

Just one stop to make first. She left Fox napping in a patch of warm sunshine at the opening of the tent they shared, stomping through a winding route to the water trail while trailing her fingers over trunks and spreading ferns as she passed. She said a silent goodbye to him as she walked, but it felt unsatisfying. Incomplete. Time was a luxury she no longer had, and that pitiful *Goodbye, friend* was all she could hope for. Maybe repeating that it was better this way would finally convince her and break the lump of guilt in her throat.

Shiloh was enjoying the mild heat, holding their small market day just outside the gates of the outpost. Aromas of cooking meats, flowers, and livestock wafted from the meager collection of carts and rough wooden tables dotting the valley. Children played with stick toys while parents strolled, absently examining wares.

Esther stood like a shadow behind the thinnest covering of foliage, studying the world she could never belong to. She kept her eyes from drifting to the road, the way to Lydia, the simple solution to all of her problems. Her shoulders tightened.

Esther's nails clawed into the logs forming the wall of the outpost, scaling it as silently as a breath of wind, gone in a moment as she dropped to the other side.

During Demon's Time the gates stood open for her and she was allowed to pass. Esther imagined the panic she would cause if the tolerated specter returned after Demon's Time and in daylight. Or perhaps they would only lose their respect for the haunting figure. It wouldn't matter much longer. Still, Esther kept to the shadows.

She only made one mistake as she rounded a corner.

Esther skittered backward but it was too late.

The little girl's wide eyes stared at her beneath wispy blonde strands, her straw doll tucked against her chest. A dainty patter of small feet in mud drew nearer.

Esther gripped the handle of her knife with a shaking fist. *What are you going to do with that?* She put the blade away, trying to breathe through the frantic thud of her heart.

"It's alwigh'," said a small voice, and a tiny cool hand touched Esther's robed arm. "You can come ou'."

Esther shifted, slipping away from the girl's hand. She drew herself up to look as menacing as possible, dropping her masked chin to her chest so the hood created a black hole in the shadow of the house. "Go. *Now!*" Esther lunged forward.

The girl let out a scream, darting away and cackling hysterically. She looked back for the black-clad figure but the alleyway was empty. Frowning, she went away.

Esther, from the hay thatched roof above, breathed out a long sigh of relief. No one would believe a child's story that she had seen the demon.

Esther picked her way around the back of the building to a leaning ladder. She scaled it easily, creeping into Jathan's small apartment just above his bar. She propped herself against the open window, slipping off her hood with a sigh of relief.

A mug burst apart as it collided with the floor. Jathan's face reddened, eyes stretching wide as he stood in one corner of the room.

Esther darted forward to clean up the wrecked mug.

Jathan watched her, his limbs frozen against the grainy wooden wall behind him.

"I'm sorry," she said, carefully picking up the jagged pieces and putting them in a wide-necked pot sitting on the floor. "I didn't mean to cause you trouble. I just need your help."

"Wha's happened?" Jathan rasped.

"I ... I wasn't honest about the man from the bar." Esther hesitated, trying to swallow past the lump in her throat.

"I know."

"You do?"

"A man knows when he's bein' lied to. I thought yeh must've had yer reasons for keepin' it to yerself, like yer past. But something's changed, hasn't it? Wha's happened?" The old man stared at her with sharp, cunning eyes.

"He's escaped to Lydia."

"Who is he?" Jathan asked, crossing to the window and checking the street.

Esther's eyes fell. "I didn't know who he was when I took him. I thought he was some rich merchant's son." She picked at the peeling wood of the window with her nail, her face twisting. "I kidnapped the prince. Threatened his life. Now they'll be coming for me. It's only a matter of time."

"And yeh didn't think this concerned Shiloh?" Jathan's great barrel chest grew with the boom of his voice. "Why are yeh still here? Run!"

"I can't! I've already thought of that. I've thought of every way out and there isn't one. Not for me, at least."

"Child," Jathan said, softening, "wha's stoppin' yeh from runnin'?"

"The only place I could go that would make any difference is Lydia. I could present myself to the king and have him do what he wants with me. That's the only way this ends well for those I care about." Esther began to pace. "Now, what I need is—"

"Tha's yer plan?" growled Jathan, crossing his arms so that his muscles bulged out against the folds of his tunic. He fixed her with a sharp stare through his untidy gray eyebrows. "To go to Lydia and sacrifice yerself for a problem yeh don't even know is happenin' yet?"

"If it saves the people I care about, yes, I think that's the only answer!"

"Who exactly are yeh saving by this? How many years have yeh been kep' hidden, safe, and yeh're willin' to throw that all away now by goin' to Lydia? Yeh don' even know if they're comin'."

Esther laughed without mirth. "Of all the uncertainties around me, the one thing I do know is that they are coming. I was young, but even I caught news of what the new royals did ten years ago when they took Lydia. They killed without mercy anyone who was a threat. I—beating the prince and living to tell the tale—have become a threat. They don't forget, and they never forgive."

"And yeh think yeh're their biggest threat?" Jathan's eyes flickered meaningfully over her. "There're things yeh—"

"I think our people have been killed for a lot less. So, the only question I have any control over is how long it takes and how many people are taken with me. I'd rather get it over with and not let them take anyone else."

"If yeh're lookin' for me to say yeh should do this, yeh migh' as well crawl back out that window." Jathan rubbed a heavy veined hand across his eyes. "I will not watch yeh destroy yerself."

Esther looked at the floor, chewing on the inside of her lip. "That's not why I'm here," she said, at last looking up again. "I need you to watch over the fox for me … after it's done. Make sure he has enough for when the frosts come. He'll need you."

"Tha's why yer here? To make sure yer bleedin' pet gets fed?" Jathan scowled. "Aye, I'll keep an eye out for the mutt."

Esther nodded. "Thank you." She planted a boot on the window ledge.

"Oi—ten years and yer not even goin' to say goodbye?"

She turned back to him.

Jathan took her face in his hands and placed a kiss on her forehead, blessing her as a daughter. "I will keep a place for yeh, till we're home among the stars."

V

Abner put his forehead against the black stallion's neck, allowing himself to lean into the smooth, silken coat for one breath before he pulled away. His fingers brushed off a few stray hairs as he glanced over the beast.

The groomers had done a decent job at getting him clean, though they had let the horse grow fat on summer grass while Abner had been gone, forcing his girth to stick out like a pregnant mare.

After Abner returned from dealing with those traitors in Shiloh, he would need to have words with them.

Feeling the king's stare on his back, Abner cleared his throat, pushing the horse's nose away.

The courtyard around him echoed with the clop of horseshoes and the last-minute bustle of a large group readying to depart. The heavy, heat-soaked air stank of too many bodies kept too close in the crowded stone enclosure.

"Sire." Dennison nodded in greeting as he mounted his large gray horse.

Abner flung his leg over the horse's back and took his seat, his muscles molding seamlessly to the stallion's side. He met his father's glare with a raised chin and a cold smile. *Have I made you anxious, Father?*

"Have a care, Prince," Dennison muttered at his side.

"You ride today into battle to secure the honor of your kingdom." The king's voice boomed within the courtyard.

The courtyard before the castle gates had been designed to amplify the humblest of voices to reverberate against the walls with unnatural force, so the king's already commanding voice was to Abner like a thundering drum that vibrated in his bones.

"May those who challenge it be treated as you will treat the peasants of…" the king checked the scroll held at his elbow, "Shiloh. Ride fast, be of good courage, and return victorious or not at all. Conquer, no compromise." His eyes found his son's as he dipped his head. "So says the king."

"Conquer, no compromise!" answered the royal guard with one voice.

Abner's horse jerked away from the sudden noise, spilling coarse black hair over the prince's hand. He ran his fingers down its neck as the drum beat began.

It calmed at his touch.

He knew this rhythm; he'd listened to it as a boy at his father's side, watching Dennison leave to fulfill the king's wishes. It was a call to strength, a call to arms, and it shook his breath as it burned in his blood. Abner's eyes turned from the king's to fix on the image of his father's house, a rearing stag, painted on a shield and fastened to the space above the gate.

Conquer, no compromise.

It was a legacy he was born to carry.

Abner reveled in the glorious attention he received as the guard wound its way through the city.

Women loosened ribbons from their hair and tossed them down, spiraling for the men to catch.

Abner tucked two into his belt.

Outside the city gates, the rest of the army waited for them. Behind the thirty horsemen of the king's guard marched soldiers on foot, organized into units; further back, a mass of servants guided pack horses. At the center of that group rode Abner and Dennison.

The heralds fell back to return to the city, their valiant chant of "Make way for the king's royal army," fading into nothing.

It didn't take long for the quiet clopping of hooves on the dusty road to make Abner's shoulders droop in boredom. The adoring smiles were gone, even the king's scorn-filled gaze had fallen behind, and the travelers, who scrambled into the ditch along the road to avoid being trampled by the guard, grew sparse. Abner had nothing to entertain him as they rode deeper into the barren plains that occupied most of Alberon's land.

The stallion felt the impatience of his rider and tossed his head, pushing his nose against the rump of the horse ahead.

Abner chuckled and pulled the reins back, having no desire to be kicked for the animal's arrogance. "Two days," he muttered to himself. "Just two more days."

"Prince Abner, Captain Dennison," said a voice from beyond Dennison's shoulder.

Abner leaned forward to see who from the riding guard addressed him. *Cantus?* "What are you doing here?"

Dennison's brow furrowed. "The guard shift their positions every mark to keep vigilant. Abner, you know this."

"Why are you riding with the guard and not walking with the other soldiers?"

"I—" Cantus hesitated.

Dennison leaned toward Abner, "Cantus has been promoted. Your father—"

Abner couldn't quite stifle his groan.

"—decided that, in light of his recent heroic service to you against so many dangers, he should be given more responsibilities. He is now a low-ranking member of the guard."

Abner looked Cantus slowly up and down, from his horse, obviously groomed in a hurry, to his ill-fitting uniform and wind-blown, blonde hair. "Really?" he said, not bothering to keep the skeptical edge out of his voice. "So, Cantus, you're going to defend the kingdom through your *heroic* service." Abner laughed, shaking his head. "We're doomed."

The sun crawled through the sky until evening and Abner was bored the whole way through. He longed to kick his horse into a gallop and ride over the rolling grassy hills they passed, but knew he had to keep his place at the captain's side for appearance's sake.

Dennison finally called for a halt and the servants rushed to ready the camp for the soldiers. Torches were lit and meals were cooked while busy hands erected tents, picketed horses, and laid out bedrolls. Abner lounged on a few cushions, his boots inches from the blazing fire lit for his comfort. He stared into the flames. The uneasy anticipation he had carried for days burned away in the crackling heat.

"Sire?" A servant handed him a plate.

Abner sniffed at the meat, his mouth filling with watery anticipation.

The elite of the guard joined him around the fire and were served plates as well.

Abner wished he could share in the surrounding laughter. He took a gulp from his flask instead, feeling like a hollow man with nothing in him but doubt and rage. That would change. Soon.

As the stars sparked to life across the sky, Abner left for his tent. Pulling aside the canvas covering, the prince was greeted by a rich perfume. Traveling as a royal had the advantage of expansive tents the size of a small suite at the castle and most of the luxuries of home. He kicked off his boots so he could feel the soft skins that had been laid down for him. A grating groan passed his lips as his sore toes were enfolded in fur-lined comfort.

Two dark eyes stared at him out of a shadowed corner of the room.

Abner stumbled back, gasping through the sudden tightening of his chest, until he could make out the form through the faint candlelight. His brow rose. "Oh. I'd forgotten about you."

The eyes blinked. The dancer turned her back, silently repositioning her thin shift to lay flat on her thighs.

Abner frowned. He crossed to the bed and grabbed her shoulders. She tensed beneath his touch.

He shoved her aside. "I'm the prince. I get the bed."

She hit the floor. Picking herself up wordlessly, she made a home in a corner, pulling one of the fur rugs to her chin. She tucked her knees into her chest, curling into a tight coil, and hid her face in her arms.

Abner turned his back and willed his mind to quiet. *I wish I'd left her behind.* He couldn't look at her without seeing himself in the same monstrous light as he saw his father. Strong but cruel. A beast controlled by emotion, driven to move like a horse with a bit in its teeth.

By the time the sun rose the next morning, his eyes were sore and itched. As he dragged his body out of the bed, the girl shifted beneath the fur. She unfolded herself with a grimace and blinked at him with sagging, exhausted eyes.

Abner rubbed the back of his neck. *You're the prince of Alberon. Stop giving ground and showing your weakness. Take back control.* "Good morning."

She shook her head but didn't reply.

"How are you?"

Her eyes widened then settled into narrow slits over her scowl. "Don't do that," she snapped.

His skin warmed. "What? Ask how you are? Yes, what a monster I am."

She sat up on her ankles, her nails scraping her loose hair into a knot at the back of her head. "I'll admit, I read you wrong. I didn't think you were one of the rough ones. But pretending to care when you don't is worse than not caring at all. I'm not interested in making you feel better about yourself." The dancer began to fold the thick rug she had slept in and tidy around her.

"The servants do that, you know."

The girl raised her brow. "I'm hoping for a promotion."

"Because being with a prince is so terrible?" Abner pushed open his tent flap and called out for a servant to make him ready for travel.

After a moment of impatient tapping, he gave up hope of someone getting to him, and he wouldn't go out looking for one like this. Since he had been taught to never do anything himself that a servant should do, his eyes turned to the girl.

"You. You will dress me."

She smirked, shaking her head. "Of course." Crossing to the trunk, she pulled open the lid and began rummaging for a tunic, breeches, and belt. Grabbing an unassuming brown garment she came to the prince's side. "Arms up," she spoke in a singsong voice reserved for dogs and babies.

"Not that one," Abner said, wrinkling his nose at the bland color.

The girl twisted the fabric around her fingers as her face slowly reddened. She stomped back to the trunk to begin her search again.

"Better." Abner nodded at the silver-threaded black tunic she returned with. Her fingers were not nearly as gentle as his servant's. She pulled the fabric roughly into place and tightened his belt with a quick, merciless yank.

Abner emerged from his tent and took in the bustle of the camp around him.

Dennison joined him as the canvas flap snapped open and the dancer emerged, combing through her dark curls with hooked fingers. "Where is your manservant? And will you need the Aftvar? I can send for the Healer—"

Abner shook his head as the girl stooped to wash her face in a basin sitting on a little table nearby. The camp was a huge sprawling mess with men and equipment scattered everywhere. *How many marks will I be standing around while the servants tidy everything up?*

"It's very odd, the boy not being here," Dennison said, scanning the camp.

"Who?" Abner asked, taking the offered plate of sausage and bread from a bowing servant.

"Your new manservant. He was hired by the king for this campaign. Surely he knows failure to report would mean death." Dennison acknowledged the food bearer with a nod, biting into the bread with the relish of a man accustomed to hard work.

What does one servant matter when I'm so close to my goal? He shrugged. "Let's be off, Dennison."

"Sire?"

"Let the army ride ahead and the servants follow along after things are packed. It's not like they'll be doing any fighting, anyway."

"And the soldiers on foot?" Dennison raised his brow.

"I'm not suggesting we gallop. They have feet. Let them run. We could reach Shiloh by last mark today and the servants can catch up when they're able."

"Reach the outpost and be too tired to fight? Abner, I've taught you better."

"We'll attack in the morning, but the sooner we arrive, the better. Anyone who's seen us can get to Shiloh and tell them we're coming. I'd rather not arrive at an empty wooden fort and have to hunt through the forest for them."

Dennison thought for a moment. "The servants have slowed us down quite a bit."

"And you put too much stock in these peasants. The guard riding ahead alone would be enough to overrun them."

Dennison scowled.

"Not that I'm suggesting that."

Abner caught the dancer's gaze. She looked quickly away.

"Well?"

"This is your campaign, Prince Abner. I'll let you decide."

Abner's chest rose with the weight of authority. "Give the order. We're leaving."

Dennison left to fulfill his wishes, pausing to instruct a guardsman to find Abner's manservant and give him twenty lashes with a promise of more upon their return.

Each step brought Esther closer to Lydia. Breaking from the trees and joining the road, she felt the protection of the forest—which had kept her hidden and safe for so many years—lift.

She was alone.

She was weak.

She was going to die.

The assurance of this final thought almost sent her stumbling into the ditch that ran beside the road. She forced her lungs to take in air, hands gripping her knees.

What would it feel like when she died? Would she be brave, straightening and looking at her killer with a calm, peaceful expression before the sword? Would she be a coward, begging for mercy, and trying to crawl frantically away? And when it was all over, where would she go?

Esther had never been optimistic enough to believe in an afterlife better than the present one, so she took comfort in the only hope she had.

Fox will live. Shiloh will be safe.

It gave her the strength to rise.

She met no one on the road that day, and slept that night in the ditch. She was moving again before first mark, and felt the sunrise warming her shoulder. *Not long now. I can see them.* The dust cloud billowed like a rainstorm over the road ahead. *I'll never see my twentieth birthday.* It was a silly thing to grieve. Her mind traced over all the things she would never see again as she walked, staring at the dust announcing her execution.

Autumn. I'll never see another autumn. Or a fresh coat of frost on the heather in winter. I wish I had known last year would be my last full view of the seasons. I would have taken more time. I'll never run with—no, don't think about that. Only happy thoughts for him ... I'll never eat again. Even prisoners in a dungeon get a last meal. What was mine? I can't remember...

Metal caught the sun, flashing like tongues of fire through the haze. It must take a great number of soldiers to stir the ground like that. *How many has the prince sent to stamp out one life?* It seemed like an army of thousands. What could one person do against something so massive?

It's harder to kill with a name, isn't it? The prince's words made Esther grind her teeth. She would not make this easy on them. Her name was her own guarded secret, but her face was something she could show. They would not slash through a formless black cloak, but a weaponless woman. The prince would have to bear the weight of that. Esther stopped to lower her hood, pulling her black mask down from her chin.

A breeze touched her cheek, as if the wind gave her a parting blessing.

She shivered. Her breath shook. She began to walk again. Her feet started to pick up speed. She kept herself going straight toward the army despite her limbs' trembling energy driving her to flee. Her breath became short, quick jabs of her lungs in her chest as they fought for the calm, controlled breathing of a person prepared for what was ahead.

Fifty paces now, the distance closing every moment.

She could make out a little of the grim faces and the mighty horses pounding the road beneath them. It was really about to happen.

Thirty paces.

Esther's fingers yanked her hood back into place. She stood, shaking in the road.

"Out of the way!" ordered the lead man, threatening her with his short sword.

Esther's foot shuffled to one side. She couldn't breathe.

Ten.

"Move, lest ye be trampled!" called a wild-looking man, sitting forward on his horse.

Esther turned away, ducking her head. The ground trembled with the weight of the army. Her legs drifted, numb beneath her. All the resolve and martyr's pride drained out of her, puddling on the ground.

They were upon her.

Esther darted for the ditch.

The lead man yelled, landing his boot on the small of Esther's back. She was flung forward, falling into the ditch. White hot pain blasted through her temple before darkness flooded every recess. She knew no more.

The fox stretched his stiff muscles, aching from the second long night spent still and watchful.

Where is she?

The fox always made sure to tuck his furry body into his human's side as they went to sleep, or she would wake, frantic and panting, searching for him. Since they had found one another they had spent plenty of daytime apart about their own business, but every night she would come back and curl with him beneath the cloth until the sun rose. The first night she didn't return, he was able to sleep but kept his ears open, listening for her familiar step. When morning came, he wasted his time tracking her scent through a mess of trails that led nowhere. As if she had spiraled through the forest to mislead him. But she wouldn't. Lies were a thing humans told one another, they did not exist between his human and him.

But, as evening fell once more, Fox had sat at the cloth opening to their home and pinned his eyes on the forest. If, by morning, his human had not returned, he would have to go looking near the other humans to find her.

The sun rose. No human had appeared. Fox nibbled at an itch on his paw before shaking out his fur and trotting through the towering gray leaves to the human camp.

What he found erased all sense and reason from his mind, and he became like other animals.

"No! No, please, not my daughter! Agh—"

Sprays of dark gray water went up from every corner of the valley.

Fox ducked beneath a heavy fern. The smells, the sounds, the sight assaulted his sharpened senses. The leaves he hid beneath shook as his body trembled with the chaos. If it wasn't for love of his human, the fox would turn tail and dart back to the safety of the forest. But the men she was afraid of were here. They were hurting people she cared for, so she was probably here too.

Fox flattened his body to the ground as the woman's voice gargled, a little girl's shriek pinning his ears against his skull.

"Mama!"

The noise beat against his ears and the smells stung through his nose. He couldn't make sense of anything until—

A cloak! A great, sweeping cloak like the one his human wore.

Fox's eyes fixed on it, everything else fading. *I've found her.* The fox darted forward, streaking through the fighting humans as if they were trees standing still.

The cloak stumbled back from a charging soldier whose hand clutched a stained sword.

Fox bared his teeth, a growl ripping through his chest as he gathered his strength. Using his powerful back legs, he leaped into the air, piercing the soldier's hand between his jaws.

The soldier tried to shake him off, keeping his grip on the sword, but it only sent the animal's bite sinking deeper into the soft flesh.

As warm life water trickled into Fox's mouth, the hood of the cloaked figure fell back. A pair of old gray eyes stared at the fox.

His grip slipped. Only a little.

Enough for the human to switch which hand held the sword.

It's not her.

Hot, wet pain exploded through him. Fox's growl echoed louder as he restrengthened his grip. The sword was withdrawn and again brought down. *It's too much. I can't ...*

He exhaled a shuddering breath as his teeth slipped.

The world went white.

Get off—get off—get...off!

Abner's nails scraped at his palms. No matter what he did the scarlet stain wouldn't fade. Panic tightened his throat as he watched it spread, dripping down his arm, mixing with the water to turn it a sickly pink. He shook with each breath, splashing the front of his tunic as he tried in vain to scrub away the evidence of what he had done.

He'd seen executions before. He learned of war and death before he'd learned his letters, but it was another thing—something else entirely—to be the one holding the blade.

Far from being relieved, his torment was redoubled.

Get off of me!

What would his father say if he could see him now? Cowering by a water barrel behind the tents, struggling through each breath, trying to forget.

This was to be his moment, his triumph.

Instead, his eyes burned with bitter hatred at his own weakness. A weight he couldn't escape.

Her eyes.

His hands curved like claws, ready to gouge out his own.

He bit his tongue, strangling the sob that threatened to spill past his lips and expose him for what he was. Weak. Unworthy. *Father must never see me like this. I will master this.* He gave up the hope of relief, resolving only that his torment would not show. He would bury it.

His mind turned to the only comfort he now had any hope in. Oblivion. To forget. "Somebody get me a drink!"

Esther's breath pulled in a mouthful of dirt. Spitting, she rose to her knees, hands digging into the dust until the pounding rhythm assaulting her temples receded.

I'm alive? But ... why?

She dragged herself out of the ditch onto the road. Her limbs shook as she swayed on weak knees. Looking in either direction, Esther tried to think like her enemy. Where would the prince go?

Crickets sang in the long grasses, the stars glimmering to life above her.

If the prince didn't come for me ... no.

Esther began to move, despite her shaking limbs and pounding head, stumbling back through the dark as her heart thumped against her chest.

Oh no. I'm a fool. Shiloh.

She hoped the crisp, summer night air would awaken her mind and give her enough speed to reach her goal before it was too late.

It was too late.

Midmark of the next day came and passed before the land dipped beside the road into the bowled valley of Shiloh.

Esther found the first body. She slid to a stop, eyes running over the massive red stain on the ground. The dust had become a sticking mass of mud beneath the pale form lying in the ditch. Flies already buzzed over him, eager to begin the feast.

Esther's hands trembled as her vision was flooded with a white haze of horror. It was too much. Her feet gave way, her palms smacking into the dirt, and she forced her lungs to keep moving, glad of the emptiness of missed meals as her stomach heaved. Ripping her gaze from the dead man, Esther turned to the rest of the valley.

Her eyes burned.

There was nowhere she could look to hide from it. The animals hadn't begun to pick at the bodies, the camped army deterred them from that, but the summer heat had already driven much of the blood into the ground. What was left stained the grass and turned the dirt into pools of red mud.

Esther scrambled into the bowl of the valley as a line of servants appeared on the road, leading pack horses in a long, stretching procession. The army grouped a distance away from the havoc they had wrought, and tents were being put up while the smell of cooking food worked unsuccessfully to cover up the wet, metallic smell of blood. It rose to the sky so strong it was a taste in one's mouth. She watched from her kneeling place in the dirt as the line of servants disappeared into the camp. Her eyes turned to the dead.

She crept through the carnage.

Shiloh was gutted. The people, most of whom Esther recognized only as a passing memory, were twisted into grotesque shapes as they had been flung into heaps like piles of slop. Her eyes raked each face, searching for the familiar features, but hoping, even though she knew it was in vain, that somehow he wouldn't be here.

The sun sank toward the edge of the world before she found him.

Jathan lay on his back, stiff arms spread over a woman and a young child, his throat gashed and left open to the night. His mouth was slack, his eyes rolled back beneath his sagging lids.

Esther slipped her gloves off and reached out to pull his eyelids down, but stopped, unable to touch him. She couldn't bear to feel this new, dreadful reality. She hadn't saved him. She hadn't saved anybody. Esther, the runaway, the outcast, the *demon* had survived while the good, normal people of Shiloh bled from now lifeless bodies. She had slept while they had died.

It was like a physical weight she carried around her neck as she struggled forward. What had she expected to find? There was no mercy in the armies of Alberon, not anymore. This proved it. Everywhere she looked was—

The weight tripled in size, dragging her to her knees. A stretch of red fur—stained, matted, and only distinguishable because of the white tuft at its end—was on the ground ahead.

No, no, no! It was supposed to be me. I don't — what happened? It was supposed to be ... me...

All feeling left Esther's body. She rushed forward, pulling him into her lap, gathering what she could of the fox and frantically struggling to push him back together. As if that would open his eyes and bring the spark of life back to him.

Her breaths, short terrified gasps, transformed her once again into the small nine-year-old girl, shivering alone in an unfamiliar forest.

As the light faded into unknowable night, she used her fingers to study the fox's last expression. *Gone. He's gone. He's...I'm alone.*

"May you—" her whisper choked through her tears, "M-make your way to p-peace. May you find," she pushed her voice to burst through the bubble of grief blocking her breath, "find your home among the stars. Un—I can't. I don't want to be alone. I—" she forced her breath into a slow steady trickle, closing her eyes. "Until we meet again." She touched her trembling lips to his jaw, her tears wetting his dried-out mouth as she rubbed her face into the fur of his drawn-back cheek. "Goodbye," she whispered, pushing the pain into a pocket of her mind, where it lay, barely contained, as she pulled him into one last, bone-shuddering embrace. "I promise," she flinched at the stab in her chest. *My word means nothing now.* "I will repay their violence done to you." Her eyes opened, a fierce light filling them as a new, burning purpose coursed through her limbs. The guilt consuming her mind was engulfed in the flames of this new thought.

Esther laid the fox carefully down, and then straightened, her hood cutting everything besides the army's camp out of her vision. Every lit campfire, every flaming torch was a mockery to the dead. Her grief was pushed farther back as her gloved hand tightened around her knife handle. She picked her way carefully through the bodies, too far out for the army to bother tidying. To any watching her approach, they would have believed every story ever told of the demon who haunted the forest of Shiloh. She seemed the embodiment of death, each step deepening and solidifying her resolve. Esther would avenge this wrong.

No matter the cost.

VI

Liara, the dancer, wrapped her arms around her waist. Her legs still stiff from days of travel, she shivered as the chill of evening settled over the camp. Stamping her feet, she raised her chin to the stars winking in and out of sight. Her eyes tried not to linger on the valley before her, but morbid curiosity kept drawing her attention back to the silent shadows, standing as sentinels of doom over the camp.

Why hadn't the army left, or at least erected their camp out of sight of the slain?

That sick feeling she had been choking back since her line came into view of the first carcass heap surged up her throat. Her hands covered her mouth. She turned away, trying to fill her lungs instead with the lingering scents of cooking.

A prickle rose up her spine.

She held her breath as she turned back toward the grim silence of the valley.

A moving shadow crept among the forever stilled ones.

Impossible. She leaned out into the night.

"Careful," said a voice behind her, a hand touching her shoulder.

The dancer jumped with a gasp, the prince's face as it had been on his return from the battle filling her mind. She began to shake.

Instead of his face, smeared with the blood of innocents, a young man stared back at her, his blond hair discolored with sweat and dirt. His ill-fitting uniform stretched between his broad shoulders as he offered her a hand.

She drew back, seeing the red stains on his palm.

"You shouldn't be out here by yourself. The prince will be angry if you are not available to serve him."

The dancer said nothing. She turned away. *Why did I try to climb off that balcony? Should've just jumped.* At least her eyes would never have seen what they saw today. *But...Tessa.*

"Are you...alright?"

"Cantus! I need you!" bellowed a raucous, drunk voice.

The young man sighed, his boots clomping through the grass as he left.

The shadow was much closer now.

Her heart drummed against her ribs. She wanted to run back to the tent, if only the canvas would hide her enough until morning, but that meant going back into the camp. Was she any safer with these murderers' wolfish expressions than standing here facing the shadow? She shut her eyes as the memories from earlier that day repeated in her mind. When she looked again at the valley, she found it empty.

Empty?

More terrifying than it making its slow, steady way toward her, was the monster suddenly disappearing.

A scream ripped at her throat.

A gloved hand slapped across her mouth, her arms twisted in an iron grip behind her.

She yanked her limbs, fighting to break free as she built air for another scream.

"One more noise and I will gut you where you stand!" whispered a fierce voice.

Liara stilled, the scream dying in her throat.

"Where is the prince's tent? Tell me, and I may let you live to see the sunrise."

Liara made a small muffled sound. The hand disappeared from her mouth, bringing a blade to meet the skin on her neck. *Curse every Fate that led the prince to notice me. How did I get here?*

"I am not patient."

"Okay, okay, stop!" she whispered, panic leaking through her eyes until the blade eased its pressure. "I can take you to his tent." She was allowed one full breath. "Who are you?"

No answer.

"A survivor from the town?"

"Take me to the tent!" The shadow released the dancer's arms. "Now."

"Wait," Liara's mind tripped over itself in its desperate dart for safety. "You, going as you are, will only get you killed. I have a better way."

Her captor growled low. "What way?"

Abner let the laughter wash over him.

On the other side of the fire, a man staggered from his drink while insisting he was fine. He tripped over his own feet and landed a pace from the curling flames. No one noticed except to laugh as he sneezed on soot.

Abner held up his mug, waving it back and forth until a servant refilled it. He gave little grunts of pleasure as the drink poured into his mouth.

Across the fire, men compared trinkets taken from Shiloh. One had a lock of brown hair, another a straw doll stained crimson. Both complained that the pickings had been meager, hardly anything worth carrying back to Lydia.

"A great victory!" exclaimed a man, standing on weak legs.

The men cheered and repeated the words, taking a long draft from their mugs for good measure.

Dennison clapped Abner on the shoulder, his eyes gleaming as he stood. "Not a single man lost!" he yelled, spilling his drink on Abner's boot as he flung out his arms.

"Not one!" yelled the men, taking another drink.

"Oh, Dennison, look! You got *your* drink on *my* boot. Your drink should be on *your* boot." Abner reached to wipe it off, but his vision swirled uncomfortably. "Oh, I have an idea." He leaned back to grin at his mentor. "Watch." He bit his dried out lips to wake them up. "Cantus! I need you!"

The boy, pale yellow-haired little pimple of a pest that he was, appeared from behind a tent. He made his slow, cautious way toward them.

Abner worked his face into a speculative, regal expression. His eyes squinted at Cantus while his lips pushed into a dignified pout.

"Yes, Sire." Cantus stopped in front of him.

Abner's expression broke for a moment as he laughed. He pulled it back, like a weaver gathering spilled threads, and reformed his kingly look. "Cantus, I have a job for you. A drop from someone's cup has spilled on the royal boot." He paused, raising an eyebrow at Dennison. "Lick it off."

Cantus looked around at the other men, all laughing at him. Even Dennison chuckled, watching the fun.

"Go ahead. Go on, Dog," Abner stood with a moment of swaying difficulty. He put himself nose to nose with Cantus. Or close to it. When did Cantus get taller? "Lick my boot until it shines."

Cantus did not move or speak.

"Disobedient dogs get beaten, you know." Abner nodded slowly.

Cantus' eyes began to dart.

"One...last..." Abner brought his knee up to meet Cantus with a force he didn't know he had.

Cantus dropped, clutching himself while his face burned red with pain.

"That's right, I don't give last chances." Tossing his gaze around the campfire, he grinned and the men cheered.

The world tilted beneath him.

"To bed!" he called.

Two soldiers helped him to his tent.

He was half asleep before they got there. The shadow in the corner clad with a thin red dress was like a whisper in an empty room. Quickly forgotten as the flood of heavy silence engulfed his mind.

Sit in the shadows, wait till dawn, then in the bustle of the camp rising steal a horse and slip away.

Esther waited in the dark, tucked under the prince's rope-pole bed. The pile of canvas cut from the back of a tent lay in a heap behind her. The fabric had made a passing disguise, swathing Esther in the sand-colored cloth so the two women could slink through the camp. The only drunken eyes that noticed them fixed on the thinly-clad dancer, who hurried on before their mouths could slur out a proposition. Esther barely had time to second-guess the insanity of this plan before the tent flap was ripped open and the man himself appeared with disheveled hair and a rumpled tunic. That disgusting mess flashed a lopsided smile at the corner where the dancer sat, before he stumbled to the bed and began to snore.

Sit in the shadows, wait till dawn...

Esther repeated the dancer's instructions to herself again and again, fighting off the urge to crawl out from her hiding place and fulfill her promise.

The girl, Liara, was a dancer from the north. Her daughter, Tessa, was in danger. Liara needed to get to her before her master, Milok, did. Though only three years old, Tessa would be forced into the same work as Liara for the more perverse men Milok provided for. Whatever else happened, Liara had to escape.

If Esther killed the prince and someone found him before morning, the girl's chance would be gone. The fierce-eyed men guarding the horses abstained from celebrating and from drink to remain vigilant. The guard would change near dawn and the replacements would likely be recovering from the night before and less wary. That's when the girl could make her attempt. She insisted they could both escape then.

Esther had no intention of escaping. Her nails clawed into the fur rugs and her muscles cramped, thinking of how long it would be till the sun was ready to rise and she could move again. The prince's snore filled the air and Esther willed time to rush forward to the moment she could silence it forever.

Sit in the shadows, wait till dawn...

The dancer dozed in the corner, her arm hooked under her knees to cradle them into her chest.

The candles lighting the room flickered.

New air flowed into the tent as a hand pulled the flap aside and a pale face looked in.

Esther studied him, unable to move lest he notice the pinpricks of light reflected in her eyes by the motion.

He was blond with no beard. His mouth twisted as he looked at Abner sleeping. This must be the guard the dancer had warned Esther about, who would probably find Abner in the morning. What expression would he wear then? He left, apparently satisfied his charge was safe and not likely to wake anytime soon.

Esther propped herself up more comfortably on her elbows as she waited for the sliver of night she could see through the tent flap to lighten.

I'm going to kill you. She listened to the snore of oblivion rattle the air above her, the lashed frame creaking as that waste-of-a-spark adjusted himself. *I'm going to watch your blood leave you. I'll see the spark go out of your monstrous eyes before the sun arrives.* This filled her belly with heat. She smiled.

At last, the light began to change. Esther crept from her hiding place with the practiced skill of a huntress. Rising from beneath the bed, she adjusted her hood, flexed her gloved hands, and looked down at the prince.

He must have changed since the massacre. His clothes, hair, and skin were clean. The only evidence of what he had done was left to rot outside. They hadn't even given a single night without fire to aid the dead.

Esther moved forward, determined to fulfill her promise.

"No," groaned the prince. Still lost deeply in sleep, he mumbled to himself. "No...Please...I didn't want this. Not like this...I'm sorry."

The whispered phrase furrowed Esther's brow. Was he sorry about Shiloh? Did that really matter? He was a murderer, his people were all murderers. He didn't deserve a chance at mercy. Her fingers wrapped tighter around the knife handle.

The prince's snoring had quieted, and the dancer unfolded herself. "Why didn't you wake me?" she whispered, struggling to stifle her yawn.

"No need." Why was she unsure? She had made a promise and had the means to keep it. Why hesitate?

Liara stood quietly, making her way to Esther with almost no noise across the fur-lined floor. When she saw the prince, intact and sleeping contentedly, her eyes narrowed on him. "You couldn't do it?"

"I can. I will." She gathered the memories of Jathan and the fox, all the faces of Shiloh that she had known by sight, filling her mind with visions which stabbed at her grief-numbed heart.

A hand touched hers.

The dancer took the knife. The soft fabric of the girl's dress swept across Esther's cloak as she made her way toward the prince. Standing over him, chest rising with every breath, Liara raised the knife above her head. Her hands gripped and released the handle, testing themselves before she would drive it through his flesh.

"Wait!" Esther whispered, grabbing the dancer's shoulders to pull her back.

She threw a cold stare at Esther. "I thought you wanted this, but if you're too much of a coward to get a little blood on your hands, I'll do it." Esther had never seen a face so beautiful become so ugly as in that moment. The girl's lips hugged the base of her nose as she formed a snarl. Her eyes popped with barely-contained fury and her eyebrows hung low over them. "You don't know what it's like," she whispered. "I'm finally taking back control."

"No!" Esther said, pulling the dancer away. Forest living had hardened her muscles, and she was able to rip the blade from the dancer's grip. "You need to get back to Tessa. You should go."

"Then finish it!" The dancer's eyes still shone with intensity, but her features quieted into the pretty mask she wore for the world.

Esther took her place and raised the knife.

"Look out!" yelled the dancer.

Esther was knocked aside and found herself locked in a battle with a uniformed guard. The object of their fight quickly became gaining and keeping control of the knife gripped in Esther's fist. He was strong. She was stubborn. Bracing her grip, she refused to give a finger's breadth of ground.

Liara, Esther could see her move in quick flashes over the guard's shoulder, began to edge toward the tent opening. Stopping just shy of the patch of gray morning light that was their only way out, she turned back. She made her way to the table where the candles sat and then was lost behind the massive shoulder of the guard.

With a heavy grunt, Esther bit the veined hand pulling at hers.

He drew back, his stubble-clad mouth grimacing.

Esther grinned behind her mask.

They both froze as a heavy choking scent invaded the air.

The guard and Esther stared at the yellow tongues of fire climbing the side of the tent for a long three count before either moved. She tried to twist away, but he gripped her hand with a crushing force powerful enough to break it from its hinge. The guard secured her wrists together with a scrap of fabric that had torn in their struggle.

As she fought her bonds and began to crawl on her knees to the tent exit, Esther's eyes raked the room for the dancer. She couldn't see anything through the smoke. Esther made it into the fresh air and her lungs gave up the choking vapor with a fit of furious coughing.

The camp stirred to aid the prince. One soldier, missing her in the graying morning light, stomped over her back as he rushed to fetch water to put out the fire. Esther pulled her face from the mud just as the guard emerged, dragging a barely conscious Prince Abner to safety with him. She cursed as she was hauled to her knees and her hood ripped back. She blinked through the mud at the stern-featured soldier, scars lining his hardened face.

I've failed.

The fabric binding was replaced with iron chains. They cut into the soft flesh of her wrists as she worked at them, clinking through the effort and refusing to budge. Heart thudding, she watched the prince be lifted to the Healer's tent where they would fix any damage that had been done to him. The guard was helped to his feet, clutching his bitten hand. As Esther was put in a cage designed for carrying livestock, she heard the call that a horse was missing.

"Must have run away when the fire started. Snapped its tether," the guard watching the horses declared. He would believe anything to save his own hide.

But Esther knew better.

Liara rode free and Esther was going to die.

All was as it should be, except the prince's still beating heart.

❖ ❖ ❖

Abner awoke to news of a fire. His tent had been engulfed while he was still inside, everything he had brought with him destroyed before the flames were contained. He only remembered being dragged from his sleep by a pair of rough hands through muggy air.

The entire camp was enthralled with the story. A mysterious assassin lurking in the shadows, and an unlikely hero coming in at the last moment was all Abner heard about that morning.

Released from the Healer's tent with a plate of food, Abner stomped through the camp in a foul mood. Dennison matched his stride as he made his way to the charred remains of his belongings.

"Got the smoke out of your lungs then, Sire?"

Abner scoffed.

Dennison looked ahead at the still-smoking husk that could have become the prince's tomb. "Fate showed favor to you, Abner. You could have very easily died. Did you see anything when you entered the tent?"

"No."

"That girl—your companion. Was she there?"

Abner picked his way through the burnt grass and charred posts with a grimace. He had nothing to wear for his triumphant return except yesterday's old clothes. His father's ever-present scowl deepened in his mind's eye as Abner led a triumphant army into Lydia wearing a wrinkled tunic that smelled like drink and smoke. "I don't...yes, I think she was. Where is she?" His gaze raked the camp for her but found nothing. He buried his relief that she, and the feelings she inspired, were gone.

"They are saying the assassin found in your tent started the fire, the girl must have run away in fright. I'm sure we'll pick her up somewhere along the road to Lydia. Come." Dennison nodded toward the horse enclosure. As they walked, the captain told the prince what he knew.

"Cantus? Dennison, you must be mistaken. Cantus couldn't have dragged me to safety. Those scrawny arms. Are you sure I didn't fight my own way out through the flames, and he just grabbed me at the tent entrance to look heroic?"

"Sire, the men are saying they saw Cantus pull you out. What happened inside the tent, no one can speak to ... except perhaps her."

The black-cloaked figure sat with her back to them, resting against the network of bars stopping her escape.

Abner groaned, striding forward. "Not you again!" He jabbed at the girl's side through the bars.

She yelped and darted away, sitting crouched at the far end of her cage.

"Take off that ridiculous cloak. There's no hiding for you anymore."

"I will die with my dignity, Prince. That's an honor you've now lost."

Abner leaned against the bars and grinned at her. "You forget, little one. You tried to kill the Prince of Lydia. Twice now. I decide how you die. And..." his eyes ran the length of her cloak before traveling back to her hood, "I've got some ideas."

Like a creature from a nightmarish dream, a gloved hand suddenly lunged at the prince, narrowly missing his throat.

Abner fell back as Dennison darted forward, wrestling a long thorn out of her grip. He held her wrist, ready to break it like a dried-out branch as he studied the thorn.

"Poisoned. I'm certain of it."

"Poison, of course. The coward's weapon!" spat Abner, pushing himself to his feet. "What were you hoping? That killing me would somehow free you from your cage?"

Dennison released the girl's arm.

She drew back, rubbing at her wrist with her other hand. "The only thing I would change about this cage would be to make sure you were dead and burned before I was put in."

Dennison turned to hide his smirk at the girl's bravado.

Abner set his feet, making sure to keep a good distance between him and the bars. "What other tricks do you have hidden in that cloak?"

The girl in black sighed, leaning her head against the bars. "I don't know." Abner imagined she closed her eyes, bored with them as she continued in a bland tone. "I'm sure I'll think of something."

"What did you do with the dancer?"

The cloaked girl turned her hood to stare at the prince.

"She was in the tent before you set it ablaze. Did you murder her?"

"Oh, no, little prince." The voice emitting from the hood sent a chill down his spine. "I helped her escape a nightmare."

"Just as we thought. Scared by the fire. We'll find her again on the road." Dennison glanced at the hooded girl as if for confirmation.

She laughed.

"What?" Abner moved forward, Dennison stopping him from getting too close. "What is it?"

The girl looked away from them, down the valley.

Abner scoffed, shaking his head. "We're finished with this useless girl. Let's move out. It's time we returned home."

VII

The two days of jolting, rolling monotony were torturous to Esther. Caged without possibility of escape, and a stubborn resolution not to even if she could unless it was to finish her task, left her with waves of frantic useless energy, busily tapping fingers, and a mounting headache. The sun beat her with relentless heat, sharpening the needles of pain in Esther's temples. Exposed and vulnerable in the vast treeless landscape, Esther tried to ignore how her cloak clung tightly to her sweat-dampened skin. The soldiers' presence beside her cage made Esther toss away the thought of shedding the heavy black fabric. Best to stay hidden. She resigned herself to sweat in silence.

The only break from this steady torture was at the changing of the guards who watched her cage through the night.

Two new soldiers marched forward, saying a few quick words of greeting to those they relieved to take up their posts at the cage.

Not near enough to grab. Esther idly watched the throbbing pulse in the younger soldier's throat.

"Do you really think it could happen?" he asked, looking sidelong at his graying companion. "What the men are saying? The invasion?"

The older guard scoffed. "Concern yourself with your charge." He thrust his chin toward the cage. "Not with the imaginings of cowards."

"But Hanson said the boats could be finished at any time, that the Keldeeman army is coming and will slaughter us all! Doesn't that worry you, even a little? We could all die, and all the king has done is—"

The younger man's persistence earned a sharp kick from his superior.

Two servants strolled by the cage, and both guards stilled until they passed.

"I don't understand why we both need to watch this cage," muttered the younger man, rubbing his leg. "It's just a girl dressed in black." He cast a look at Esther, eyes narrowing as he took a step toward the bars. "She's not so terrifying." Unsheathing his sword, he took another step. He stuck the blade between the bars, slowly creeping toward her.

Esther went still, every muscle loose and ready. Waiting.

"Hello?" he called, wrapping his hand around a bar and pressing his face between two others. "Is there anybody under there?"

"I wouldn't do that," warned the older man.

The young soldier touched Esther's knee with the sword tip, grinning.

Esther struck like a snake. She landed a heel on the soldier's nose—the bone snapping beneath her boot—while her hand pinned the blade flat to the floor of her cage.

The soldier dropped the sword and stumbled back with a steady stream of curses and threats. Blood spilled from his nose, and he worked to staunch it with the sleeve of his uniform.

The older soldier turned to the cage, unsheathing his own sword.

Esther tossed the blade to a far corner and refolded herself in her cloak.

Surprise flitted across the man's expression as he reached carefully through the bars and pulled the sword out of reach of the prisoner. "Go get yourself cleaned up, and stop your crying!" barked the older soldier, eyes narrowed. "If I didn't have such an idiot for a nephew, your face would be whole and well."

"She should be punished—killed—burned for that!" whined the young soldier, stomping away.

The older guard looked at the girl in black, huddled in the deepest corner of her cage. "She will be."

Just not for that. She had tried to kill the prince. Worse, she had failed to kill the prince. If she didn't think of something soon, she would die for nothing. As the guard turned away, Esther rubbed her fire stone, used to warm so many cold nights in the wild forest, against her palm. *It isn't enough.*

The young guard was replaced with a silent one.

The rest of the night passed in fitful sleep cut off only by the early rising of the sun. Then came the several marks of travel, just as monotonous as the day before. As the road became more populated, Esther's guard increased. She curled on the floor of her cage and watched the sunlight glint off of the gold design on the soldier's uniform walking beside her.

He shuddered at her stare.

Grim amusement twisted her lips into a smile.

"Cantus!" a soldier called, the quick trotting hooves of his horse punctuating his words as he rode back toward the cage.

Esther sat up.

"The captain needs you riding with the guard at the head of the line."

The soldier, Cantus, grimaced. "The prince thought I would be better used back here. We're missing a horse anyway."

The soldier on horseback sighed, shaking his head. "I'll let the captain know."

A shudder passed through Cantus as he saw the black hood fixed on him. A single bead of sweat dripped down the back of his pale neck, his skin pocked by goosebumps. This was the soldier who had stopped Esther from fulfilling her promise. Fear and disgust flitted across his features as he avoided her gaze. From the look in his eyes, he had no great love for the prince either, yet he had dragged him to safety when he could have easily fled.

Esther leaned against the bars of her cage, studying the tall, blonde soldier.

At last. Something I can use.

Abner straightened, dressing his face with a smile, as the land opened up to embrace the sea and Lydia came into view. The stress of the road was probably what made him so uncomfortable, and now, returning home, he could celebrate his victory and the weight would lift. His father would be proud of him, leading his first battle, gaining his first kill. The fanfare blasting from the castle walls as the lookouts saw the army approaching made his smile almost authentic. He adjusted his tunic, brushed some road dust from his boot, and patted his hair to make sure everything was in place.

The procession made its long spiraling way into the city.

Flower petals and ribbons rained from the houses above him as the line worked its way to the castle at the city's center. Abner caught a ribbon cast off by a maiden with long blond hair which curled loose in the wind. She giggled, hiding her face, and Abner smirked, looking at the gift in his hand as he ran his thumb along the black fabric. A flash of memory—red stains spilling from his palms—made him drop the ribbon. He blinked and his hands were clean again.

As they entered the castle courtyard, Abner's eyes searched the balcony for his father's proud face.

He was not there.

In fact, the only people populating the viewing area were servants waiting to begin their work of packing the army equipment away, getting the horses stabled, and whatever else a servant does with their time.

Abner tried not to let the stinging hurt show on his face, but his father's absence made his chest tighten. *Why did I expect anything else?* He swung off of his horse, catching his weight against the beast's neck as several marks of riding had not been kind to his knees. Abner marched toward the throne room, Dennison at his heels.

The heavy doors struck the wall behind him, making the cluster of busy servants inside jump.

"Where is he?" Abner demanded.

An elderly servant took a few hesitant steps forward, dipping into a nervous bow. "May it please Your Highness—ah—who?"

"My father, the king! Who else would I be asking for?"

The servant's chin bobbled hesitantly.

Abner grabbed the old man by the front of his tunic. "Where is he?" Anger felt easier than hurt, and Abner invited it in to burn through his mind as the servant stuttered.

"I b-believe the k-king is in the council room."

"The war council room? I haven't seen him use that room in years."

Dennison moved forward. "My prince, we should hurry."

Abner let go of the servant and followed Dennison's echoing footsteps out into the hall. He hesitated as Dennison closed the door behind them.

"To the right, Sire."

"Yes, yes, I know!" Abner waved a hand. "Although my memory is a little dull after this turn. I haven't been to that room since..." Dennison took the lead and Abner lengthened his stride to match the old captain's. "I think the last time was when we tested my mock battle plan. Do you remember that?"

"You were twelve."

"I did very well on that test. Father wasn't impressed, but I was able to route around your troops by letting you take that weaker unit."

"You lost 300 men, if I recall, but yes, you won the battle." Dennison turned sharply down a small staircase. "We're almost there."

The door at the base of the stairs whined on its hinge.

Abner stepped into a hallway heavy-laden with dust and old air. He coughed into his sleeve, pulling the fabric over his mouth. "Why haven't the servants aired out this wing? It's awful."

"The king must not have expected to use the room. Whatever news arrived during our absence has him nervous of unknown ears." Dennison glanced over his shoulder and Abner understood what the captain could not say. They both picked up their pace before arriving at a large black door, its silver studded planks coated with neglectful grime. "My prince, I wouldn't—"

But Abner was already pushing the door open and marching inside. "Father! I, Prince Abner, have returned ho—"

"Quiet, you useless child!" snapped the king, frantically shuffling through his papers. "Now, repeat it again, exactly what the message said."

The handful of old bearded nobles gathered in the shadows behind him shifted on tired feet.

"My lord, the esteemed true king of Lydia and the country of—"

"No, no scribe! The important parts. Skip the introduction!"

The scribe's fingers shook as his eyes scurried across the scroll. "Ah, I–I bring grave word related to the doings of King Echnor. The boats you burned as you left have been replaced. Your brother by union, the king, is preparing his army and will be sailing to Alberon. He will take everything you have gathered over the past ten years and end your line, if he can. I would be killed if it were discovered I had passed words onto you. My lord, every day grows more dangerous for me here. I ask to be given sanctuary at—"

"Oh, I don't want to listen to the spy's whining." The king dismissed the scribe with an irritated wave.

Abner's father, the man he had looked up to all his life and who had never bothered to look down at his son except to scold, raked shaking fingers through his hair. A wild pulse beat in the king's throat. Dennison was right. The king was afraid. "Father I—"

"Don't speak to me, you pathetic pimple-faced whelp! If only you had succeeded and gotten a dragon to defend us. But you failed, as you always will. I've given up hope for you. Stupid child. Stupid, stupid." He muttered to himself as he shuffled through papers. "And this, this is all the soldiers we have? What if we arm the villagers?"

"I don't think that's wise, Highness." Dennison stepped out of the shadows and the king's outraged words died on his lips. "There is unrest in your people's minds. Shiloh may not be the only pocket of it. And, from the letter, I do not think we have time to train farmers into soldiers before the army arrives."

"Then we can use them as human shields, I don't care. He must not be allowed to set foot in this castle alive." The king pounded the paper-clad table with his fist, sending several maps and charts cascading to the floor. "Dennison, old friend," the king's voice took on a pleading note, "What do I do? How do I stop this?"

"I don't know that it can be stopped, but I will command the charge to defend this castle. I will die trying. Long live the king." Dennison bowed his head and fixed Abner in a stare of intense purpose.

Abner bowed, along with the other occupants of the room and murmured with them, "Long live the king."

"A lot of good that does me," muttered his father. The king's eyes darted around the cobweb-strewn rafters, as if danger crouched in every shadow. With a shudder, he began to dig through the papers again, muttering nonsensical words to himself.

A full mark of the day later, Abner was released to wash the road dust off of him and, as his father said, "change into some decent bleeding clothes."

The bolt to lock his chamber doors was stiff and rarely used.

Abner cursed as his fingers strained to slide it into place past its groaning protests. The door at his back now secure, the prince crossed to the balcony and shut those as well.

Alone. I'm finally alone.

No one to overhear him, no witnesses to his weakness. Flashes from the battle stormed against his mind, driving him to his knees. Abner blinked, trying to dispel the memory, to fight it off as he had a hundred times since the slaughter at Shiloh. Even drinking himself into oblivion the night following the battle had not stopped the dreams from coming. He scrubbed at his brow with fingers bent into claws. On the outside his skin was clean, yet he could still feel the sticky stain of life blood that had only been covered up by soap and water.

He was not clean.

He never would be again.

Her full brown eyes, staring up at him through a sea of salted water, with a wordless plea for mercy were weights on his breath he would give anything to remove. Abner had felt that familiar tug to weakness, the pull to back away making him hesitate. He had to bite his lip to keep from screaming with her as his sword had come down. Her body gave up her breath and Abner still waited to stop feeling like he now borrowed his.

He thought of Dennison, the monster regathered into the man, and wondered how his mentor kept that calm demeanor when he had such a savage beast inside who hungered for the spilling of blood and ripping of flesh. Was everyone just monsters locked in the careful pattern of practiced civility? If only he could forget or somehow become like Dennison and learn to enjoy it. Abner longed for sleep or some magical oblivion that could wipe his eyes clean of what he had seen, the disloyalty that had pushed him to it, and the nagging unease that still drove his thoughts to anxious places.

A part of him wished the assassin had succeeded.

The iron chains bit into Esther's wrists. Her eyes kept straying, unbidden, to the high walls of the castle as the pack horses were unloaded. The tail of the procession had taken most of the day to wind through the city. Now that it had at last reached the castle, the sun already dipped toward the last mark before nightfall.

The waiting was almost over.

A servant pulled a crate from a pack horse's leaning saddle, opening the top of one of the bottles to check the contents. He stoppered it loosely and set it down, muttering about another crate of oil he had just seen and wandered off.

Not close enough to use. Unless...

The soldiers stationed themselves around her cage with swords drawn, the toe of one's boot almost touching the bottle of oil.

Almost.

The cage opened and Esther allowed the hesitantly reaching hands to grab her cloak and drag her out onto the straw-strewn ground.

Fear was something she knew well, and these men stank of it. The nervous twitching of several pairs of eyes and the uncertain grip on their blades gave them away as cowards and easily spooked.

Glancing around the courtyard, she saw only servants and her small entourage of soldiers. The fire stone sat warm, clutched inside her glove. Slipping it out, she held her shackled hands together, hiding the stone between her palms.

Esther dropped her chin, a rasping breath rattling from her hood. She lunged at the soldier near the bottle, and he flinched away, swiping at her with his blade. The oil spilled, the puddle creeping toward her feet.

"None of that," said Cantus, edging forward with his sword, the ring closing with him slightly. "No tricks."

"I?" Esther's voice whispered out of her hood as she took a few slow steps to one side, giving time for the oil to pool. "The Demon of Shiloh has no need for tricks."

Esther struck the fire stone against the metal links of her chains, flooding the ground with sparks. Flames sprang up between her feet, emboldened by the spilled oil.

Above the empty bottle, the guard yelped as the fire bit at his booted feet, darting back to keep it from catching onto his tunic.

The cloaked girl disappeared under the cart that had been her cage and sprinted into the crowd. They parted for her, the servants leaping aside lest they be caught in the fray, as soldiers charged.

Esther ran, using her gloves to stop the fire singeing the hem of her cloak before it could catch and consume the fabric. She led the soldiers out of the courtyard gates, darting like a rabbit through a thicket. The armored arm reaching for her missed by a full armlength, the weight of it clanging behind her as she buried herself in a line of trudging men carrying goods up to lavish homes. She climbed a vine-covered trellis bound to the side of one of the gleaming white walls before she could run into a dead end in the unfamiliar alleyways.

Esther settled back to watch which way the soldiers ran, plucking a fistful of grapes from the trellised vine below and smirking at the ridiculous metal clothes catching in the sun. Their clanking step made tracking them laughably easy. The city was built on a hill, so most of the streets stretched out like a parchment map below her with milling bodies to populate it.

Her eyes turned back to the castle as she slipped down to search for a way to scale the walls before the soldiers returned. After all, why would anyone escape death only to break back into the home of the most powerful evil this land had ever held? The best place for her to hide until she could finish her task would be in death's own shadow.

Despite the hampered reach of her bound wrists, she was able to stretch her grip enough to scale up the stone wall, with the aid of some wood scaffolding that leaned against it. Her feet found footholds as her fingers clung to the wooden frame, nearly slipping once before she caught herself against a tethered beam. At last, she slipped over the top and broke her fall on a lush green hedge.

Esther bolted to a servant's side door and picked her way carefully down the hall, ready to blend into the shadows at the slightest sound. As servants made their way down the corridor, Esther strained to catch a few whispered conversations, though most were maddeningly trivial. An age seemed to pass before she overheard anything of use.

Down a long hallway with fewer doors and more lanterns, soft footsteps made Esther hold her breath. She tried a door to her right but it was locked. Her pulse pounded in her ears, blocking out the footsteps getting closer by the moment, as she backed up a few paces to try the handle of another room.

It gave a small groan but opened.

Once inside, Esther held the door almost closed, but not quite, as the footsteps were now accompanied by voices.

"Think we're far enough now?" A girl, maybe just younger than Esther, puffed out.

"I reckon so. No one but us servants come down here."

The girl sighed and let something heavy thud onto the floor. "Then can I just say, this stupid prince of ours has more clothes than any man should have. Do you know how many marks I spend scrubbin' out his unmentionables?"

Her companion laughed. "He is a vain one."

"And that's just the start of the day. After they dry, guess who has to lug them up to the third floor to put them all away?"

"I thought Bernie was helping you with that."

The younger girl scoffed. "Bernie doesn't lift a finger now that he and I are—well, he doesn't think he has to try so hard anymore."

"Since when has that been going on?"

The younger girl lifted her discarded load again with a groan. "Maybe a fortnight? I didn't mean for it to happen, but ... well it's better than the sixty-year-old pig keeper my mother wanted to sell me off to."

"*Sixty?*"

The footsteps passed Esther's room, but she waited for their laughter to die away before she allowed herself to breathe properly again. The third floor, that was where the prince's rooms were. At last after listening to so many pointless, gossiping, drudging conversations, some useful information was gleaned.

Esther glanced around the abandoned room. It wouldn't be long before nightfall. Navigating the more traveled halls of the castle in a black cloak lit only by torchlight would give her a greater chance of getting to the third floor and finding the prince without being spotted. This was as good a room as any to wait until the darkness allowed her to move. Until then, she picked through the items left in the room.

Long forgotten by time, huge trunks sat coated with dust, their rusted latches hanging open. Inside one trunk she found some oil and candles. Parchment paper, yellowed from neglect, lined the bottom. She pulled each item out carefully and laid them on the ground next to her. The other trunks were filled with clothes. Long, flowing dresses in vibrant colors, along with sashes, belts, and shoes. Esther pulled out a gown of shimmering red, grimacing at the gaudy fabric before dropping it back in the chest.

Her eyes lingered on the flask of oil, her fingernail tapping lightly on her chains. She snatched the flask off the floor and popped it open.

The air filled with a sweet heavy smell.

Esther fought back a sneeze. She pulled off her glove and rolled back her cloak before pouring the oil over her exposed arm. The cold honey-like liquid flowed over her skin, intensifying the smell almost beyond what she could bear. Once coated, she put the flask to the side and worked on pushing the iron clasp off of her wrist. It didn't slip off as she had hoped, but eventually, after coloring her arm white with scratches, she pried herself free. The other wrist gave her more trouble as her gripping fingers were now slippery with oil.

By the time the shackles were off her clothes were covered in the stuff, smeared in her struggle. She quietly retched, the smell overwhelming, and knew that the odor would remove any possibility of stealth through the castle.

Esther took off her cloak, her boots, her breeches, her tunic, and cast them in a heap on top of her discarded gloves. She scrubbed at her arms with the red dress to lessen the smell of the oil.

Esther could barely look at the trunks bursting with clothes, but she had no choice. She stuck her hand into one, grabbing at random.

Esther's fingers closed on a soft line of fabric, flowing cool and delicate beneath her hand as she traced the trail of a long forest-green gown. The black flow of fabric beneath the green made this one much more modest than others in the trunk. Much less conspicuous. The colors reminded Esther of home. Green and black had been her life for the last ten years, the forest and the demon were her safety. And now they would be the mask she wore to fool her enemies. She slipped the green dress over her head, swimming up through the folds of fabric to find the open air again. She grunted, tugging the strings at the back so the dress didn't hang off of her shoulders. She found shoes in the chest as well, and slipped them on while she worked through the knots in her hair with hooked fingers. Giving up, she stuffed the oil-soaked chains into the folds of the red dress and shoved them into the trunk.

The sky outside the open window filled with glowing reds that told of the darkness to come as the sun sank below the horizon. When the red faded to a deep purple and she watched the first stars spark to life, Esther made her way as quietly as possible to the door. She tugged at the clothes, her nervous fingers readjusting the fabric again and again as she struggled to listen past her own pounding heart. Esther winced as the door squealed through its hinges. Guessing on the most likely direction to encounter stairs, she marched forward, her ankles bending uncomfortably in her loud clacking shoes.

"Oi!" said a voice, and something thumped to the stone floor behind.

Heart pounding a wild, savage beat against her ribs, Esther turned.

"What are you doin' down here?" asked a servant, gathering the washing back into her basket.

Speak. Her mouth ignored the command, and hung open, utterly useless.

"Now you best come with me, Miss. Come on."

The old servant set the basket against her aged hip and gestured impatiently to Esther.

A well-placed kick would drop this old sack of bones and allow Esther to escape, but short of murder there would be nothing she could do to stop this old woman blathering to other servants about the strange girl she found roaming the halls.

She had only one real option.

Drawing herself up to her full height, Esther followed the aged servant, being careful to lock her feet into a calm, steady stride.

"Look at the state of you now," tsked the woman to herself. "You look as if you've been crawlin' through the castle rafters, but I'll set you right. Which rooms are you stayin' in this summer, love?"

"Oh," Esther's thoughts scurried, searching for something plausible. "I'm not quite sure, I only just arrived."

"Ah, so you are one of the Hildren House? They are the only ones to arrive today."

"Yes," she said, hoping the lie wasn't obvious in her quick reply. "That's it."

"I'll get you cleaned up then, and show you the room you'll be stayin' in."

"Perfect," Esther forced the word past clenched teeth as with each step she was more certain of the trap closing around her.

This was not the plan.

VIII

"Presenting the famed beauties of the North, Ladies Giselle and Rosemarie of House Jurut."

The young women curtsied to the court, fluttering long cloth fans against their dark cheeks, both sets of eyes fixing on Abner's with a narrow, aggressive hunger.

The prince readjusted his slouching frame and looked away from the dark-eyed women, just in time to catch several other ladies from far away houses casually turning their backs as if they had not been watching him a moment before.

"Well I do hope they find that creature soon," whispered a noblewoman to her gray-haired husband. "I shall not feel safe with some masked mad thing running around Lydia ready to attack our carriage at every breath. Have you been listening to what I've said? I heard—"

Abner discarded the gossip as he did the people. The news of the girl in black's escape was a relief, though he would never admit it aloud. He doubted he could bear the weight of more blood on his hands so soon. Abner's gaze bounced over his familiar dull world for anything that could fill his thoughts so his mind had no room for anything else. The prince mostly avoided pursuing noble-house daughters, too many expectations attached, but having these women as house guests for a full season every year made it hard to completely ignore them. His chin fell to his palm.

"Presenting the lady—what was it?"

The cane-wielding Master of Ceremonies who, in all of Abner's time knowing him, had never mispronounced a name or missed his entrances, now stumbled over his words. Boredom made even this small wrinkle in the typically smoothed cadence of court worth Abner's eye flickering to him. The cane tapped at the old man's ankle as he paused, clearing his throat to recollect himself.

"Presenting Lady Tessa of House Hildren."

Abner's lips pressed together, his smile rising high up his cheek as he took in the girl slowly making her way into the throne room.

She wore a dark green dress which made the skin of her shoulders gleam in the torchlight of the hall. It was in an older style, cut thinner to her form. The other ladies' dresses needed a wide circle of clearance, but this girl was able to slip around the milling group with quick sweeps of cloth. She pinned her back to the wall, displaying the full length of her neck as she tipped her chin to take in the height of the room. Her blonde hair was wound intricately on top of her head and her lips looked soft and full in their painted red sheen.

Abner had never paid much attention at meals with the surrounding nobles, but shouldn't he have remembered a creature like that?

The prince pushed himself to his feet and strode forward.

The crowd parted for him except for a few hopeful girls who curtsied in his path, playing a daring game to try to draw his eye before their dresses were snagged beneath his boots.

Each had to step aside, unsatisfied.

He stopped just shy of the girl. Her hip leaned against the wood framing a servant door, and he took a moment to appreciate the smooth curve.

Her eyes found him, a sudden gasp filling her chest.

"If I didn't know better," Abner pushed through the distance between them as he leaned a hand against the door. He looked down at her with a smirk, catching a light scent of something sweet that he couldn't place, "I'd say you were trying to escape."

The girl's eyes narrowed and she raised her chin, studying his face.

He studied her as well. Now that he was closer, he could see the powder on her face was hastily applied, the sheen on her lips imperfectly blended. Even still, the imperfections in her court-inspired finery only heightened his curiosity.

"Do you speak?" Abner asked, only half joking. That could be the reason he didn't remember her.

The girl paused. "When I have something to say."

Her quiet voice pulled at some memory in Abner's mind. He dismissed it.

"What does the Prince of Alberon want with me?" asked the girl as Abner continued to stare.

"Titles bore me," Abner said, letting his hand slip off the door and offering it to the girl. "I am Abner."

The muscles in her face tightened. Her hand trembled as it accepted his in a loose grip. Rough skin against his smooth cream-treated palms only stoked his interest.

When she met his eyes, hers were filled with some kind of blue fire. "Tessa," she said. Tessa dropped his hand and turned away.

She's leaving. "Would you like to walk with me, Tessa?" The words rushed out of his mouth. Too quick, too eager. Collecting himself, he fixed his conquest with a practiced-to-look-easy smile, but his eyes betrayed some of his fear that she would slip away and leave the evening to return to the dull event it had been before her.

The girl turned back and took a moment to look over his fine clothes before giving a small nod.

Pleased, Abner offered an arm.

She ignored it, striding toward the exit and out the gilded golden doors, leaving Abner to follow.

Obviously lost as soon as they left the throne room, Lady Tessa allowed Abner to lead her to the castle gardens. The curling roses and vibrant moonlight had aided him in making an impression on more than one coy maiden. As they emerged into the open air, Lady Tessa's shoulders rose with a deep breath of the crisp summer night.

"Are there many flowers where you're from?" asked Abner, stooping to pluck a rose from a low bush.

"Yes, but not many like this." She cradled a bud ready to open in her hand.

Abner presented the flower to her with an exaggerated bow. "My lady."

Esther struggled to keep her eyes from straying again to the dagger clasped at the prince's hip as he dipped into a bow. She could end this now if she could just get that knife. Ending the farce of Tessa, the long-lost niece of Hildren House, would be a mercy in itself. Her feet hurt, these shoes were ridiculous, and that servant had tightened her dress to a merciless degree. Luckily the rooms had been empty while the servant worked on her, so Esther hadn't yet answered any questions about herself to Hildren House. She hoped to be done with her task before that moment came.

The prince offered her a flower. He had taken her out of the party, away from any witnesses, of his own will, to die.

How sad.

How just.

Abner glanced up at her, checking her face for amusement.

Esther wondered if the smirk of triumph she couldn't keep from her mouth looked to him as if she were playing along with his joke. She took a step forward.

Snap!

Esther froze, her eyes swiveling toward the twig breaking under a heavy step.

The prince had been followed. One witness. A soldier. Young. Blonde. The same one who had wrestled the knife away from her in the tent. Cantus. Of course, he would be guarding his precious royal charge.

Abner must have found him watching as well, throwing several colorful words at the soldier lurking in the shadows.

The spilling red in Cantus' cheeks announced his embarrassment and a far door burst open, drawing his eyes.

Abner seized Esther's hand and pulled her out of sight, down a little lane that was bordered closely by tall hedges. Around another corner, several similar avenues branched off in different directions. Abner took the middle one, his eager stride leading them both further from any witnesses, deeper into the moonlit greenery. Checking over his shoulder, the prince grinned at Esther as his stride slowed. His hand brushed some stray hairs away from her eyes and, seeing the opportunity of the moment, she allowed him to close some distance between them.

Her fingers found the hilt of his dagger.

His teeth pinched his lip as his gaze dropped to her mouth.

She studied the sparks of yellow embedded in his dull brown eyes as she crept his dagger out of its sheath. She almost had it, just another—

"Oh!" The old woman drew back a pace toward the corner she had emerged from.

Esther's body recoiled with a snap, freeing the blade. She held the old woman's sharp gaze to keep herself from looking for where the knife had landed, silent in the thick grass.

The elder was propped by a cane and dressed in a muted purple gown, her blue eyes the only thing about her that seemed lively and not about to crumble to dust with a passing breeze.

"My prince." She bowed her head.

"Lady…" Abner hesitated.

"Hildren, Your Highness. Of the Hildren House."

"Lady Hildren," Abner nodded. "If you'll excuse us."

"My girl, what are you doing out this late?" The old woman fixed Esther in a stare of such sharp, layered intensity that her eyes could have popped from their sockets.

Lady Hildren. A tide of dread washed over Esther, flooding her gut. Had this woman been present when she was announced? "I was just…"

"No daughter of Hildren House will soil its reputation by being the receptacle for some illegitimate child. Now come along with me, my girl. We bid you good night, Prince."

Without seeing a way to plausibly remove the old woman, find the blade, and stab the prince, she took a place on Lady Hildren's right and followed her out of the spiraling hedges. Esther was so frustrated she forgot to be relieved that she hadn't been revealed. The prince followed a few paces behind as Esther studied the wrinkle-lined face of her unintentional co-conspirator.

Reaching the rose-filled garden, Abner was hailed by two ladies, the plumage of their attire filling every bit of space between the rows of flower beds. They leaned out from the arching pillars which marked the entrance to the garden, holding their dresses back from being shredded against the thorns.

"Prince Abner!" called one, her black hair rolling across one eye as she fluttered a fan toward her dark cheek. Her companion blushed behind her fingers, twittering a whisper like a fledgling in the speaker's ear. "We were afraid that you were," the lady's eye strayed to follow the line of Esther's gown with a narrow look, "retired for the evening."

Abner slipped forward, past Lady Hildren, with a last look at Esther. "I hope," he paused.

"Come dance with us, Prince Abner!" giggled the two girls.

"Go, Prince." The elderly woman rubbed the handle of her cane with a long gnarled finger. "Enjoy the ball. My great niece and I have much to discuss."

"You will be here tomorrow?" Abner pressed, walking slowly backward toward the castle entrance.

Esther said nothing.

The girls threaded an arm through each of his and led him back to the noise and the lights of the party.

Cantus hesitated before following the prince and his giggling companions.

The crickets chirped into the stretching silence.

Palms moist and breath shallow, Esther glanced at her companion.

The old woman watched her with sharp eyes and a wrinkled mouth tipped to one side.

"So, Aunt—I—"

"None of that." Lady Hildren drew her lips together in a hard line. "I lied for you. I am not stupid enough to think you are actually related to me."

"Then why?"

"There had to be a reason you would invent such a story. I wanted to see what you would do. You made quite an entrance with my family name inside. But finding you in the garden with him, I admit I am disappointed." A puff of stale breath wafted to Esther as the noblewoman sighed. "Just another girl looking to become higher than she ought, trying to grab a prince to wed."

"What? No, I—" Esther's stomach curled as a sudden sour taste flooded her mouth. Her lips sucked in a breath, and she worked to compose her face. "I—I mean, yes. That's right." Pushing past the popping tension in her shoulders, Esther nodded.

"I don't know what I was really hoping for. What other reason would bring you here?"

"Nothing I can think of," Esther said in a tone of deep regret.

"Well," Lady Hildren said, sizing Esther up. "I've already vouched for you, you are here under my name, therefore I must do something with you. We'll dress you up for the festivities tomorrow, and then tomorrow night an excuse will be given and you will depart. You will have your day in the sun, as long as you are able to behave properly. Then you shall go home, wherever that home may be, I do not care."

"Why would you still vouch for me?"

"Tessa was it?" Lady Hildren nodded as she turned away, bringing that topic of conversation to a jarring end.

Not knowing what else to do, Esther followed her. Her eyes lingered on the spiraling hedges as the door closed, shutting out her opportunity to get the knife back. She thought she would be brought to the throne room and submerged again in the sea of satin, ribbons, and frills, but Lady Hildren passed the large gilded doors without a glance. Collecting a practiced handful of purple fabric from her dress, the old woman traced the tall staircase leading up to her rooms with sagging, exhausted eyes.

Esther extended an arm, and the elder, with a look of surprise, wrapped her aged fingers around the offered elbow.

Lady Hildren let a small amount of weight lean on her young companion while the cane wobbled in her hand on the uncertain staircase footing.

Esther caught a fistful of her dress and hugged it to her chest, searching for her feet. The layered fabric tugged at the seam on her waist, dragging under her shoes more than once. At last, safely at the top, both women looked down at the treacherous climb with a breath of relief.

"Why they housed an old woman on an upper floor I will never understand." Lady Hildren clicked her tongue and began her slow plod down the hall and toward her room. "Come along, my girl."

Esther followed, working to memorize every corner and passage of the castle as they passed it. "Why didn't you want to rejoin the party?"

Lady Hildren let out a soft breathy chuckle. "When I was a younger woman I would have stayed and danced until the morning. But now, I see a little clearer. And I think I saved you from some trouble coming upon you and the prince when I did. I wouldn't send you back into that wasp nest in a hurry."

Having encountered literal wasp nests, Esther couldn't help but smile. Navigating the pompous prince's pretend world was nothing.

Besides, it would all be over soon.

IX

The morning was dark and cool.

Esther slipped out of her room before the sun broke over the horizon. She crept silently down the now memorized route to the castle gardens. A shiver rifled her shoulders, her skin pocking in the cold beneath her thin white shift. She met no one on the way, thankfully, and once outside amid the perfume of the red blooms she savored the sweet free air. All the gilded finery in that stone tomb behind her couldn't compare to the invigorating crispness of a summer morning. Even the stretching pillars lining the throne room which Esther had craned her neck to see the top of the night before were weak imitations of the massive pines of her forest.

Esther's eyes tightened through a sigh. *I'm sorry Fox. Sorry that I'm here to breathe in another morning but you're gone. It's not right, but I'm going to fix it ... and then I'll join you.* Stirring up the water droplets clinging to the grass stems as she passed, Esther followed the path she had walked the night before. At the opening of the clearing her feet hesitated, her eyes stretching large as twin moons, searching the ground for the telltale glint of reflected silver.

"Yes!" she hissed, stooping down. The cold metal bit her chilled fingers as she pulled the knife out of the grass.

"Early for you to be out, isn't it?" said a deep voice from too close behind.

Whipping around as she pressed the blade into the folds of her night shift, Esther's panicked eyes landed on the soldier. *Cantus.*

"Are you alright?"

"Oh." She dressed her voice in the fluttery, whimsical manner of the other women at court. "I just thought I ... the gardens are lovely this ... do you not agree?"

Looking at her as if she had sprouted an extra head, Cantus rested his hand on the hilt strapped to his waist.

Esther let her speech fade into an awkward giggle, her eyes darting above her tight smile.

"I just thought," Cantus said, stopping her feet as they began to edge away, "you might be more comfortable in this." He unclasped the heavy black cloak from his shoulders and held it out to her.

"Oh, thank you. I was cold," Esther admitted, taking it from him. She folded it over her arms, keeping the knife out of sight.

"I thought you'd appreciate wearing something you're used to."

Esther's lips parted, and she sucked in a breath.

With a smile, Cantus stepped back, unblocking the path.

Esther walked slowly back to the castle, feeling a pair of eyes on her back at every step.

She waited in her room until the sun was bright in the sky and Lady Hildren rapped on her door. "Wake up, my girl!" called the old woman. Without waiting for a response, the door was opened and several servants followed the noblewoman into the room.

Esther feigned sleepiness, stretching to cover the motion as she tucked the blade more securely out of sight under the bed.

"Arise, arise," commanded the old woman. She gestured for Esther to come to her and snapped at a servant to begin "making her up" for the day.

Lady Hildren gave instructions as Esther's hair was pulled, her body clothed, and her face painted. Esther tried to take in the information, knowing it was vital to escape detection long enough to complete her task, but her mind kept going back to what Cantus had said. *Something you are used to.* He knew. What other explanation could there be? If so, she was already marching toward the executioner's block.

Lady Hildren stepped back to take in Esther's courtly white dress and intricately pinned hair. She frowned. "Too much cream on her face. Again."

Without a word, Esther was wiped clean and the servant redid her work but only dabbed at a few spots on her skin.

Satisfied with the second attempt, Lady Hildren turned to leave, calling Esther with her.

"I will be right out," Esther promised, "just have to ... relieve myself."

Lady Hildren sighed and left, followed by the troupe of servants. Esther slipped to the floor and grabbed the blade, watching the door as she wrapped the metal in a light purple scarf that had been laid out for her and tied it to the inside of her thigh. As she turned to leave, her eyes caught her reflection in the large metal sheet leaning against the wall. It was the first time she had bothered to think about it, but Esther's fingertips traced along her skin and her carefully pinned yellow hair. She gave a small smile, despite herself.

The two women made their way down to the Great Hall for the first meal, as was customary Esther learned, and Lady Hildren continued her lessons on how to avoid the disaster of using an improper fork for the present course of a meal. She sighed, saying she could not expect Esther to learn a lifetime of manners in a single sitting, to which Esther was grateful because she didn't remember any of it. Her eyes kept straying to the paintings on the walls, the little statues of fierce-looking animals and stern-featured men tucked into each corner, and the rich deep rug beneath her feet.

Once inside the hall, Esther searched for Cantus. He met her gaze with a raised chin, and Esther's brow bent as she struggled to guess his intentions. Intrigue did not exist with animals. Her eyes lowered to the ground, shrinking from the impenetrable stare.

The air laid heavy beneath a load of contradictory, confusing scents. Esther's temples felt bound into a vice as her mind fought to sort them out. She strained her breath through pursed lips.

Matters were made worse when the king, upon noticing their arrival, demanded Lady Hildren and her charge be made to sit at the head table across from himself and the prince.

Lady Hildren's cane tapped into the unnatural quiet as they maneuvered around the smaller tables and blooming skirts to the offered chairs.

Cantus moved to stand silently behind Prince Abner.

Pleasantries, which neither seemed to find pleasant, were exchanged between the king and the noblewoman. Abner said nothing, but his eyes rolled over Esther with a wolfish smile that made her wish for her sling and a good smooth river stone.

A gentle steam rose from the dishes set before them, distorting the air. It pushed all other scents aside and Esther drank in the smell of sizzling meat and fresh warm bread, her mouth filling with eager water. With Lady Hildren's practiced fingers beside her as a guide, Esther began the careful excavation of what delicacies the rich hoarded on their golden plates behind their high white walls while begging hands just outside went hungry.

"And Lady Hildren, I hope you will introduce this lovely young blossom you have invited to my court. Who is she? Where did she come from?" The king arched his brow when the elderly woman hesitated. "Is she really such a mystery?"

"My niece. Great niece. We haven't met for many years, but she came to me and, yes, now she is family." Lady Hildren patted Esther's arm with trembling fingers.

Esther glared at Abner, challenging him to break his stare.

His grin stretched wider at the attention.

"Interesting." The king leaned forward, his eyes moving quickly between the two women. "Yes," he said, finally relaxing. "Yes, the resemblance is subtle, but present. So, my dear," he turned to Esther, the intensity of his gaze pinning her still, "you are the future Lady Hildren. There is a lot of history with that name, yes? Quite a lot of influence with the people."

Esther drew a shallow breath through her constricting chest. Her eyes checked her view for some unseen danger. "I suppose."

"But," continued the king, "I'm sure that has hardly crossed your mind. You must be so pleased to be reunited with your family again. Still, you should understand the consequences of whatever choices you make."

Lady Hildren met Esther's eye for a brief moment before she flourished her fan, breaking some of the tension by commenting on how splendid was the meal they were enjoying. "I have always told my nephew of the importance of starting the day with a well-cooked egg and a hearty meat." Her eyes drifted over Abner's shoulder.

The king regarded his own plate with a bored expression. "Indeed. I have heard the same. You must be comforted, knowing he is well-fed in our army."

"True, I dare say we are—ah—grateful for the esteem of his position."

"As you should be." The king nodded and signaled for his glass to be refilled.

Just as Esther's dress was beginning to feel the strain of her stuffed belly, the king stood to conclude the meal.

Abner rose, smirking at her.

"No." The king snapped his fingers under his son's nose as if he were a disobedient dog. "No time for that now. You must come talk with Lady Hildren and me."

Esther jumped as an avalanche of chairs scraped over the stone floor and a cacophony of voices began to chatter. The forest was not always a quiet place, but this sudden noise where it had been muted made every muscle in Esther's body spring to life.

A shade lighter, Lady Hildren stood with shaking hands pressed against the table.

Esther extended an arm to help, hoping her quick, jolting movements were not noticed.

The king shook his head. "My dear, I beg you to go explore the grounds. Enjoy the sun. Surely one of the guards can escort you…"

Esther made a quick exit, excusing herself hastily before a guard could be volunteered. As it was, she noticed Cantus slowly follow her out of the hall as she worked her way through the pressing crowd. Esther angled toward the castle gardens, longing for a breath of air that didn't carry the choking musk of scent, but was tracked there by a giggling horde of courtly women. They called out to her, and Esther sighed, lingering in a blink before turning toward them.

"Now, my dear," said one girl, striding out ahead of the other five in her band. Esther remembered her by the rich brown tone of her skin and the clever slant of her eyes, accentuated by shimmering powder. "What scheme are you working on with our dear prince?"

Abner leaned his hip into the table while the Great Hall emptied, his fingers bouncing on the wood. *What does Father possibly have to say to this old crone of the court? And why must I be here when he does?* His chest released a heavy sigh as the door closed behind the last straggler.

Lady Hildren stood before the king, leaning on her cane in her faded purple dress. What could she have possibly done to warrant such special attention?

"I don't think you are at any loss for why I wanted a moment to talk." The king paused. He folded his hands in front of him, his smile cocked to one side. "I have an interest in that niece of yours."

"In Lady Tessa?" Abner wrinkled his nose. "Father, you can't be thinking … she's so much younger than you and she's—besides what about—"

"Still your tongue or I will still it for you," snapped the king. He refocused his spark-penetrating stare on Lady Hildren, the intensity of which rose as each moment of silence was joined by another. "I wish for our houses to be united. The prince and your niece, new and old kingdom."

Lady Hildren's lips pressed together until they became a thin wall of white.

The king drew up to his full height, towering over her. "It is an honor I am offering you."

Abner straightened as well. *What honor? To be offered like property—a thing to be traded? No! I will not!*

The king's eyes stayed fixed on the noblewoman.

Finally, Lady Hildren cleared her throat. "My king, I—we have already given so much. Why not another house? There must be another, a better match here in the court. My niece, she is due to leave tonight and I fear she is an unsuitable companion for your son."

"Unsuitable? I decide!" declared the king, grabbing the cane from Lady Hildren.

Her feeble bones swayed, fighting for balance.

"You will say yes. She will marry my son. She will win the people's favor. An old kingdom noble, returning from disgrace, and the sovereign family graciously welcoming her back to unite our lines will be enough to get the people to ... it'll be enough. Yes." The glint of frantic desperation returned to the king's eyes.

If Abner didn't get control of this, his father might do something that couldn't be undone. The mark of which would last longer than any bruise. "I'm not—" Abner ventured forward a few paces, "I don't want to be married."

The king turned. "Did I ask for your consent?" He hooked Abner's neck with the handle of the cane, yanking him forward until his breath blasted hot against the prince's face.

Abner's eyes grew round, every muscle stiff.

"You hear, you obey. Else what good are you?"

Abner stumbled away as soon as the grip was released, rubbing at his neck.

"What then?" The king turned to Lady Hildren, brandishing the cane with wild eyes. "What do you say?"

"I—" Lady Hildren paused, breathing shakily, "I will inform her of the change in her circumstances. She is to be Queen—"

The king's eyes flashed.

"—someday. Thank you for exalting my family name." Lady Hildren worked her tired old lips into a pretense of a smile.

Abner marched from the room. Cursing, he kicked the wall, then uttered a worse word to soothe the throbbing pain in his toe. The prince put some speed into his step, as if he could outrun his father's decision to sell off his freedom. He made his way through corridors at random until, tired of every eye lingering on him, he slipped out into the castle courtyard.

It was empty except an old man scrubbing at a large black stain on the stone with soot-crusted hands.

Abner avoided his gaze and turned to the gate blocking the castle from the rest of the city.

Closed, locked, and guarded as ever, the gate was no escape for Abner.

He turned at the sound of the castle's main entrance creaking open.

Cantus peered around the side and checked over the courtyard. Seeing Abner, he straightened and gave a low bow.

The prince tossed his chin up, calling the inferior to approach.

As the soldier made his way forward, his eyes bounced across the courtyard, up to the viewing deck, and around Abner.

"Where have you been lurking, Cantus?"

Cantus' forehead creased. "I ... nowhere."

"Convincing." Abner ground the flat of his foot into the dirt. "Where is Captain Dennison? I haven't seen him this morning."

"Preparing for our departure, I imagine. The king has ordered a portion of the guard out to gather supplies for the Event."

Abner let a rush of air escape his nose as he folded his arms.

"We should be departing by midmark."

"Well, I need him. He helps with strategy and I—things have advanced. The king has..." Abner paused, picking at a loose string on his sleeve. "You should congratulate me."

"What's happened?"

"I am promised. To be married. For my life to end. I am traded away for the *people*." His nose wrinkled. "For their comfort. So they are happier to die while my father protects his own skin."

"Who are you supposed to marry?"

Voice flat, Abner said, "Lady Tessa of Hildren House."

"That—no—that isn't right." Cantus shook his head.

"And to think, if Lady Hildren hadn't found us in the garden we could have taken our pleasure from each other and then been done with it. Instead, we are to be shackled permanently together."

"No, Abner, that can't happen." Cantus' sudden intensity propelled him forward a step. "You have to stop this."

"Oh, you forget. I'm only the prince." Abner spat the bitter taste from his mouth. "I don't have any power to defy the king. Lady Hildren and he have agreed, so I guess I'm knotting the cord. The trap is closing upon me."

"Lady Hildren gave her support of this?" Cantus gave back his ground, his eyebrows folding together in thought. "Then her reputation, the house name, is tied to this union already."

"She didn't have much of a choice," Abner admitted.

The servant gave up on the black stain and slowly rose to his feet. Perceiving the prince's gaze, he pushed his tired legs to stumble out of sight.

"Has Lady Tessa been told?"

"I have no idea." Abner rubbed his face with his hands. "What does it matter? It's done."

"Maybe if you asked the king—"

"You don't know what you're talking about!" snapped Abner, heat rising under his skin. "What do you know about anything? You have never had to sacrifice anything in your life! You're a coward—a worthless, fatherless coward who has no future beyond what I give you!"

They stared at each other as the echoes faded.

At last, Cantus bowed.

Abner waved him away. Once alone, he felt the tide of a thousand thoughts pull at him, calling him to oblivion.

Esther was silent as the ringleader of the flock of women launched on another long pointless story. She had tried repeatedly to melt out of the group, but was always called back at the last moment. After the third failed attempt, she cleared her throat.

"Well, I'm going to leave." She nodded into the abrupt silence and walked away.

The women didn't bother waiting until Esther was out of earshot before they began to exchange opinions on her plain dress and obvious lack of any real beauty. How others they knew were so much more deserving of the attention she received.

Heat rose behind Esther's eyes as color filled her cheeks. What should she care if they thought she was ugly? What did looks matter on a corpse?

She began to wonder if she should seek out the prince with some pretense to draw him away, when Cantus rounded a corner ahead of her. She froze, frustration flashing through her at having forgotten about him.

Without a word and hardly a glance at her, he caught her arm and dragged her into a closet filled with wash basins, moldy towels, and pastes in clay jars lining the narrow walls. "You," he began, his lip pulling up over his teeth.

"Let go of my arm," Esther said.

Cantus ignored her. "What are you planning? Whatever it is, you need to abandon the idea. You are going to leave. Now. While there is still a chance."

"A chance for what? I'm just a guest of Lady Hildren's." Esther realized her eyes were probably too wide, and she blinked to hide her awkwardness.

"Who arrived mysteriously unannounced on the same day a girl in black who has a death wish and a vendetta against the prince escapes? How many times have you failed to kill him already?"

"I—that's just a coincidence."

"Really? Then I suppose this news will be a pleasant surprise for you. The king has decided you are to marry Prince Abner."

The wave of burning bile stung Esther's throat. He already knew. What was the point of pretending? She spat to one side. "I must say, I'm surprised. You have gotten bolder, cornering me like this. And you haven't told him. Why?"

Cantus looked away. "It doesn't matter. You need to leave."

"I can't do that."

"You risk an old woman's life if you stay. Do you really want more blood on your hands?"

"And why would that matter to me?" Esther pulled her arm out of his grip. "But what do you mean?"

"The king will assume she planned with you to conspire against him. You die and so does she for vouching for you. She doesn't deserve that." A fine mist spread over Cantus' eyes, and he swiped at his nose with his now free hand.

Esther's gaze narrowed. "Why didn't you tell the prince about me?"

Cantus would not meet her eyes, instead pushing the toe of his boot into the floor and watching it spread dust.

Some floating pieces of information about the nephew of Lady Hildren, in the army, and given an esteemed position finally reconciled in Cantus' averted gaze. "Oh, hello cousin."

Cantus' eyes snapped to hers. "We are not related."

"But you and Lady Hildren are. I suppose I should have wondered how they picked the royal babysitter for the prince." Esther smirked.

"None of this matters. You need to leave and then things can go back to normal. She'll be safe."

Esther took a step closer to Cantus, letting her eyes shine with intensity and pulling her lip up into a snarl.

Cantus took a half-step backward, staring at her. "I'm sorry," he said, holding up his hands. "Are you trying to be intimidating?"

Esther leaned back.

"You, without the cloak, dressed like that? No, that doesn't work."

Sliding her foot back to test her space, Esther raised her hands like twin knives. "I'm not leaving."

"Then you will let her die for your plot?"

Esther threw her weight forward, leading with her fist, and struck Cantus in the chest.

He remained maddeningly still.

When she drew back to strike again, he caught her hand, twisted it, and Esther found herself on the ground. "Let go of me," Esther's voice rattled behind clenched teeth.

"I don't have time for this," Cantus said, leaning over her. "Leave or I will make you."

"What makes you think she will be safe even if I go?" Esther twisted her arm, forcing Cantus' grip to loosen. She slipped out of his grasp and sprang to her feet, giving him a sharp kick to the knee to win herself space.

He stumbled back against the wall, breaking several clay jars.

"When have you ever known a royal to willingly let go of a conquest? Is torture over information preferable to death in your eyes?"

"Another attempt on the prince's life will mean definite execution, whereas that is only a possibility."

Esther edged herself toward the door.

Cantus extended a hand in warning.

"I'm not leaving. I will try to protect her, if I can. But more important than anything else, I have a quest to complete."

"Quest? This isn't a quest, it's a vendetta. You doing this, sacrificing an old woman's life so you can use her like a human shield, makes you just like the king." Cantus watched Esther grip the door handle, but the noise of a passing servant made him stop talking.

Esther put a finger to her lips and gave a mocking smile before slipping out. She didn't allow herself a moment to breathe or collect her thoughts, instead setting off with heavy clacking footsteps, more than once almost rolling her ankle in her haste. She needed time to think of a way out of this, how to succeed now that it was not just her life at risk. Fox's face haunted her thoughts.

I must set this right. No matter the cost.

It was around fourth mark when Abner opened his eyes, blinking against the late-dipping sun. A breath away, a pile of auburn spirals reflected the glaring light as it caught the curls. The stale taste of old drink coated his tongue. His stomach curled as he pushed himself to sit up. A cup of old wine helped to clear the musk and quiet the throbbing of his head.

The girl rubbed her eyes. Squinting at him, she smiled. "My prince."

Abner's nose wrinkled as he tossed the servant's frock to her.

Her eyes spilled silently. She slipped the clothes over her head and stood. "What would you like me to do, Your Highness?"

"Leave."

The bed creaked as she rose.

"Find the Healer to fix it. Tell no one."

The door closed and he was alone.

Abner pulled breeches over his waist before walking out onto the balcony to lean over the side. He rubbed his temples, muffling his groan into his palms as the last pleasant numbness of the drink faded away.

Somewhere around the third bottle, he had considered pulling one of the court ladies from the herd, but the thought of having to convince her of any good intentions had made his limbs heavy. Upon retreating to his room, he had found a servant girl leaving with a basket of soiled garments on her hip. She was young and not ugly, and this offered the perfect release for the depression he felt.

Or so he had thought.

Now that it was over, and his mind stretched ahead through the long years when he would only have a wife and perhaps some chance meetings like this one, he felt worse than ever.

Why was Fate so cruel to him?

❖ ❖ ❖

Esther slipped into her room and leaned her head on the door as she let out a shaky breath.

"Well, my dear, we have made quite the mess."

Esther spun to face Lady Hildren sitting on a chair next to the window ledge. Her skin seemed to sag more than usual, as if it was tired of holding together.

A light wave called Esther forward to sit down on the bed.

Lady Hildren looked out over the city. "I suppose I should tell you what has happened." She rubbed her mouth with a bent-knuckled finger. "I ... well, you are going to be staying a bit longer. It seems the king has taken a liking to you and wants you to marry the prince."

Esther forgot to feign surprise.

"The wedding will be held after the Event. That should give us enough time."

"Time for what?"

"To prepare you. Do you not understand what this means? You will be the future queen, you will birth royalty. It is an honor."

"Then why don't you look ... honored?"

"Did you know," said Lady Hildren after a moment of ear-ringing silence, "I did actually lose a niece, a grand niece. She escaped during the king's ascension, I think. She was only five—no, six years old. She had blonde hair, like you. I don't know how she got out but I never saw her during the—she could still be alive." Lady Hildren's sad old eyes turned to Esther. "Where did you come from?"

"I lived in the forest to the East."

Lady Hildren studied her, then nodded. "Well, you could be her then. Who's to say, really? As long as we play our part well, nothing bad will happen." Lady Hildren tapped her nose with her finger. "That is your first real lesson. You must play your part. Don't be concerned whether you love the prince or feel like a queen. Act like it and you will often grow to."

This began a steady stream of instructions and advice, all of which Esther ignored except one piece that caught her attention.

"And you will find that your passion for something may wane. Passion always does eventually. Stick to it anyway. Don't become complacent in your task, especially your duty to others."

Fox's white-tufted face filled her mind and Esther's shoulders dropped. What real progress had she made toward her goal? How had plot after plot gone wrong, and yet she kept repeating her actions and expecting it to go differently? She needed time to formulate a good plan, something that couldn't be circumvented by a chance interruption.

Maybe allowing the wedding to happen would give her that time.

"Now, my dear, it is important that you..."

Lady Hildren's voice faded in and out of hearing as Esther watched the old woman talk.

"...and if you ever..."

Esther imagined what the noblewoman's execution might be like, picturing that mouth being forever stilled because of the choices Esther made. Could she really allow that to happen?

Before she had an honest answer, the servant troupe assigned to ready the nobility each night arrived to help them dress.

As she was remade, Esther resolved to play her part as best as she could.

The troupe left with Lady Hildren after working on Esther, leaving one girl behind to finish the job. Esther couldn't help but admire the skill in the young maid's fingers as she twisted every lock of hair into perfect placement and pinned it for good measure. The girl avoided Esther's eyes as she worked, her fingers darting in and out of view in the smooth shine of the metal plate propped in front of them.

"What's your name?" asked Esther.

The girl jumped, her brown curls bouncing. "I'm called Ava."

Esther smiled, struggling to find something to say. "Do you like to do hair? You're very good at it."

Ava's eyes narrowed as she stared at her work. "I suppose."

"You seem ... not content."

"If your hair wasn't so uneven I could give you nice curls and—" Ava's gasp brought both hands over her mouth as her eyes grew wide with horror. "I'm—apologies, Lady. I misspoke. Such beautiful hair."

"It's awful," laughed Esther. "But you have done a good job with the mess you were given."

Ava's smile broke through her fingers as she struggled to stifle her laugh. "I've had much practice."

Esther grinned at the maid's reflection. Her attention strayed back to her own image, eyes seeking out every flaw. The slight discoloration of her teeth, the red dot on her chin, everything would be covered over by the skillful hands to which she entrusted herself.

"You're very pretty," Ava acknowledged, seeing Esther's perusal.

"Really? You think so?" Esther tried to see it too.

"Most of the girls here," Ava leaned down to whisper in Esther's ear, "they have worn pasted makeup every moment of their waking life and their skin is riddled with blemishes they're hiding. The more they try to cover it up, the more they have to hide." She rose back to her full height and began slowly picking through the pins in Esther's hair. "You don't have as much to hide."

Esther let the compliment ferment in her mind. She savored this frivolous concern, as a child might enjoy a sweet treat. The kindness was a new experience to her, and the honesty it showed was unheard-of in this place. Ava's face wore her feelings openly, and it was a relief to not have to work at dissecting her true intentions within every veiled word.

"Do you live here in the castle?"

"No," Ava said, bringing her canvas bag of supplies to the table beneath the metal sheet and setting up to apply the cream paste. "Only the year-round servants do. I'm just brought in over the summer when there is company to appease."

"And the rest of the time?"

"A neighbor has a large vegetable field outside the city that often needs tending to. I pull weeds, mend the fence, all that sort of thing." Ava's mouth tightened, as if the memory of the work brought a pain. "We do alright though. My mother gets a bag of gold from my brother regularly and we are usually able to keep bread on the table until the next one arrives." Her dark eyes met Esther's. "It's not an easy life."

"I know what that's like," Esther said.

Ava's eyes sparked with interest.

Esther shook her head to try to brush past it. "I mean ... I have gone through hard times as well."

"I heard you're a long-lost niece of the lady?"

"Yes." Esther tried to gather into her mind all the information she had been piecing together about her put-on identity. "Lady Hildren is my great aunt."

"So where have you been all these years?" Ava took her time choosing what shade of pink to spread on Esther's cheek.

"I'm not sure exactly where. I wasn't in a town. I had a friend who helped me get supplies and I lived on my own."

"You were alone? But how did you escape? And who helped you? Did you know who you were?"

Esther wasn't ready to give so many details. "It's ... I'm sorry, could you get me something to drink? My throat is..."

Ava's enthusiasm was pulled back with difficulty. "I'll run and fetch it." She disappeared out the door with one lingering look of curiosity.

Esther moved to the window, hoping for a breeze to cool her face. She traced a path of escape down the castle wall. A small drop from the spreading awning to the ground was simple enough, a bar jutting from the stone wall would get her to the awning, and she was confident she could slip from the window ledge she leaned against and land with her balance on the wooden bar. Glancing down at the voluminous folds of her dress she shook her head, turning from the window.

The silk gown rustled pleasantly as she sat down on her bed covered in fresh sheets. Her fingers pet the whisper-soft fabric of the canopy hanging down her bed posts. Esther had never known luxury, had never imagined anything man-made could be so delicate as the items gathered in her little room.

It will all be over soon.

Esther opened her eyes as Ava returned with the drink. She had apparently mussed her hair leaning her temple against the post holding up the canopy over her bed.

Ava reset the mislaid hairs.

The conversation after that was patchy and Esther did not try to reignite it.

Ava's hand paused before adding a last brush of powder along Esther's cheek. "Smile please, m'lady." Her narrowed eyes assessed her work with a frown. "I think that'll have to do."

Esther let her smile drop. "You still don't seem content."

Ava lifted a shoulder as she clasped the powder and dropped it into the canvas bag with the other used beauty supplies. "I never am."

"Thank you, Ava."

The servant bowed, stepping away from her position as friend to one employed to help. The awkwardness of this invaded the room.

Esther admired Ava's work in the metal sheet, turning her blemish-free chin from side to side as her eyes took in every detail. "I think you did wonderfully."

Ava leaned forward and pulled one strand that had wriggled loose of its pin back into place and forced a smile. "You look beautiful. I think Prince Abner will be pleased." She turned away before displeasure twisted Esther's features, freeing the other of the need to explain. Slinging the clattering bag against her shoulder, she walked to the door.

"Can I help?" Esther asked, standing with her.

Ava turned back, her head thrust forward and her features pulled into a slant of confusion. "No?" She shook her head and left with a chuckle.

At the last mark meal, Esther and Abner couldn't look at each other. The king talked to her through every bite however, smiling amid the steam of his soup as he slurped it from the bowl. She had hoped Lady Hildren and she would be able to slip into a back table and avoid notice, but the king had given instructions to the servants. They were led through the choking cloud of scents to the head table as soon as they entered the hall.

Esther now sat opposite to the king, and, more than ever, she wished to have her cloak back to hide from his eager eyes. When he rose and spread his hands before the court, Esther's heart jumped against her ribs as a thousand voices rumbled to life.

Lady Hildren cocked her chin and Esther mimicked her bowed posture.

"You, O King, are infinite. Let your eternal light shine on us for another year of glory, blessing us by your continued reign. Every sacrifice and honor to you, ruler and decider of Fate." The chant—deep, reverent, and strange—drew Esther's muscles to coil. "May your glory never fade."

It was an exhausting evening, feigning interest in things she didn't understand or places she had never been. The king sought constant affirmations that everyone listening felt blessed and honored being included in any conversation he thought to bring up. Her cheeks ached from nodding and smiling.

Curse every Fate that led Abner to notice me. I could probably be done by now, Fox and Jathan and the rest appeased, if I didn't have so much attention fixed on me every moment. Perhaps being forced into this promise is the price I must pay to complete my task. Surely there will be benefits to it.

Maybe she would gain access to the kitchen, poison their meal and murder the whole treasonous bunch of nobles!

Her grin faded when she bid good night to Lady Hildren after their careful climb up the stairs and now second nature task of navigating the halls to their rooms. How many people trying to survive amid dreadful circumstances did her actions risk? Was it worth it to stop the voices in Esther's dreams? Head rattling with doubt, Esther closed her door with a sigh.

At the midmark meal the following day, Abner strode to meet Lady Tessa as soon as she entered the hall. The older woman was already seated before the king, her fan fluttering like a bird's beating wings to make a breeze for her cream-smeared wrinkles. The flashing movement worsened the headache pounding his temples. Even a morning spent sparring with the guards who were left hadn't made him feel any better.

Those nearby quieted their conversation, subtly watching as the prince halted in front of Lady Tessa.

With a mocking smile that made his face twitch, Abner bowed.

She dipped into a clumsy curtsy in reply.

"How would you like," Abner began, moving his lips as little as possible to make the gossips work harder, "to eat elsewhere today?"

"Where?" Lady Tessa's eyes narrowed as her chin tipped to one side.

I'd settle for a dunghill at present. Anywhere to be away from my father and the host of staring eyes. "My rooms. I have a balcony that has a nice view of the city. I can have servants bring everything out to us. It's no trouble."

"To you," Lady Tessa whispered, then shook her head and dressed her features in a smile. "Why not?"

"Excellent. I'll meet you outside." Abner caught the arm of a nearby servant as he was about to pour a drink for a noblewoman.

Her eyes flashed at the interruption of her service.

"Grab a few plates, food, all of it. Get someone to bring it to my room."

The servant hesitated, his trembling hands clutching the wine pitcher.

"I'll take that while I wait," Abner said, pulling the pitcher out of his grasp. "Go!"

The apron-belted man scurried away and Abner met the noblewoman's stare as he took a swig of wine straight from the pitcher's mouth before sauntering from the hall.

Where is she?

The corridor was empty. Abner's brows folded together, his teeth grinding. Taking a guess at where the Hildren rooms might be, Abner leaped up the grand stairs three at a time. Rounding a corner, his boot slipped over a soft shoe.

The servant girl yelped, stumbling back as she gripped her toes.

"Watch where you walk," Abner snapped.

"A thousand apologies," she said, her cheeks pinched pink in pain. She swept an auburn curl from her forehead.

Oh, it's her. "Did you see the Healer as I instructed?"

"Of course, Your Highness."

"You know what my father would do to you, *and to it*, if you lie."

"It's done, my prince."

Lady Tessa's quick feet clicked across the floor.

"Where did you go?" Abner folded his arms. "I've been waiting for you for half an age!"

The servant slipped past him, her neck tucked between her shoulders as she hurried out of sight.

"I'd forgotten something in my room. I'm ready now."

"Shall we?" Abner offered an arm.

Tessa strode past him.

Eyebrows raised, Abner reclaimed the lead. The balcony was open and a table prepared beneath the awning's shade.

The guard standing in the corner of the room was a silent irritation Abner struggled not to notice.

Lady Tessa, obviously uncomfortable, stared at the room, her brow tightening at a table stacked with spilling scrolls that Abner had forgotten to put away from his self-guided lessons, neglected during his long absence.

"Forgive the mess," Abner said, stepping around her to block the view. "An unfortunate side effect of being a future king. Lots of busy work. Do you like to read?"

"Uh ... some ... sometimes."

Abner sighed. "Shall we?" He gestured toward the balcony.

"They set all of this up so quickly," Tessa said, brushing a finger across the fresh flowers overflowing out of a metal mug at the center.

"There's a network of passages in the walls the servants use. It's a little unnerving actually." Abner looked at the spread critically as he filled both their glasses with the pitcher of wine. "Well, sit. Might as well get this over with." He collapsed into the chair—comfortable and high-backed—that had been moved out from his room for him.

Tessa slowly took the seat opposite his, which creaked as she sat.

They stared at each other for a long moment of silence.

"So, Lady Tessa..." The weight of the years ahead of him hung as an overladen pack strapped to his shoulders, dragging him to the ground. "Tell me about yourself." He didn't like listening to answers to these questions at the best of times, but this was compounded now. Every answer gained lessened the mystery of her which was all he had left in this exchange. Still, custom was custom.

"I ... there's not much to tell."

"Just as well," said Abner, popping a round red fruit in his cheek and taking his time to chew it noisily into the deepening silence. He swallowed hard and reached for another, his hand pausing just before he touched it. "You can eat."

She jumped, broken out of her trance-like stare.

"I know," Abner said, interpreting her look with a pained smile, "my table manners are atrocious." He chewed through his words as the second fruit split between his teeth, "Blame my lack of female influence." Waiting for a look of amusement or sympathetic understanding that never came, Abner sighed, flicking his finger free of the small green leaf that clung to it. "So you seem ... nice? Anything else I should know about you?"

Lady Tessa looked into the room toward the guard silently watching. She cleared her throat. "Does it really matter?"

"Lady Hildren told you?" The awkwardness of his position covered him like a stifling blanket. "Are you not honored?"

Lady Tessa did smile then, her lips pressed tight together as her eyes looked over the city.

"You are to marry the future king. Can you really hope for better? If you have to give yourself away, why not to royalty?" Abner waited for a blush, a chuckle, a shrug of acknowledgment, anything to tell him she appreciated the honor of his hand and did not feel trapped into marrying him like he did to her. Instead, she stared wordlessly at the city spread before them and Abner gave her up as dull. He set to eating his food without bothering to look at her, irritation making him chew with more than necessary force.

Pain lanced through his jaw as his teeth missed their mark. His hand slapped the table, the other cradling his bitten cheek. *Bleeding! Stars above, that hurt!*

He caught the smile Lady Tessa worked to hide and frowned at her. "Amused are we?"

She fixed him with a cold eye, her lips curling ever so slightly. "Not at all, Prince." At last, she began to eat. Her teeth ripped meat from the bone as voraciously as he did.

Perhaps there was more to her after all.

He had his entire lifetime to find out.

XI

Two weeks of failure. Esther allowed the realization of how long she had waited, trying to think of a plan to finish the prince, to steep in her mind as she was fixed up for the day. Even the discovery of the exact path to his rooms did little to help as there was always a guard standing silent in the shadows. Her little knife would only scratch up the guard's armor like a cat's claw on a rock face. The passages within the walls were promising, but, try as she might, she couldn't find an entrance. So she waited.

All she was required to do here was wake up, allow herself to be made 'presentable', and then wander and amuse herself with company or alone. The long absence of the soldier, Cantus, made this much easier. She told herself repeatedly, whenever the guilt of her inaction occurred to her, that it would be easier and probably more efficient to remove the prince when she had more access to him. Whenever she saw him now he was accompanied by a guard, and during their planned and enforced time together, though both tried to think of a way to disappear, that watchful presence was always lurking at a quiet distance. Even if she had to wait till the wedding night, when she was sure to have ample time alone with the prince to complete her task, the job would be done. *I am not a failure. I just need more time.* Repetitions of this sentiment coddled her uneasiness until it faded away again.

While she waited there was no harm in enjoying another *scadia*, a Keldeeman treat of light layered bread and mashed fruit, which she had asked to be delivered from the kitchen to her room for the past six mornings. Esther frustrated the women working to assemble her face for the day by sneaking small quick bites whenever their backs were turned. It was bursting with tangy, sweet fruit that left red smears of evidence on the corners of her mouth.

Hiding their emotions in masks of indifference, the practiced fingers would remove all traces and resume their work until the next surprise scuff on their masterpiece.

"Which corset would you prefer today?"

Esther stared at the stiff, fringed fabric held up for her examination. Both the pale blue and the pink looked like some kind of torture device.

"I've never had to wear one before."

The maid hesitated. "The king wishes it."

"The king has an opinion on my underclothes?" Esther leaned away from the corsets even farther.

A little red spilled over the woman's cheeks. "Apparently he has a preference."

"Well," Esther slapped her thighs as she stood. She chose the blue and was strapped in. "Hmm." She let out her breath, her belly pushing against the unyielding garment while her waist stayed the same thin, molded shape. "It's not too bad actually." She let a hand rest on her hip. "Kind of like a hug."

One gray-haired woman leaned forward. "Give it time, love."

The ladies in the room chuckled good-naturedly.

"Which shoes today, Miss?" asked another servant, gesturing to several frilly options.

"I..." Esther struggled to have an opinion. "Honestly, I have no idea. What do you think?"

The woman hesitated.

The room stilled.

"You ... you want to know what I think?"

Esther nodded.

"Well, if it were me—which of course it couldn't be—I'd pick ... this?" she pointed to a shoe with a wide low heel. It was smooth and white with only a single ruffle of lace. "You seem to like to be active, and I think of the three, this would be the most comfortable to move in." Her cheeks filled with color. "Begging your pardon, I didn't mean to declare any opinion of your—"

"Perfect. I'll wear those." Esther smiled, accepting the help to slip into the pair. These were nothing like her rough boots whose heels stuck in the mud every rainy season and left sores on her feet when the water leaked in. These were sensible, comfortable, and lovely. "Thank you."

"Thank you, madam." The maid dipped into a quick curtsy, unable to stop the smile spreading across her face. Her glassy eyes danced with sparks of early sunlight as she excused herself with the others.

One old maid tutted to another just before the door closed, "Sweet girl, real shame."

Esther took a moment to admire herself in the metal sheet one last time before following them out the door.

The day would probably follow the same pattern of arbitrary pursuits of pleasure, and Esther found herself musing about a morning walk in the garden. It was easy to ignore the prince's presence while she planned her route through the labyrinth, but more difficult to put out of mind was the king's narrow, pursed-lipped stare. Her jaw chewed through the crunching fruit and sticky cheese laid out for her.

"I think, Abner," the king spoke so loud and sudden that the knife jumped from Esther's hands to clatter onto the floor.

Her cheeks warmed as she retrieved it.

"Don't do that," the king snapped.

Esther met his severe scowl with a forced calm as a servant appeared behind her and whisked the blunted knife away. A moment later, a new polished utensil was slid into place beside the others, awaiting her use.

"That's what they are there for." He took a breath to settle himself. "I think, Abner, you must need some help with your betrothed. You will go on a ride in the enclosed pasture."

"Help? I don't understand."

"You are wasting everyone's time." The king sighed. "If it were me, Lady Tessa would already be heavy with child. It's important for the people to see you two as a strong couple, and an heir will lend you some sorely-needed strength."

Lady Hildren stifled her shock by dabbing her mouth with a napkin, her eyes hardening.

"I'm your son, not a horse for breeding," Abner whispered, his lips pulling tight over his teeth.

"And yet, you're failing on both accounts." The king laughed, those around him breaking from their conversation to join in without bothering to understand the joke.

Abner's face reddened. "It's not my fault! You expect me to make an heir with an audience watching? Your guard follows us every moment, and she—" Abner's eyes found Esther's and his voice fell silent.

The king's lips pulled into a tight smile. "Yes, maybe this is a conversation for another time, since you insist on being so explicit." The king ignored Abner's start of indignation. "I don't expect to see head or rump of you until the day's end, and will have a full report from your escort. Leave after the morning meal."

Esther tried to convince herself that it was fortunate her morning walk was canceled in favor of time with the prince. Maybe there would be an opportunity during the ride, a chance to make the charade end. That was a good thing. Wouldn't it be nice to not have to play pretend? To stop dancing around the truth and enjoy one moment of glaring honesty before she died? Isn't that what she wanted? Finishing her meal with a last regretful bite, Esther brushed her hands on her dress as she stood.

"Where are you going?" Abner demanded, his face pinched into a sulk.

"I assumed I would need to change. Can't really ride a horse in this." *Can't really ride a horse at all, but how hard could it be?*

"Well, do it quickly." Abner tossed his fork onto his plate, leaning back. "Apparently we're in a hurry."

Esther left the hall. A servant, whose freckle-lined cheeks returned Esther's smile, fell into step beside her.

"A moment if you would, Lady."

Esther almost missed the gray-haired man leaning against a wall behind the door.

His lips pulled up into a tight smile over his shockingly white teeth.

"Hello," Esther said uncertainly, extending a hand.

The older gentleman took it and placed a scratchy kiss on her knuckles. "A true and glorious pleasure, Lady Tessa."

Esther pulled her hand away and looked around the deserted hall. "Do you need help with something?"

The man glanced at the servant standing at Esther's shoulder as he closed the distance between them.

The servant understood the subtle cue and vacated the hallway.

"As a matter of fact, I do. You seem like such a bright young girl. I have a problem that I think you could help with." He paused, inclining his head toward her. "I should probably introduce myself. Sir Rowan of Avery House. Old, old family, like yours."

Esther nodded vaguely.

He smacked his lips. "I have taken on the honor of introducing a more modern water system to the city. The wells we have now are being horribly over utilized. You see the problem, don't you? We must bring water into the city."

Esther nodded again.

"To that end, I've drawn up plans to construct a huge cistern that will collect the rainwater during its given season and then to have every street dug up and a massive network of interlocking metal to bring the water to certain points within our walls. Of course the lower quarter only needs diverted water from the river tributary, which will be the next phase to tackle."

"I don't understand."

His smile slipped into a sympathetic wince. "You don't really need to. It is complex. All I need from you is to talk to the king about funding. That is all that is holding us back. Of course his armies are a priority, certainly. But how long will we last in a siege without water, eh?" He ran a hand through his gray locks before resetting the smile on his lips. "I think I could be very useful to you here. If you can find a way to be helpful to me."

"You want me to talk to the king?"

"If the moment arises." The nobleman bowed, catching Esther's hand in a kiss once more. "You will do well here, young one. With help."

His clacking footsteps echoed down the hall and carried him out of sight.

Esther had to jump out of the way as the door burst open and a stream of nobles poured forth. She was swept along with the tide, riding it to the stairs which led up to her room.

Esther didn't try to kindle a conversation with the freckle-cheeked maid. Instead, she was quickly clothed in a voluminous dress of muted gray with the efficient fingers of someone who knew the motions of their work by feel more than thought.

The maid stopped to fluff out the layered fabric. "These extra folds will keep you covered more modestly in your sidesaddle, Lady. Just have a care not to fall or you could get tangled up in them."

Esther swallowed. *How hard could it be?* The waiting maid held the door for her as she exited the room just as the morning was starting to warm.

Abner waited by her door, shocking her with his sudden presence. "Ready?" He struggled to smile. "Off to the breeding stocks we go then."

Following him down the hall, Esther tried to reason herself out of her worry. "I have a confession," she said, breaking the silence of two long hallways.

Abner looked back at her, eyebrows lifted.

"I ... don't know how to ride."

"Of course you don't," Abner sighed as he turned away. "Most women of the court only learn enough to go on little walking trails and stop altogether once they're married."

"I'd like to learn, maybe. I'm just giving you a fair warning ... how are you even supposed to ... with a dress and all?"

Abner chuckled. "I wouldn't know what that's like. I can teach you some basics though. I've been told I've got a good seat. Barely ever fallen off."

"But you have fallen? Hmm."

Abner's eyes ran across Esther's mask of contrived tentativeness.

"I just wonder if you're really the best teacher then."

His grin was slow but wide. "You ... are bold." Abner paused at the doors which led out of the castle. "Lesson number one: falling is a part of riding. You learn a great deal by failure."

Esther ruminated on the words as they were engulfed by the sudden noise of a bustling city with thousands of cares. A carriage waited at the lowest step to the courtyard and a stern-faced guard held it open for them to enter. She hesitated to follow Abner into the dark door.

"I thought we were riding?"

Abner's head popped back through the opening. "We don't keep the horses here at the castle unless we need them. They're brought in from the pastures outside the city. We'll be taking a country ride."

The guard gave a forceful nod for Esther to climb in.

Mouth tight at the need for obedience, she picked the furthermost corner from Abner as her seat. The carriage leaned as the guard joined the driver on the raised bench. They jolted forward, the steady clopping of hooves announcing their passage through the city. She tried to breathe through her drumming nerves. Couldn't she do it now? A glance at Abner, staring out the window, sent the idea drifting from her mind. *Not yet.*

The sound of hooves filled the space between them.

"It's not something I've really thought of before, but being enclosed in buildings all your life can be suffocating. It's almost a relief to be outside of the castle." Abner stared out the window, his eyes darkening as he blew a heavy breath through his nose.

"I wouldn't know," Esther said, drawing his eye.

"Where *did* you come from?" he asked, as if the question had never occurred to him before.

A bump in the road saved Esther from needing to answer as the door bounced open.

Abner caught it, his hand slowly pulling it closed. "I have an idea."

Esther tilted her head, willing him to continue.

"It's dangerous." Abner leaned toward her. "Let's jump."

Esther glanced out the window as the city sped past their view. The carriage made its own way through the spiraling streets, people darting out of its path as it rolled down the hill with near-reckless speed. A fall would hurt, and yet ... every moment of hesitation would be a missed opportunity to get lost in the thicket of buildings. Time alone, just like she'd planned. She nodded.

The light spreading across Abner's features as his face pulled tight into a grin must have been an expression left over from childhood, before selfishness and corruption took hold. Pushing open the door, he waited.

Too long. Esther opened the opposite door and slipped onto the road, her weight's sudden disappearance making the carriage teeter uncertainly as it rounded a shallow corner.

The carriage rocked to two wheels as Abner followed, bounding out to freedom. He ran back to Esther and snatched her hand as the guard called for the driver to stop. The horses' fierce neighs echoed after them as Abner and Esther sped down the narrow alley, hand in hand.

One turn, then another.

Abner took each corner with ever-increasing speed, nearly bent in two from laughing. In his glee, Esther realized as she tracked the turns, he was leading them straight back to where they had started.

Esther pushed ahead, pulling him down the opposite path. "This way," she insisted. "Trust me."

Any resistance Abner had felt melted from his hands. He was led down the ever-darkening alley by this mythical, confusing creature. Lady Tessa, he mused, as she swiped her forehead with the back of her free hand, leaving behind a smudge of dirt to stain her face. Two weeks had brought them into a forced closeness that he was beginning to enjoy. She slipped her hand from his, and he thought he caught a blush on her cheek.

Tessa's eyes traced the rooftops of the middle-wealth houses lining the alleyway, as if searching for a place to perch. Dragging a large crate to form a step beneath a lower awning, Tessa kicked aside her dress and hopped into the air. Her fingers caught the metal braces which attached the awning to the house, her knuckles turning white with effort, and then her body went rigid. "This," she said, looking down at herself still hanging from the awning, "is not ladylike."

"Not at all," Abner agreed, gripping her waist to help her down. His hands would have lingered if allowed, but Tessa moved quickly away.

"I doubt he's still following." She coughed. "I think the dust from the road dried out my throat."

"Let's find something to drink."

Abner led the way to the sun-beaten street. His chest puffed and his chin rose out of habit.

Tessa kept close to his elbow as they made their way through the crowded city, the middle-wealth neighborhoods free of the begging hands in the lower quarter.

He liked the feeling of her there, but would have felt better if he had been able to find the dagger he normally wore at his hip. It had been misplaced somewhere, and now, being on the streets without a guard and no weapon, his eyes roved the crowd uneasily. They came across an opening between buildings, framed like a courtyard. Vines grew along the walls and up the sides of the well that stood at the yard's center, with some tools and a ladder pushed into a corner.

Abner wrinkled his nose as Tessa picked her way toward the well. "Plain water?" he said, doubtfully. "I've heard it's not safe to drink."

"Well, you don't have wine on hand." Tessa grasped the rope threaded through a wheel at the top of the well. She set her feet, her arms popping forth muscles he hadn't noticed before, and pulled up the heavy bucket brimming with water. She drank from a cupped palm.

Abner drew out a careful handful of the brown-tinged water.

A ghost of a smile tugged at one corner of Tessa's mouth. "I guess that old noble's plan doesn't sound so terrible now."

Abner leaned back. "What?"

"Um, Avery House I think? He wants to build an underground water system of some kind—"

"And he told you about it to—what? Bring it up to me?" Abner's jaw locked as he tossed his eyes.

"Your father actually."

Abner's hands gripped the side of the well with crushing force. *Of course. Why would he bother bringing it to me? I'm just a placeholder. Waiting on my father like everyone else, a slave to his will.*

"I mean, no. I didn't mean to say that. He just wanted someone to consider it. I don't think he meant—"

"Stop." Abner pushed off the well and stepped away, shaking his head.

Tessa's eyes shone, watching him like he was a snake about to strike, her breath punching from her chest.

Abner blinked away the red stain that only he could see. "Never mind him. I could do something about it, of course," he shrugged, "but I don't want to think about politics today, the castle, or anyone in it."

Tessa's shoulders relaxed. "Okay." She brushed her hands clean on her dress. Her smile died as her brow bent. "Where is?" she spun in a circle, kicking the fabric away to search the ground at her feet.

"Did you lose something?"

Tessa's mouth fell open. "What could I have lost?" she seemed to be thinking aloud. "Nothing, it's fine. I'm fine. This is fine. Not a waste at all."

"I'm glad a day outside the castle with your prince isn't a waste to you." Abner moved forward. "Would you like to make use of it?" *Let's get this over with.* His body warmed out of instinct as he took her face in his hands.

She slipped out of his grip, the powder from her cheek smearing on his fingers. "That's—no."

Abner's brow bent into a hard line over his eyes. "Didn't you hear my father? He wants me to have an heir as soon as possible."

Tessa puffed a breath past her lips. "Then let this be your first act as a man. Don't do it."

Abner lunged forward, catching her arm. "Watch your words with me!"

Tessa leaned back, eyes jumping wide before they settled into a hard, narrow stare.

"You think I want to be ... this? A prop my father sets up when useful? You think I have any choice?" Abner's jaw was a knot of muscle. "I do nothing without his approval. Now he's even managing—it's humiliating."

Tessa's eyes loosened. Her jaw stayed locked.

Abner released her arm, swiping his face with his hand. "You won't? Really?"

Her gaze narrowed again. "Are you going to try to make me?"

"I—no." Abner turned away. "It may look like a weakness, but I've never had to and I won't start now." He turned back to her, finger raised. "But understand, this is not you winning some victory over me. I'm choosing this. I don't want you to think after the ... when everything is settled, that you will have some power over me."

"That won't be a problem."

Satisfied, and a little relieved he didn't have to go through with it, Abner pulled more water from the well bucket. He splashed it over his neck. The beads dripping down his back extinguished the embers of anger burning in his chest. His eyes landed on the ladder leaning against a far wall. He pulled his face into a tight smile, trying to salvage some of the day at least. "How about a view?" He tested his weight on the worn rungs before nodding for her to climb up.

"After you," Tessa said, gathering her wide dress into handfuls.

Abner climbed to the roof easily. He settled himself on the worn, mud-baked tiles and looked out over Lydia. The city's design of an upward climb to the castle allowed him an excellent vantage point of the winding streets. A baker in the middle quarter had just finished placing the last of the day's bread on a little stand near his cart. A young boy, not a quarter of Abner's age, slipped a loaf from the end with an easy hand.

Abner smirked. *Little runt.*

Tessa joined him, settling the knots of fabric she had tied to help her climb up the ladder back into wrinkled layers. She made sure to sit at a distance.

Lydia sprawled at their feet, a mess of houses and shops, baking white in the late-summer air.

"I can't believe how easy it was to lose our escort," Abner mused, searching the streets for him. "He is going to be so angry," he laughed.

"Is this the first time you've slipped away?"

Abner paused, brushing the powder from his fingers with his clean hand. "My father is not a tolerant man. Certain things he ignores."

"Like what?"

Abner laughed through a scoff. "Me." His brow folded. He cleared his throat. "My education he's left mainly to other people: Dennison, Achor while he was still around."

"I have no idea who those people are."

"Achor was assigned to teach me books. Learning mathematics, politics, sciences, to read." Abner paused. "He stopped when I was ten years old."

"Why?"

Abner's eyes squinted at the sun. "I was ten when we left for Alberon from across the sea. Achor stayed in Keldeema, and my father seemed to never think about it again."

"Do you remember your old country?"

"Only pieces. And it's all—" he shook his head, "My mother used to—" Abner's throat closed as his face pinched together. *I haven't even looked at her portrait in ...* "We don't really talk about it."

"Why did your father come here?"

"We don't talk about it," Abner repeated firmly. Swiping away the moisture gathered in his nose, he brushed his hands on his breeches. *Why did we come here? Why did she*—"My mother turned against my father and me. Maybe she hated him ... and me by association? But she tried to get us executed by manufacturing a story about my father conspiring against my uncle, the king of Keldeema. Her brother would have believed her, so my father saved us by taking those loyal to him who knew the truth, and setting sail. I don't think he knew where he was going, but we ended up here."

"And he ended up King."

Abner shrugged. "I was a boy, I don't remember much. I do recall the old king giving me a toy rolling horse on little wheels that I started carrying around. My father saw me playing with it after ... everything. His eyes were ready to pop out of his head, he was so angry." Abner rubbed at his shoulder, a phantom pain making him wince. "It got burned."

"And by all this you think you deserve ... pity?"

Abner stared at Tessa, who pulled her face into a challenging frown. "No. I don't even know why I'm talking to you about this." He let out a shaking breath. "I'm breaking every rule today."

"I would have thought you lived a rule-free life."

Abner picked at a tile by his feet.

"Oi! You!" yelled a voice from below. "What in bleedin' glory you doin' on me roof, yeah?" A man, his barrel belly sticking out a clear hand's breadth over his widespread feet, stood glaring at them from the street.

"Oh, I'm sorry!" Tessa scrambled toward the ladder.

"You best be sorry and fork over the gold it'll take to repair them shingles you messed with!" declared the man, spitting at the dust at his feet.

Abner didn't move, his eyes locked on the man. "You don't recognize who I am?"

"Should I?"

Abner laughed. "Should you?" He descended the ladder and strode toward the dirty man, Tessa following close behind. "I'm only your future king."

The man's face grew slack. "You—nah, it can't be. Where's your escort? The fanfare? All of it? You pullin' me leg?"

"I'll pull your head from your neck if you don't—" he glanced at Tessa and cleared his throat, arranging his mouth into a benevolent smile. He brushed some dust from his tunic that had faded the fabric.

The man's chest seemed to collapse as he measured the fine cut of the prince's tunic against Abner's features. "Well ... bleed me dry."

"I will consider this matter past. Be gone with you."

The man's eyes scurried between them before he darted into his hovel, snapping the door shut behind.

The prince caught Tessa's eye and winked. "Did you like that?"

Tessa sighed, moving past him up the road.

"I thought you might," Abner smiled, falling into step beside her. "We should return anyway. You're a mess."

Tessa ran a hand over her hair, not looking at him.

She did look disheveled from the day, but this only heightened his interest. Her hair was slipping slightly loose from its pins, the ruffled look to the layers of her dress, and the wearing away of her "done up" face made it difficult to keep his eyes and tone casual.

When they reached the castle, having a clear view of it always uphill ahead of them, they were greeted by the furious, dirt-crusted face of the soldier set to guard them that day. A raised eyebrow from the prince made him remember his place. The king would certainly use some blows to communicate his feelings on Abner's behavior, but that was later, and that was the king.

The soldier had to repaint his expression into one of forced indifference as he said "Glad to see you safe, Highness. Was your outing ... fruitful?"

Abner winked at him as he moved past. "That was," Abner paused to let the large iron doors of the castle courtyard be pulled closed behind them as he searched for the word, "an interesting day."

"It wasn't too horrible."

Abner laughed. "Not so much of a monster now, am I?"

Tessa said nothing.

Abner cast a final look over Lady Tessa from hair to heel. "See you for the last mark meal? After you get cleaned up?" The prince left her in the courtyard, feeling lighter than he had in years.

Esther picked up the knife, hidden under her mattress for safety, and glared at her reflection in the smooth silver blade. Of course, the one day that killing the prince would have been laughably easy, she had forgotten to tie it on under her dress. She was so nervous about falling off a horse, she hadn't remembered to check that she had the blade. Maybe she could have beaten his head in with a brick, plenty of those littered the alleys they ran through, but the days of a full belly and leisure had slowed Esther's movements. She would only get one chance as Lady Tessa.

The long day in the sun had baked away all her energy like a dried riverbed in high summer. Esther lay down on the freshly spread blanket. *Just for a moment. I am not going to sleep. Only resting.* Quiet snores filled her chamber and strange visions crowded her head.

Fox.

When her eyes burst open again, waking in the castle of her worst enemy was a welcome relief. Esther rubbed her sweat-lined temples, her breath shaking past her lips. She buried her face into her hands, willing the voice of justice to stop ringing through her mind the call to finish what she had started.

Prince Abner must die. For Fox, for Jathan, for Shiloh.

She nodded into her palms. "I know. I will." *Just not yet.*

Ava entered, knocking softly on the door before peeking around it with a tentative smile. "Care for a scent cleanse, m'lady?"

"A what?" Esther grimaced as she stretched to rearrange the pinching fabric of her corset.

Ava's mouth tipped to one side. "A bath."

"How have you been?" Esther asked as she was led through the halls.

Ava stared at her with lips pressed tight together.

"I haven't seen you in a few days."

"I've been fine, m'lady."

"Any news from your brother? I think he was away working or…"

"He's in the army." Ava checked over her shoulder. "You shouldn't talk like that."

"Like what?" Esther retraced her words. "I'm sorry if I offended you."

Ava stopped walking to stare at Esther. "That's what I'm talking about. Your 'sorry if I offended you' attitude is getting you a lot of attention from the staff. People are noticing. They *like* you."

Esther had never been liked before. She couldn't help the smile spreading her mouth wide. "Thank you."

"No, that's bad!" Ava sighed. "You're new here," she said, checking they were alone again. "You may not understand the king's … temperament yet." Ava shuffled closer, her whispered breath hitting Esther's cheek. "I have seen nobles gain fame, even the hint of a following … it isn't long before some contrived mild disobedience gets them summoned and their head ends up on a block. So, please, treat us like everyone else," she backed away with a meaningful nod to Esther. "Invisible."

"You're all just living in constant fear, aren't you?" Esther fell into step beside her.

"Not at all, m'lady," Ava put on a voice of quiet indifference. "We all know the pleasure of serving well and the reward that follows."

As they rounded the corner, another servant hauling a basket heavy with clean sheets paused to dip into a curtsy. Her eyes sparkled at Esther before they moved quickly past her. Down a previously unexplored hallway, Ava led Esther to a large stone archway devoid of any door.

"The steam," Ava explained, noticing Esther's stare, "tends to rot the wood. This way the warm air gets out easier. Now inside, if you please, and I'll get you undressed."

Esther waited as the water warmed and Ava picked through the laces of her corset. Each loosening string brought a rush of blood and sensation back to her torso and her bones ached with it. Ava grabbed fistfuls of flower petals from a crate in one corner, tossing them into the steaming water filling the tub as if she were making a giant pot of stew. Next to the crate were strange plants with small ridges that transformed each leaf into a tooth-lined jaw. Esther had never seen a plant like that before in all her forest wanderings.

Ava led Esther to the steaming water. At the edge of the large, overly-ornate bucket, clinging to her white slip which she insisted stay on, Esther shivered. She had waded in forest pools enough to know she wouldn't drown but the steam spiraling up from the water reminded her of the patchwork of burns her hands had gained as a child learning to cook over an open fire. Petals spiraled over the water's surface, filling the air with a sweet soft scent.

Ava dropped her smallest finger into the bath, and, shaking it dry, nodded to Esther. "At your leisure, m'lady."

Esther climbed into the tub. The flood of warmth through her skin as she sat against the side of the wide metal basin made every tired, tightened muscle slip loose under the water's gentle massage.

Ava cracked a leaf from the stalk of the toothed plant and sliced down the length of it, extracting the clear sap. She rubbed it into Esther's shoulders and arms. "You got a little sun-touched on your last excursion. This should help."

Esther closed her eyes. *What magic is this?* Cooling relief, instant and enrapturing, drew a quiet sigh from her lips. Burns from the sun had been such a constant presence in her life they hardly registered anymore, but the relief she felt as they were lifted away was a pleasure few things could touch.

Ava appeared with a thick washing rag. "Perhaps you might be more comfortable now without the slip? It will make you cleaner."

Esther gave it up and Ava began to gently scrub at her, the cloth scratching every itch from her back. She coated her hair with oils, her nails digging into Esther's scalp as she massaged them in. Once clean, Ava asked Esther to relax in the water while she ran and fetched some things to help Esther dry off, cursing quietly at the empty shelves that hadn't been restocked.

Esther's eyes slipped closed, the gentle eddies of the water rocking her back and forth. Her sigh filled the room.

"Apologies, I wasn't expecting anyone. I—" Giselle, Esther had learned her name after many forced excursions together, hesitated in the doorway. Her dark eyes narrowed on Esther. "Oh, it's you. I didn't recognize you without all the…" she passed a hand over her face.

"Well. Nice seeing you." Esther pulled her knees to her chest, pushing a wave of water to the floor.

Giselle smiled. "So innocent," she said, striding into the room.

She was followed by a middle-aged woman. The old servant's wide eyes looked as if they had seen too much in this life and her stooped neck bore the weight of it.

"You're almost done, aren't you? I'll wait." She leaned against the wall, kicking a bucketed plant out of her way, her dress brushing against jars of creams and oils. Her eyes roved over Esther, head tilting to one side as the silence stretched to an unbearable tension. "I have to admit," Giselle spoke at last, "seeing you, *seeing you*, I just don't understand."

Esther stared at the doorway, willing Ava to reappear, and cursed herself for giving up the slip. It lay discarded on a table. Out of reach, useless.

"Has the prince actually seen what I'm looking at?"

Esther's jaw tightened.

"I mean, he has, hasn't he? He should know what the kingdom is getting in trade for their heir. Just so you know, until the king officially announces his intentions, this can all go away. When Rosemarie told me the rumors and I saw how much attention you were getting ... after the years of waiting for him and now the crown goes to some ... what are you again?"

"Apparently," Esther said, meeting Giselle's eyes at last with a pained effort, "I am your future queen. I'd speak carefully." She hated leveraging her pretense of power to stop the girl talking, but Esther's preferred method of snapping her perfect nose with one strike might raise questions. Giselle was not worth discovery. Still, the thought made her smile.

Giselle's mouth closed and she, with eyes burning through a fierce, narrow stare, dipped into a slow curtsy. "Apologies," she said through her teeth. "I misspoke. I am so very glad you have come to court. Such a happy union."

Ava reappeared at the door, her hands stocked with a tower of heavy folded cloth. "A thousand apologies, m'lady," she said, rushing in to set down the cloth, saving one to hold open in front of Esther for her to exit the tub and be patted down with.

The shock of cold air on her skin made Esther's arms pull into her sides as Ava swept away the moisture as quickly as possible.

Giselle watched with a smile.

Slipping a clean dressing gown over her head and a warm shawl over her shoulders, Ava rolled Esther's dripping hair into a towel and gathered the discarded clothes.

As they turned the corner, Giselle's anxious order to "Make sure you scrub every bit of that tub before I get in," echoed after them.

Unstung, Esther raised her brow at Ava with a smirk as her stomach announced the need for a snack. When Ava returned with a butter-smeared *scadia*, Esther grinned, devouring it in three large bites while Ava combed through her wet hair.

The last mark meal was an awkward time.

Like a dog beaten into submission, Abner stared at his plate. When he finally hazarded to pick up his fork, it was with gritted teeth and a sharp breath, as if the motion brought a sharp stab of pain.

"So," the king's voice boomed.

Abner dropped his fork onto the gold plate, sending a mess flying toward his neighbor.

The noble hid his disgust quickly as he apologized to the prince for being in the way and wiped at his sleeve.

Abner ignored him.

The king cleared his throat, drawing Esther's stare away. "Lady Tessa, I was curious what you thought of the day's excursion. Was my son properly diverting?"

Esther forced her lips to smile and her chin to nod.

"I find it quite charming how economical you are with language. Never a wasted word with you. Nothing is worse than a prattler." The king rose and spread his hands. The room quieted.

"You, O King, are infinite..." Esther pretended to recite the chant with the others, mouthing the unfamiliar words with a ducked head.

The king dropped his hands. "I invite you, guests of our royal court, to open the envelopes tucked beneath your plates. It is time once again."

The hall was filled with a rustling noise, like a thousand paper wings taking flight. Esther freed the little card from the folded paper, taking care to keep pace with Lady Hildren beside her. Writing scrawled in long looping letters adorned the card. Her cheeks colored.

"Well, my dear," the king said, resuming his seat with a raised brow, "what do you think?"

Esther had no idea what the letters said or what answer she could give in response to it. The eternal moment, as everyone within earshot turned to watch her struggle with a reply, was finally shattered by Esther forcing her mouth open and words to spill out. "Sounds lovely."

The king's tight smile was shadowed by his heavy brow, hanging over his eyes. "Quite. I agree. Abner, she's going to join us. Doesn't that sound

"... lovely?" His attention was pulled away by a noble who leaned in close to the king's ear and faced the back wall to hide his words.

What did I agree to?

Abner's eyes stayed on his neighbor's laid-down card, running over the words again and again. His face had grown pale.

Esther strained to catch whispers of conversation around her, to separate the voices and glean an understanding of what was happening, but the jumble was too much as the hall resumed its full-force volume.

At last Abner stopped reading and rose.

"I am not hungry, at present," Abner stated to no one in particular. He gave a nod to the king, who did not acknowledge him at all, and left.

Esther stared at her plate for a moment, precious time wasted by indecision, before springing to her feet and following him. Her eyes searched for Abner along the carpeted corridor, but he was gone. No guard had accompanied him, it would have been the perfect moment to strike. Now he could be anywhere among the winding passageways and hidden network of rooms. Her feet ached from the day, despite the bath and rest before the meal, and her fire for revenge was cooled by the thought of her bed and sleep. *Perhaps tomorrow there will be a better chance.* Slipping through her door, Esther set the bolt to avoid anyone following and leaned her forehead against the wood. She sighed. She would struggle through undressing herself.

"You walk exceptionally slowly," said the man hiding in her room.

Esther turned with a yip of surprise.

Cantus pushed himself up from the chair at the window. He leaned against the framed canopy of Esther's bed.

"You're back." She fought to regain her breath.

Cantus scoffed. "And you're still here. You seem to have settled in. Dug a nice little hole for yourself."

"Your aunt has been very kind to extend an invitation to share her accommodations with me."

Cantus' mouth twitched. "You have no idea what you are doing, do you?" He crossed his arms, assessing her coldly. "What makes you think you can fool a whole kingdom of people that you are something you're not?"

"I don't have to fool them for long."

Cantus rose to his full height, breathing deeply through his nose.

Esther tensed and withdrew a step, ready for his attack.

With a flourish of his hand, Cantus dipped from his waist into a bow.

Esther nodded, unsure what differentiated a good bow from a bad one.

The soldier held out a hand, waiting for Esther to take it. When she did not, he snatched hers with a coarse sigh and dragged her stumbling along with him as he began to glide silently around the room. "Thought so. You'll need to learn how to dance."

"For what?" Esther planted her feet, wrenching her arm out of his grasp.

Cantus let out a slow, trickling breath, recovering the distance between them. "I've decided ... I'm going to help you."

Esther blinked, not sure if she had misheard his barely audible whisper. "What are you talking about?" She found herself whispering as well.

"We are going to kill the king."

XII

"Get out," Esther said, slipping around him. "I'm too tired to sort out whatever games you're playing right now."

"You're not getting anywhere on your own. Partly because you're fighting the wrong enemy." Cantus glanced over his shoulder, as if the stone walls had grown ears to listen. "The king is the real evil haunting this land. He ordered the attack on Shiloh. He murdered Hildren House—your pretend family. He's a monster. Every injustice you blame on the prince, his father is the real perpetrator."

"No, the prince—"

"Until Abner finds a way to remove the king from power, he will have no real say in anything except his outfit for the day. You murder the prince, the king will just wreak havoc on the land and his court. He'll find a new woman and then his new heir will doubtless carry on the same horrible legacy. You need to stop the line."

Esther's chin tipped, her mouth bending into a smile. "And I suppose I should spare the prince. Exile him so he can return to kill again?"

"Not if you want to be thorough, no." Cantus' face hardened. "I have given everything to protect what's left of my family."

"And now you give all that up? Why?"

Cantus sighed, a furrow creasing his brow. "I—I can't say." He stared at the floor. "I never knew where they came from. They were just ... people. I thought—It needs to stop." He met her eyes. "More importantly, without me you're only going to succeed in getting everyone killed. Lady Hildren has refused to flee, so my only hope is to get her to safety by whatever means necessary when the king and his son are dealt with. Promise me, and I'll help you."

Pride kindled, Esther scoffed and turned away. "What makes you think I'd trust you, or need your help?"

Cantus' eyes darted over her in a quick assessment. "You may be able to trick superstitious villagers into thinking you're some kind of demon but a lady of the royal court? It's only by the grace of a kind-eyed Fate you've lasted this long."

"I've been doing fine on my own."

"And yet ... the prince still breathes."

Esther winced.

"And you have not exactly been subtle. What was that hesitation before?"

Esther's fingers released the parchment still clutched in her fist to stare at the indecipherable scrawl once more.

Cantus gave a low chuckle, shaking his head. "Of course."

Esther glared at him.

"Of course the fate of one of the very last people under the stars that I care about hangs on your ability to convince an entire court and you ... can't ... read." He snatched the paper from her hand, his eyes raking over the mess of letters. "The king is inviting you to the Event. It's in three days." He tossed the paper back toward her. "I don't know if that helps or hurts us at this point."

"Us," Esther said, retrieving the paper from the ground and placing it on the table beside the reflective metal sheet. "No. There is no us. I don't need you. You're just trying to distract me from my goal. To kill the prince. That is what I'm here to do. Simple."

"Then why isn't it done?" Cantus spread his hands to encompass her room, nodding toward the frills and finery. "Are you starting to get a little too comfortable?"

Esther's hand tightened at her side.

"Maybe marrying Abner doesn't sound that bad now. Wanting to get fat with his babies and live your life in oblivious luxury while the kingdom suffers at—"

Esther punched him in the throat.

Cantus fought to quiet his sputtering.

She brought her stinging fist back to her side, mouth twisting into a smile. She relished the release of rigid control in the snap of her arm.

He forced himself into a shuddering calm, a quiet admiration lighting his eyes. "We can help each other. You've made this mess, and now—"

"The prince made it!" hissed Esther.

"We can do more than you could achieve alone. But you need a plan. One that gives lasting change."

Every muscle itched to punch him again, but the impulse died before a move was made. Was there some truth to his accusations? She traced over every missed opportunity, every hesitation, her stomach sinking to the floor. *Cantus*. He wasn't Fox, nothing could match their bond now severed forever, but at least she wouldn't be alone. Esther sighed, her limbs sagging heavy. "What's your plan then?"

He spoke through a wide smile. "Sit. It's going to be a long night."

In the morning, Esther opened her eyes to a hand touching her shoulder.

"Time to rise, m'lady," said a voice, and Esther blinked away the glaring sunbeams to reveal Ava's face pulled into a heavy frown. "Sorry to wake you. Your plate is here. I thought I would let you rest since you didn't stir when I checked on you earlier, and they're already cleaning up the Great Hall."

Esther pushed herself up to sit. "Thank you, Ava. I think I may spend a little more time in bed this morning." She rubbed her cheek as a yawn popped her jaw.

"Apologies, but that is not permitted today. You've been summoned by the king. You are to make yourself suitable to appear before him as soon as you are able. I would have gotten you up sooner, but I only just heard of it."

"It's fine, Ava. I'll get up."

Ava twisted her fingers together, chewing her lip.

"Is something wrong?"

Ava shook her head, pushing her gaze to meet Esther's, and her eyes flooded. "Lady Tessa, forgive my boldness. Please, just ... be careful." She blinked, sending one heavy tear slipping from its lid to thud on the carpeted floor.

"I'm fine, Ava."

"Of course, Lady Tessa." Ava dipped into a quick curtsy, staring at the ground. "But if I have done anything to put you in danger, I'm sorry. I just want you to know that, whatever happens," she lowered her voice and came forward a step, meeting Esther's eyes with a fierce stare, "you are a good, honest person. It has been an honor."

Ava pressed her forehead into Esther's hand.

Esther blinked, leaning back from the girl kneeling at her feet.

"Until we meet again among the stars," Ava whispered the ancient blessing for the dead.

Esther's heart began to pound.

The maid rose and dressed her charge in silence, applying the creams and color to Esther's face with a blank expression and loose hands. As Ava opened the door, Esther snatched her arm, pulling her around to face her.

"What is happening? Why are you so afraid?"

"I've told you everything I know." Ava's eyes darted to her wrist pinched in Esther's fist. "I've just seen enough to know nothing good comes from private meetings with the king."

Esther released her grip and followed Ava down the hall, irritatingly aware of the echo of her shoes clacking on the floor and her own pulse battering her eardrums.

Abner was not allowed in the hall after the first mark meal. He was informed of this by a servant in his ear while his father sat beside him. "Why would I care about that?" His eyes drifted once more to Lady Tessa's empty chair.

Catching the stare of a pair of dark eyes beyond, Abner's attention wandered over Giselle who, although never shy, had grown bolder in her attention to him with each visit to the castle. She smiled, her eyes fluttering long dark lashes like a peacock's tail to keep his stare.

"—given your arrangement with Hildren House and Lady Tessa—"

Abner's attention snapped back to the servant. "What was that?"

"The conversation with Lady Tessa is something the king thought it best you be absent for and—ah—"

"What is this about?" Abner demanded, turning to his father.

The king halted his conversation with a stiff jaw, and faced his son.

"What do you mean by interrogating Tessa? She's mine, isn't she?"

"That," the king said in a low voice, "remains to be seen. We really know nothing of her. Nexus thought—"

"Nexus?"

"You need to learn your nobles' names, Abner. I'd wager you couldn't name half the people in this room. An appalling fact." The king relished the scold before continuing. "Nexus, our patriarch of Tillman House, advised me yesterday that some further questions may be necessary to ascertain the girl's intentions. A formality, I think, but one that takes little effort to satisfy. I admit I am quite curious to hear more about our dear little miss of Hildren House."

Abner didn't see the point, but didn't see the harm either, and so he finished his meal and declared to his father he would spend the day training with the guard since he was not wanted for kingdom business.

Followed out of the hall by Giselle, Abner sighed, readying his ears for the onslaught of talk her company brought.

"Oh, Prince Abner," Giselle said, feigning surprise as she slipped her arm through his. "How do you do?"

"I don't have time for games, Giselle." Abner dropped her arm, putting some space between them. "I have training today. I've been getting behind on that lately."

"Well, you've been distracted." The weight of anger burning in Giselle's coal-black eyes made her smile stiff. "What is it about this new Lady Tessa that has you so obsessed?"

"I'm not obsessed. Just—my father's not made the official announcement, so I can't say anything more."

"But it's true, isn't it?" Giselle's lashes pinched over her eyes as they filled with shining moisture. "You're promised to knot the cord?"

Abner's shoulder twitched, sending a shock of pain lancing through his back as it hit on his recent bruise.

Giselle blinked. "It happened again?"

Abner let out a shuddering breath, putting on a smile. "What are you talking about?"

"Your father's gotten better at leaving bruises where people won't notice." Giselle touched his shoulder, frowning when Abner couldn't cover up the twinge of pain. "You really shouldn't train today."

"I'm fine," Abner insisted, slipping past her.

"Abner!" she called after him, but he didn't stop until he was out of the castle doors and into the courtyard. He shook himself free of the draw to weakness compassion always tugged him with, before passing through the narrow alley around the far side of the castle.

Across the lawn, Dennison and the elite guard ran drills. Picking a blade from the weapons stand, he joined in the line. His mouth pulled into a one-sided smile as Dennison acknowledged him with a nod. Abner set his feet and let his mind quiet as his body fell into the motion of the familiar set.

When the guards were paired off and Abner faced his man, he pushed the twittering voices in the viewing stands on the far side of the lawn from his thoughts. Wary of the bruises spread like pox over his strong arm, Abner switched his single fist training sword to his off hand and gestured for the bearded man to bring his best attack.

❖ ❖ ❖

The gilded gold frame on the doors of the throne room stung Esther's eyes.

Ava bowed and disappeared without a word, leaving Esther to face the throne room alone. As the doors rattled open, all conversation within halted as heads turned to watch Esther walk into the room. The king sat on his grand throne, an empty seat beside him, and a gathering of white-bearded men stood huddled below on either side.

Her foot caught, almost sending her to the floor, as their stares pressed on her like a weight strapped to her toes.

"Ah, excellent." The king held up a hand, stopping her. "Stay right there, dear girl."

Esther ran her hands over her dress, reassuring herself of the blade still tucked into her underclothes from the night before. Cantus' plan still echoed in her mind. "I believe you had expressed a wish—"

"Yes, this is just an informal conversation." The king flapped his ring-studded hand at her. "A chat really."

A white-haired noble cleared his throat with a tilt of his head. "May I?" the noble asked, gesturing to the space between the king and Esther that remained empty.

"Please."

"Lady Tessa of Hildren House," the noble paused, as if expecting her to contradict him. When she did not, he continued, "I, Nexus of Tillman House, will be asking you some questions to ascertain with what intentions you have set upon the court. Is this agreeable?"

"I ... yes?"

"Where were you born?"

Esther's face colored as she said, "I don't remember. I was only a baby after all."

One noble chuckled but covered it with a cough.

She continued quickly, before Nexus' frown could deepen, "The Hildren Estate I would imagine, though. It's to the north along Greenway Road." *Thank you, Cantus.* "Do you know it?"

Nexus pouted his lips, sucking in a breath through his wiry white beard. "It would make things easier if you would refrain from questions, jokes, and such. Simply answer what I ask—"

The king made a noise behind Nexus.

"—d-dear girl."

The king pushed himself to his feet and stepped forward. His mouth twisted into a smile as he paced a slow circle around Esther.

The old noble stood awkwardly in front of her with a roll of parchment smashed between his age-spotted fingers as the king began his own line of questions.

"How did you leave the castle? That night Hildren House was dealt with."

Esther raised her chin, her mind tracing over the practiced story. "I had help. It was dark so I didn't see who. I was only a little girl. The person led me through a door with a wooden latch. I climbed out through a hole meant for washing water. I don't remember much else about it."

"And the person who helped you? You must recall something." He was behind her, his voice curling over her shoulder like fingers clutching her in a bony grasp.

Her back tingled.

"A voice, a shape."

"No, I don't know anything about them." When his hand did touch her shoulder, her arms sprang in surprise. She bit her tongue to keep herself from ripping out of his grasp. Her chest held her breath hostage. *Get. Off.*

"Very well. What about afterward? Surely you had someone help you. Should they not be rewarded for keeping you safe?" The king moved in front of her, watching her features struggle to answer.

"I told a family in Aalah I was an orphan. Abandoned. They knew nothing of me or where I was from. They did nothing wrong."

"Of course not," the king said, his eyes sparkling. "What are their names?"

"I never learned them." Esther resisted the urge to break his stare by raising her chin. "To keep them safe."

"You carried quite a bit of fear—of hatred—with you. For one so young."

Her words were sour in her mouth, her jaw locking around them. "Not at all. I knew that the power my family once had was gone, and with that protection removed I had to find a new way to protect myself. I think anyone would understand me being cautious, given the circumstances."

"Extraordinary," the king said, his stare bouncing over Esther's face, "to have wisdom like yours. In one so young and ripe. Almost a waste, really." He returned to his seat. "So you bear no ill will toward your king, do you?" He reclined on his throne, one booted foot looped over the other as his fingers drifted across his mouth.

"None, Your Highness."

"Be on your way, sweet Tessa." The king waved his hand, and Esther turned, weight shed with every step she took out of that nest of adders.

"But, Sire, forgive me. That can't be all the questions you have—"

"Quiet, Nexus!" snapped the king. "Bring Lady Hildren to me, the rest of you nobles may leave. We have plans to discuss."

His last words were stifled by the doors closing behind Esther, and, although they echoed in her head with a vague worry that there was something wrong, the rush of relief to be out of that room and away from that stare pushed the feeling from her thoughts.

Cantus leaned against a wall, worry written on every line of his young face. He matched her step and grabbed her arm, pulling her once again into a closet filled with cleaning supplies.

"Are you alright? What happened?" His voice forgot to be quiet.

"Your concern is touching. Truly." Esther twisted out of his grip.

"What did the king ask you? What did you say?"

Esther hesitated, trying to summarize their interaction in a way that wouldn't leave Cantus thinking her incapable. "He wanted to know how I got out, if I had help, where I went. All things we discussed last night."

"And your answers were ... sufficient?"

"Well, he let me leave." Esther shrugged, kicking an old rag away from her skirt. "I didn't mention the old cook giving me a bag of food. It just didn't seem to fit at the time."

"What about the others in the room? Were they satisfied with you?"

"I think the one who was supposed to ask the questions had more he wanted to know, but the king cut him off. Really though, what does it matter if they believe me? All I need to do is convince the king long enough to—"

Cantus clapped a hand over Esther's mouth.

She turned away at the tang of salted sweat.

"Not here," he whispered, rubbing his hand clean on his tunic. "We have to think of something normal for you to do with the rest of your day, somewhere you can just melt into a crowd."

"Seems like a waste of time," Esther said.

Cantus nodded to himself. "You can go watch the guard train. I noticed a group of ladies going to the training lawn, so you can just join them. Tonight, we begin with the plan."

"You mean..." Esther couldn't keep the smile from tugging at her mouth.

"I'm going to show you how to walk through walls. Now act normal." Cantus opened the door.

"Where am I going?"

"I'll escort you, Lady Tessa." Cantus drew himself up to his full height, leading the way outside.

As Cantus promised, the seating by the lawn was filled with flowing dresses and gushing ladies, all whispering together.

Esther's feet slowed as they drew near, her face coloring under the thin layer of paste.

Giselle dropped her conversation to watch her approach. Her nostrils flared as she sighed through a tight smile. "Tessa, dear! Come sit next to me," Giselle tipped her chin to one side. She elbowed her friend viciously in the ribs until her companion gave up her seat with a sour smile.

Cantus nodded with some force when Esther hesitated, taking her elbow and giving her a subtle shove. "My Lady."

Esther dropped into the offered seat.

Cantus withdrew, his eyes pinning on the men fighting in pairs.

Following his stare, Esther found the prince in the foremost group, noticeable as he rolled his shoulder and his opponent waited with his sword point hanging over the dirt.

With a yell, Abner swung wildly at the guard. His unfocused eyes seemed to be somewhere else as he put all his strength behind his strike.

Deflecting the blade, the guard paused, waiting for the next blow.

Although Abner was the loudest fighter, it became quickly apparent he was not the most disciplined. The precision of the other guards' motions, their feet planted and then moving with breath-taking dexterity as they twisted around one another made it so Esther couldn't look away.

"Handsome, aren't they?" whispered Giselle. Her stare pierced through Esther's skin, whose cheeks burned beneath the fiery glare. "Take care you don't develop a liking for any of them. That would be ... dangerous, for a woman like you." Her voice turned away. "Right Elena?"

"I'm sorry?" the girl said.

"I was just saying Lady Tessa should be careful who she gives eyes to. That falling in with a guard would be ... well, you know." There was a long moment of silence before Giselle laughed. "But all that is past now. You don't still like him."

"Of course not."

"Oh, Cantus," Giselle called with a wave, "I almost didn't recognize you. How perfectly ... delightful to see you here."

"My lady," Cantus replied with a stiff bow.

"I just love it when you call me that, Cantus. I feel as if I haven't spoken to you in years. How are things?" Giselle laughed as Cantus moved away. "Can you believe that dog used to be nobility?" Giselle whispered to Esther. "One of the wisest things our king has done is whittle down *that* family." She paused. "No offense."

Esther didn't reply as Abner drew her eye once more, flapping his stunned hand behind him.

"That's match!" announced the head guard, tossing his scar-lined chin as the soldiers lowered their weapons. A standing barrel held water for them and they congregated around it, ignoring the girls fluttering their fans and a few calling out to them. Abner cut through a group of red-cloaked commanders to speak with the head guard, rubbing at his shoulder as he walked.

"You know, I don't really consider a man married until he actually knots the cord. To that end," Giselle's gaze flickered over Abner with a slow smile that pulled her sun-darkened cheek up to crease the corner of her eyes, "good luck."

Giselle rose and, with her, the ladies of the court. They trailed after her sweeping skirt like ducklings behind a mother duck in search of water.

Abner grimaced as the head guard clapped him on the shoulder.

Esther's eyes narrowed.

"Go find the girls," Cantus said through barely opened lips as he passed her. Joining the men at the water barrel, he was greeted with nods and grins.

Esther grimaced, following the path the women had taken with quick trotting feet.

XIII

At the last mark meal, Esther was seated directly across from the king. His lounging, booted foot invaded her space, forcing Esther to pull her legs completely beneath her chair. Lady Hildren had not come to Esther's room to walk down with her and she wondered at her empty seat.

When the king rose with a wink at Esther, Abner abandoned his food with his spoon midway to his mouth. His eyes bounced from his father, to Esther, to a third someone behind her, his face coloring.

"My dear friends," the king spoke into the low roar of conversation.

It gradually quieted, and all eyes turned to the front of the room.

The king took his time walking around the head table to stand before the court. "I have an announcement to make. Some assembled here may have noticed an addition to our court. This..."

Esther struggled to keep her disgust hidden as the king's soft, plump fingers closed over hers and pulled her to her feet to face the crowd.

"This is Lady Tessa, the lost niece of Hildren House, finally returned home to her family. As a mark of good faith to this honored lineage, we will accept her into the royal line through marriage."

Esther was certain everyone could see her dress trembling with her knees, every flaw she had carefully cataloged through the crowd's assessing eyes. She pushed her back straight, staring at a far corner of the room. Her mouth went dry.

"Lady Tessa of Hildren House," the king turned to Esther, lowering his forehead to her hand, "I honor you with *my own* hand in marriage. May you make a worthy wife and Queen."

The clapping hands and scraping chairs echoing into the cavernous hall were muffled by the buzzing beehive filling her ears. *What?*

Quietly to Esther the king said, "We'll talk over details later, sweet Tessa."

He dropped her hand, exiting amid loud congratulations by all he passed.

Esther's fingers found the table behind her, steadying her feet as she turned toward her chair.

Abner stared after his father, strangling his spoon in his heavy veined grip. The lower lid of one eye twitched as he scoffed through his tight smile. Muttering to himself, Abner left the table.

Esther searched for Cantus, but he was lost amid the sea of stunned smiles and raised eyebrows. The buzzing in her ears swelled beneath the pressure of so many faces.

A scratchy cheek brushed against Esther's, the pop of a kiss too loud in her ear. The noble from Avery House lingered as he gave her hand a slow pat. "Congratulations." He turned to kiss her other cheek, his voice low. "You're in dangerous waters now, my girl. Best to be careful and look to those willing to help."

Behind him the line of well-wishers stretched without end.

Esther was forced to accept kisses from each of them, her mind still foggy as all their work planning had just been ruined by the king's sudden change in direction.

"Father!" Abner's voice echoed down the empty corridor.

The king did not pause his stride.

Abner ran to catch him. "Why?" he threw his hand back the way they had come.

"You can't really be surprised, can you? Abner, I'm doing you a favor. I thought you didn't want to get married."

"I didn't. Don't. But now she's to be my mother by union?" Abner's face twisted. "I don't want that either."

"That doesn't concern me in the slightest. It's what's best for the kingdom. You should thank me. It was obvious you couldn't handle her. Like that horse you couldn't break when you were fourteen."

"I didn't think you remembered that."

The king sighed. "Every one of your failures is burned into my memory. And to that end, Abner, I knew having an heir, looking toward being king when times are so uncertain, would be too much for you to handle with grace."

"And so you make her Queen through an illegitimate marriage? What of—" Abner snapped his mouth closed, cutting off the words that would have landed him a broken rib or worse.

Even still, the king's eyes burned like black coals set aflame in a deep dark hearth. "You know the penalty for speaking of that she-devil."

"I didn't." Abner took a step back, hands in front of him as if to calm an animal. "But, you are still married. The law—"

"I make the law!" snapped the king, his hand punching his own chest. His beard quivered beneath his tensed jaw. "Your mother was a filthy, cruel woman who betrayed me. She caused everything that happened, if she had only listened—" his hands formed claws as he stared between them. Blinking, his eyes refocused on his son. "If you only knew what she used to say behind closed doors about life with you ... you would not miss her."

Abner swallowed, his eyes hot.

"I don't want to hear any more dissent over this matter. I have spoken. So says the king."

Abner raised his chin. "Long live the king."

As Abner's face hardened, the king's brow rose. "Good," he said, the word measured with dark comprehension.

Images of what it would be like when his father was finally gone flooded Abner's mind as the king turned his back. *King Abner. I would hold the power, the crown. No one would be able to touch me. Nothing would be out of my reach. I would be just ... like ... him.*

Abner marched to escape the flood of nobles before he could be engulfed with questions he didn't know how to answer. He eventually found himself wandering a long circuitous route around the castle border, taking the familiar snaking lanes through overarching greenery with a slow heavy step.

"Abner!" A voice called to him out of the growing darkness behind.

"Dennison?" Abner noted the dirt covering the captain's clothes as the elder smoothed his ruffled hair. "Where have you been?"

"I went into town after training to deal with some business that got mishandled while I was away, so I missed my meal. Feel like walking with me down to the kitchens?"

Abner fell into step beside him.

"I was hoping to get a chance to talk with you. I've heard from the servants that while I have been away there's been some ... developments. I know this marriage isn't something you want, but—"

"Stop."

"—it could be of real value to you in the smooth succession of power. Having an established heir, a link to the old kingdom, not only tightens up the king's power, but gives you some of your own."

"That's probably why the king announced his engagement to Lady Tessa at the meal tonight."

Dennison stopped to stare at Abner.

"And the law," Abner shook his head, "is made by the king. Apparently he won't even play by his own rules anymore."

"Abner, this is—are you sure?"

"Nothing could have been clearer!" Abner kicked at a tuft of grass missed by the gardener with his heavy boot. "He told me after his surprise to the court that he didn't think I could handle the responsibility of it. As good as called me incapable of anything."

"There is much more at stake in this news than your vanity." Dennison's brow bent as Abner tossed his eyes. "Don't you understand? The king could produce an heir."

"He already has me."

Dennison sighed.

"What do you keep hinting at, Dennison? What do you want me to do?"

"Enough playing foolish, the time for games is done. This is what I've been preparing you for every day of your training. I think you may have run out of time to wait."

Abner's eyes fell to the ground, the weight of indecision sitting heavy on his brow. *I could be just like him. Is that what I want?*

Esther looked up as the door opened.

Cantus let himself into her room, greeting her with a stiff smile. "Ready?"

Esther nodded, her eyes straying back to the horizon through the window as she let her arm dangle over the ledge.

Joining her to peruse the sky, Cantus' brow cast a heavy shadow over his eyes as it knotted. "Did something happen? You seem..." he let the words trail away.

Tired. I'm already tired, knowing you'll want to stop everything to discuss how to adapt to this. I'm tired of sitting. Tired of this useless waiting. Tired of the weight of it. It's time to move. "Where were you during the last mark meal?" she asked, picking at a loose thread in her night shift.

"Errands for the captain of the guard. My presence at the training ground volunteered me for the job."

"How exciting," Esther said, dryly.

"Did something happen at the meal? Did Abner—"

"No, nothing. Nothing new. Just the same awkward game." She stood from the ledge and walked toward the door, followed at a respectful distance by Cantus. "Let's move."

If he held suspicion, her eyes didn't catch evidence of it.

Esther's hand rested on the door handle and an unaccustomed pleasure buzzed at her temples. She was adapting to life here, and her lies were improving.

Taking the lead, Cantus straightened as he strode down the corridor.

Esther slunk behind him, missing her cloak in the darkened walkway.

He stopped as they reached the grand staircase, catching her arm. "If you want to go unnoticed where you shouldn't be, act as if you belong. Straighten up."

Pulling her arm away, Esther stood tall, tossing her chin as her cheeks warmed.

Cantus glanced down the staircase before descending in quick steps. They walked through several long hallways in silence.

The main servants had gone to bed, the corridor empty except the dancing light cast by torches in brackets along the stone wall.

"Here, I'll give you a boost." Cantus stopped at an unlit one and gestured up toward a small latch just below the ceiling.

"That's the entrance?" Esther raised her brow.

"Not my normal one, but the cooks in the kitchen might have questions if I brought the prince's intended through the wall tunnels at night. This is the one without an audience. Now put your foot here and I'll boost you up." Cantus bent his knee, making a kind of step for her.

Esther blew a breath past smiling lips. She pushed him out of the way and wrung her hands together. Grabbing the unlit torch like a branch, Esther walked up the wall. Her nightgown raised to her knees as she hoisted her weight onto the torch, crouching against the wall as she opened the latch above her. With a last smirk at Cantus, she disappeared into the dark.

"You can climb." Cantus jumped to grip the stone ledge beneath the little door and hoisted himself up to sit beside her, before enclosing them in complete darkness as he snapped it shut.

At least I'm able to stand without stooping in here. But ... it's very dark. Esther followed Cantus' shuffling step, her eyes stretching wide in their sockets to collect the nonexistent light. An echo of water droplets dripping somewhere ahead filled her ears with an unnatural weight.

Nerves tingled in her fingers as her mind stretched for senses to ground her. Her feet skidded on wet wooden planks and Cantus caught her, placing her hand on his shoulder to guide her.

"Did they teach tunnel finding in your guard training?" Esther pushed dust from her nose with a heavy puff of breath.

His voice was stretched by a smile. "I grew up here, and exploring is just ... something little boys do."

"How did you..."

"Lose everything?" Cantus paused. "Edge along the wall here."

Esther's hand brushed moist stone, her mouth twisting at the sudden dampness on her white shift as she followed Cantus' shoulder scraping against the wall.

"There's a leak from somewhere above, it's rotted through the floor. Abner and I learned that the hard way."

"Abner?"

A few slivers of light crept through worn cracks in the stone. Esther could make out Cantus' vague shape and the shrouded rough walls stretching ahead.

"Almost there," Cantus said, shrugging her hand off his shoulder as he rounded a corner.

Esther let her question drop with her hand.

"This treasury," he said, stepping over an old post that had fallen with barely a glance down. He turned to help Esther as she slipped unaided to his side. Cantus shook his head. "It was used by the old king and queen. Rather than relocate the treasures to a different room, Abner's father just cut off access to this section of the castle and allocated a few guards on rotation to watch for intruders."

"And there's something in there that will help us?" asked Esther, following the path of Cantus' feet through the holes in the floor. He put out a hand, pushing distance between them as the floor creaked beneath his weight.

"Apparently I've gotten heavier since I last walked this way." He smiled. "Recently the guard was sent to catch a counterfeit money lender. We knew someone had been circulating false crowns but it had taken time to narrow down the source. I was one of the men who raided his house."

"What happened to him?"

"Oh, executed, of course." Cantus shook his head. "He was clearly a criminal. But I was also tasked with cleaning out the supply room under his home." He paused, as if to foster suspense. "There was quite a lot to sort through. Mostly tricks to entertain the masses and earn him gold. But there was a box under a table with—well, you'll just have to see it."

Esther huffed impatiently. "Weren't we almost—"

Cantus turned, waving emphatically for her to fall silent. Continuing again, his steps were slow and deliberate, albeit heavy.

Esther slunk after him. A quiet cough from the outside made Esther freeze.

Cantus paused, listening with his ear to the wall. With a steadying breath he pulled aside a long tattered sheet, to reveal a small latched door like the one they had used to enter the tunnel. Lightly padding the handle, Cantus released the clasp on the door.

The treasury of the king.

There's ... so much. Gold, precious stones, and piles of strange objects laid enshrined in dust. Esther bit her tongue. *Every frost Shiloh had to break their backs and work their hands raw to not starve, while the castle hoarded this weight of gold to sit and rot.* Her eyes fell to her feet, to her soft slippers and flowing white gown. *I might be sick.*

Cantus called her to him with a tip of his chin. Putting a finger to his lips, he bent his head toward a tower of coins and treasure. With careful steady hands, both began to pick level after level off the tower, setting it aside. At last, they found the stone floor and the item that drew them to the king's guarded horde in the middle of the night.

It was a box. Rough, wooden, and covered in strange symbols and spirals. He eased open the lid to check the contents.

Esther leaned forward to see, as the lid snapped closed.

Cantus left the gold, the jewels, everything except the box tucked into his arm as he crept back toward the little door.

Esther's eyes raked the room, alighting with surprise on the shining ruby winking in the polished silver pommel. Her mouth twisted at the memory of all the pain that sword had brought into her life. She snatched it before disappearing into the tunnel.

When the guards were far enough behind, Cantus let out a heavy sigh.

"That went well," Esther said.

"We're alive," Cantus agreed.

"So, what's in the box?"

"Later," Cantus said over his shoulder as he slipped across the fallen beam. He didn't offer her an arm this time, but paused to watch her maneuver easily over it. "Some lady of the court."

"Oh, I'm sorry." Esther's eyes narrowed, putting a hand over her heart, her voice adopting a breathy, displeased tone. "As a lady I must ask for assistance in climbing through the bowels of the castle at night. How terribly improper of me."

"Truly," Cantus said with a smile, being steadily swallowed by the dark as he made his way forward again.

Esther followed close behind, still unaccustomed to the route.

"You did well. I'm—well, you're alright. For a demon."

A smile spread through her cheeks and Esther didn't try to stop it.

They shuffled quietly together through the black.

"So, today at training..." Esther hesitated as Cantus' breath caught. "When I first met Abner, he told me he had never been beaten in a fair fight, but today every opportunity the guard had to strike, he didn't."

Cantus let his trapped breath loose. "What's your point?"

"They're holding back with him."

"Of course we are. Who wants to get beheaded because you beat the prince in a training exercise?"

"So he lied then."

"No, he's telling the truth. He's never been beaten in a fair fight because he's never been in one."

Esther laughed, stifling the noise with her palm.

Both stood and listened.

"Sorry," she whispered, satisfied that no one had heard her blunder. "I guess we'll all find out how good he is then."

"I hope not."

"What do you mean?"

"When it comes, I hope he has no idea. Just a shock ... then it's over." Cantus filled the passage with a sudden burst of light as he pushed open the little door with his boot. The light was cut off by his frame as he hopped down, landing with a heavy thump on the soft carpeted floor.

When he was clear, Esther slipped out after him. She braced herself against the bracket and swung down, her dress hem gaining a tear as she hugged the sword to her side. "You're very merciful to someone who hates you," she said, brushing herself off.

Cantus hesitated. "We'll talk more tomorrow." He took the sword from her, shaking his head as he slipped it into his belt. Laying a fold of his tunic over it, Cantus gave her a quick bow and left.

"But, the box!" Esther whispered at the disappearing figure. "What's in the—"

The following day, Ava was the only person who seemed glad to see Esther. Throwing propriety to the winds, she jumped forward and hugged her, arms trembling.

"I just heard the news. You're okay. You're going to be okay. The king wouldn't execute a woman he's promised to. You're going to be alright. I'm so glad!"

Esther worked her face into a smile. "I'm fine. You don't need to worry."

"And you shouldn't worry either. Being married to the prince may have been more appealing, but being Queen, it's a far safer promotion of your standing. And you'll hardly ever see the king, he's so busy. Some parts ... might be awful, but this is good news. You must have really impressed him."

Esther broke away from her beaming face at the door of the Great Hall. She was greeted by two men glaring at her from across the table and apologies, delivered to her by a servant, from the king for his absence. Abner's twisted scowl confused her, but Cantus' dark stare emanating from the shadows sent a chill down her back.

"So," Abner said, breaking her eyes away from Cantus with jarring force, "pleasant dreams?"

"What?"

"I assume your head's full of visions of what it will be like as Queen Tessa? Or should I start calling you Mother?" He tossed his knife forward, sending it clattering against the dish he had hardly touched. "We're all just interchangeable for you, I suppose." His fingernails scraped against the plate, his hand curling into a fist.

"What has you so upset, Prince?" Esther asked, forcing a calm she did not feel to her grip as she took a sip of juiced fruit.

"You." He leaned forward. "How can you be—I guess I was naïve for thinking that—never mind." He stood up from the table, his hands splayed flat on the wood as he leaned still closer to her. His mouth bent into a sneer. "I hope you are very happy with your choices."

Exiting the room with swift, angry strides, Abner barked for people to clear out of his way.

Cantus followed the prince, allowing Esther at last to draw a full breath as she straightened in her chair and took a careful bite of her fruit-filled *scadia*. She ate slowly, not eager to leave the safety of the crowd. Exiting with everyone else, Esther spotted Giselle leading her flock to the garden. She winced at the thought of joining them, and looked up the grand staircase, measuring which was worse.

As she entered her room, she faced the window with a forced smile.

Cantus' dark stare emanated from his perch in her chair.

Esther raised her chin to meet it. "I assume you have something to say?" Her brow rose in challenge.

Cantus pushed himself to his feet, crossing her room in two long strides. "You," he said the word like a curse, "do not lie to me! I'm risking my life, everything. I need to be able to trust you, and the first opportunity you get, you betray me."

"What are you talking about?" Esther demanded, shoving his chest in an attempt to gain more room.

He allowed himself to be pushed back a step, his mouth pulling to one side. "Nothing's changed? Really? You don't think you becoming the very near future queen worth mentioning? This changes everything. What are we going to do now, hm?"

Esther sighed, staring at the wall. "We were finally going to make some progress, so I kept what I knew to myself for one night. Can't we continue as planned? They both have to be dealt with."

"But you've lost your access to the prince. The plan hinged on the prince being taken care of, and then the king drawing in the guard for protection. Abner won't respond to his father's death the same way the king would to his son's." Cantus blew air into her face as he cast his eyes around the room. "You've ruined us."

"What did I do?" Esther's chin stuck out as tension mounted in every muscle. "I played my part. I did what you wanted. It's not my fault he's a fickle, selfish—"

The door creaked open and Esther stopped talking to stare at Ava's wide eyes and hanging mouth.

"Apologies, my lady. A thousand—I should have knocked. I thought you'd be out, since it's such a nice ... I'll leave you alone."

Heat spread slowly across Esther's cheeks as the door whined closed behind Ava.

"That's a problem," Cantus said, his eyes on the closed frame of wood.

"No. I'll talk to her." Esther shook her head. "It'll be handled."

Cantus ran a hand over his stubbled chin, softening the hard line of his mouth. "I realize you didn't want this. Any of it. You didn't make the king change his mind. But you lie to me again, I will let you flounder on your own. I'll think of a different way to protect her. Understood?"

Esther's nod was forced out from a stiff neck. "What was—" she paused to gauge their standing, "what was in the box?"

Cantus' eyes lit with surprise. He took a breath, shoulders loosening. "Here," he pulled it out from under his belt.

Esther stared at the bubble of fabric from above his waist and wondered how she hadn't noticed it nestled there.

He popped open the box, a slow grin creeping up his mouth as he turned it to face her.

Esther leaned forward, eager despite herself. She rocked back on her heels and stared at Cantus, her grin slipping away from her wide eyes. "Is that?"

Cantus nodded, slowly.

Oh.

XIV

The desert of sand stretched across the expansive arena separating the nobility and the royal viewing box from the commoners in the stands. Esther perched on the edge of her chair, her eyes flitting from the small door to the left side of the arena with whitened animal bones nailed over the frame and the iron grates to the right where a barely distinguishable path led underground.

"What a fine day it's turned out to be, eh?" The king slipped a hand over her knee.

Esther stared at the rounded fingers, wondering if she could make breaking them look accidental.

"Yes, I don't think I've ever seen so fine a day for enjoying the Event. Although, that may be because of the company beside me." He arched his brow when she didn't reply.

Abner, sitting an aisle lower in the royal box, glared back at them with a tight jaw, his nostrils flaring as he turned away to watch the arena.

Giselle, seated next to him, raised her chin to give Esther a long, slow smile as she slipped an arm through his.

"And, you know, as my seating companion you are honored with the best view of the sands. You'll get to see every moment of it, unless your delicate sensibilities drive you to cover your eyes." The king leaned in closer to her ear. "Let me know if you are frightened, and I'll hold you till it's over."

Throat stinging, Esther bit her tongue.

The king's fingers squeezed her knee.

A sudden blast of a trumpet released her from his touch. Esther almost fell off her high cushioned seat from the bolt of energy the noise sent jolting up her limbs. She kept her fingers gripped on the wooden sides of her chair as a dreadful masked figure bounced out onto the sand. The mask he wore looked like a bird, with a long crooked beak and black feathers sticking out in odd directions. From his arms hung a collection of skull bones that clacked together as he ambled out in a jerky contorted gait.

"My lords," the bird man said, bowing to the royal box. "My ladies." He bowed to the nobility seating. "My victims." There was a pause as he slowly turned to regard the peasantry seated behind him. "I am Death. I have come on this, the tenth anniversary year of His Majesty's eternal reign to offer a humble gift. With Your Highness's permission," the masked man swung a skull-garbed arm toward the royal box and the king waved his acceptance, "we will begin."

Bang!

Esther's head whipped to the right as the metal grates cranked and ground through their gears, opening onto the sloped path.

The crowd clapped as a large cat emerged, its heavy body covered in black stripes.

Esther held her breath as the cat stalked slowly to the center of the arena. Her eyes barely took in the iron chain looped around its neck or the red-haired man behind it. His long agile stick flicked periodically at the cat's side.

Upon reaching the center the cat stopped, pulling back its white whiskered cheeks to snarl. An audible flick from the handler made the cat sit up on its hind legs, with its front paws folded together as if to beg. It held its balance.

Two bears ambled forward to join the cat. Esther was familiar with these large beasts, having sacrificed more than one meal over the years to their greedy stalking of her camp. She had never seen them move like this, however. They bounced from one paw to the other as a quick drumbeat began. The five drummers marched with huge barrels strapped across their chest, their exposed brown skin glistening with sweat as their arms beat an infectious rhythm. A ring was brought to the masked man, and he trotted toward the cat, holding it out at his shoulder.

"I don't know of any other kingdom that has such a magnificent tiger as ours," said the king in Esther's ear, his lips practically touching her neck to be heard over the noise. "They are brought over the land from across the sea. Very expensive, but such a beast."

Esther shifted away, eyes still on the animal. *Tiger.*

"You're very enjoyable to watch," remarked the king.

Esther comforted herself with the knife's presence, warm against her calf, as her stomach twisted.

The king and his cloying voice were forgotten however, when the tiger—stripped of its chain—launched into the air and passed through the hoop. Muscles rippled beneath the stripes as its bulk sank onto its paws, its white-whiskered mouth slipping open to hint at the massive teeth within.

Death dropped the ring with a flourish and the drumbeats intensified.

The tiger trotted along the wall of the arena with the human keeping pace beside it, while the bears performed tricks at the arena's center. They stood, balancing against each other's paws, and roared on command. If Esther wasn't watching it herself, she wouldn't have believed such tricks of precision and agility were possible for these massive animals.

All the while, the cadence of the drums beat on.

Forgetting the king beside her, Esther lost herself in the spectacle. She stood to clap with the rest of the crowd as the tiger, completing its final circuit of the arena, gathered its bulk and leaped. It arched over both bears standing on their hind legs, while a pop sent a shower of golden paper slips cascading down behind them. The rolling drum beat led the animals dancing back through the iron grate. Esther resumed her seat.

A flood of dancers spilled from a door hidden below, and the drumbeat changed from the wild furious rhythm to a rolling swell of noise that quieted and grew again with building waves rocked by the fury of their movements.

Esther had never seen dancing like that before, and she studied the bouncing bodies with a confused tilt of her head.

The king cleared his throat, making a point to stare at her instead of the dancers.

She blocked him from her thoughts and leaned forward just as the drums rang out a last note and the performers disappeared, waving to the crowd.

"And now," the masked Death came out a little less jovially, "a thank you to the generosity of our king. O people," his voice leaked enthusiasm with every syllable, "do not fear tomorrow, because the king has rescued you from every danger. He is god, giver of all you need, master of your fate. Believe in him and you will prosper." As he spoke, the peasantry seats began to buzz with activity as hunks of bread were passed between them from servants at the end of each aisle. "He gives you bread. Life. Are you not blessed?"

Emerging from the door marked with bones, pairs of fighters replaced him on the sand. Their presence awakened the crowd to give a collective roar of excitement as swords were drawn, spears struck shields, and whips cracked the air. They formed a line on the sand, heavily muscled arms extended in salute to the king.

"We, the warriors of the arena, give our lives for your favor. May you delight in our sacrifice, O King of Alberon. May your glory never fade."

The king kept them holding their stiff posture for a moment before he, with a dismissive wave, signaled them to begin.

With a bow, two fighters broke away from the group and moved to the center of the arena, while the others filed out of sight. Facing one another, each man dug his heels into the sand. One wore a heavy iron mask, and his hardened muscles made the sweat sparkle on his exposed chest. The other wore no helmet, his blonde hair bound at the neck to hang down the back of his metal coat. He banged a rolling beat with his short sword against his shield as his opponent roared behind his mask.

A shiver ran down Esther's spine, her eyes straining forward to see better.

The masked man's ax sliced through the air and the crowd responded with a roar. As the ax man charged, Esther pulled in a breath and leaned away. The ax blow was knocked aside by his opponent's sword. Rolling with a spray of sand, the ax came again. The swordsman dodged and the masked ax man screamed as a spray of red wet his side and stained the ground. Stumbling away, the masked fighter used his ax handle like a cane.

The swordsman paused, raising his blade to allow the spectators time to celebrate his victory.

"Death! Death! Death!" chanted the people.

He turned to face the crowd, smiling through his heavy yellow beard as he pumped his sword in the air.

"Death! Death! Death!"

Blood stained the sand at their feet. The yellow bearded head fell to the ground a moment before the rest of his twitching body. The masked fighter rose, ax dripping into the red mud as he laid his boot on the back of his decapitated foe.

Cheers swelled for their surprise champion.

The masked man raised his ax, clutching his side with the other as blood seeped between his fingers.

A frame of stretched canvas, bound between two poles and carried by running servants, loaded up the dead man and his head to take them out of sight through the bone-lined door.

Death bounced forward, skulls clapping against their neighbors as he celebrated with the crowd.

The victorious man stumbled after the dead one back through the yawning door marked with bones.

The next pair were called to fight, followed by another and another.

With every passing challenge, Esther sat more forward in her chair, her hands gripping her knees tighter, and her blinking slowed as her eyes fought to catch every detail of the exchange.

Her favorite was a small man, covered from hair to heel in black. From every fold of fabric he produced a weapon, small and cutting. His agility kept Esther's breath captive in her chest as the man darted around his opponent doing little slices of damage, but always sliding out of reach before the other could land a returning strike.

After a long while of furious, fruitless swiping at his attacker, the dagger-wielding opponent stood in the center of their sparring circle, chest heaving through each breath as a steady trickle of life seeped from twenty different wounds.

The man in black, still untouched, appeared behind him.

A few crunching awkward moments of struggle made the daggers fall and the opposition go limp.

"Boring!" The king threw a bone picked clean by his teeth down from the viewing box at them.

Esther heard the word like a murmur in a crowded room, far away and not quite real.

The black robed fighter stood over the vanquished and bowed to the king's viewing box.

Esther couldn't tell if he was looking at the king or if his black eyes glared at her, but she had to look away from the pooling darkness of his stare.

"Another!" The king's voice boomed across the sand as he stomped his foot for good measure.

Death obediently bounced back to his place as the body was carried away. "Our final competitors. Champions each." Death gestured for them to come forward, while the victor of the previous match slowly turned and left. "With no fear of death, and no hope beyond the pleasure of their king, they present their bodies as a sacrifice to you, O Great One."

The two fighters flourished their weapons and bowed low.

The king yawned heavily, staring down at the scarlet wine in his cup.

Death whispered in a servant's ear and sent him sprinting to the iron grate. The feathered announcer backed away toward the bone door as the two fighters circled each other. The echoes of the first clanging blows had hardly faded before a roar drew attention to the grate.

The lion growled as a guard jabbed its flank with a long spear. Metal screeched as the door was hastily rolled into place, locking the beast in the arena.

The two swordsmen looked at each other.

Death was nowhere to be found.

The gasp of the crowd recaptured the king's attention. The lion's chest dipped to the ground, its heavy mane brushing the sand. Seeing the great cat begin its slow circle of the men, the monarch's eyes sparkled. "Mhm..." he stroked his mouth with a finger. "You may enjoy this, my dear." He winked at her.

The gate on the other end of the arena marked with bones began to creep closed. The competitors turned from the lion at the sound of the door and sprinted toward their only hope of safety.

Esther knew it was a mistake.

The lion launched after them, powerful muscle propelling it forward over the sandy ground.

The men put on a burst of speed, racing the beast and each other.

"No!" yelled one fighter, dropping his weapon and shield as he threw himself down to slide under the door. Too late.

The door snapped his leg bone like a dried twig and, despite his desperate tugging, trapped it beneath its crushing metal grip.

The other caught up a breath later. He joined in the effort to move the metal barrier, but a look back sent him rolling with a spray of sand.

The lion rose up and enclosed the trapped man's neck between his jaws.

The survivor had a few moments to properly panic as the lion mauled the other. Some from the crowd of peasants called to him, thumping fists on the wooden stands and reaching hands down for him to grab. He didn't hear them, running in a wide circle through the arena in his desperate search for a hole to hide in.

"Nowhere to go," laughed the king, his mouth barely containing the hunk of thick-crusted bread his jaw worked to chew. "Not a bad runner," he added to Esther with a chuckle. "Shame."

At last, the fleeing man spotted the peasants' hands extended to help. They screamed for him to hurry, the furious pounding on the stands swelling as he sprinted toward them. He didn't notice the lion startle at the noise and leave its prey, still twitching in the sand, to stalk after him. He jumped toward the hands reaching for him and planted his foot on the wall to swing up to safety.

Too late.

The triumph of nature was swift as the lion's claws dug into the man's chest, flaying it open as he was dragged to the ground.

The peasants fell back with screams and curses.

Esther leaned forward to study the lion as it pulled the man by his broken neck back toward the other victim. "Why would it do that?"

Like Our Enemies

"What do you mean? The lion killed the men. That, my dear, is the hard law of nature. It may be difficult for someone of your sensitivity to understa—"

"Not like that," Esther insisted. "It had its meal, why risk its first kill because it was startled by a noise?"

"Oh, that." The king took a large gulp from his wine, clearing his throat loudly. "Probably has something to do with its training."

Esther stared at him.

The king's head tilted as his hands stroked his oil-soaked beard. "You're adapting well here, you know. As if you were always one of us."

"What training?"

"What? Oh, that. Well, we can't have lions eating people here. They'd turn on their handlers. So we train it by delivering pain if it ever goes beyond the kill."

Esther turned back to the arena as the lion was jabbed away from the fallen men by five soldiers with spears and flaming torches.

The great cat sank low to the ground, trying to find a way around them as it let out a desperate sound from deep in its massive chest. Eventually, after a strong smack to the face with a torch and several hard jabs to its flank by different spears, the lion began to retreat and was herded back into the lair where they kept the poor beast.

Esther stood, her whole body heaving with every breath.

"I'm going to go freshen my face, or something." She cast the sentence to the king as an afterthought as she brushed past him.

The king grabbed her wrist, his hand slick with oil. "Don't be too long," he said, running a thumb along her skin.

Slipping her hand out of his grip, Esther couldn't stop the shiver which rifled through her shoulders as she tried to forget the feeling of his touch.

Breathe. Just bleeding breathe. You've seen blood before, you've seen all of this before. It doesn't matter. It can't touch you. Just breathe. Abner swallowed, pulling shuddering gasps of air through his nose as his hands clamped over his ears, struggling in vain to shut out the noise that shook the wooden scaffolding around him.

He hadn't made it past the first cut. Instead, he'd fled into the hidden servant's passages threading around the arena that he hadn't visited since he was a boy. At least Giselle wouldn't find him here. No one would. He crouched on the ground, hiding like a coward. His palms pounded his temples, nails biting into his scalp, but nothing he did stopped what he saw.

The blackened spray of blood, the dreadful memories of what Dennison and the rest of his men had become. What he had become. The blood followed him, haunting him, still only covered up by soap and water. How long until they all saw it dripping from his palms?

His hands covered his mouth, stifling the groan of misery that escaped his throat.

Breathe, you bleeding weakling! He laid his head back against the wooden post.

A hand, cool and strangely sticky, met his.

Abner jumped away.

"Tessa?" Abner's shoulders dropped some of their tension. "What are you doing here?"

"I thought I heard—" she hesitated, eyes running over Abner. "What are *you* doing here?"

Abner didn't have an answer he could share. Instead, he stared down at their knees which were almost close enough to touch.

"I didn't see you leave," Tessa said, the intensity in her eyes seeming disjointed from what she was saying. "When did you get up?"

"First cut." Every muscle in his face tightened in a vice grip. "I thought I could watch, but I'm apparently too weak. Like he always said I was. Like I always have been. He knew, and he—"

"Are you ... mad?" She leaned away.

"Insane? Maybe. Probably." Abner closed the distance between them, desperately searching for something he couldn't name. "I see it. All the time. Everything. The things I have done, over and over in my mind. I can't make it stop. I don't know how to make it stop."

Something softened in her eyes, the glimmer of compassion drawing him in.

Her eyes—

Abner jolted back against the wooden beam. He remolded the skin over his forehead, attempting to hide his misery in a passive mask. "You should get back. The king will be missing his seating companion."

She scrutinized him, unmoving. "If you were the king, today, what would you change?"

"I can't change anything."

"But if you were king, you could."

Abner paused. "I don't know. I've never really thought about it."

"What have you been doing all your life?" Tessa's face pinched in frustration. "You knew this was coming. You don't like how things are, why aren't you making plans to change it?"

Air hissed through Abner's teeth as he breathed out a laugh. "You think because I'm the prince I have any more power than you? Well, that may be a bad example. Any more power than a common soldier?"

Eyes narrowed, Tessa opened her mouth to respond but was cut off.

"I am nothing unless my father says so. I have nothing of my own. Not even you."

"Me? Why would that matter?"

"Why wouldn't it?" Abner threw his arms out. "You were supposed to be mine. I'd just gotten used to the idea and..." he stopped himself, unsure of what to say to explain his thoughts. They had both known that he hadn't wanted to be in this position, but now—

"And now things have changed." Tessa shook her head. "Maybe it's better this way."

Abner's jaw tightened. "Is it?"

Fanfare blasted through the wood above them, the crowd hidden from view roaring and cheering at some new spectacle.

Tessa looked over her shoulder.

"You should go," Abner said quietly.

Drums beat a heavy driving rhythm.

Tessa hesitated.

"I'll follow in a moment." Abner nodded toward the little door that would lead her out to the walkway opening to the king's box.

The girl in white disappeared.

He won't forgive me if I miss the tribute. Time to go.

"Ah, my dear, you are just in time."

Esther resumed her seat next to the king. The crowd's noise sent the wood thrumming beneath her feet. "What's happening?"

Posts had been dug into the sand, and a score of peasants clothed in thin rags shivered together in a group on the far side.

Death paced in front of them, striking a few at random with his beak before moving to stand by a wide-necked clay jar closer to the center of the arena.

"The main event." The king winked at her.

The crowd quieted, as if all held their breath together.

Death bowed to the king. "The final drum beats now, the last of today's glory we offer to you, O Rightful and Everlasting King." He moved to the peasants, followed by a servant lugging the clay jar. Death scooped handfuls of heavy oil, dumping it onto the peasants' heads. They shook as it hit their scalp but did not dare move as the guards encircled the group with swords drawn. After the last peasant was prepared, a small girl with matted brown hair who looked as if she hadn't eaten for weeks, the guards began to move.

"Please!" begged an old snow-haired man, "Please let the child go! Have me, just me, but let—" His voice was stopped by a metal-clad strike to his mouth. He whimpered, holding his jaw.

He looks ... I couldn't have met that man before. No one survived Shiloh.

The swell of the crowd grew.

The peasants were forced to stand around the posts, tied together with their backs pressed against the wood.

The king rose.

The wood. The oil. Oh, no—he wouldn't!

The world faded away, Esther's eyes saw nothing but the torch being brought to Death on the sand.

"May their sparks—" Death took the torch, "—light your glorious reign for another year."

Horror turned Esther's stomach into a pit of roiling snakes. *He's not only taking their life, but their sparks. He's stopping their existence, taking away any hope of eternal rest. The king is a monster.*

Kindling had been laid at the peasants' feet and, although they now fought furiously against their bonds, their cries were overwhelmed by the crowd.

"DEATH! DEATH! DEATH!" the people shouted.

The king raised his arms.

Death went down the line and lit the fires.

The tongues of flame spat at the peasant's feet, their oil-soaked clothes catching quickly.

The king's shoulders rose and fell with waves of obvious pleasure as he spread his hands, extending them to embrace the arena and the moment and hold onto it forever. He sucked in the smoke beginning to curl through the air with a vicious hunger.

The crowd roared.

The drums beat.

The people screamed.

"I am your god!" The king joined in the roar of the crowd.

Each of the twenty victims were now a thrashing column of fire burned at his altar.

Esther did not think, didn't plan, darting forward with quick precision. She freed the knife from her calf, driving it into the king's shoulder before a breath had passed. She clutched his soft blue tunic to her chest, grinning at the spreading red stain as he screamed. Her eyes fell to Abner seated below.

"Father?" Abner's expression spiraled in fury and confusion. "No—Tessa! Guards! No!" He lunged at her.

Esther twisted the blade, relishing the king's strangled cry. An iron grip yanked her away, the knife ripping free from her grasp as she was tossed to the side. Her knees struck the rail in her struggle for balance. Esther's desperate thrashing sent her body flipping over the wooden barrier to the sands below.

The fall was over before she could scream. The crunch rattling through her bones pulled her eyes closed as a horde of flashing metal descended upon her.

XV

D*rip.*
Khh.
Drip. Drop. Drip.
Khh.
Drip. Drip.

Esther's mouth twisted. The tang of old blood sat heavy on her crusted lips. Glaring light streamed through the solitary window, intensifying the pulsing beat at her temples. Cold stone cradled her pounding head as she turned away from the glare.

"Guh," her throat buckled in protest as she pulled her deadened arm out from beneath her waist and pushed herself up. Pain lanced through her shoulders, the muscles awakening with regret. She tipped back onto her heels and leaned against the slime-slicked stone wall. One eye was unwilling to open, but the other sat blinking at the room around her. Dim, save for the streaming light which formed irritating flashing rods through the bars enclosing her, and dirty.

"Finally awake, then?"

Esther winced at the lancing pain the sound sent jarring her nerves. She blinked at the light winking off the crown held between two thick-veined hands. Her sight traveled up the line of the man's forearm, to his tunic, to his face. Her head bobbed weakly as she tried to focus.

"Ab ... ner?"

His thumb rubbed at a ruby stuck in one of the spokes of the crown while the prince sat in the dirt with his shoulder pressed against the bars of her cell. "And who are you?" He fixed her with a glare, the anger smoldering in his gaze awakening Esther's limbs with a slow heat. "You're the girl in black, aren't you?"

Esther's lip lifted into a crooked smile, one side still tugged down by the weight of her exhaustion.

"Hm." Abner turned from her. "I had been wondering where my dagger got to. It never occurred to me that you'd stolen it."

"What did you ... expect ... Prince?" Every word was a colossal effort, draining her energy like a bucket with a hole punched through the bottom. "Think you could run ... and it wouldn't matter what you—" Her chest broke through her accusation with a fit of coughing. She choked past the heavy glob at the back of her throat before spilling her stomach with violent force on the ground next to her. The mess began to seep slowly toward the boundary of the iron cage she was locked in. "Ugh," she groaned through her burning throat, too tired to wipe her mouth clean. She leaned against the wall.

"You tried to murder my father." Abner read the question in her eyes, the words too much of an effort. "No, he isn't dead. Not yet. In the meantime, I'm supposed to make a decision on what to do with you."

Esther's foggy mind began to sharpen. "What else would you do?" *Of course I'll be executed. It's over. I've lost.*

"It's not that simple." Abner set the crown down on the dirt floor beside him. "As the demon girl, yes, kill you in a heartbeat. You mean nothing to me. But, as Lady Tessa, I ... I don't want to see you die."

Esther drew in a deep breath, needing to get every word out before another fit of coughing could strike. "I was only ever Lady Tessa to get close enough to kill you."

Abner shook his head. "I don't believe that. There were plenty of times when you could have done something. You didn't. Maybe it wasn't me, but something made you want to stay."

"No—" She abandoned the effort to control her head mid-shake and let it roll against her shoulder. *How is it possible to be this heavy?*

"Something in you must have wanted you to live. And for reasons I don't want to think about, so do I." Abner stomped at something near his foot, popping Esther's chin up from her chest. "I hoped seeing you might make my decision clearer, but it's only confused me more. There's no worse feeling."

I could name a few worse ones. Pain lanced between her temples, drawing a weak groan from Esther's throat. She bit at the crust on her lip, pulling her hand up to scrape it off her tongue. "All your life," Esther said, forcing the words out through shallow breaths, "you've wanted to have power to do something. Now your moment is here and—" she broke off as a wet cough spewed from deep in her chest, "you do nothing." Her head fell back.

"It's pathetic." Abner's jaw became a knot of muscle as he used the bars enclosing Esther to pull himself to his feet, the other hand retrieving the crown from the dirt. "This was a waste of time." His forehead almost touched the bars of her cage. "Goodbye Tessa." He set the crown on his head, his gaze dropping from hers.

The fog crept back over Esther's mind as his boots clomped beyond her hearing. Before her eyes fell closed again, she looked directly across from her into another cage, where an old gnarled hand wrapped around the bars and a pair of sharp blue eyes stared at her from the darkness.

"Please, Sire, I would beg you to take this matter seriously. The king—"

Abner pushed past the noble.

"Prince Abner!" called another, his ring-coated fingers flashing as he waved.

"My lord," Giselle slunk to his side and slid one arm through his.

Abner twisted away, his face forgetting to hide his displeasure.

Giselle let him escape through a small break in the horde of older men vying for his attention.

"Prince, that land was promised to me a month ago, and I believe it would benefit your future cr—"

"Abner!" Dennison extended a hand to forge a path for his escape.

"Prince, please!"

"We need to know what—"

The captain held back the flood from spilling past him as Abner rounded a corner.

Puffing a grateful sigh, the prince ran to his room. He only wanted a moment to think, to breathe before the pressure descended again. On the balcony, Abner squinted at the city's white walls, which glared back at him in the fading sun. A breath of wind carrying the changing season blew, and he rubbed a hand over his face. Abner's fingers found the crown hanging on his brow and he pulled it from his head, dropping it on the small round table behind him.

Talks of his coronation and the smooth succession of power plagued him, as well as each noble viewing this transition as an opportunity to push whatever agenda they had been scheming to move on. He had allowed the old nobles to place the gold weight on his brow— apparently the formal one he would don in the ceremony was even heavier and set with more precious stones—to show the kingdom that there was no gap in authority or succession. Alberon was secure.

At first, he had been angry at how quickly the noble with the long white beard had produced it, dusted from whatever corner they kept the heavy symbols of power, as if the king was already dead and Abner had already replaced him. Now he was numb to anything except the weight of it. How many pointless, unreasonable decisions did he have to make before they would all just leave him in peace? Abner pinched the bridge of his nose between his fingers, his eyes closing to allow the throbbing pain in his temples to recede.

Two warm brown hands slipped around his waist, traveling up his chest.

Abner twisted away.

"My prince?" Giselle raised her eyebrows at him, a self-satisfied smirk planted on her lips.

"How did you get in here?" Abner heard the snap in his tone, but didn't bother to smooth it over.

Giselle pushed a sigh through her lips. "No one notices a woman. I move wherever I please." Her laugh grated against his ears. "You look skeptical. Would you like me to prove just how far I can go?"

"I'm not in the mood for games, Giselle. Just leave." Abner turned to stare over the city.

"I think I could get you to sing a different tune if we—"

Abner shoved her hands away.

"I don't understand you," Giselle snapped, irritation winning at last. "One would think you weren't even happy. Everything you've been waiting for has fallen into your lap. You didn't even have to lift a finger and—" she picked the crown up from the table, holding it reverently, "—you're practically King."

Abner snatched it from her hand. "My father is dying!"

"Your father—"

"Get out!"

Giselle's icy wall of civility and coy attention gained a large, wide crack as her eyes swam in tears. "I've always—"

"I don't care! Get out!" Abner threw his hand toward the door.

Giselle gathered her skirts and marched away. Pausing before she exited his room in a furious whip of cloth she said, "You will regret this, Abner. We could've been ... but now you've ruined everything!"

Eventually Abner, having grown tired of staring at the city, exited the balcony to sit in his great chair and stare instead at the bare hearth, twisting the crown in his hands until the sun began its descent toward night. As the first streaks of red and gold lit the walls of his chamber, he rose from the chair, placed the crown on his head, and left his room.

His eyes raked the familiar halls.

At the door of the king's room, the prince pushed out a breath, ran his hands over his tunic, and slipped the crown from his head. His shoulder ached.

The door's gold handle was warm beneath his fingers by the time he pushed it open to enter the chamber.

"Father." Abner was a boy again.

The colorful tapestries lining the walls, the ocean waves rolling far down at the beach, and the glinting of precious stones embedded in nearly every surface faded away at the sight of the king's labored breathing. His cough was a hollow echo in his cavernous chest, but not enough to stir him from sleep. His arm hung off the bed beneath the yellow-smeared bandage wrapped over his bare shoulder.

Abner shifted forward slowly, the awkwardness of standing in his father's room with the king unaware made the prince's heart hammer loud in his ears. He set the crown carefully on a little table and perched himself on the bed at his father's side.

The king strained to gather each breath through his wiry, unoiled beard.

He looks so old. So tired. I think I understand that now.

Abner's hands twisted together anxiously in his lap, until, for something to do, the prince wrung the cloth from the basin at the king's side and dabbed at his forehead.

His hand had almost drifted to peel back the bandages folded over his father's wound when the old monarch's eyes snapped open. They stretched, glassy and round, at the sight of his son. His mouth moved without sound.

"It's okay, Father. It's me. There was ... something happened. But it's okay. I'm with you."

The king's chin bounced through a cough.

"I should go and let you rest. They've been hounding me to make these decisions. I don't—"

A whispered word croaked from his father's lips, one eye twitching with the effort.

"What?" Abner leaned down.

"Trai ... tor," the king's voice strained through his wheezing chest.

"Yes, she lied to us." Abner's stomach settled like a stone.

The king's brows pulled together.

"I'll deal with it."

"You," he punched the word through whatever fog had descended over his body. "Filthy trai—" Yellow bile sprayed from the king's lips as a cough rattled through his bones again.

"Healer!" Abner cast the call over his shoulder as he wiped frantically at his father's mouth.

The king's hand found his son's cheek, fingers shaking as they touched his skin.

Abner turned back to him, surprised. A shock of pain bit him and he jolted backward.

The king dragged his clawed fingers to his chest, two of the nails stained with speckles of red.

Abner's hand probed the wound on his cheekbone as he stared at his father.

"If I..." whispered the king, his eyes screaming though his voice could not. "I'll kill you."

"I didn't—I wouldn't betray you. I'm innocent," Abner pleaded, leaning toward him.

The king took a wild swipe with stiff claw-like nails as soon as Abner was within reach, missing his son and sending himself smacking onto the rug-laden floor. He screamed as blood seeped from his wound, staining the woven purple threads beneath him.

"A curse on—" he roared from the ground as Abner's feet raced to the door, his speech broken apart by a guttural cough, "kill you—"

Abner whipped into the hallway, slamming the door on his father's words, just as the Healer and Dennison rounded the corner ahead.

"Prince Abner," Dennison said, hailing him with a hand.

A gut-churning cough from the room behind him, followed by the king's croaking cry of "Traitor!" slowed Dennison's step.

"Abner?"

The Healer hurried past him into the room.

Abner slipped by Dennison, sprinting down the hall as the noise of the overwhelmed physician trying to settle his rage-filled charge echoed after his pounding boots. The familiar halls and doors of the castle passed in a blur. This was no longer his home. He could never be safe or comfortable here again. His father wanted him dead. Descending the grand staircase was the next thing that he was really conscious of. He tripped on the last stair and had to catch himself on the banister.

A hand gripped the back of his tunic and pulled him through a narrow door. Abner crashed into a clay jar of scented spices, smashing it with his hip and flooding his nostrils with the stinging powder. He sneezed, blinking as the wrinkled visage of a guard's uniform pulled Abner to his feet.

Cantus stared down at him, his mouth a hard line.

"What?" snapped Abner, pulling away. "Come to take your bite of flesh too?" He drew the dagger—recovered from the girl in black—at his waist.

Cantus' breath flared his nostrils as he drew his sword.

"So be it." The prince's face twisted as he readied his muscles to lunge forward.

Esther was first aware of her breathing.

Khh ... Khh ... Khh ... Khh...

The heavy air pushed past her lips for an eternity before her eyes understood anything that she saw.

There was a window.

A single window lighting the room, now painted with evening colors.

She twitched a finger.

It bent. Straightened again.

Whatever shock had cocooned her mind during the prince's visit seemed to be falling away. Her ears caught a quiet murmur of conversation beyond the doors, her nose stung with varieties of smells she didn't want to name, and her exhaustion was muted by pain.

Esther pushed herself to her feet. A wave of pressure broke against her back, flooding down her legs as she flailed, fighting for balance. She lost the battle, pulling herself up spitting dirt a moment later.

She started on her knees for the next attempt. Slime coated her fingers as they gripped the wall beside her, bracing against the swell of her churning stomach.

Not again. Esther swallowed hard. She climbed to her feet. Her moistened hands yanked the strings of her corset, pulling her waist in further and straightening her back.

At last, she could breathe easier, the crushing discomfort lessening.

She pulled the string again, harder, her eyes turning from the window to her cell bars which did not quite reach the ceiling.

Today is not the day I die.

Abner cursed, eyes darting between their weapons. His dagger was little better than a kitchen knife against the long-reaching sword, unless he could use the lack of maneuverability in the cramped room to his advantage.

Cantus held up his hand. "Come with us."

Abner's gaze narrowed on the ruby glinting beneath Cantus' fist. "That sword ... that belongs to me."

Cantus pulled back.

"Are you a thief now, Cantus?"

"You aren't safe here, Abner. The king will turn against you. Come with us. Help us."

"Us? What do you mean?"

"Lady Tessa and I."

Abner's jaw fell as he shook his head. "I don't—you? You were a part of this?"

Cantus' mouth disappeared, pressed into a hard line, his furrowed brow deepening.

"How did you even—"

"No time. Are you with me?"

Metal boots marched through the hallway beyond the door and both men turned to the sound, frozen as they listened.

"You there!" a voice echoed to them. "Where is the prince?"

"I wouldn't know, Sir."

"Another servant saw him descend the grand staircase. The king wishes him brought. If you see head or hide of him, you find one of us."

"I will, Sir. Always a loyal servant, I am."

"Be on your way," said a second soldier. "He can't have gotten out. We may have to search room by room, but we'll find him eventually."

"The rabbit has lost his burrow, time for the foxes to have their way," the first soldier said with a dark chuckle.

"Foxes? Why did you pick foxes?" The metal feet began to stomp away.

"They hunt rabbits."

"They're tiny." The voices began to fade. "Wolves. Wolves hunt rabbits and sound much better."

Ear-ringing silence invaded the air between them as Cantus and Abner studied each other.

"What do you say?"

"How do I know you're not trying to kill me too? That this isn't a trick?"

Cantus offered him the jeweled sword, hilt first.

Abner, eyes narrowed, snatched it from the Cantus' grip. His hand tightened over the sword hilt, staring at Cantus' empty fists.

"I remember what it was like before." Cantus kept his hands stiff at his sides. "This isn't how our lives have to be. Change it. Come with me."

Abner sighed, dropping the tip of the blade to the floor. "We're getting Tessa out too?"

"I promised her. Along with my aunt, who we'll have to find." Cantus turned to the door and eased it open, nodding for Abner to follow.

Lady Hildren? How many conspirators lurked under my nose?

"Of course," Cantus shook his head, "she decided to do things her way and muddied the whole plan." He set off down the hall toward the kitchens. "Reckless girl."

Abner searched for something to ground him. For anything to be familiar, normal. Nothing around him felt real. His father did not feel like his father. His home was no longer his to claim. His enemy was now one he risked his life to rescue. And the dutiful soldier now led the exiled prince down the path of treason.

Cantus yanked Abner through the kitchen door as soldiers entered the hallway with swords drawn. He backed toward the fireplace, nodding to the servants preparing trays to be sent to all the nobles' rooms in the king's absence. Seeing the prince at his side, their faces grew white, conversation dying on their lips. Cantus pushed Abner to the hearth, the muddy gray ashes of the fire still sending a slow spiral of smoke up the chute.

"Say nothing," Cantus whispered to them, stopping one old cook's trembling mouth. "Please."

Abner waited while Cantus twisted a brick out from the surrounding wall within the fireplace. Through the newly-formed hole, Abner spotted a wooden lever.

"I didn't know this was here," Abner said as the lever was pulled and a rattle of gears brought the back wall of the hearth swinging forward.

Cantus lifted it with a grunt and threw his head to signal Abner to enter the tunnel beyond.

"How did you find this without me?" Abner ducked into the darkness.

Cantus led the way with quick expert steps.

Abner tried to keep up, but his stumbling boots sent him tripping into the back of Cantus' heel more than once.

"Can't believe I'd rather have the girl with me," Cantus muttered as he kicked out his freshly-bruised ankle.

"I don't understand," Abner said, finding the wall to guide him. Drips of water had created a path for trickles of light that now allowed him to see enough to move with a cautious stability. "How did the most obnoxiously yes-sir-no-sir, never disobey, boring soldier in the army fall in with an assassin? I mean—"

Cantus glared at him as he edged around a leaning support beam.

As Abner slipped around the rotted wooden frame, he was struck in the mouth by falling water, the ping of salted dirt making the corners of his mouth seize.

"It's complicated," Cantus said as Abner spat his tongue clean. "It seemed the best way to protect the only family I have left."

Abner kicked away a loose brick. "Seems like an awfully big risk for an old woman."

Cantus' gaze narrowed, curled fists at his side. "I'd die for her."

Abner held up his hands. "As you wish it."

Cantus turned back to the tunnel again. "Where are you keeping Tessa?"

"Tower prison. She's in the cell on the left, if that makes a difference."

Cantus shook his head, muttering a curse. "There're no tunnels in the tower. I think we will need to go through the guards. But I'm sure by now they have orders not to let us pass."

Abner's eyes darkened, unsheathing the dagger and handing it to Cantus. "We won't be asking permission." His grip flexed on the gleaming handle of his sword.

Cantus' mouth tightened, staring at the blade. Finally, the soldier nodded and continued into the semi-darkness.

Slipping from the tunnel up onto the corridor's carpeted floor coated Abner's hair in dusty spiderwebs. Swatting himself clean, he stood with Cantus. Together they faced the stone steps that would lead them spiraling up to the tower prison.

The guards were stationed at the door of the two-part cell and their wood backed chairs faced the stairs at all times. Abner had never caught one of them sleeping or distracted, save a dice game to pass the time, which made their job now all the more difficult.

Cantus' expression changed when the two soldiers came into view. He hid the dagger beneath his heavy black cloak.

"Behrn." Cantus' eyes glanced over the thick-bearded man who dropped his fistful of dice onto the table. "Nathaniel."

The younger guard's brow pulled together as his smile slipped to one side.

The prince and the soldier closed the distance to the guards.

"Cantus?" Nathaniel rose and clapped him on the shoulder. "How are you, you old stalk?"

"Well enough."

"Still no luck with the ladies, I take it?"

Cantus tried to appear casual as he held the dagger stiffly beneath his cloak. "How's Ava?"

"Hands off my sister," Nathaniel warned with a grin.

Cantus chuckled.

"She's well enough, I suppose. I haven't seen her either. It's these cursed—" Nathaniel's eyes moved to the prince. His face flushed. "Highness." He bowed.

Abner raised his chin. He buried the sting of pain that this may be the last time he would hear himself addressed as royalty. "I need to see the prisoner."

"Again?" Nathaniel's eyebrows rose. "As you wish it, Sire." His eyes strayed to the drawn sword clutched in the prince's hand.

Abner brushed past him. News to the far corners of the castle apparently came at a slow trickle.

Behrn watched him go with dark eyes, his jaw slowly chewing on something unseen.

Cantus clapped Nathaniel on the shoulder again before enclosing them in the dungeon with the girl in black.

Or rather, her empty cell.

Abner's gaze darted over the space. A crumpled mass of purple cloth balled up in the second cell and an old trunk tucked into the corner behind them were the only things in the room.

Cantus let out a rough breath, and pulled at Abner's shoulder. He pointed to a far corner, where a wooden beam stretched to support the weight of the floor above. Clinging to the scarred grains where it met the ceiling, like a nursing babe to its mother, was Lady Tessa.

"Get down from there," Cantus whispered, pointing toward the ground with a scowl.

"Why is he here?" Tessa's eyes darted between the two men.

Cantus shook his head, "Later. Now—"

Voices filled the hallway outside.

Abner, Cantus, and Tessa all froze to stare at the thick wooden door.

"Now we have to go," Cantus said in a rush.

"And the king?"

Abner's face hardened. *I cannot stay here. He'll kill me. My only options are to run or die.*

"We can't do anything about him now." Cantus' words were rushed, breathless. "There's a score of men guarding his room and Captain Dennison looking for Abner. We need to escape, get my aunt safe, then—"

Tessa dropped to the floor with a thump. She clutched her stomach, squeezed tight by the corset wrapping her waist.

Abner pulled his eyes from her chest rising and falling on the swell of each hurried breath. His gaze landed on the large trunk in one corner with an old rusted latch.

Pushing herself to her feet with a growl, Tessa slapped Cantus' offered hand away. "Plan." She yanked the laces of her corset, knotting it into place.

"I haven't got one," admitted Cantus, his eyes darting around the room.

I might. Abner laid down his sword, setting his shoulder against the large box. It weighed enough to be filled to the brim with heavy stones.

Cantus joined him and together they pushed the box in front of the door.

The voices were louder outside.

"There," Abner said, rubbing his hands free from the sting of brief intense work. "Now no one can get in." He retrieved his sword.

"And we can't get out," Tessa's voice dripped with venom. "Good plan."

"Enough," Cantus said, "that won't help anything."

"Window." Tessa moved to study the small square of light. She leaned out, sizing her shoulders against it.

A bang rattled the box into the space of the room by a step. Abner and Cantus leaned against it, trying to hold it in place.

"This is just putting off the inevitable," Cantus' voice strained through muscle as his heel was pushed back with the latest blow. Grunting, he moved himself to the middle of the box and reset his shoulder against it.

Tessa brushed past them and Abner caught a drifting whiff of her hair, the sting of bile rising to the back of his throat at the smell. She measured Cantus' shoulders against her arm before darting away again.

The next knock came blasting through the door, cracking the wood, and both men strained to hear the argument being fought on the other side. The bangs stopped, the pressure momentarily lifted.

Abner took advantage of the pause. Joining Tessa at the window, the prince peeked over the ledge. "So, we jump?"

Tessa stared at him, her chin pulling to one side beneath her tight mouth. "It's five levels to the ground. We'd never survive that."

"Aim for the hay?" Abner gestured to an open-topped supply wagon, spilling over with yellow bundles of grass.

Tessa shook her head, turning from the window. "That is the worst idea I have ever heard." She strode across the room and dropped to her knees in front of the box, Abner trailing behind her. There was no lock closing the hasp so, with a grunt, Tessa flipped open the lid.

A mess of coiled chains lay within.

"That'll work," she nodded, grabbing a fistful of iron and dragging it out of the box. "Well," she threw the chains clanking across the floor to unknot the coils, "aren't you going—"

"Please," rattled a voice.

The hair lining Abner's arms pulled straight, sending a shooting prickle up his back. He shivered, slowly turning to face the room.

The mass of purple cloth in the right-hand cell moved. It transformed into a curled, hunched figure. The age-spotted hand reached out from a heavy purple sleeve, and the bruise covered eyes drew Abner's stare. "Please," the wrinkled mouth said.

"Lady Hildren," Abner said in shock.

"Pl ... ease." Her chin drooped to the floor, exhaustion sucking the strength from every muscle.

Cantus turned from the door. His brows furrowed, his eyes shining with a fierce light. He fell to his knees before the cage. "Aunt Olivia," his fists shook the bars, the noise drawing her eyes open. "What have they done?" His hands desperately yanked at the lock. He barely flinched as an outcropping metal piece sliced his palm. "I can't—we need to get this open!"

Tessa's eyes were hard shining orbs of ice, her features set in an unyielding grimace. She began working at the chains again.

Abner joined Cantus, tugging on the metal, but it was as unyielding in his grip as in the soldier's.

"This," Abner pulled at Cantus' arm. "This isn't working. We need to go. Cantus!" He shoved him back. "I order you to stop!"

Cantus growled at Abner, his hands balled at his side, "Move out of my way."

"We need to go, we can't—"

Ping!

Thunk.

Cantus dropped to the ground.

Tessa stood behind him, a few lengths of chain wrapped around her fist. There was no sound except her heavy huffing breath as they stared at one another. "Today is not the day I die."

He watched her slip an end of the chain beneath Cantus' waist, and wrap it around his torso a few times.

"You need to help!"

Abner dropped beside her. The two worked together over Cantus' unconscious frame.

Twisting a knot in the chain, Tessa stood and peeked out the window again. "There may not be enough now. It's our only option. Let's go."

Lady Hildren's voice drifted—a whispered groan beneath their words.

"Out the window? With him?" Abner nudged Cantus with his foot. He didn't move.

"I don't see how—"

"We're going to lower him down, then repel down ourselves. There might be a bit of a drop at the end, but—" she shrugged.

"It doesn't sound safe," said Abner, eyeing the window ledge and the darkening sky beyond as his stomach churned.

Tessa didn't argue with him, taking an opposite end of the chain and wrapping it around one of the bars of Lady Hildren's cell. She couldn't avoid the old woman's stare anymore. Her mouth tightened, her breath flaring through her chest. "I," she swallowed. "I'm sorry."

Lady Hildren gave her a long slow blink, pushing her face up from the dirty floor. "A curse on the day I met you," she said in a slow grated voice, her eyes narrowing. "Selfish girl. I tried to protect you against him, and you—a curse on you."

Lines of muscle sprang from Tessa's shoulders as she gave the chain a last strong tug to test its placement. Without a word, she turned from the cage.

Bang!

Abner's shoulders jumped. "Out of time," he said, stumbling into the cell bars as he pulled Cantus up against his shoulder.

"Hurry up!"

"He's very heavy," Abner grunted, sinking under the soldier's weight. Setting Cantus against the ledge, he fought to regain his breath.

Bang. Crack!

Abner didn't turn to see the damage. Up and over the window ledge, he let the chains slide through his hands as he lowered Cantus out of the tower and toward the ground.

"Start climbing," he grunted, the chains sliding faster, despite his effort to keep a steady pace.

"What about—"

"I'll follow, just hurry up!"

Crack!

"Halt!" called a guard's voice.

Tessa popped up, clutching the stone ledge beneath her like a cat on a wall.

The metal bit Abner's palms as it scraped through his grip. He clung tighter to slow it to a stop.

She nodded and began to climb down.

He did well for a few moments, passing the chain through the window, hand over hand, until a thump from behind startled him. He glanced back to see the black eyes of Behrn sear into him through the hole in the door. They glowed from across the room as a hungry sneer bent his mouth.

The chain slipped from Abner's hands.

Tessa yelled from below, and he slammed his boot against the window, trying to pin the quickly disappearing links in a wild effort to stop them sliding away.

Keeping his boot planted, Abner leaned over the ledge to check if Tessa was still alive.

She had both hands and feet wrapped around the chain, swinging with Cantus at the bottom like a ticking weight.

The guard's voices were louder behind him. There was only a bit of chain left, held in place by his boot when a guard spilled into the room over the open chest, snapping the lid closed with his body as he fell to the floor. Grunting, he pushed himself to his feet.

Darting to one side, Abner retrieved his blade.

The man's glare turned into a smile.

Backing a step at the look of vicious pleasure mirrored between Behrn and the lead guard's face, Abner's foot snagged on the chain sending him skidding back toward the ledge.

More guards burst through the broken door.

"No, no, no, no." His hips hit the ledge on the stone window, letting him flail wildly for balance for a moment, before his failure to find it sent him falling into the air in a terrifying spin of his vision. His fingers strained to grip the chain as the last bit of slack snaked out of the wall's opening. The metal caught him in a knot, the bite drawing a cry from his chest. His mangled fingers bent in the chain, and Abner's jaw locked under the crushing pressure.

A guard lunged for him, blue and gold flashing from his chest.

Abner pulled to swing away, his finger crunching in the coil of the chain. He sheathed his sword.

Tessa screamed from deep below. He had just enough sense not to look down at her, pulling his hand free of the twisted metal as his knees wrapped around the chain and it began to steady.

The other guards above tried to haul up the chain, but it caught against the ledge and even with all them pulling together, it barely shifted. Cursing commands to heave it up echoed down before the effort was abandoned.

The black stare glaring after Abner was lit with a creamy red glow from the darkening, color-soaked sky. The guard cursed, lunging for him again but nearly toppling out of the window in his effort.

"Let the rabbit go," said another, catching the guard's chest. "He won't get far. We'll hunt him down."

Rabbit? Abner's mouth twisted at the comparison, but the thought was soon drowned by rough metal pinching his fingers, the steadily mounting throb from his left hand, and the breeze rocking the chain's occupants in a gentle lull. As he made his way down the wall, every joint from his hips to his ankles began to shake and his arms burned. He was certain at any moment his injured hand would slip, that his feet now planted against the wall would lose their footing, or a passing bird might club him into an unexpected free fall. He knew the last was ridiculous, still he glanced over his shoulder to check the empty sky.

Just when the burning in his forearms scorched his muscles into seizing with such strength that he was sure they would never loosen, the chain knocked against his thighs at a sudden shift in weight.

Tessa dropped to the ground, Cantus swinging above her. Rolling across the dirt, she slowly straightened, her hand yanking at the strings guarding her torso.

"What are you doing?" Abner yelled at her.

Tessa ran to the wagon loaded with hay and freed it from its bracket before dragging it forward to wait beneath the slow swaying chain. Abner grimaced at his curled fingers, slices of pain catching his breath as he quickened his descent. *Almost there.*

Tessa ducked down to check her placement with her thumb as Cantus rolled lazily in his iron swing above. "Make him land here," she instructed, pointing to the center of the hay.

Abner hugged the chain to his chest, his knees clinging tight as he clawed at Cantus' knotted bonds. *It's too tight. Bleeding stupid chain.* The sting of his fingers was becoming unbearable.

Tessa glanced over her shoulder. "Hurry up!"

"I can't!" Abner snapped, pulling at a random stretch of chain with a vicious jerk for emphasis.

The chains began to uncoil, loosening around Cantus enough for the soldier to slip free.

Abner swung an arm around his chest before he fell. Closing one eye for aim so Cantus' body wouldn't splatter on the dirt, Abner took a breath and let go.

Cantus landed with a heavy thump and a groan.

Abner dropped beside him in a spray of hay. Popping up from the yellow grasses, Abner leaned over the side of the wagon. He grinned at

Tessa, his chin resting on his good hand. "Worst idea you've ever heard, eh?"

Tessa's glare made his smile stretch wider.

Cantus blinked blearily at the sky.

"We need to go, Cantus." she said, shaking his shoulders. "Can you walk?"

Cantus nodded, then promptly emptied his stomach.

Tessa darted away to avoid the splashes of vomit.

Abner held on tight to his last breath of fresh air.

"Help him. Let's go."

Tessa didn't wait for Abner to agree, ripping Cantus' guard uniform over his shoulders, leaving the white, sweat stained undergarment to cover him. She buried the soaked uniform and his heavy black cloak in the hay and began to pull at Cantus' arms.

Abner joined her, letting Cantus settle against his shoulder as he dragged him away from the cart toward the courtyard doors which were sure to be locked as the time for the night watch approached.

"What's your plan now?" Abner said with a grunt. The greatest barrier to freedom was still ahead of them, the guard tower overlooking the gate looming heavy in his thoughts as they crossed the training lawn.

Tessa paused, chest swelling with a breath before she ripped her corset tighter. "We go forward."

XVI

Esther kept herself still, eyes staring through the narrow slit beneath the edge of the canvas.

The passing guard glanced over the wrapped goods she had burrowed beneath.

"—why he's so upset is beyond me. All I have asked for is what I was promised!"

The two guards dragged the thin man between them.

His heels strained to snag on something that would stop their progress. "An entertainer of my caliber cannot perform what I do and not be paid! The cats alone—let me only speak a moment sir about how much those animals *eat*! That is only—" his words cut into a yell as the guards tossed him down the steps like a bucket of waste from an upper story window. He rolled, the many clasps and buckles on his short black tunic clinking together.

They stood in the doorway laughing at him.

Esther jumped as Abner's shifting weight nudged a basket. It spilled a bedroll onto a thin plate of metal. The muted clatter drew the performer's eyes toward his waiting caravan.

"You're lucky, little man," called one guard, his jaw tipping into a tilted grin. "The king's yawn during the Event should have cost you your head. Instead, it was only your coin."

The entertainer flipped his black, oil-dampened hair from his forehead as the doors slammed shut. His empty hands formed tight fists. Sighing, he dug out the cloth pouch which sagged empty from his silver-studded belt. Pausing behind the second to last wagon in the line, the thin man shot his face through the opening, ripping off the canvas they had hidden beneath.

"Well, hello there."

Esther pulled back at his sudden proximity.

"What are you doing in my caravan, young miss?" His eyes lingered on her dirt-smeared corset and thin slip.

"She's with me." Abner leaned into view.

The thin man stumbled a half step backward, a look of startled surprise rewriting itself into a wide smile. "Why if it isn't Prince Abner—they're looking for you, you know. Your father—"

"Get us out." Abner said. "Get us out and I'll give you coin."

"Ahh…" The entertainer tapped his lips with a long white finger. "I could do that. Committing treason to save you could make quite the story, but I think the far simpler path would be to hand you over to the guards and accept the reward your father is sure to pay for your safe return."

"Don't do that." Esther leaned forward. "Please."

"Ooh, beg me again," he said with a quick wink, his tone bringing a deep red to Esther's cheeks.

Abner jerked her arm back, keeping a firm hold on her wrist.

Esther winced at the skin pinched between his fingers before wrenching herself free.

"You really think," Abner said, "that the king will just decide to pay you for me when he didn't pay you what he agreed to? I'll educate you on the man another time, but he isn't the type. You will get nothing unless you help us."

"Are you still here, little man?" a voice called down the steps of the castle.

An ember burned behind the black stare as the entertainer took a long moment to weigh their fates.

"You need to clear the courtyard."

The black-haired man turned from them.

Unresolved energy clenched Esther's hands, the pressure on her back receding to a far corner of her mind.

After a pause that lasted a lifetime, the caravan leader opened his hand behind his back, and Abner slipped forward, dropping coins into his fist.

"Have you been struck dumb?" called the guard, his voice getting nearer. "Be on your way."

"But of course," the man dropped into a bow.

"So we've been here all day and received nothing?" growled a rough voice from out of sight.

The entertainer smiled at Esther. "I wouldn't say nothing." He drew the canvas curtain, blocking them from view.

Abner relaxed at her side, leaning back against a sack that spilled feathers as he shifted.

It was narrow and cramped in the wagon. Most of the space was taken up by a large boxy shape with a heavy gray cloth tied over it. Dragging Cantus between some barrels and the large covered box was the best they could manage to hide the soldier. Abner and she were forced to duck out of sight and hope no one looked in just the right place.

Their breath made the air wet against her cheek. Her nose stung with the smell of them, made worse by the stifling heat.

Esther had to bite her tongue to choke off her angry growl as Abner's boot pressed against her leg.

Obliviously, he counted the coins left in his belt, muttering to himself.

As the caravan of six heavy-laden wagons rumbled to life, Cantus grunted in his sleep. His breath came out in heavy huffs of air.

"El ... lay ... na."

His voice was mostly drowned out by the grinding wheels, the heavy creak of the horses' harnesses, and the clopping of innumerable hooves. Esther slid past Abner to look out the front fold of canvas, stretching to catch a glimpse of what was coming.

Outside of the sparsely guarded courtyard gate, which they passed through without incident, Lydia dipped down to meet the plains beyond. The city was full of soldiers searching the alleyways and homes for Abner, the time since his last sighting making the commanders assume he had escaped into the city somehow.

The last mark of light faded as the day yawned toward night. None of those shadowed figures carrying torches on the streets paid much attention to the trundling passage of the wagons. Nodding in recognition, they urged the drivers on with quick, dismissive waves.

While Esther stared ahead, Abner looked behind. He sighed, muttering something, as they edged closer to the gate bordering the city.

Cantus breathed deep and heavy somewhere nearby, lost to the world.

Esther wished she could sleep too. She was exhausted. Her back hurt. She decided if they were able to get past the guards and were not killed in the next few moments, she was going to sleep. If they survived, she planned to sleep for years.

"Just a few moments more, little miss," said the thin man who had saved them. He glanced at her from his raised driving seat, keeping his mouth as still as possible. "Watch you don't peek out too far."

The first wagon was through the gate. The guards gave the back a quick glance before waving the driver on.

What would happen when the attending guard peeked into the fifth wagon in line?

"Do you have a plan?" Esther whispered, eyes darting between the driver and the sword-bearing men ahead.

He smiled at the leather strips in his hands, rubbing his thumb over them.

The second wagon was through.

"What are you whispering about?" Abner asked her, coming closer.

"You should at least have some idea what you're going to do," Esther said.

The entertainer picked at a spot on the seat next to him, giving her a quick wink. "Not to worry, little miss. It'll be handled."

"How?"

The third wagon exited through the gate.

He didn't respond.

Cantus mumbled again.

The driver shifted in his seat to cover the noise.

The guard's attention did not stray from the fourth wagon as his eyes grazed over the back with a wave.

"Okay, under the blanket. Quick now." He dug out a heavy roll of fabric from just behind his seat.

"Really?" Esther muttered, checking that Cantus was still well covered behind them. Abner flung the blanket over their heads. "That's the plan? Hiding under a blanket? We could have done that from the beginning."

Abner and Esther's breath intermingled in hot coils as the forced blindness and the muted sounds of the guard's questions made each heavier. They lay side by side, almost touching, frozen by the need to be as still and small as possible.

"No, nothing of note. Oh, except," came the driver's voice, "well I wouldn't peek too far into the back of this one. Tigers can be awfully feisty if woken up. I'm mostly sure I locked her cage."

A muffled reply pulled Esther forward to hear better.

"By all means," answered the driver to the unintelligible question. "Just don't go poking about with your sword. They are rather expensive to replace." The wagon rocked on creaking wheels and Esther braced against the floor.

The clinking metal footsteps marched beside the wagon.

They were behind her now, and she dared not breathe.

"Behold and wonder," the performer said.

Esther's hands curled into fists. *He's about to betray us.*

Esther heard a blanket whip away and her eyes clenched shut. A warm hand touched hers and she cringed, waiting for the cleaving sword to descend on her back.

"Stars. I've never seen the like before." The guard's voice echoed into the wagon from the back opening.

"Indeed," answered the performer. "She had to be transported by caravan across the desert to the north and before that over the sea. She is only three years of age. Half that time was spent getting here."

Esther peeked an eye open.

The blanket still obscured her vision.

She strained her relieved sigh into a trickle through tight lips, her head swimming.

"We're okay," Abner mouthed.

Esther turned her chin to listen.

"Just going to resettle this blanket, if you're alright with that, and we will get out of the way. I'm sure you have plenty of—you know—guarding to do without us cluttering up the city gate."

"What about the rest of it?" asked the guard.

Abner's hand tightened his grip on Esther's.

She wished she could rip her fingers away. Her face slowly filled with heat, and she became painfully aware of every muscle in her hand.

"Oh, just supplies, extra miscellaneous things needed for the show. Whips, bed rolls, costumes. The tiger is the main thing I care about here, feel free to poke about the rest."

"Ah," the guard said, "be on your way with my thanks. She—it was she, right?"

"Yes. Esmeralda we call her."

"Well she's a fine animal. Never thought I'd see one up close."

"Thank you, sir. A pleasure."

The wagon groaned as the entertainer resumed his seat and clicked his tongue, tapping the horses into motion. "All's well this side of the stars," he said after a few moments of clopping hooves and creaking wheels. He reached down and ripped the blanket off of the two stowaways. The sky was an inky purple now, the last light of the sun sinking below the line of the world. "Made it out safe so far. I'll be taking my next payment now."

"Next payment?" said Abner, sitting up to cross his arms and glare at the driver's back. "I think you are confused."

"Oh, should I go and let the guard know I just found two traitors hidden in my wagon? I'm sure he would come to see."

"And the gold I gave you, how will you explain that?"

"I already had it," smiled the man, pulling the harness of the two horse team until they stopped in the road. "Shall I turn around or do you have something to give me?"

"Vulture," Abner muttered, digging out another handful of gold from the belt on his waist.

"Well," the entertainer said, snatching the gold from him and counting it in his palm, "I prefer my stage name of Death, but Vulture has a certain intriguing effect as well." He paused to fill his satchel and light the swinging lantern near the wagon front.

Lydia was at last behind them, the bare plains stretching ahead.

Once free of the city, Esther edged over Cantus and made her way to the back of the wagon to peek under the blankets. She found the cage and rolled the heavy gray cloth onto the top of the bars.

There she was. The great cat huffed heavily in sleep from her wide open mouth, her orange and black striped chest rising and falling with the weight of her powerful breathing.

How had she not noticed the giant's noise? Glancing at Cantus, she heard his quiet whisper of air and could now separate it from the noise of the cat beside her. She hadn't expected the cat so all she heard was Cantus. But here it was, in all its wild glory.

A tiger.

Esther was mesmerized. She longed to slip her fingers through the bars of the cage and brush the white-tufted fur beneath the tiger's jaw. Instead, she tapped the floor in front of her knees. The cart rocked as a front wheel struck a stone and the tiger growled in its sleep, sending Esther tipping back on her heels.

"We'll drop you in the nearest village," Death called back to them in a jolly voice, clinking the pouch of metal near his ear. "Ah, sweet music!"

"Brennon might be a bit too easy to track us to. Wouldn't it be better to—"

"Not my problem," sang Death, giving a kissing sound to urge the horses on faster.

Abner's reply was coated in irritation, spoken through a tight jaw and a cocked head, "And what would it cost to make it your problem?"

Death paused, turning back toward him. "I'm listening."

"Everything has a price with you, so what would it cost to take us to—say—Merdian Point?"

"Oh, more crowns than you could fit into your belt. So sorry, little prince. Not enough gold in the castle treasury to make me pass through that stinking fish hole again."

"Why?"

"None of your business," snapped Death.

"So how far can you take us?" cut in Esther, sitting down with as generous a gap as the narrow wagon would allow between her and Abner.

"Honestly, Little Brennon is not a bad place to get lost in. The neighboring city is quite large and difficult to track anyone through. But Brennon is as far as I will risk my head for this little venture."

Abner sighed, tossing his hands in the air. "I suppose I'll figure something out. It'll be fine."

"How far is Brennon?" Esther asked.

The carts in their line turned off the main road to Shiloh and one by one descended the path onto an unexplored stone-knit roadway, turning their progress into a symphony of hooves and creaking wheels.

"I think we should be able to disband our little gang of conspirators by the second mark of the day tomorrow."

"Not soon enough," muttered Abner.

A stir behind Esther made her turn.

Cantus was muttering in his sleep again. His face drifted closer to the bars of the tiger's cage as he resettled himself into slumber, shifting the blanket that covered him.

The tiger huffed in sleep, blowing Cantus' hair back from his forehead.

Brows pinching, Cantus rubbed at his face.

The tiger huffed again.

With a groan, Cantus opened his eyes. The yell that ripped from his throat as he crashed backward against some netting, which held a bundle of shields, made everyone jump.

"What happened? Agh," he cradled his forehead against his palm, "I can't even see straight. Where—"

Cantus squinted at Abner and Esther, the strain of focus clenching his jaw to the point of breaking.

"You're safe," Esther assured him.

"For the moment."

"Shut it," Esther snapped at Abner. She knelt in front of Cantus. "We're all okay."

Cantus' eyes scanned the wagon, the supplies, the driver. He let out a long breath. "That's ... good."

Esther nodded.

Cantus' brow furrowed. "I—there was something I was..." He looked down at his hands, his jaw grinding his teeth together. "Why can't I think?"

Esther and Abner shared an uneasy glance.

Cantus would want to know what had happened to his aunt, why she wasn't with them now in the caravan. What would he do when he learned the truth—that they had left her behind?

"You should rest," Esther said. "Get your strength back. You took a hard knock to the head."

"I did?" Cantus' head dropped onto a blanket roll sticking out by his shoulder. "How?"

"Doesn't matter now. Just rest."

Cantus swallowed, his mouth twisting to one side. "Ugh. That doesn't feel good."

"What can I do to help?" *Please don't get sick again.*

Cantus blinked slowly. "Can you sing? I remember ... someone singing when I used to…"

"Ah, a duet! How about it, little miss?" Death grinned at her. "I'm sure your tender notes will meet with my deep rich tone beautifully. Do you know the mountain song?"

"No," Esther vigorously shook her head. Pain bolted down her back.

"A solo performance then, just as well. I don't much like the first verse, so I'll start on the second."

"Kill me," Abner muttered, leaning his head against the canvas lining as Death warmed up his voice. "Not literally," he smirked at Esther.

Soon after the last note faded and Cantus snored quietly in a corner, Death knocked on the wagon's side with a large hammer. The sound was apparently a signal, as the four lighted wagons ahead of them echoed the noise and then pulled their teams to a halt. Dismounting, the troupe laid out bedrolls and built a fire. Their practiced hands were not troubled by only having starlight as their guide until the crackling yellow flames sprang to life. Death watched the scene with a smile. He turned to the two travelers as the fire was lit.

"May want to join us, give your companion time to sleep. Seems like he's had quite the day. Or is he just one of those touched in the head?"

Abner looked at the assembled misfits. Their wild hair, heavy limbs, and pale, dirt-lined faces made his mouth push into a pout. However, when a pale skinned, wild haired man used his heavy arms to produce several brown bottles sloshing full of liquid, Abner's features lit with interest.

Death waved for him to follow.

"You should stay here," Abner said, stepping over Cantus' feet to hop off the end of the wagon. "It's not proper for ladies to be around drinking."

Esther hadn't been sure what she would do, until he said that. Stopping only to snatch an unrolled blanket from the floor to wrap her shoulders against the air turning cold, she slipped to the ground and marched to the center of the group. She raised a bottle, making sure to catch Abner's eye before she took a long, deliberate drink.

Abner's eyes pinched over his smile, raising his bottle to her. He took a draw from it, daring her to drink again.

The stuff was awful. It tasted like muck left to bake in the sun and burned its way to the pit of her stomach, already empty and uncomfortable. She took another drink, unable to keep the twitch from her eye as she swallowed in a hasty gulp. It burned her insides clean.

Abner tilted his own bottle back, keeping his face relaxed as he swallowed. "Ah," he sighed with a smirk. Clearly he had more practice at drinking than she, but it didn't matter.

She took another drink.

Matched.

Another.

Matched.

Another still.

The world began to tilt. Odd. *Abner's smile ... why is he smiling?*

A hand touched her blanket-wrapped shoulder and she was led to a mat. Her hands found the ground, trying to ride the tilt of the world and keep from falling off.

Abner drew his hand into his side as someone brushed between them, his sharp breath a hiss.

"Having some trouble with your hand, Friend?" asked a man on the other side of Esther. His red hair stuck out like a thicket of hedgehog quills.

"Twisted up the bleeding thing on some chain today." Abner grimaced at it. "Just been ignoring it but I think it's—" Abner held up his left hand. The fingers pulsed, two swollen at the joints and leaning in odd directions, the skin bruised.

Esther chewed through invisible food, trying to quell her uneasy stomach.

"Eh, Clive!"

A short, bald man stomped over.

"Take a look at his hand there. Can you fix it up?"

Death's laugh rang dimly from another circle gathered on the far side of the fire. The flames looked invitingly warm and Esther swayed toward them, only drawing back when the smoke changed direction and stung her eyes. She blinked, Abner and Clive reappearing.

"Ooh, I haven't seen one this bad in a long time. What happened?"

Esther belched, thankful that all that came up was air.

Clive had his tongue stuck between his teeth, his hand carefully probing Abner's disjointed fingers. He nodded, his teeth now gripping his lower lip as if it was in danger of falling off. "You may want to take another pull from your bottle," he warned, "this is going to hurt."

Abner's eyes widened, staring at his hand. He rolled his shoulders. "It takes stronger stuff than that to make me lose myself." He nodded. "Just do it."

"Here's one," said Clive.

Abner cried out as his finger was grabbed, tears leaking from his eyes when Clive pulled. Abner's panting breath quickened as Clive's attention passed on to the next finger.

"This one's a bit worse. There's a break here, and the bone is out of place. Deep breath now."

"Wait, wait, wait." Abner pulled his hand out of Clive's grip. "Wait. A moment, please."

Clive handed Abner his drink.

Abner gulped several pulls from the bottle. Brow furrowed over red eyes, he set down the drink.

"Are you ready?"

Abner's face crumpled, but he nodded. "Do it."

Clive's hands reset the bone in one fluid motion. "I'll get something for that break."

He left Abner clutching his hand to his chest beneath streaming eyes.

Bored by Abner's whimpers, Esther turned back to the fire, the smoke obligingly curling away from her so she could stare at the flames. As the night marched steadily colder, Esther edged closer to the fire. Her chin sank to one side. Uncomfortable, she laid down.

Just for a moment. I am not going to sleep, just resting...

The morning was gray when Esther's eyes snapped open, a yip of pain springing from her throat.

"Where is she?" Cantus demanded, his frame filling her vision as his fingers pinched the bones in Esther's hands together with crushing force.

Esther tried to twist herself free, face tightening in panic.

His eyes were hard, glaring at her with a shine of understanding that replaced her pain with a flood of cold dread down her back.

"Let go of her!" Abner hit Cantus like a battering ram and the two launched out the back of the wagon.

"Bleeding—" called Death from the front, as the wagon driver behind struggled to control his horses.

The animals screamed and tossed their heads, stomping to avoid the men suddenly beneath their feet. Somehow not a single hoof landed on either man's head or hand, but there were several narrow misses.

Esther jumped from the back of the wagon after them.

Death hopped from his perch, sprinting to the men. "Here!" he called to the driver of the wagon behind his, diving toward the two brawling men to pull them apart.

"Busy!" barked the other driver, shushing the horses while he yanked them off to one side. They nearly climbed up onto one another's backs in an attempt to relieve the sudden pressure. "Easy now, ho ... ho now ... ho."

Esther darted around the stomping beasts.

Death wrapped an arm beneath Cantus' chest and pulled him to his feet.

"Let go of me!" Cantus bellowed, elbowing Death aside. "Where is she?" He turned to Abner, hands already fists. When the prince didn't immediately reply, his eyes moved to Esther. "Where is she?"

Her mind was frustratingly blank, filled with a heavy ringing silence she couldn't disperse.

Abner stepped forward, holding his bandage-wrapped hand close to his chest. "We tried. You were knocked out when the guards broke down the door—maybe a piece of it struck you. I didn't see."

Cantus' eyes narrowed. "Keep talking."

"They fired arrows through the hole before coming after us with swords. Both missed their marks: one was wide and went out the window, the other went through the bars and hit Lady Hildren." Abner watched Cantus' expression, adjusting his tone to soften as the soldier's eyes loosened. "She was gone quickly, no real pain I could see. We left out the window with you wrapped in the chain. Bargained our way onto this caravan, and now we have nothing left to do but run."

Cantus' eyes hardened again. "You left her body behind."

Abner shrugged a shoulder. "We barely escaped with—"

Smack!

Abner fell back onto the grass. He touched his jaw, wincing as it reddened. "You—you struck me." He pushed himself to his feet. "How dare you strike me!"

"Get used to it." Cantus stepped toward Abner, pulling his red-knuckled fist stiff to his side, the snarl on his lips making his nostrils flare. "You aren't the prince anymore. I owe you nothing. You left her and now her body will be burned. She'll be nothing, her spark will cease, because of you!" He pushed Abner out of his way and stomped back to the wagon, disappearing around the far side.

"And ... this is where we bid you goodbye, I think." Death pushed his mouth into a smile.

"What? I paid you—"

"To get you out of Lydia, and I have. Rather flawlessly in fact. But this fighting in your group is a danger to us. It draws attention and replacing any supplies you break while you work out your ... differences, that'll cost what little coin I have left. I've already been—"

Abner counted out coins into his hand. "Have us go in separate wagons then." He dropped the gold into Death's waiting palm.

Death's fingers curled over the crowns. "Your reasoning is ... compelling. The girl rides up front with me. Madus, take this one into your wagon."

The rough-voiced driver of the last wagon in line nodded to the back of the canvas-covered cart.

Abner hesitated, turning back to Death after a few steps toward his waiting wagon. "You keep your hands to yourself, understand? That is Lady Tessa, and she is above your touch."

"Is she?" Death said as Abner turned away. "Well, my lady," he bowed to her as a mocking smile bloomed across his cheeks. "Your royal carriage awaits your pleasure."

Esther perched at the very edge of her seat, trying to ignore the sounds of Cantus in the back of the wagon. Perhaps the anger only gave a temporary reprieve so gut-wrenching grief could have its turn, but the loud sniffles and deep sobbing coughs from the soldier made Esther wish to be anywhere she couldn't hear it.

Death, meanwhile, had all the appearance of delight. He tapped the horses' backs with the leather strips running through intricate buckles and rings in the harness holding the team together, humming to himself. His eyes stayed fixed on Esther. His ever-present grin grew even wider as her face heated.

"I thought I recognized you from the Event."

Esther's jaw locked.

"You look quite different without all the frump from court. I think I prefer this look for you though, despite the—"

"I remember you from the Event too," Esther said, her eyes borrowing the burn from her cheeks.

"Really? I love it when I make an impression."

"I especially remember the part where you burned little children alive while the people chanted your name."

Death sat back, the smile slipping to a subtle smirk held in place by willpower. "Ah."

"I'm sure you feel so honorable, making coin for yourself by letting innocent children die."

"Technically I didn't make anything from it."

Esther glared at him, and his smile slipped away all together.

"I wish we lived in a world where such things weren't necessary, but I have myself and my people to look after. I have no other way." He paused, his brow tightening. "I've survived another year. That's enough to keep me grateful."

"You're a bleeding coward," Esther crossed her arms, looking ahead as they began to wind between two small hills, the smattering of trees along the roadside becoming thicker.

Death seemed unaffected by the insult. "You don't get to the age of thirty and two years by giving every sad story you hear a bite of your life." He glanced at her, his smile slipping back into place. "I hope I haven't offended you too badly."

Esther brought her knees to her chest and turned resolutely away.

"Shall we turn to pleasant topics more suitable for those lovely feminine ears?" He waited, but Esther didn't change her folded posture. "No? Perhaps you're struggling too much under the weight of your own guilty conscience, eh?"

Esther stared at him.

"It doesn't take a master pretender to see that the story woven for our other passenger wasn't quite what happened."

"I don't know what you're talking about," whispered Esther, looking back into the wagon.

Cantus sat rocking with his forehead pressed to his knees, facing away from them.

Esther breathed a heavy sigh.

He hadn't heard.

The driver smiled wide. "The prince is surprisingly good on the stage but you may want to rehearse your side. You'll have to give your performance soon, I imagine. And who is this woman he mourns? Some deceased romance? What a tragic story."

"No," Esther said, "It wasn't like that."

"Then?"

"None of your business," snapped Esther.

Death laughed. "One night out of the castle and you're already as hard as any peasant woman. What a fascinating creature you've turned out to be. When I looked into my wagon and saw you, I'll admit I only noticed the shallow things." His eyes traveled down her torso again. "Speaking of, might want to cover over the goods if you don't want to get robbed." Reaching into the wagon behind, the man pulled out a long length of rough brown fabric. "Wrap this around your shoulders and secure it to your waist with—hang on, it was here—" his arm dug into the mess behind him again. "Ta ta ta DA!" he imitated the sound of a trumpet as he laid a strip of worn leather and the brown drape on the bench beside her.

Esther pushed them back toward him. "I don't think I could afford anything more from you."

"Consider this one a gift, just this once." His cocky smile stayed rooted in place but his nod seemed to carry meaning. "From one survivor to another."

The sudden benevolence was passed over with no further explanation as—with a smile—he called out the last bend of the road before the village of Little Brennon came into view.

A short walk from the furthermost house, the wagons stopped, the drivers dismounting to discuss where they were headed next. The consensus was to turn north, and so, with hardly a glance at the strangers, the other drivers returned to their seats and prepared to resume their journey.

"Go give our miss Esmeralda her morning medicinals, would you, Clive?"

Clive dug in the back of his wagon and strode to the tiger's cage.

Death stood before the three stowaways, who formed an awkward triangle, facing vaguely away from him and looking anywhere but at each other.

"Well," Death clapped his hands together, drawing their eyes, "have a grand adventure, you three. Hope you make it out alive. And I'll be taking my last—"

Abner's eyes narrowed. "Go."

Death winked at Esther. "Always worth a try."

XVII

"So," Abner said, rubbing at his bruised jaw and wincing, innumerable tiny hairs scraping against his palm. "We should probably talk about—"

"Don't." Cantus' jaw locked.

"We're just going to avoid it forever?"

"Abner, stop," Tessa whispered, looking between them.

"She won't ever be at rest! What is talking about it going to change?" Cantus threw his hands out. "That was the one thing I had left. The only thing I cared about. And you're letting it burn!"

"Would you rather be dead? *I* got us out. I paid to have us smuggled from the city, while you snored on the floor!" Abner rose up tall, his chin tipping toward the cloud-filled sky. "You owe me your life!"

"Yes, because you did everything?" snapped Tessa, folding her arms.

Abner waved her off, eyes never leaving Cantus. "You may hate me, but you're alive because of me."

Every muscle in Cantus' body shook. He spat to the side. "I know."

"Because if I—what?"

"I know." Cantus sighed through a tight jaw. "I didn't get us out. I was nothing more than extra weight for you to lug around. You could have easily left me behind. I know." Cantus passed a hand over his face. The silence between them thickened. "The king is the one who put her in a cage. Not you. Let's go on to Little Brennon."

Abner set his eyes toward the first house along the road. It was a moment before he realized he walked alone.

Behind him, Cantus and Tessa spoke quietly together. Cantus put a hand on her arm and Tessa shook her head.

Abner turned away, pretending he hadn't seen, as anger burned quietly in his gut. He kept the heat from his eyes as they caught up to him on the road.

The house was unusually quiet for a farmstead in the morning. A washing line held several tunics, all various shades of brown and yellow.

Abner sniffed at one, the smell stinging his nose. "I think we can find better if we—"

Cantus pulled a tunic over his head, Tessa adjusting her clothes to do the same with a long frock. "Better would be worse for us, if we're trying to blend in," Cantus said, his tone cool. He grabbed a strip of rough leather from a bracket and slung it around his waist. "Where did my belt go?"

The peasant frock hung like a used sack of grain from her shoulders as Tessa pulled her hair out so it could spill down her side in a messy twist. "I think it was left with your guard's uniform. You got sick on it."

"I did?" Cantus shook his head. "I have no memory of that. Well, then I'm out of coin. Abner, anything?"

Abner brushed his hand along his belt, the hidden compartments much emptier than they were yesterday. "Not much."

"Let's have ten copper bits to leave on the front step of the house then. To pay them for these." Tessa nodded toward the farmhouse entrance.

"Ten bits?" Abner stared at Tessa, then at the stained garment in his hand. "These aren't worth half that."

"We should probably save what we have," said Cantus.

"You two have never lived in want. They need everything they have to scrape by." Tessa wrapped her shoulders in the brown fabric she had appeared with that morning. She belted it in, cinching and then recinching it even tighter across her waist with a grimace. "Better," she whispered, holding her back.

"Then if I'm paying, I'll be taking this as well." Abner snatched a cloak from further down the line.

Cantus lifted a shoulder at Tessa, who sighed at the sky.

Tessa would not allow them to leave without making their offering on the step, so when Abner at last set down the stacks of copper coins, she gestured to the road, giving her permission for them to continue.

Little Brennon was nestled between dense, tree-lined hills. Its changing leaves blew across the road and crunched beneath the travelers' feet, stirring smells of childhood in Abner's mind. Tessa stooped to gather a small bouquet of the dried leaves, slowly shredding them and letting the growing breeze carry them away. He thought about starting a leaf battle, long-lost memories of Cantus and he terrorizing the other children every autumn with surprise attacks drawing a smile, but the quiet ember of anger still smouldering in his gut burned away the impulse.

They turned a bend and the road opened onto a bustling street market. Abner was glad of his cloak as he pulled the hood down over his eyes. People, *so many people*, chattered and yelled to one another. Children raced, animals sang in their many voices, and the busy flurry of activity blew past them with the rising wind. Either side of the stone-cobbled road was a mess of little wagons, stalls, and goods. Abner's back prickled as they slipped into the crowd. He made sure to keep the other two in sight as the milling shoppers pulled them apart.

"Oi travelers! Not seen you round here before. How about a necklace for your young lass?" said a vendor, offering a jade pendant to Cantus. "It would look striking against those beautiful, sea-blue eyes, no?"

Cantus and Tessa shared an awkward smile. He shook his head with a raised palm.

"Then how about a drapery other than that worn brown one? Only five bits. Surely she deserves to be lavished with something soft as the weather turns." A woman leaned from the neighboring stall toward them, running her fingers down the woven fabric she offered.

"No, thank you," Tessa said.

"Is that?" whispered a voice near Abner.

His face warmed, his shoulders rising higher with each breath.

"No, Ezra. It couldn't be."

"It is!"

The man—Ezra—pushed between two women haggling with a stall owner over some eggs, striding toward Abner.

Finding the hilt of his sword under his cloak, Abner swallowed. The man was very large.

Ezra shouldered Abner out of his way, not even looking at the prince as he dropped to a knee in front of Cantus and Tessa. "Lady Tessa," he said, "is that really you?"

Eyes drifted to them from every corner of the market. Whispers of 'who is she' and 'it can't be' spiraling out like ripples after a stone is thrown in the middle of a lake. Cantus looked at her, eyebrows pinching over his eyes.

"Lady Tessa?" asked a woman draped in a long dirty frock. "Is it? Are you?"

Tessa's eyes were large, round. Her mouth opened, but no sound came forth. The moment dragged on.

Cantus nudged her side, tossing his chin.

"I am," she said at last in a small voice, pushing her back to her full height.

"What are you doing here?" asked the man who first recognized her. More dropped to their knees and bowed their heads.

"She probably needs our help. Several of us were at the Event, Lady. We saw the blow you struck for our freedom. We've waited—just ever-so long for someone to do something against the king."

"Death to the king and to his line!" shouted a man, his gray beard quivering from his chin as he raised his fist.

"Death to the king!" chorused the villagers, punching the air.

"Don't!" Tessa stepped forward, hands raised. "Don't talk like that. You can't—Shiloh did nothing and they—you need to be careful."

"We are ready," insisted a young man, clutching his smithing hammer in an iron grip.

"The time for being careful is done," agreed a voice in the crowd.

"Hear! Hear!"

"What do you need?" asked the large man.

Tessa looked at Abner and Cantus, her wide eyes and high shoulders drawing Abner forward to speak. He dropped his hood. "We need supplies for the road. Clothes, food, packs. Horses if you have them. And a map. Most of all we need your silence that we were ever here."

All eyes turned to Abner, and those on their knees sprang up. Doors slammed as a few on the fringe of the crowd darted inside. Others planted their feet and balled their fists.

"Lady, behind us," said Ezra, a hand reaching out to shield her as he squared his shoulders at Abner.

"Wait," Tessa said, shaking her head.

With a high, screeching yell, the youth with the hammer came barreling forward, hand drawn back to club Abner's head in.

The prince stuttered back a step, heat burning his ears as his injured hand twitched in its bandage.

The youth tripped, over committing to his swing at Abner, and crashed into the stone road. He scrambled away, wiping blood from his chin. Another attacker came from the right, swinging his fists wildly while still out of reach of Abner. Cantus jumped forward to knock the blow away.

"Stop!" Tessa said, pushing her way forward. "Enough!"

The crowd stilled.

"The prince isn't a threat to you, not anymore. You're not to harm him."

"But, Lady, he is—"

"He travels with Lady Tessa," Cantus said, his voice taking on a weight of authority it had never possessed before. "He will not be harmed."

"As she wishes," the woman in the drape said. "What else can we do to help you, Lady Tessa?"

Tessa bit her lip, twisting her fingers together. "Oh, it's fine. Really. Just what they've already said."

The older woman blinked at her. "It would be our honor to do anything we can for you."

"Well," Tessa looked between her two companions, "if it's not too much trouble, maybe ... a bath?"

"Most certainly. I dare say—" the woman said, smoothing her frock. "Jezzie, heat the water! And you, Tara, go pick some flowers to scent it! You men, scrub out one of the troughs at my home and bring it into the store room." The woman's hands shook as they reached for Tessa's. "The village of Little Brennon welcomes you."

Cantus and Abner were directed toward troughs standing in the field beside the storeroom where Tessa was taken. They were each given an old rag to use, and Abner grimaced at the green-topped water. Cantus found the elderly woman and thanked her for the village's hospitality.

She waved away his apology at the inconvenience. "No trouble, no trouble at all. But, a moment, sir." She pulled him away a few paces. Abner still caught her whispered warning. "Watch that prince, Sir. Lady Tessa will need your protection from him yet, I think."

Cantus' eyes drifted to Abner, who stared resolutely ahead, anger burning his ears. "I will keep her safe."

"Swear it, Sir."

"I swear."

"Good man," the woman said, nodding. "You two make a fine couple, you know. Some people just don't look right together, but you ... your babies would be beautiful!"

Cantus stared after her, face beating red.

Abner wished there was something around for him to break. Instead, he ripped the tunic up over his head, struggling with only one usable hand, and threw it to the ground. Swirling the trough's contents to clear the mire of green slime, Abner flung handfuls of water over his shoulders. The chilly trails dripped down his back.

"So," Abner said, putting his hip to the side of the trough.

Cantus pulled off his tunic.

"We need to speak."

"I'd rather we didn't."

"I don't care." Abner narrowed his eyes. "I want to know how long it's been going on. How long have the two of you been sneaking around together and making me look like a fool?"

"Abner, don't. I did what I had to do. It's not what I wanted, but it was the only way to stop the king. Or ... so I thought."

"And at some point things changed, didn't they? You started to have eyes for her. Admit it. That's why you helped her. You've been bedding *my* woman this entire time!"

"What? No, Abner. That never happened. It never would happen."

"Really?" Skepticism brought a bite to Abner's tone. "So you risked your life on a treasonous plot for nothing in return? Even the ever-honorable Cantus is not that stupid."

"I did that to save my aunt."

"And?"

"And nothing else," Cantus' hand slapped the water as he thrust it out for emphasis.

"I don't believe you."

"Have you forgotten why I was demoted from nobleman to soldier?"

Abner shrugged. "You slurped your soup too loudly? Forgot to compliment his majesty's shoes?"

Cantus' laugh was brittle. "I asked your father for permission to get married."

"Married? To who?"

"Elena." Cantus' voice was soft, as if even her name was too much for the soldier. He waved off Abner's bemused face. "You would only know her as one of Lady Giselle's tagalongs. She was never striking enough to earn your notice." Cantus paused, his eyes drifting down to the rippling water at his fingertips. "But I liked her."

"You should have done something about it then."

Cantus looked at him.

The prince shrugged. "If you liked her so much, you should have—I don't know—invited her to run away with you. Proven your love and all that." Abner breathed a long sigh, gathering his thoughts. "So you ... don't have eyes for Tessa."

Cantus shook his head. "We're friends, nothing more."

"I don't understand. What's wrong with her?" Abner looked toward the wall that hid her from view. "You don't think she's nice to look at?"

"I suppose," Cantus said, with a shrug, "but no more than other girls I've seen."

"And you've seen so many."

Cantus scooped a double handful of water into his face and scrubbed it through his hair. "My point is she's a friend, and that's all."

"A friend," Abner muttered, grabbing a cloth slung on the side of the tub and dunking it into the water. "Never heard of such a thing." He scrubbed the dirt from under his nails, avoiding his injured fingers. His smile stretched high up on one cheek.

The two girls spent a long time preparing Esther before she entered the bath. While the water was heated and petals were added to concoct the stew that would make Esther clean again, they rinsed her hair with pitchers and chatted to one another. The grime of the prison had seeped into her skin, turning her hair into a briar and her odor like the victim of a skunk's spray. She was grateful for every pitcher poured over her head, knowing it brought her a little closer to clean. The empty storeroom, meager bits of old grain caught in little rivers at her feet, made Esther's cheeks warm with shame. How could she take more from these people?

"Mmm, smell that lavender?" one girl said, sending handfuls of petals to swirl in the water. She stirred it with her hand. "I had these by my cot at home to help me sleep. To think they're to be used in a noblewoman's bath! What do you say to that, Jezzie?"

"Apparently you have noble flowers," Jezzie raised a brow, setting aside the empty pitcher to wring out Esther's long wet hair. She gathered it in a twist down Esther's side. "Arms out please, Lady Tessa. Going to get those clothes off so we can wash you properly." When she reached the corset, Jezzie paused. "A hand, Tara. It's full of knots from beginning to end."

"I'm sorry," Esther said, embarrassment pinching her cheeks. "I didn't have anyone to help adjust it. It's been a busy few days."

"Not a care," Tara said, joining Jezzie's fingers to pick away at the knotted threads. "We'll set it right."

The corset began to loosen, bringing a heavy pulsing pressure that pummeled her back. The more the strings were unwound, the stronger and farther the pressure reached, and the firmer she had to grip the table in front of her. The giant squeezing her back did not relent. Her eyes lost focus as she swayed.

I think I'm—

Esther blinked at the ceiling above. She was lying on the ground, the pain echoing down her sides. She sneezed the foul nipping powder from her nose. Or most of it.

"There she is. Just coming round, now."

Her hand froze on its way to rub her nose clean.

The face of every woman from the village leaned over to stare at the girl lying bare on the ground save for her dirty white slip.

"It's alright, Lady Tessa. Just us. You ought not wear the corset so tight in your condition." The older woman stroked back Esther's hair. "Now, how many months along is it, dear? No shame in it."

"I—" *have no idea what you're talking about. What happened?* Why couldn't she make her foot shift underneath her to stand up? Why did her words fail her?

"Have you felt a kick yet?" Tara laid a hand on her stomach.

Esther flinched away. Stings of pain raced each other down her legs.

"Tara!" chided her dark-haired friend, Jezzie, leaning into view to elbow her hard in the ribs. "It'll bring the eye of an evil Fate to ask a new mother that. You know the stories."

"I'm not," Esther shook her head.

The old woman tipped her chin to one side. "You're not ... with child?" Her darting eyes grazed over Esther's prone form. "Then what is it, dear?"

"Maybe the corset was just too tight?" volunteered Jezzie, picking up the discarded fabric. "It was all knotted."

"We should tell her companions that she's hurt, maybe they'll know what's happening." Tara rose to her feet.

"No," Esther said. "Don't—tell."

"Well," the old woman blinked thoughtfully, "let's dip you in the water, and see if that doesn't bring your body back to you."

Esther was lifted and half-led, half-dragged, to the tub's edge. Her skin burned at their touch as the women lowered her into the tub. Pitchers of fresh steaming water were added, bringing the mostly cold bath to a comfortable warmth that sank into Esther's bones.

The women, having settled her, began to disperse.

Esther breathed easier with fewer eyes on her. The pressure receded at the warm water's touch, and she held the sides of the trough to float, no heavier than a leaf gliding on the surface of a smooth stream. Her eyes drifted closed. As the bath began to turn cold again, Esther rose. Her skin stung, like a thousand tiny insects were nipping at the soles of her feet. She thrust one foot over the side of the tub.

Fresh linens were brought to her, patting her dry. The pressure began its march down her back again as Esther shivered under her wet hair. Before they slipped the dress over her head, she pointed to the stained corset, its strings frayed to near oblivion.

"I need that as well."

Jezzie brought it to Tara, who wrinkled her nose as she wrapped it around Esther's waist.

"Are you sure, Lady? They aren't terribly comfortable and this one is—"

"It helps." Esther pulled a breath high into her chest as the two girls slowly tightened the vice around her. Letting the air slip loose as the stiff fabric clung snug to her hips, Esther could have wept with relief. The pressure was there but contained. She could bear it. The peasant's frock was embroidered with flowers on the hem, and Esther smiled through her thanks, running her hands over the soft threads.

"My friends have coin to pay you for this," she said, "though it's probably—"

"Lady," Jezzie said, her mouth drawing into a hard line, "do you really think we are so low as to ask payment of you? It is a gift."

"But—"

Tara shook her head. "No argument now. We haven't time."

Esther missed Ava and the skill of her gentle fingers as the two girls righted the mess that was Esther's hair. They pawed at the knots with long-toothed combs. Jezzie was abrupt, yanking the hairs into order, while Tara absentmindedly stroked the strands, leaving them unmoved. One thing both girls excelled at was braiding, and they twisted Esther's hair out of her eyes, letting half of it flow down her back in loose curls. Satisfied with the look they had created, the girls led the way outside. Esther gave a nervous tug, tightening the band that secured the folded drape around her waist, before she followed.

Ignoring the sting of weakness at her heels, Esther blinked at the high sun.

Cantus and Abner stood by three horses saddled and bridled with worn brown leather, their whiskered noses pushing into the men's shoulders. A pile of packages sat at their feet.

"Did you fall asleep in the bath?" Abner smirked, eyes bouncing over her.

"This is ... too much," Esther said, looking at the gifts.

"We'll make it work," Abner said. "You'd be surprised how much a horse can carry."

"No, we can't take all of this from these people. They'll need it, with the weather turning."

"They gave it away very happily," Cantus said, uncertainty pulling his mouth into a frown. "It should be alright."

"It's not!" Esther snapped, grabbing a package. *How could they give this to us when their own storeroom sits empty?*

"And how did you get your supplies as The Demon of Shiloh?" Abner's smile made Esther's shoulders stiffen, her eyes narrowing. She dropped the package. "Exactly."

Striding forward, Esther grabbed at the clasp securing Abner's belt.

"What are you doing?" he jumped back, blocking her sudden assault on his middle.

"We need to pay them for it, so they can buy what they need!" Esther insisted, lunging forward. A sting down her legs made her suck in her breath.

Cantus caught her shoulder. "Let them be generous, Tessa." He shrugged. "That money is going to have to last us a long way. We can't afford to reject offers of kindness."

Esther pulled out of his grip. She crossed her arms, glaring at the pile at their feet. "I can't ride," she said, raising her eyebrows and shrugging. "I don't think horses are going to be much help to me. You may have to leave me behind."

"Nonsense," Abner said, rubbing a horse's white striped nose with his palm. "We'll just have to teach you."

"That might be difficult on the run," Cantus said, his mouth tipping to one side.

"Until then, we'll just ride slow. Anyone can sit on a horse while they walk in a straight line. You'll manage, trust me." Abner clapped the horse on the neck. "Unless," he said, raising an eyebrow at her with a smile, "You'd want to ride with me. You would have to hold on to me very tightly, but I'd make sure you didn't fall."

"I think I'd rather be dragged behind the horse," Esther said.

Cantus chuckled.

Abner bit his lip, smiling as well. "Give it time."

XVIII

"Arise!" Esther snarled at the boot nudging her thigh, swiping wildly at the unknown attacker of her sleep. Every muscle from her neck to her ankles ached, her knees throbbing worst of all. How could a day of sitting on a horse be so much work? Even with her corset keeping her back straight, balancing in one position for however many marks of the day they had ridden across the barren plain should not make her feel like this. She wanted nothing more than to curl on her mat and snooze away the morning. The gentle buzz of grass bugs thrummed her mind quiet as she began to drift.

"No, not back to sleep. Up!"

Two arms dragged an unwilling Esther to her feet. Snapping her eyes open, Esther twisted away from Cantus.

"Finally, we get to see those beautiful sea-blue eyes!" mocked Abner with a laugh. The fire at his feet sent the first smells of the meal wafting to Esther's eager nose.

Cantus handed her a wooden stick a little longer than her arm.

She took it slowly. "What am I supposed to do with this?"

"Defend yourself." Cantus whipped his stick at her shoulder.

Esther threw her stick at him, tripping backward.

Cantus sidestepped it, and it thumped away across the grass. "Not like that," he said, retrieving it. He held a hand to Esther. With a scowl, she was dragged to her feet. "Again."

This time Esther was able to watch the blow coming. The crack of collision hit her ears like a whip. She smiled, triumphant, but Cantus was already in motion to deliver the next hit. He stopped just short of her shoulder while she flailed wildly away from the strike.

"Okay," he said, catching her arm before she fell again. "So that was—"

"Bleeding awful," laughed Abner from behind Cantus.

Esther threw her stick at him.

He ducked, covering his head, but it struck his forearm anyway.

"We'll work on it. Nice aim though," Cantus nodded. "You just need to breathe. You're trying to do too many actions at once. One at a time."

"You just came at me," Esther said, crossing her arms. "I wasn't ready. It wasn't fair."

Abner put on a high-pitched, lofty voice, "Well, life hardly ever gives us a fair fight, so—"

Cantus turned. "Abner."

Abner looked up. Cantus' arm was already a blur of motion as the wooden stick hurtled toward the prince's head. Abner rolled to the side, toward the fallen stick, tucking his bandaged hand into his stomach before planting his feet. "Oh, are we playing now?"

Cantus adjusted his grip, eyes narrowing.

Abner grabbed the stick from the ground. "Come on then! Pay attention, Tessa, and I'll show you what a trained man can do."

Crack!

The sticks splintered on their first impact. As the soldier struck another blow, they cracked visibly. The third collision brought Cantus' stick to half its height, the top half flying off to strike the old oak. The bent-fingered branches that sheltered their camp shuddered.

"New sticks?" Abner suggested, dropping his badly cracked branch.

"And maybe we should hit a bit softer this time," Cantus agreed, and the two went hunting for them among the oak's fallen limbs.

"So you can both swing sticks at one another. Congratulations." Esther raised her hands with mocking joviality.

"I don't think you understand what will be coming for us if we're caught," Cantus said, returning with a freshly broken branch.

Esther folded her arms. "You forget, I lived ten years in the forest. On my own."

"And how many trained swordsmen did you encounter as a hermit in the woods?" Abner challenged, stomping his heel on a branch to make it short enough to use.

"You need to learn to defend yourself."

"Let's go again," Abner said, returning. "I haven't had a good match in—" he raised a brow. "Well, it is you I'm fighting. I'll probably still be—"

Abner's words were cut by Cantus' stick slicing the air at his knees. He darted out of reach, raising his brow with a grin. Back and forth they fought, Abner sometimes taking the initiative and striking at Cantus, while other advances left the prince giving feet of ground to the assault from the soldier.

Esther picked at the oak's gnarled bark, sighing at the sky.

Abner's scowl of concentration tipped into a one-sided smile. Ducking a swipe, he edged to his left and aimed a strike down the soldier's side.

Cantus fell, unable to balance his shifting weight. His backside had hardly hit the ground before his hands were ripping off his boot.

Abner stood a few feet away, breathing hard, but the smile on his face stretched to meet his ears. "I saw you—you were holding yourself more on one side. I saw it and—did you—Tessa? That—that is how you win a fight!" He threaded his hands through his hair, stretching to catch his breath.

Cantus' shoulders rose through a sigh as he pulled something wrapped in animal hide from his boot. "It's alright, it didn't break. It's alright."

"What is it?" Esther asked, coming forward.

"Nothing." Cantus stuffed the animal hide back into his boot but Esther had already caught the shape of it before it slipped out of sight.

Has he really kept that this entire time?

"Now, you," Cantus said, pushing himself up from the ground and facing her. "Show me what you've learned."

Gone was the cool breeze and changing colors of the hills which hinted at the season to come. On the plains everything was dull, dry, and dead. The sun rose to glare at the three travelers before Cantus allowed her to stop. If Esther thought she was in pain after the previous day of riding, it was a whisper compared to how her muscles screamed at her now. The pressure beat on her bones until she felt she would crack like the hill of sticks they had made use of and discarded.

The food was now cold.

Esther grabbed it from Cantus, not bothering to thank him for it, and turned to stomp away.

The ground swung at her, hitting her hard on the cheek. Yells jostled the air above her. Esther was lifted off the ground, her back set against the oak.

"What do we do?" Cantus' voice was a muffled echo.

"I don't know."

Abner stared at her as he slipped in and out of being with her failing vision. "Water? Get some water."

Her chin fell, exhaustion pulling every limb down to crushing oblivion.

"Water. Okay. I can—I can do that."

"Tessa, can you hear me?" Abner gripped her face between his palms.

The warmth of his hand pressing into her cheek flowed through the skin. Esther blinked to find his eyes.

Cantus returned with a cup, sloshing in haste.

Abner pulled a square of fabric from his belt and dunked it in the water. He dabbed at her forehead, hands shaking.

"I'm ... fine."

"Shut it," Abner said, shaking his head. He squeezed some water against her neck, the droplets spilling down her back and making her skin stick to her dress. "You are most certainly not fine." He dunked the rag in the water again. "People who are fine don't fall on their faces for no reason."

"Do you know what you're doing?" Cantus asked. "What's wrong with her?"

"I was a prince, not a Healer! I have no idea!" Abner snapped. The tremor in his hands intensified.

Esther's eyes drifted closed. She couldn't bear the weight of them anymore.

Fox.

His honey golden eyes were gone, half-eaten and hollow, blackened by decay. The white fur on his chest was clumped together with dirt and crusted with old brown blood. His paws moved toward her in a jerking jarring motion. His head lolled to one side, tongue rolling out from an open jaw.

Tick. Tick. Tick. Tick.

Fox's head ticked down farther toward his shoulder, held unnaturally straight.

Esther's chest tightened and she pushed herself away until her back hit a wall. Walls sprang up around her. The room was filled with shadows and black mist.

The fox ticked closer. His nose stopped a hair's breadth from hers. Fox's head began to right itself, shuddering. Slowly. Painfully.

Errrgh, the groan pushed from the blood-crusted throat.

His head snapped into place.

The silence pulsed.

The sight of the hollow black eyes filled Esther's with heavy tears. Her breath stuck in her muddy chest. The fox's rattling air dragged pieces of Esther away with it through his dry gray nose.

You betrayed me.

Esther shook her head, tears leaking from her eyes. The words choked her like a chain wrapping around her throat.

You're a liar. A coward.

Esther turned away, trembling mouth clenched tight, but the fox was there too. Everywhere she looked, his face flooded her eyes.

"I—please—"

You know what you have to do.

Esther shook her head. "I tried."

You know what you have to do.

The fox's chest began to unbind itself, in a moment standing raw and open as it had when she found him in the valley of Shiloh.

"It's all my fault," Esther whispered. "I can't—I can never make up for it."

You know what you have to do.

"It won't fix anything! Please!"

The fox's mouth began to stretch wide.

Esther screamed.

The fox was everywhere, the stretching black cavern now a gaping jaw lined with teeth, the throat looming large enough to swallow her whole.

"Get off! Get off me!" Tessa thrashed blindly at Abner. Her fist struck his jaw.

His eyes flashed as he leaned away from the sudden assault.

"What happened?" Cantus asked, running forward.

"Nothing! I—I don't know!" Abner rubbed his jaw, pushing down the burn to strike back. "I didn't touch her and she just went wild. She struck me!"

Tessa breathed deep through her nose, her terror-soaked eyes never wavering from his face.

He checked over his shoulder for whatever monster she was seeing.

Her breath shook. "Stay away from me."

Abner's brow jumped. "Fine!" He stomped toward the curling, smoky remains of the fire.

Cantus took a seat next to him.

Silent tension hung like a rope stretched too tight.

"What did you do?"

"Nothing!" Abner insisted. "She—" he looked back at Tessa, her face now buried in her knees, hugged to her chest, "just went mad out of nowhere. I did nothing."

"Okay," Cantus said, standing. "Then I think we should move camp to those trees near the road and stay for the night."

"What? We'd lose the entire day. We can't just—"

Cantus tipped his chin toward Tessa, raising his brow.

Abner groaned. "This girl has brought me nothing but trouble."

The sun was about to rise. Esther could feel it in the chilled air. That quiet energy that thrummed through her breath in the moments before a new day began. She needed to move quickly.

Esther slipped free of the canvas tent the men had discovered yesterday as they picked through supplies and argued about how best to load them. She studied the camp. Nothing had changed since she had crawled in to hide from the weight of guilt stacking heavier on her chest at Abner's every look. The very fact he was still breathing was a knife blow to all those Esther loved.

Even still, a treasonous whisper curled in the back of her mind. *Not yet.* The before-dawn chill sank to her bones.

The grove of birch trees they took shelter in cut the road from view.

The horses ripped grass behind her, while the men slept with boots set out toward the ashy remains of the fire.

It was Cantus' boot that drew her forward on silent padding feet. She stared at his steady waves of breath as she pulled open his discarded shoe. Ignoring the smell, Esther dug through the leather down to the toe. It was empty. She glanced at Abner, sleeping with his back slumped against a tree as she checked the other boot.

Empty.

Replacing the boot carefully beside its mate, Esther sat on her heels.

Cantus slept sprawled on his stomach, his long legs spilling over the side of his mat and his arms tucked up to cradle his head.

She moved to sit in front of him. A brown tuft of fur peeking out from beneath his splayed fingers pulled Esther's mouth into a wide smile.

There.

She just had to get it out. There was nothing the same shape that she could use to replace it, and the angle would be near impossible to get right without him waking. Her fingers landed on the small bit she could see with no more weight than a feather. Gently pinching a few strands of fur, Esther began to slowly pull.

Cantus shifted.

Taking advantage of the motion, Esther pulled half the object free, allowing him to resettle onto his half. She slipped a breath out. Another. Flexing her fingers by her sides, she set them on the object again. Her legs cramped at the slow steady pace, but each pull of progress brought the object closer. They were numbed deadweight by the time Cantus' last finger dropped to the mat.

Finally.

Her fingers stumbled to untie the cord holding the wrapping closed. Esther released the animal hide, letting it fall away.

The long, yellow-lined tooth sat heavy in her hand. Pointed, curved, and double the length of her palm.

She ran her other hand along it, her fingers walking the trail of natural grooves and testing the sharpness of its point. Not as cutting as she had hoped, but Cantus said there would be some old venom stored away in it to help get the job done. Paying off the Healer to extract it was no longer an option, so stabbing would have to do. *Dragon venom has no cure. If this really is a dragon tooth, if they ever actually existed, there's no turning back from this moment. This will be the end of Abner of Lydia.*

Esther ignored her pulsing back and stinging feet. Her eyes turned to Abner, her mind gathering the memories of his crimes. The faces of Shiloh filled her sight.

Jathan. The little girl with the doll. The old guards. The flower girl. The seamstress.

Her feet began to move.

Fox.

Esther's mouth twisted as she stopped in front of Abner. The prince slept unaware, his mouth hanging open on one side. New images filled her mind.

Abner gripping her hand, laughing as he ran through the alleys of Lydia. His hand on her cheek, the warmth of it bringing her back to reality. His smile, both inviting and challenging, as he raised the caravan drink to his lips.

She whipped her head free of those thoughts, sending a lash of pain across her back.

He deserves this. This is justice! This is—

Lady Hildren's eyes—bruised, dirty, and pleading for help that Esther refused to give—made her fingers falter.

Behind her, Cantus shifted and resettled himself to sleep. The soldier would have as much right to stand over her clutching a poisoned fang as she did to Abner. She had betrayed his trust, abandoned Lady Hildren to death, and let an entire village fall for her mistake. She had delayed and stalled, stretching her time in luxury while others suffered.

Liar. Coward.

Lady Hildren's sharp blue eyes, not the Fox's blackened empty ones, flooded Esther's vision as she turned her back on the prince. *I can't take justice. I'm just as wretched. I don't deserve to feel better.* There would be no relief from it, the tortured face of the fox would greet her every time she closed her eyes, but perhaps that was as it should be. Pulling in a shaky breath, Esther dropped the fang back on the animal hide and left the camp.

The prince's gentle snore continued on.

XIX

Esther snapped the palm-length stick in two, hurling both at the gnarled oak trunk. Her weak hand went wide, but her strong hand struck with deadly accuracy. She missed the easy power of her sling.

The sun's slow climb into the sky had chased away most of the mist over the plain, exposing the grove of white birch trunks surrounding the camp.

Snatching another twig from the ground, she spun to fling it over her shoulder, aiming at the knotted trunk.

Thwack! The stick bounced off the gnarled bark to thump into the grass.

Esther sighed. *It's time.* She had considered leaving, disappearing into the fog before the men woke, but there was nowhere to go. Everyone she cared for was gone. There would be no relief from that even if she traveled to the farthest edges of the world.

Reentering the grove, Esther jumped at the low guttural eruption from the throat of one horse, while another lashed its side with its long whipping tail. Abner was a misshapen mass of blankets piled so tight against the morning chill that his breathing was imperceptible. Cantus snored quietly into his mat, his feet sticking out toward the gray ashy remains of their evening fire. Esther folded her arms, shaking her head at their snoozing bodies.

Swish. The horse's tail gave another lash, drawing Esther's eye to a third figure standing by the farthest horse's neck. The shock of the unexpected stopped her breath and froze her limbs. Her body thawed as her eyes narrowed on the intruder. She picked a path through the sparse fallen leaves, limbs gliding in the practiced stalk of a hunter. Using the dense white trunks to mask her progress, Esther bent to watch the figure beneath the horse's barrel gut. He dug at the inside of the horse's hoof with a long narrow dagger.

He's trying to make the horse lame, strand us in the wilderness.

Esther caged the growl building in her chest, holding her breath behind clenched teeth.

"Ho ... ho," the deep murmur soothed the horse, relaxing its leg until it stopped trying to jerk away from the blade.

Esther slipped under the beast's neck.

"Away from the horse!" she barked, driving her heel into the intruder's back.

The horse screamed through a neigh, popping up on its hind legs as much as the rope tied over its nose would allow.

Esther tripped back from the snorting beast.

A stream of curses flowed from Abner's mouth as he spun, gripping his back.

"You—no, you were sleeping." Esther studied the pile of blankets behind him.

Abner threw out his hands. "Not sleeping." He winced, stretching to one side. "That is going to smart all day."

"What were you doing?"

The horse still danced nervously against its bindings, a rim of white showing around its eye as it leaned away from Esther.

Abner ran a hand down the horse's side, calming both the animal and himself with the touch. "The horses should be groomed before and after each ride. I don't have the tools I need but I'm making do. Now stand back, and if you kick me again, I will return the favor." Abner snatched his dagger from the grass and ran his hand down the back of the horse's leg. He clicked his tongue and pulled on the beast's ankle.

The hoof stayed planted.

"Come on," Abner said, pushing his shoulder into the horse's side to shift its weight, "Give it here. Have to get that rock out." The leg bent under Abner's gentle coaxing, and he set the horse's hoof on his knee so he could resume his careful excavation of the knuckle-wide stone.

Esther folded her arms against the creeping chill, sitting in the damp grass to watch Abner work. "How did a prince who probably never changed his own undergarments for himself learn to care for a horse?"

The animal must have held some calming magic in its flank, as Abner glanced at her with a smile. "I was eleven when my father first let me ride. In Keldeema, outside of war, horses are rare and only used to pull carriages and work fields. Most of the country is big, loud, and cobblestones wreck horse hooves. Better than riding, I liked going down with Dennison and taking care of the horses. I haven't done it in years. My father was furious that I was being taught peasants' work." Abner's mouth flattened. His voice softened to a whisper, his fingers brushing some stray hairs from the horse's coat. "I always thought Dennison was right. An animal needs care to work well for you. Taking part in it helps you feel connected. And," his voice brightened as he clapped the horse's neck, running his hand under its mane, "since I'm nobody now, what does it matter what my father thinks is 'princely behavior'?" He reached for the next hoof and paused, holding the horse's back ankle. "Would you like to try?"

Esther shook her head, sending a ping of pain down her back.

"Suit yourself." Abner pushed into the horse's hip and set the acquired hoof on his knee. "But there's no better feeling."

"Really? No better feeling?"

Abner raised his brow then shook his head. "It's," he paused to carefully scrape around the border of the hoof with his blade, flicking away dirt clods and pebbles as he went. "It's peace. You have to calm yourself, for the horse to settle. And eventually, you really do feel it. Everything else gets quiet and there's just this peace."

"That ... sounds nice."

Abner set down the hoof and nodded to her. "Come here."

"No."

"I won't make you pick up the *scary* feet." He held out a square of fabric, already coated in dirt, his fingernails black.

Esther chewed her lip, moving to his side.

Miming the motion as he spoke, Abner instructed her, "Follow the hairline down with slow gentle strokes. And, that's it," Abner laughed as the horse dropped its chin, that low guttural sound rumbling from its throat again.

Esther's hand jumped off the horse's side, her breath flaring her nostrils wide.

"No, it's alright, you're alright." Abner had one hand on the horse's shoulder, the other out to Esther. "That sound just means it feels good. You're making her happy."

A smile crept up Esther's cheeks as she returned to the horse's side, brushing across its smooth coat with more confidence.

Abner nodded, watching her. He bent to pick up the waiting hoof, scraping it clean. The morning birds sang in the branches above and the air began to warm. "This is," Abner paused, a chuckle escaping his throat, "very strange for me. I've never just spent time doing something with one of you before. It's nice."

"One of you?" Esther asked, her hand slipping down the horse's hip.

"Watch the hairline there, it changes," Abner warned as he stepped around her to finish off the last hoof. "I mean, a girl. I've never just had a friend who was a girl. I don't know how to act."

"Well, what would you normally do?"

"Normally I would try to get you to bed with me," Abner said, the bluntness of his words seeming to momentarily surprise even him.

Esther cleared her throat, slowing her hand to carefully arrange each splayed hair running up the horse's side. "What if I was a boy?"

"Probably make a joke about bedding a woman, maybe punch you in the arm? I don't know."

"How is it," her hands wound through the horse's stringy mane, picking out the odd twig or foxtail, "I lived alone in the woods, and yet I have an easier time making friends than you?"

"I never had to make friends," Abner said, straightening. He stretched his arms over his head, his hands clasped together and pulling his muscles to life.

Esther blinked, turning away.

"I was royal and powerful. I didn't have to try to convince people I was worth their time to be around. I sort of inherited popularity."

"My, how tragically difficult for you."

Cantus stirred, yawning noisily as Abner moved to the next horse.

"Where is it?" Cantus popped to his knees, empty hands searching. His darting eyes landed on the discarded fang and he sank into a heavy sigh, wrapping it in the animal hide again.

"Lose something?" Abner hardly turned his chin from the horse hoof in his hand.

"No, no, it's fine." Cantus said, still breathing heavy. "Tessa?"

She ducked under the horse's nose and waved to Cantus. "Right here."

"Don't—"

The horse snorted, jumping to one side and twisting its nose to keep Esther in sight.

Abner pushed his words through an irritated sigh. "Just—move, I'll settle her. Ho, now..." He rubbed the horse's shoulder.

"Feeling any better?" Cantus asked, his gaze flicking over her.

"Oh, she's feeling just fine! Gave me a solid kick to the back this morning, so I'd say she is right back to her usual self."

"I thought you were trying to hurt the horse," Esther said.

"But I wasn't."

"What are you looking for? An apology?"

"Actually yes, I wouldn't mind one. For once."

"Well, savor that disappointment, because—"

"This is going to waste another day," Cantus interrupted. "We should keep moving. Can you ride?"

"Well…" Abner's mouth twisted, his eyes pinching.

"I'm fine," Esther said, her chin sticking forward.

"Not what I meant." Abner smiled at her. "You still have a lot to learn, Lady Tessa."

"Teach her as we go," Cantus said. "I, for one, want to put some distance between us and the road today. I'm getting nervous that we'll be easily tracked."

"They're probably still combing the alleys of Riverton for us," Abner said, pushing the words through a grunt as he scrubbed a circle along the horse's flank.

Esther slipped her dress off her shoulders to tighten the strings of her corset, anticipating the day of jolting, aching monotony ahead. "I can't—can you help me with this?"

Abner's full attention snapped to her.

"No," Esther threw out her hand, "Not you. Cantus, just tug on these strings."

"I don't think—" Cantus stared at the ground, his eyebrows pushed to his hairline.

"It's not my ideal either, but I can't tighten it enough on my own."

Cantus raised his eyes with a sigh. "Let me know if I hurt you," he tugged tentatively.

"You'll have to pull much harder than that," Esther said, holding her breath up high in her chest to get a more snug fit.

Cantus huffed behind her.

The corset pulled her bones into a firmer line, and she sighed as the tingle in her feet receded with the pressure.

"Is that—"

"Good enough. For now." Esther said, slipping the top of her dress back over her arms as she turned to Cantus. "Thank you."

"What happened yesterday? Are you ill?"

"It's nothing."

Abner went back to grooming the horses, his hands a little rougher than before. "I'm fine. It's nothing. You're full of lies lately."

"It happened in Little Brennon too," Esther admitted.

The men both stared at her.

"During my bath. I don't know why, but the corset seems to help. I don't feel as much when it's on."

"So it'll stop it from happening again?" Cantus said, nodding slowly. "You just never take it off and you'll be—"

"It keeps coming loose so I have to tighten it over again, but—" Esther shrugged.

"Good enough." Cantus pulled on his boots before stomping to the horses with a saddle spilling over each arm.

Abner tossed his rag onto the ground behind the last horse, standing at her shoulder as Esther pulled the canvas tent apart. "We should go back to Brennon or Riverton and see if there's a Healer there."

"No," Esther said, not bothering to look at him.

"It's not worry for you," Abner said, crossing his arms. "But it could slow us down, you suddenly falling out of a clear blue sky. Especially with riding, you're going to break your neck."

"Your concern is touching," Esther spoke through a tight smile, "But I'm handling it." She gathered the canvas into a hasty fold, pushing it into his shoulder as she slipped past. Her eyes turned to the ground and the messy trail of footprints that would have to be swept away. Esther bit off her sigh of irritation at the broken branches, trailing prints, and obvious path they left off the road and into the trees. These men had never had to hide, and if she wasn't watching, they would leave a trail even a child could follow. She got to work covering traces of the camp, following the path out of sight of the men.

Crrrch.

An unexpected footfall on the leaf-strewn ground made Esther's limbs jump beneath her skin. She dragged in a slow calming breath. *I've already been tricked once today. Not again.*

"I told you Abner, I'm fine." She turned around to face him. "Go back to—"

Not Abner.

A long green cloak stood silent between the dense white trunks. A hand shifted.

Esther moved in a flash of instinct. She seized the figure's wrist, twisting it back as she plowed the heel of her hand into the cloaked chest. The figure and she both crashed to the ground. Ignoring the pain stinging down her legs, Esther reached into the hood and grabbed a fistful of wild brown curls.

Ava?

Esther let go, slipping off to pull the girl to her feet. "What are you doing here?"

Ava coughed, rubbing her chest where she'd been struck. "I came to find you."

"How?"

"I followed the rumors until—" she coughed again.

"And ... why? You were safe in the castle."

"No one's safe in the castle. But I came for you, because ... we're friends."

She pulled Ava to her chest. "You shouldn't have come."

"I'm sorry, Lady, if I—"

"But I'm so glad you did." Esther smiled at Ava, surprising herself by the sting of tears in her eyes. "They're useless, you know. I had to have Cantus tighten my corset this morning and—well—it's good you're here."

"Cantus?" Surprise threaded through Ava's wide eyes as she followed Esther between the trees. "Cantus is here?"

"And Abner, unfortunately," Esther said, pulling apart two interlocking branches. "Abner, Cantus, this is—"

"Ava?" Cantus' hands dropped the mat he was binding. It rolled slowly flat in front of him. "What—what are you doing? Here, I mean. What are you doing here?"

Ava's freckle-lined cheeks lifted into a forceful smile. "I'm here to help. If you'll have me." Her eyes danced between the three.

"Oh," Abner said, smiling as he glanced over her. "I'm sure we'll find something for you to do."

"You touch her, I will castrate you," Esther warned.

"Jealousy, Tessa? I'm flattered."

Cantus folded his arms. "I'm not sure this is the best idea, Ava. What did your brother say about you coming out here alone?"

Ava shrugged. "Doesn't matter."

Cantus raised his brow, his eyes slipping to the ground as he shook his head.

"I didn't tell him. It should be my choice anyway. It's my own neck I'm risking, no matter what the 'Head of House' has to say."

"And oh, what about your mother?" Esther's worried eyes made Ava pull in a tight breath. "Doesn't she depend on you for—"

"Why doesn't everyone just let me worry about my family and my decisions? I'm here. How can I help?"

"Can you ride?" asked Abner, strapping a pack onto the horse's saddle, his fingers struggling over a knotted buckle.

"No, not really."

"Alright, you can ride with me." Abner winked at Esther.

She took a step forward, mouth tight.

Ava touched her shoulder, flashing Abner a quick smile. "No offense meant, but I don't trust a rabbit to keep me from falling. Cantus, mind if I ride with you?"

"Fine," Cantus shrugged, "but we'll probably be sending you home in the morning."

"I wouldn't count on it," Ava said, giving Esther's shoulder a squeeze.

"Again with the rabbit?" Abner muttered to himself.

Ava slapped Abner's hand away from the saddle strap, her clever fingers easily righting the twisted leather. After the camp was properly loaded, the three companions watched Ava stroke one horse's brown nose, giving it a kiss.

Esther was at least able to mount without help this morning, Abner clutching her reins in his fist as he swung his leg over the horse's back. Ava had to scramble up with the help of Cantus' arm. She perched with her knees tucked together, her hands holding on to his tunic for balance.

At midmark, they stopped for a meal. Ava put together plates, Cantus falling in to help beside her, while Abner worked with Esther on her riding. She would have preferred the chance to burn her hands in the fire trying to heat a meal, rather than listen to his constant demand for "Heels down!"

She pulled the horse to a stop and dropped the reins. "I'm tired. I'm done."

"No, you're not." Abner crossed his arms.

"Heels down, chin up, chest out, I can't keep track of all the unnatural things you want me to do all at once! It's uncomfortable. It shouldn't be this hard. Why can't I just sit on the horse?"

"You just sit, you're going to fall. We can't stay at a walk forever and you not knowing how to ride is slowing us down. It's something your muscles will learn to do, but here." Abner wrapped her ankle in his hands.

Her eyes narrowed.

With a smile, he jerked her heel down, holding her toes in place in their iron seat. He adjusted her hips and her shoulder into a long straight posture. "Now, stay in that line, look where you want to go, and work on moving with the horse. It's about balance."

Esther looked down at him.

"And don't look at the ground unless you're looking for a soft spot to land when you fall."

She pushed her eyes up.

"Squeeze her forward."

Esther's heels lightly pinched the horse's sides.

The beast's neck rose as it began to jolt forward.

"No, no, no, no." Esther bounced around the saddle.

"Balance," Abner called, running after her. "Just find the rhythm."

At each pop of the horse's stride, Esther rose out of her seat, landing only to be popped forward again. She began to predict the motion.

"Now put weight in your seat," Abner said, jogging beside them.

"I don't—know—what—that means—"

"You sit, kind of fuller?" Abner shook his head, still at a jog with them. "I'm not sure how to explain it. Uh—"

"Ready!" Ava called, waving to them. "Come back before it gets cold!"

Abner put a hand on the horse's neck, grabbing the reins from Esther's grateful fingers. He slowed her gradually and then led them back to the group.

Esther slipped down. Her feet stung as they hit solid ground, but the relief of not bouncing out of control eclipsed the pain.

"Make sure the knot's tight but let her have enough slack to drop her head and eat," Abner said, letting the reins fall into her hand.

Esther led the horse to the solitary tree where the other two horses were secured, tying it beside its companions before turning to rejoin her own. Ava smiled, handing Esther a flat metal plate.

"I can't believe you had time to pack cutlery before fleeing for your lives," Ava said as she stooped to grab her own. She lowered herself down next to Esther, shaking her curls out of her eyes.

"These didn't come from us," Esther said.

"No, they were gifts from Lady Tessa's adoring fanatics in Little Brennon!" Abner swept his hunk of bread in a broad flourish as he dipped his head. "I wouldn't be surprised if they started work on your statue as soon as we left."

Esther scoffed, pushing the bread and meat together to bite both at once.

"Oh, I didn't—" Ava frowned.

"I've been thinking about them too," said Cantus, staring at the bite mark he'd left in the dried meat. "I didn't know such passionate opposition to the crown existed."

"Yes, isn't it inspiring how many people would love to lop off my head?" Abner snapped.

Cantus lifted a shoulder, looking back over the way they had come. "I wonder…"

After everyone had finished their meal, the day of travel continued on.

Esther's knees shuddered gratefully when they stopped as the sun reached the last mark of daylight and the four hurried to set up camp before they lost the light. They didn't bother looking for much cover as the day's travel had distanced them from the road and the likelihood of someone happening upon their camp seemed small.

Ava set to work on the meal with the occasional frustrated noise as she made do with their limited supplies.

"Alright, I've decided I can't wait any longer." Abner's sudden breaking of the quiet drew all eyes to him. "Why does everyone keep calling me 'Rabbit'?"

"Rabbit?" Esther's eyes skipped over his face. "I don't see it."

"Thank you," Abner nodded, crossing his arms.

"Weasel maybe," Esther squinted at him.

Cantus barked a laugh behind her.

"No, *skunk*!"

Abner opened his mouth to lash back, but Cantus spoke first. "It has nothing to do with your courage or anything, Abner. I wouldn't worry about it." He prodded the flames with a long stick, sending a flurry of sparks into the empty, purple sky.

"*You* knew about this?"

"It's," Cantus paused, a smile breaking across his mouth, "It has to do with how you sort of hop around when you fight."

"I don't hop!"

Esther muffled a laugh against her palm. "You do actually." She pinched her fingers together. "A little bit."

"I *do not* hop!"

Cantus chuckled. "It's fine, Abner. You're ... enthusiastic is all."

"Besides, what does it matter what nickname they had for you," Esther shrugged, planting herself by the fire with her knees to her chest, the warm glow melting the icy skin of her calves. "The Prince Abner who lived in the castle and had servants is gone. You have to figure out who you are now. So, you don't want to be a rabbit? Don't hop." Her brow raised at Abner's quiet stare. She shook her head, still laughing at him.

Cantus nodded. "We should all think about who we want to be from here. None of us can go back to our old lives. Unless…"

All mirth died from Esther's lips. She glared at Cantus from across the flames. "Not that again. Don't say it."

"Abner," Cantus turned so every line of his face was lit by the fire's glow, "Do you believe in dragons?"

"No weapons," the doorkeeper at the tavern turned his narrowed, dark eyes to Esther and Ava, "and no women."

"Just as well." Abner grinned, undoing the buckle of his jeweled sword and tossing it to Cantus, who caught it with barely a blink. "She can't hold it anyway."

"I'll keep an eye on them." Cantus attached the sword to the knotted cord of leather around his waist.

Ava sighed. "You can go drink. We're not children."

Cantus ignored her.

Abner shrugged a shoulder before disappearing through the door.

"Be on your way then."

Naamah was a crisscrossing web of wide stone-cobbled streets and narrow dirt lanes lined with shops and houses. Large carriages were the only things to break up the crowd of busy people hurrying to nowhere. The muck lining the street beneath the homes, where house women tossed it from high windows, filled the air with a musk that made Esther long for the barren plains behind. She coughed as Cantus turned to face them.

"He'll be in there awhile, trust me," the soldier said. "Any idea what you'd like to do?"

"Getting stronger corset strings for Tessa should be the first thing." Ava scanned the signs hanging over people's heads. "We just have to find a lady's shop."

Cantus nodded. "While you do that, I could use—" his hand brushed the strip of leather looping around his waist. He smacked a palm to his forehead. "I forgot my belt was gone. Should have asked Abner for a few coins. I'll go in and—"

Esther slipped a small pouch out from a fold in her flowered drape, clinking the coins inside with a smile.

"Where did you get that?" Cantus asked.

"I didn't want to have to argue Abner into doing the right thing again. So I took it." Esther shrugged. "Been slipping a few coins out of his belt after he hangs it up most nights since Little Brennon."

The other two stared at her, their lack of admiration drawing heat to Esther's cheeks.

"I left him some ... I think."

"I just—" Cantus paused, his mouth chewing through an unpleasant taste, "I find it very unnerving. The idea of you sneaking around and digging through things after I'm asleep." He shook his head, his shoulders shivering involuntarily.

"Well, I'm not putting it back," Esther crossed her arms, the satchel of coins in her fist, "so are we going to use it or let it go to waste?"

"Let's go," Ava said at last. "We have things we need." She threaded her arm through Esther's and pulled her to her side.

The knife hanging on the wall looked as if it had been recently used, a smear of oil along the cutting edge drawing Abner's eye to its shine. The tavern was loud and dim, and Abner found himself alone at the bar counter.

"Pocket Empty Negotiator," the bar owner said, pausing in his coin count on the far side of the bar. He nodded to the blade. "Someone orders and drinks what they can't rightly pay for, we all sit down and have ... a wee chat with Penny there." He paused, looking Abner over. "You have coin?"

Abner nodded.

The man became instantly friendlier. He tossed the crowns he had been counting into the large black sack from beneath the counter before tucking it back out of sight. "What would you fancy then? Drink, hired woman, or both?"

Abner's brow shot up. "A drink would be plenty."

"Another for me as well, Seth!" said a young man, leaning over Abner's shoulder to thud his mug on the counter. Abner turned to tell the newcomer to move off when a wet cold something touched his hand, sliming his palm. He bolted off his stool, mouth twisting in disgust.

The fur-lined face peeked out from around Abner's vacated seat, one eye obscured by coarse black fur, the other by shaggy white. A pink tongue lapped the air toward Abner's hand between heavy panting breaths.

"Dogs are allowed, but not women?" Abner asked.

The owner, Seth, flashed the mutt a smile, filling the stranger's mug and grabbing an identical one from beneath the counter for Abner. "Dogs are usually the better behaved of the two." That earned a general chuckle from the room. "Just got tired of watchin' my coin bein' dragged out the door by the ear because some little skirt needed somethin' done. More trouble than they're worth, the lot of 'em."

"I'll lift a drink to that," muttered Abner, resuming his seat and pulling the offered mug to his chest. He tipped it back, gulping down half before coming up for breath.

"Ah, they're not all bad, are they?" smiled the young man, who looked barely old enough for his first set of whiskers. He settled in, leaving a gap of one stool between his seat and Abner's. His hand rolled over the dog's ears, the animal bending its neck back to lick the man's palm.

Seth gave a gruff noise from his throat before walking down the length of the counter, an oil-blackened rag in his hand as he scrubbed at the wood.

The stranger watched him leave before claiming the seat next to Abner. He leaned in close and Abner's jaw locked.

"You may be too young to know, but you should leave a gap—"

"I would run," the young man said, his voice barely perceptible and framed toward the wall. "He does not joke about the 'chats' with Penny. Unless you want to walk out of here a few fingers lighter—" his voice cut suddenly as the bar owner walked past them, giving both a nod before moving to check on his other patrons.

"What are you talking about?" Abner's hands strayed to his belt which sat flat against his waist. *Empty*. A chill ran down his back as he felt for his sword. *Gone*. His half-drunk mug sat on the counter in front of him. He cursed, quietly.

"All done, Sir? Would you be takin' another?"

Abner tested his injured hand under the counter. Held immobile by the wrapping Clive had put on days before, Abner was not sure if it had regained any strength. He would probably find out in the next few moments.

"No more for me," declared the younger man, pushing forward his empty mug. He tossed a gold crown to the owner.

"And you, traveler? Any more?"

"No," Abner said, tension rising in his shoulders.

"Ah, very well." The owner's eyes narrowed as they glanced over Abner. "You seem ... nervous, stranger. Somethin' wrong?"

"I—"

Abner bolted from his chair, flinging himself toward the door.

Too slow, as hands from every direction seized him and dragged him back. They tossed him forward to face the bar owner as he pulled the oiled blade down from the wall.

"Yeh now have two choices," the thick-bearded man said, anger making the accent in his voice stronger as his breath puffed from his chest with a quick rhythm. "Yeh can come with me into the back and face yer fate like a man or yeh can plant yer feet and I'll take 'em both. What'll it be?"

A bark was the only warning before the dog launched at the owner's hand. He whipped out of the way, knife clutched in his fist all the tighter.

"What is this, Petra? Call the mutt off now."

"You know me, Seth. Why don't we let this one walk, eh?" Petra said.

The dog continued to growl and pace in front of the bar owner.

"Aye, I know yeh. But Penny, here? She hasn't been introduced." The bar owner pulled his upper lip tight over his teeth, knocking the dog aside with his hip as he lunged at Abner, knife poised to strike.

Abner took advantage of Seth's distracted feet. He knocked the strike wide, his other hand following the knife to try to wrestle it to the ground.

Seth twisted free, and Abner's hands gripped air, missing his sword as the bar owner lunged again.

Abner grabbed a three-legged stool and slapped the blade away before pushing his arm through the wooden legs, pulling it to his side. The training shields he had practiced with were now a distant memory. He only hoped his muscles recalled what to do even if his brain was too slow. He hit the side of the makeshift shield with his hand. "Come on, then!"

The other patrons of the bar backed a step as Abner took his stance, his training showing in every muscle.

"Yeh really want to test my mettle against that stool, do yeh?"

The shield served as a brace for his hand, the force of the blow being taken in his shoulder rather than his fist, as Abner brought the stool under the strike from the knife. He rammed it into the bar owner's exposed throat.

Seth stumbled back, hand nearly dropping the blade as he gripped the counter for balance.

Abner wasn't done. He brought the side of the stool down on Seth's wrist, cracking it.

The knife clattered onto the floor.

Seth's cry of pain was muted as Abner was overwhelmed with striking fists.

He had forgotten the rest of the men in the room. Some fought to slip by him, grabbing as many bottles as they could stuff in their arms before darting out the back. Others fought for control of the knife which sat between Abner's feet.

Petra reappeared by Abner's side, his fists raised and ready as the two pushed the crowd of men back.

Abner had only one objective as he knocked aside a man with the stool, chipping another's tooth with his elbow. He needed to get out.

Largely helped by the dog running through their legs to bite at the leather boots, Abner and Petra began to edge toward the door. When they reached the wall, their progress became easier, only attracting a stray fist as the majority of the room's attention was now fixed on the liquor.

The doorkeeper dragged Seth away from the fray as he spewed curses at his patrons, most specifically by name, and gripped his wrist, hugging the black sack of crowns to his chest with streaming eyes.

Abner and Petra bolted out into the sunlight, the dog at their heels, and didn't stop moving until they were around the corner from the tavern.

Breathing hard, Petra shook his head. "You couldn't have picked a worse tavern owner to try that with." He extended an arm. "I'm Petra."

"I heard," Abner threaded his hands behind his head to stretch out his shoulders, sweat making the underside of them radiate a sticky heat.

"And you?"

Abner glanced over the young man in front of him. About the same height as himself but thinner in the arms, his dark brown hair tied against his neck. "How did you know my belt was empty?"

"I—you seemed nervous. I took a guess."

Abner looked down at Petra's hands. "You're a thief, aren't you?"

"I didn't steal anything from you."

"Only because there wasn't anything to steal." Abner crossed his arms. "It's all right, I won't be turning you over to the guards."

"Of course you won't," smirked Petra. "They'd be more interested in getting you than me. That belt? It's what made you worth that bump at the counter to check you over. It's not from around here. The king's guard, the royal family, and the nobles are the only ones who wear 'em. And they're all in Lydia until the weather turns. Everyone else just cinches up some leather and carries a bag."

Abner shrugged, turning away.

"Which means you," Petra said, trotting to keep up, "are somewhere you aren't supposed to be. But not to worry, I won't turn you over to the guards either." He stopped, the dog halting beside him. Abner was about to round a corner when Petra called out, "For your help, by the way, I thank you! Had my eye on this piece for a long time."

Abner glanced back at Petra before returning to the main road. The sun winked off Penny's well-oiled side.

❖ ❖ ❖

"How is he even supposed to find us?" Esther kicked away a ball of horse dropping from her skirt. "We can't just wait here all day."

"Finally," Cantus said, gesturing to the door of the hay-floored barn. "He's—what happened?"

Abner smiled with one side of his mouth, holding the other end of his freshly bruised jaw stiff. "Glad to see you remembered where to meet, Cantus." He winced.

"Who won?" Ava leaned against a stall, her fingers idly braiding the leather straps hanging down from the bars.

"Me, of course," Abner said, pulling his chin up.

"Did you ... hop on your guard?" Esther asked.

Abner groaned, shaking his head. "We may have a problem," he said, quietly. The sweep of hay being moved around a faraway stall by the old stable hand made Abner drop his voice even more. "My belt is empty."

"You spent all the coins in your belt at the tavern? Really?" Esther scowled at him. "How could you be so—"

"No, it was empty before I got there. I had to fight my way out of a mob because I couldn't pay. The owner tried to knife me."

Cantus and Ava glanced at Esther, quickly pulling their eyes away.

"So now we need to find a way to get our stuff out of here with the horses and not get dragged to the city leader for not paying."

Esther sighed, digging out the satchel of coins from the fold of her drapery. "Here," she said, tossing it to Abner. "There should still be enough for that."

"How?" Abner asked, thumb running across the fabric. "How did you get this?"

"It's mine, from my castle wages." Ava raised her chin to meet Abner's stare. "I brought it with me when I came."

Abner nodded. "My thanks."

Ava lifted a shoulder. "Not a care. Now, Cantus had one more stop to make, but he was worried we'd miss you when you were done drinking, so why don't we all go now?"

"What could you possibly need, Cantus?"

The soldier stretched taller under Abner's scrutiny. "Whatever happens, this is not going to end peaceably. I'd rather not die with my hand empty, and needing to borrow your dagger isn't much better."

"So you want a sword," Abner said, holding out his hand for the return of his own. "Very well. Might as well have someone at my side equipped to fight since our group has become a caravan of women."

"There's a place we passed, not far, that had some simple pieces on display." Cantus nodded to the door. "It doesn't need to be fancy, just reasonably strong."

When the four companions were able to slip away from the crowd of bustling hot bodies and enter the candle-lit sword shop, all blinked through the dim haze flooding their vision. The wall was lined with brackets holding different weapons from the floor up to the top of the ceiling. There was a chest with a heavy padlock on it, and a man perched cross-legged on the lid.

"No," he said. "One at a time. One in, the rest out!" He waved a finger, his gray-whiskered face eyeing them through a narrow stare.

"I'll be out in a moment," Cantus said, extending his hand for the bag of coins.

"Don't spend it all." Abner said, liberating a crown before he dropped the pouch into Cantus' palm and then left the shop, planting himself on the step outside.

Esther edged around Abner to lean against the wall. She stretched her back. The exhaustion and ache that had been growing each day like a weight behind her eyes now pulled her features to sag toward the ground.

The prince studied his bandaged hand, his other twirling the single crown. Standing, he slipped forward, pulling his shoulder to one side to navigate through the crowd.

"Where are you going?" Esther leaned after him.

"Let him." Ava drew Esther back with a hand on her arm. "He'll come back after."

"And meanwhile we're stuck waiting for him," Esther blew out a breath, touching her head to the wall. "Selfish." She winced.

"Are you alright, Lady?"

"Three days of riding straight through with hardly a break to get here was just more than I was ready to take all at once. I'll be fine when I'm able to rest."

"These new strings should help. They won't slip around as much, so we should be able to get you an even tighter fit on your corset."

"That would be nice." Esther's eyes lingered in a blink.

"Here," Ava said, slipping down to sit on the step. "Lean on me and close your eyes."

Esther shook her head, "It's okay. I'm just tired."

Ava tossed her eyes to the sky, as she clamped Esther's wrist and pulled her down next to her.

Weakness had been running a slow, steady invasion over Esther's body that day. It overwhelmed her mind as she let her head droop onto Ava's soft shoulder. Long humming notes sent vibrations murmuring through Esther's cheek. She was wrapped in soft arms and rocked in a gentle rhythm, and with her eyes closed, she could almost imagine that the last ten years had not happened. That, instead of Ava, her mother swayed her gently, comforting her through the noises of a storm.

Snapping her eyes open, Esther jolted off Ava's shoulder.

"I'm sorry, did I hurt you?" Ava asked as she rose, glancing between Esther and her own hands.

"No, I—"

Abner returned, clutching a bundle of rolled white linen and a clay jar sealed shut under his arm. "Isn't he finished yet?" His fingers probed his bruised jaw, drawing a hiss through his teeth.

"OUT!" screamed a voice from inside.

Abner leaped through the doorway, dropping the items to free his hands so that he could draw the sword Cantus had returned at his hip. The clay jar burst apart, filling the air with a sweet smell and the steps with a sticky cream. Esther edged around the mess, following him inside.

"Out of my shop! You—you traitor!"

"Apologies—I just—"

"You dare speak ill of our king in my shop? In *my* shop! He has lowered the tax for commerce on the land routes. Do you know how much I'd had to pay to the crown in the old reign for the right to my own wealth?"

Cantus held a sheathed sword but refused to draw it as the shopkeeper whipped at his knees with his cane. The stick smacked into the wall and a fistful of black arrows slipped from their bracket to clatter across the floor. Cantus knelt to replace them.

"Hands off, Sir, or you'll find just how quick these old bones can move! I'll gut you!" He jabbed Cantus back with his cane.

"Alright, alright. Where can I leave the coin? For this?" He held up the sword in his hand.

"Drop it right where you stand, then back toward the door. No sudden moves, now." The old eyes, sharp as an eagle's, watched Cantus slowly open the sack and lift a stack of crowns out. They fell to the floor, one rolling toward the old man's feet. He didn't stoop to retrieve it until all three left through the open door, Ava trotting quickly after them down the street with a roll of bandage clutched in her arm.

"What could you have possibly said to make that old man so angry?" Abner's voice stayed low as the press of people grew tighter on the main road.

The dust was less, but the sun glared off the stone, making them squint.

"I just asked why he had everyone else wait outside. Apparently, there's been groups of young men flooding into shops, taking what they want by overwhelming the shopkeeper. It seemed strange the soldiers here let that happen, and I said something about the king not acting on his people's behalf. That was all."

"Naamah is well taken care of by the crown," Abner said, shaking his head. "I'm not surprised their loyalty runs deep here. The principal land route into Alberon of course ends in Lydia, but its first major stop is here. That brings a lot of commerce to this region. They owe all their growth to it."

The other three stared at him.

"You think I got to twenty-and-one years as a prince without learning the basics of the country I was to inherit? Not all my days were spent bedding women."

"Wasn't your tutor left behind when you came here?" Esther said, remembering their conversation on the roof.

"Dennison thought it important for me to keep working, so as a boy I would have training in the morning and studies, self-guided of course, after midmark every day. Sometimes there were a few marks to play, when my father needed Dennison to do other things, but mostly I spent my childhood preparing for a role I'll now never take on." A breathy laugh passed through his lips. "What a waste."

"Ho there! Stop!"

The guard's armored shoulder flashed as he waded through the crowded river of people toward them.

Abner seized Esther's hand, dragging her into the thicket of bodies who dammed the stream to watch the trouble. There wasn't time to glance around for Cantus and Ava as her feet struggled to find their balance behind Abner's surging steps.

Another metal man parted the crowd ahead of them.

Abner cursed at her side.

Esther slipped forward, tugging Abner deeper into the crowd.

"The alleys?" Abner said, nodding toward a narrow lane.

Esther shook her head. *Safer in the crowd.* Phantom insects bit her heels. She stomped her feet, ignoring the nipping tingle as another guard made her change direction again.

Ava's wild curls bobbed between plodding shoulders far on their left.

Esther's breath loosened, one worry put aside.

The guards seemed to ignore the other two, exclusively hunting Abner and herself. Their continuous calls to "Halt!" beat the air behind.

Esther ducked down, pulling Abner's arm, to submerge them beneath the spilling crowd. Her back throbbed. The ribbed fabric keeping the pressure at bay buckled around her bent frame. Their scuttling steps cut through the crowd, drawing a few curious eyes.

"Bleeding coward!" one guard called from behind.

Esther smiled. *These men are poor hunters.*

"It's you!" A large man stepped into their way. "Leia, bring the stick!"

Abner straightened, elbowing the man aside.

The guards surged forward.

Whispers rippled.

"Prince Abner."

"It's him."

A woman clutched the arm of her companion, "What's he doin' here?"

Esther glanced at Abner.

No smile of recognition curled his lips as his dark eyes narrowed under his heavy brow. He pulled her toward a long dusty alley.

She sent a stack of crates toppling to the dirt as they passed, buying them a few extra moments. Esther checked behind for flashing armor as Abner turned a corner. She tripped on his heel and crashed into a pile of garbage, upsetting the rats.

"Come on! Up!" Abner said, grabbing her shoulders. "This is why we should've found you a Healer. You're useless this way!" He turned his back to the brick wall dead ending the alleyway. Snatching her wrist, Abner yanked Esther behind him.

A guard huffed, hair a mess and nostrils flared wide as a work horse's, just behind.

Abner's injured hand twitched.

"You're lucky," the guard said. Two others stood behind his shoulders blocking any hope of darting around him. "The city leader doesn't want blood messes on the streets anymore. So I'll be taking you in whole. Face the wall."

If he can't kill us, maybe I can knock him senseless and we'd have a chance that way. If I draw my sword, so will he. And unless I kill him, our chance will be gone. Abner set his feet, raising empty fists.

The guard smiled, matching him.

Abner threw the first punch. This was not a tavern owner, used to cutting up someone without a blade to return the favor, or villagers, who had never held anything sharper than a cooking knife.

The guard's answering strike gained Abner's bruise from the tavern fight another stinging layer.

Still, Abner was able to drop one of the flanks with an elbow to the jaw before his arms were caught behind him. He swallowed to keep his stomach from spilling out of his mouth as his gut was pummeled. "My father hits harder than you." He coughed. "You might want to work on that."

The soldier's mouth twisted. He reached to grip Abner's bandaged hand, ripping it the wrong way back.

Abner dropped to his knees, pain tearing through his throat.

"Enough of this!" Tessa jumped forward, taking advantage of his distracted hands to unsheathe a guard's sword. He twisted away but kept a tight grip on the prince.

"You know how to use that?" The lead guard smirked.

"Why don't you come find out?" She lunged, slashing wildly.

The soldier dodged, eyes narrowing.

She swung again, grunting to lend the blade power. Her feet were wrong, the motion clumsy.

He ducked under the blade, striking her chest to send her crashing back into the brick wall.

The sword slipped from her hand. She struggled to draw a breath, eyes sliding down to shut.

"Tessa!"

The shackles bit into Abner's wrist, his face rammed into the brick beside Tessa's crumpled form. He knew it was over. Pain radiated through his body in pulsing waves. There was no plan. No way out. *I'm trapped.*

Tessa stumbled beside him as, shackled together, they were led from the alley.

The crowded cell was cleaner than the one at the castle, though a vague unpleasant smell drifted through the air. Esther leaned her head against the gray brick wall and sighed, wishing she could strip off her dress and adjust her corset. The prince and she shared the cell with six other men who, for lack of anything better to do, kept looking at her. What if that snap in the alley was the corset string breaking? The new one was with Ava, and Esther doubted she had the strength to stand without it bracing her back straight.

"Why didn't you draw your sword?"

Abner glared at her.

"If it was some idiotic code of honor—" Esther scoffed.

Abner's nail picked at a loose piece of bandage on his wrist. "Maybe I've grown tired of bloodletting."

Her gaze slipped to his hands. "Are you alright?"

Abner smirked. "I'm used to worse." His unbandaged palm rubbed at his shoulder. "You?"

The guards returned, opening the cell door and tossing a man into the cage before they slammed it shut.

"Denny, Lenny, always a pleasure!" the newcomer said, sitting up and brushing his breeches clean of dust.

"I don't know how many times I need to say this, little snot, but my name's not Lenny!"

"No, of course not. You're Denny." The man chuckled to himself.

'Denny' stomped toward the cage.

"Leave it," the other said, bored.

"Petra." Abner sat forward.

The stranger faced Abner with a warm smile of surprise. "Why, if it isn't the prince of the land!"

Abner stiffened.

"Turns out we needn't have bothered about turning each other over, since we both wound up here anyway." He threw himself onto the seat beside Abner, filling the respectable space the latter had left between him and the next man. "I had wondered about you, but had no idea you were quite so interesting until I saw this." He pulled a parchment from inside his shirt, spreading it out for Abner to see his own face staring back at him.

Abner ripped it from his hands. "I don't believe it! Traitor to His Eternal Majesty? By signet assured: one thousand crown bounty to any sword that delivers the head of Abner of Lydia!" He tore the parchment into tiny pieces until every word was indistinguishable. "So says the king." A final scrap fluttered from his fingertips to the floor.

Every eye had turned to them.

Esther elbowed him in the gut.

Petra shook his head, spreading his feet wide as he settled back against the wall. "No, good sirs, I wouldn't do that. In a moment we will all have the opportunity to be out of this cage. If you want to get back to the sunshine, keep your hands to yourself."

"Oh, no," the guard, affectionately known as Denny, said, "you won't be. You notice the locks?"

"I did see you've upgraded since last I was in town."

"Should've hung you three times over, boy," the other guard said, bored still.

Petra smiled.

"Nigh unpickable, they are! Even for your thievin' little fingers." Denny nodded. "Like to see you get out of this trap."

Petra's smile only grew.

"I'm getting tired of the city leader's order though. Look how crowded the cell is getting with this 'no killing without a trial' nonsense. It's just his way of getting power separate from the king."

"I know, I know," sighed his companion, leaning back on his stool to fold his arms and stare at the gray ceiling.

"I'm only sayin—"

"The same thing every day. And if you can't complain about the city leader, it's the crowds on the street, or your woman goin' mad on you. It's exhausting."

"Fine, maybe I should just keep my mouth shut around you, eh?" the guard glared at his companion, tucking himself into a corner.

Petra began to whistle, a slow high-pitched tune that set everyone's teeth on edge. A dog barked outside, probably driven mad by Petra's chirping air.

"Shut it," Lenny growled, pinning his palms over his ears. "Boy, hold your bleeding noise."

"Ho, look!" the other guard said, "Out there. Is that smoke?"

Lenny jumped to his feet. "Bleedin' glory, you left the lantern out near the hay. It tipped over! Come on!"

"I'm sure I didn't!" the other said. "You don't think?" He tossed his chin toward Petra.

"Did he start it with his mind somehow while he's been here locked away?" Lenny said, already almost out the door. "And what does it matter? A fire is burning, and we need to put it out."

Denny paused, tugging on the lock to assure himself it was secure before stomping outside.

Petra counted moments on slow ticking fingers. He pierced the air with another whistle. A patchy black and white face appeared at the doorway, its floppy ears held back from its panting jaw.

"There's a good boy," Petra said, moving to the lock. The men craned their neck to see what he would do. "Nigh unpickable, huh? Time to find out." Petra dug through the dog's fur hanging down from its belly, revealing a harness strapped to its chest. He pulled a pouch of tools from the harness and set to work on the lock. After a few moments of his tools scraping gently in the mechanism, Petra leaned back. "Well, they bleeding did it," he said, shaking his head. "Time for the brute force method. A hand, one of you?"

No one moved.

Petra sighed. In the buckles of the harness was a double-handled tool with a metal claw at the end. He gripped the lock with it, extending his hand as far back as possible.

"Keep your nose out of it," Petra warned the dog. He blew a quick note and the dog looped around, settling on the floor to watch its master work. Petra slipped a string off his neck, a small fabric pouch hanging from the end.

Abner stood to see better. "What is that?"

Petra poured some fine, gray powder from the pouch onto the ground.

"You'd think they would've started checking you over before locking you up," said a black-bearded prisoner.

"Don't go giving them ideas," Petra smiled. "I need cloth of some kind. Anything."

"Bleed me dry," muttered the black beard, ripping off a strip from his long sleeve.

"My thanks," Petra said. He spit into the cloth before smearing it in a careful circle through the gray grains on the floor. Petra lifted it to the lock.

At first nothing happened.

He repeated the motion a few more times, gently massaging it into the metal.

Hiss.

"And now I should be able to—" Petra grunted, pulling at the long-handled tool. Abner lent an unbandaged hand to help. "Pull!" The bar securing the lock broke and the two men fell to the floor.

The cell went quiet.

The six other prisoners charged out of the cage and through the door to freedom.

Petra dusted his breeches, retrieved the lock from the ground, and called his dog to his side.

Smoke curled through the hazy air.

Esther pushed herself to her feet, her mouth flattening into an unbreakable line. *I am not useless.* She shuffled forward, out of the cell.

Abner glared at her. "This is a waste of time." He scooped her up, forcing her back to curve and her corset to bend, pinching the soft skin of her stomach.

A grunt escaped her lips.

"I assume the door is the only way out?" Abner's eyes fixed on the thickening fog of smoke.

Petra tipped his chin, fitting the tool back into the harness. "All of those men are running right into a swarming hive of soldiers. We'll be going out the back." He led them out of the room into the long narrow entryway. Turning his back to the open door, Petra got on his knees to push aside a wooden crate large enough to sit on, with a round hole carved in the top.

A knee height window was revealed. The vague unpleasant smell became rancid, stinging, unbearable as it spilled through the hole in the wall.

"Let's go." Petra nodded them forward.

The dog slipped out into the late sunshine.

"Ugh..." Abner's nose wrinkled as he tightened his grip on Esther. "What is it?"

"Don't you dare put me in there," Esther spoke in a deadly whisper, every muscle tensed.

"I think Denny's meal had an argument with him on the way out. Now come on, there isn't much time." Petra bent at his waist, gathering the loose folds of his cloak into his fists, and disappeared through the opening. "Mind you don't slip."

"Hold your breath." Abner took a deep breath of his own.

"Don't—"

He tossed her through. Petra caught her a moment after her backside was enveloped into the squelching, sticky brown mess.

The smell burned her throat and Esther struggled to blink away its sting as Petra pulled her to her feet. She retreated a few stumbles to rip some long fern leaves growing out of a wide bucket. Esther swiped as much of the muck from the back of her dress as she could reach.

Abner swallowed his groan of disgust as his boots sank into the muck.

The dog trotted to Esther's side and sniffed the stained fabric, sneezing into it before knocking her hand with its wet nose. Her fingers folded into the shaggy fur, smiling at its amber eyes.

I've missed this.

"We have one stop to make, then I suggest we leave town." Petra stretched to drag the box back into place, blocking the hole.

"You're coming with us?" Abner yanked his feet free of the muck.

"Course," smiled Petra. "I won't be able to run my usual tracks here for a while after this mess. I've just the place for us all to drop out of sight. Besides," the dog loped to his side as Petra began walking, nose stuck to his hand, "anyone who causes this much trouble to our dearly beloved king is a man worth helping."

The ache echoed from her hips to her heels, but Esther kept it from showing as she marched after Petra around the back of a long line of buildings. "Where are we going?"

"I can't afford to leave this town empty-handed," Petra paused before reentering the crowded cobbled street. "And I won't be leaving without Penny."

Petra slipped his hood over his head, Abner following suit with his peasant's cloak. Esther rearranged her drape to cover her hair, pushing down the urge to cover her face as well. She kept a sharp eye bouncing over the crowds for Cantus or Ava. They were nowhere to be found. The smoke billowing into a storming gray tower above the prison had drawn most of the city guards from the streets, so their progress to an old storage shed was uneventful. The thin metal walls were peppered with flaking red dust and it leaned a little to one side. Petra paused at a back corner that peeled away from the neighboring wall like old parchment. Gripping the ripped metal, he tugged. A thin crack that ran to the top of the shed opened a door in the wall and Petra ushered them inside with a hasty wave.

"The owner of the inn I've been staying with has sticky fingers." Petra picked his way through the mounds of items before them. "Besides, you don't always know when something will be useful. Best to take what you can."

Esther trailed after the dog, whose paws clicked a snaking path through the piles. Petra seemed to have every item and teetering stack memorized as his hands stuffed the rough sewn pockets stitched inside his cloak full.

"Here we are," Petra said, slipping a long bladed dagger into his belt. Last, he slung a scabbard with a large jutting wood piece over his back.

Abner paused in his fingering of a heavy golden bracelet to cock his head at Petra. "You know you can't draw out a sword like that. Your arm's not long enough and you'll cut off your head trying to get it back in."

"Can't I?" said Petra, bending down to pick up a few coins that had fallen out of their pile, and replacing them gingerly on top. As he rose, his hand grabbed the hilt over his shoulder. He whipped the blade out, swiping the air. Abner's eyes looked ready to roll from his head.

"What is—what is this magic?" Abner studied the scabbard.

"There's an opening at the side, so you draw it half-way and then tilt it out." Petra demonstrated slipping it back into the scabbard with an easy hand, using the jutting wooden board as a guide. He grinned at Abner's open mouth and wide eyes.

Esther buried her pain in irritation. "Fascinating really. But shouldn't we—"

"I've never seen anything like it! I want one. I need it! All the walking and riding we do. It'd be perfect! Where can I get one?"

Petra laughed, shaking his head. "Not from Naamah. It came in on a caravan from the north. I think I have the only one in Alberon."

"I'll buy it from you. Just—" Abner's hand drifted to his empty belt. He cursed. "I'd forgotten."

"You'll get used to that. But you couldn't convince me to part with this, not for a thousand crowns. It's helpful, looks amazing, and is out of the way when my hands are busy."

"All of this can be said later!" The pressure in her back was building and, although she had been able to shuffle beside Abner through the crowd, they had no idea where Cantus and Ava were. She had no certainty when relief would come. This intensified the pain, making it unbearable.

"She doesn't understand." Abner blew out a slow breath as his fingers traced the scabbard.

"All the same, we should go before the fire's properly taken care of and the guards return to their usual patrols." Petra blew a short breathy whistle, calling the dog to his side before pushing open the wall to let them back out onto the street.

Abner followed, eyes still on the scabbard hanging off Petra's back.

"Alright, so where's Penny? Will she be hard to find?" Esther asked as Petra replaced the wall.

Petra's chin tipped. "Where's Penny?" He lifted his cloak, hanging heavy off his shoulder with hidden treasures. "Got her right here, lovely."

"The knife?" Esther said, raising her brow.

"He's attached, although I don't know why." Abner said.

Petra smirked, resuming a place in the crowd. Abner and Esther followed. At their request, Petra altered his route to take them past the stables. Of the three, Esther seemed the least likely to stir up trouble by being recognized, so she went in to see if Cantus and Ava were waiting for them there. The stall was empty, their packs were gone. Esther returned to the men waiting outside.

"That's good. They probably got out and are waiting for you somewhere." Petra pulled a yellowed bone from one pocket in his cloak, lowering it to tease the dog.

The animal bounced around him, chasing it.

"Let's see if we can find them outside the city."

"And if we can't?" Esther challenged. "Do we come back for them?"

"I think," Abner glanced at Petra who was laughing at the dog's antics too much to listen to him. He dropped his voice lower, "we decide that when the time comes."

"I'm not leaving Ava," Esther declared, raising her chin.

"You say that now. But did you plan on leaving—"

"Don't." Esther's voice lashed the air like a whip.

"I just—"

"Shut it!"

"You don't know till the moment. That's all I'm saying!"

"Ready then?" Petra called, voice bright and cheeks pink from running circles in the heat.

Abner raised his brow at Esther.

She set her jaw. "Ready," she said, and followed the two men toward the city gate.

The guard held the crowd waiting to leave Naamah with glaring scrutiny. The people were funneled into a slow trickle.

Esther's eyes darted as each pull of breath became harder.

Abner lifted his chin, hazarding a glance over their heads. He ducked down, a muscle popping in his jaw. "They're checking under cloaks and have parchment in their hands. I think they're looking for me."

"Which means we'll just have to be a little more clever." Petra slipped from the line. Abner and Esther followed him around the back of some small huts. Petra began ripping strips of white bandage with his teeth, stomping them into the dirt until they were coated with grime and red dust. He picked up his wadded bundle. "Beautiful. Now, tie this around your eye."

Abner pinched the stained fabric. He blew some of the dust off before gingerly wrapping it around his head several times.

Petra helped to cover every bit of Abner's exposed skin on his hands, neck, and cheek with the dirty bandages.

Abner coughed. "I don't see how covering me in mud helps us."

"Wish I had some blood to smear but—ah—no one checks over these people too carefully." Petra tied a last clean strip of cloth around his upper arm.

"What are you talking about?" Esther glanced between them as Abner's single visible eye lit. "Who?"

"Just go ahead of us out the gate. You should be fine. No one's looking for you." Petra nodded.

"I don't—"

Abner sighed and pushed her out of the shadowed cover of the building.

A whistle sent the dog pelting toward the gate, gone before the guard had properly noticed he was there.

Esther shook as she waded through the queue, but the guard's eyes rolled past her, oblivious to anyone but the prey he hunted.

Abner blinked against the mud clod sitting on his eyelid.

"Make way!" Petra's voice rang out. "Make way for the sick!" He led Abner forward by the arm.

The crowd parted, some tripping over themselves to give the pair a wider berth.

"Make way!" Petra said again, splitting the crowd still further.

The guard's eyes narrowed. "Healer," he said, glancing over the torn bandage fluttering from Petra's arm. "What is this?"

"Eastern sickness. Have to get this poor wretch away from the healthy as fast as we can."

"I didn't know the eastern sickness was here," the guard said, his features pulling wide. "He doesn't look sick."

"Back!" commanded Petra. "A single cough can share it."

Abner coughed, drawing a frightened gasp from the crowd.

The guard stumbled back, covering the lower half of his face with his arm. "Be off with you! Take that disease out of here!"

"Come on, Henry, there's a fellow." Petra patted Abner's dirty tunic as they passed through the gate.

"I think we're far enough now," Abner said, ripping himself free of the dirty strips of cloth.

The dog reappeared at Petra's side, panting past its lolling tongue.

The air beyond the crushing press of Naamah's crowded streets was fresh and crisp. Abner filled his lungs with it as a man dying of thirst would drink from a mountain spring. Leaves crunched beneath his dust-coated boots as Esther joined them on the road.

Petra glanced back, a smile twisting across his face. "I am honestly surprised we still have all our limbs." He nodded at Tessa. "I didn't have time before, but I'm Petra."

"Ah—T-Tessa."

"I'm sorry?" Petra said, leaning forward with a hand to his ear. "What was it?"

"Tessa, my name's Tessa."

"Well, a pleasure to meet you Tessa. Glad I could help you not die today."

Her brow pulled together, turning from Petra's smiling face.

"He takes some getting used to," Abner said, "but he's useful."

"Oh such flattery," Petra dipped his head. He laughed to himself, drawing a small smile from her.

The smoke from a fire, curling up between a group of trees, made the camp easy for Esther to find. Ava sat next to the rock-lined pit, holding her forehead in her hands, while Cantus stood close by. At the sound of Esther's call, Ava popped to her feet and enclosed her friend in a fierce hug.

Petra strode into the firelight. "Hello, I am Petra." He extended an arm. "I saved your friends' lives today."

Ava jumped back. She drew a breath, hand clutching her chest. Her eyes dropped to the ground. "Aw, you have a dog?" she said, bending low with a hand extended toward it. The dog's tail swept the air as it trotted forward to have its fur ruffled and its ears scratched. "What's her name?"

"His name is Lord Emperor Josias Hildefount the third. But I just call him Joss."

Ava smiled, taking Joss' face in either hand to stare at his black and white patched fur. "Well, I think you're just lovely, Joss."

Petra's eyes flickered over Ava as she sat before the dog and rubbed her hands through the dog's fur. "I think he likes you, too."

"I'm sorry but, who are you?" Cantus crossed his arms and pulled his chin up high.

"Petra," Petra said.

The soldier shrugged his shoulders.

"I'm a thief."

"But a useful one," Abner stepped forward as Cantus' mouth tightened. "He's helped several times today. He's worth keeping around."

"You can't just decide to bring people in, Abner. We don't know if we can trust him."

Abner's jaw clenched, popping a hard muscle to the surface. "Of all people, Cantus, you should not talk about being careful."

Cantus leaned back.

"We were taken in right after you blathered to some old man about how the king is evil. You don't think those are connected?"

"I think more likely they were searching for you because your face was plastered in every other shop along the main road." Cantus reached behind the stump he had been sitting on and pulled up the parchment with Abner's portrait. "We found that when we ducked into a shop to get out of sight of the guard."

"You need to watch your words," Abner spat.

Cantus blew a breath through flared nostrils. "I didn't say the king was evil. I said he wasn't serving the people."

"In commoners' minds that's the same thing!"

Petra extended a hand. "May I?"

"No!" both men shouted.

Petra shrugged, sitting on the ground next to Joss. He took out the unpickable lock from the prison and began running his fingers over the mechanisms, pulling the tools from his boot to poke at it.

Ava's hand rolled over the dog's ears, her eyes watching the arguing men.

Esther shook her head, resolved to ignore their bickering and went to sit near the fire.

"What are we doing here, Abner?" Cantus demanded, throwing out a hand. "What exactly is the plan as we wander through the kingdom?"

"What are you talking about? We escaped. We are surviving. That's the goal."

"That's not good enough!" Cantus snapped. "You need a plan!"

"Why? Why do I need a plan? Why is it me that has to come up with one?"

"Because you're the bleeding prince!"

"Not anymore!" Abner's hand cut the air, drawing Esther's eyes back to him. "I'm Abner of Lydia," he said, staring down at the parchment, one eye twitching as he grimaced. "I'm no one's son. I'm not the prince. I don't need anyone looking to me for anything. Least of all a plan."

Cantus rubbed at his jaw. "What about—"

"Cantus, if you say one more word about dragons—" Esther broke a twig against the dirt at her feet.

"I know you don't believe me, but I found a dragon tooth just like in the old rhyme. It had to come from somewhere."

Petra cursed quietly, the tool slipping in the mechanism.

"It doesn't matter if you found a dragon tooth," Esther said. "You both looked for news of them for weeks and found nothing. There *is* nothing because they aren't real. At least not anymore."

"Maybe if we—"

Ava rose from the dog. "Let's just leave it for tonight. Have you three eaten?"

Petra looked up. "I can always eat."

Abner tossed his chin. "I'm not hungry." He stomped out of the ring of firelight to stand by the horses.

Cantus returned to his stump.

Esther watched Abner's back rise and fall as he put a forehead to the horse's neck, while Petra's voice seemed to soften and fade away.

"Tessa?" Ava touched her arm. "Can I fix you something?"

Esther stood to brush herself off. A pulse beat through her hips. "Actually Ava, could we put on the new string? My back's—"

"Oh," Ava's cheeks colored. "Of course! Why didn't I think to do that earlier? Come on, we'll go over here."

"New string? I thought—" Petra said, sighing weakly. "But ... food." He glanced at Cantus.

The soldier continued his study of the fire.

Petra shrugged a shoulder, picking at the lock in his hand. "Come on, open, you bleeding little—"

XXII

Esther tore the long-bladed yellow grass into thin strips.

"Watch it, not too much pressure," Petra said.

Ava pulled her lip between her teeth.

Click.

The lock bar snapped up.

"Ho ho!" Petra clapped his hands together, as pleased as Ava at her success. "We'll make a thief out of you in no time."

"So I am now a master at lockpicking—"

"Obviously."

Ava laughed, curls bouncing against her cheek. "What else is there to learn?"

Petra lifted a shoulder. "The pressure check, feeling out your next target, basics of picking pockets, the switch, I could go on."

"Oh, please do, wise master."

Petra's brow rose, his smile doubling in size.

Ava tipped her chin, reset the lock, and went back to work. A grin broke through her look of intense concentration.

Yesterday's argument still rang loudly in the back of Esther's mind. There was a tension between Abner, Cantus, and her that seemed as if it would continue as a heavy weight forever.

At least Ava was able to find something to amuse herself with.

Petra did not seem to mind the interruption as the unpickable lock sat forgotten next to him while he watched her practice on the simple one.

Joss sat panting at Petra's feet. His eyes met Esther's, and he pulled himself up to pad over to her, looking for a belly rub.

With a smile, Esther's hands scratched through the deep fur, her fingers knocking against the harness. She thought about slipping it off the dog, but it was wound and threaded into intricate knots. It would take a week for her fingers to pick apart. She scratched down Joss' sides.

The dog's tongue lolled out as he stretched for Esther's hands to sort out every itch, smiling at the sky.

Abner had left camp as soon as it was raised, promising to be back before dark. He hadn't bothered to saddle the horse, his leg fitting seamlessly along the slick coat with every muscle held in perfect balance and precision. The beast had carried him out of sight.

Maybe Abner is a rotten teacher, but he does know how to ride. Next time he decides to teach me, I should listen.

Cantus was sharpening his new sword, every giggle from Ava sending his shoulders jumping up toward his ears. The scrape of his whet stone paused. The soldier stared across the grassy plain beneath the gray, darkening sky. There were no trees for shelter tonight, but Petra assured them tomorrow would be different. "Abner should be back by now."

Esther's fingers slowed so her ears could listen.

Joss resettled near Petra.

The rustle of wind. Grass bugs buzzing. She closed her eyes, pushing herself to hear farther. *A bird calling to its mate.* Esther sighed, leaning back against the new strings of the corset. "I'm sure he'll be fine."

"He should know better than to go off on his own."

Abner returned after the sky had filled with purple ink. The hoof beats on the grass drew Cantus and Esther's eyes with begrudging gratitude. He slipped down the horse's side, its coat wet with sweat, and tied it to the stake thrust in the ground. Rubbing the sweat marks off with the corner of one sleeve, Abner thumped the horse's neck before turning to the waiting group.

He tossed a stick to Cantus.

The soldier caught it in the air, putting aside his blade to roll the wood between his fingers. "What is this?"

Abner set his feet at the edge of the firelight, raising the other broken branch. "Let's sort this out like men."

"Abner," Cantus shook his head, "me beating you over the head with a piece of wood won't change anything."

"But won't it feel good?" Abner said, raising an eyebrow. He poked Cantus hard in the shoulder. "On your feet."

Cantus shook his head again, rubbing his thumb along the stick's blunted end.

"No, I don't believe you!" Ava laughed behind them.

"What, you don't think I could do it?" Petra said.

"I don't think you can touch someone without them noticing, no. I would notice if I was touched."

"Really?" Petra's smile stretched his tone. "I've been meaning to ask when you wanted this back."

Ava gasped. "No! When did you? That's my bracelet!"

"I've had it most of the day," Petra said. "And you did not notice the touch."

"Okay," Ava slipped the bracelet back on her wrist. "Do it again. I want to see."

Petra sighed. "The technique relies on ... distraction."

Ava raised her chin. "Then distract me."

Cantus' stick whipped through the air and collided with Abner's. The *crack* echoed.

Ava gasped.

Smiling, Petra slipped the bracelet back into her palm.

"Not fair," she swatted his shoulder, "I was—"

"Distracted?"

The wood seemed ready to split apart with each strike echoing through the camp.

Abner's face twisted. He met blow after blow from the soldier, letting Cantus work out through his muscles whatever tension he was carrying in his mind.

When Abner's stick finally did break, bursting apart in his hand through a seam in the middle, Cantus reeled himself back, working to calm his breathing.

Esther had gotten a little lost in the spectacle, never seeing Cantus use the unbridled power of his arms before.

"I don't have a plan," Abner massaged his wrist that had taken the beating. "I don't want to just take my father's power and continue in the same legacy of blood. I don't want to be him. If you have any other way, I'll listen. But I'm—"

"In this case," Cantus said through a heavy breath, dropping his stick, "no action is the same as evil action."

"Why now, why me?"

"Because it's not enough to just save ourselves, we need—"

"There has to be some other way—someone different who hasn't—"

"You *are* different since we left the castle. Don't mistake me, you're still an ass, but you're less of a royal one."

"What about all the years that you were a soldier? Why is it now that we must act or we're evil, like my father?"

"Because this is the moment a stand to change things might actually work."

"You have more confidence in the swordsmanship of peasants than I do, Cantus." Abner folded his arms. "I've been in a few fights since we left the castle. They'd be slaughtered."

"So we teach them."

Abner threw his hand out. "Like we're teaching Tessa? Who, no offense to her, is not ready to face even my father's slowest soldier."

"Why would I not be offended at that?" said Esther.

"She's not being taught to take on soldiers, but to stop them from killing her so easily until we can step in. Besides, she's injured, and so are you. None of us are at our best right now, but it's the only chance that's come in ten years to fix what your father broke when he took power."

Abner shook his head. "A civil war would destroy more lives than it would save. Let's not die for the privilege of causing the world to burn."

"How much of this is concern for the people and how much is your own selfishness?" Cantus folded his arms. "I think you enjoy playing at the simple life. I think you'd like to just disappear forever and abandon your people to whatever fate the king decides for them."

A muscle popped in Abner's jaw.

Esther came between them. "We know where we're going tomorrow, don't we? That's enough for now."

Both men shrugged.

Though no decision was made, the tension was lifted. They left the sticks on the edge of the firelight, no longer needing them.

Abner lay stretched out on the far side of the fire as Cantus poked at the ashy embers. The girls had linked arms and disappeared into the tent as the night turned cold, with Cantus sitting guard at the entrance.

Petra didn't seem to notice the soldier's dark glare. "I think I've changed my mind," he declared, folding his legs in front of him. His tools picked at the unpickable. "About our destination tomorrow."

Abner and Cantus stiffened. "I thought you had a safe house that we could use in some town to the south," Abner said.

"I do. But safe is, well, a relative word."

Cantus' fist tightened. "Are you trying to trick us, Thief?"

Petra deepened his voice, "Easy soldier." He gave a little laugh that no one shared and then sighed. "This is a *safer* house. The way you two talk, I only heard pieces, but you need all the help you can get. Besides," his eyes shifted away from Cantus to something behind, "I'm beginning to care for all of you." He grinned at Abner, "You bunch of adorable, scruffy-faced traitors!"

Abner touched his jaw, the stubbly hairs scratching his fingers.

"And I believe it was Abner who was supposed to have the watch tonight? Cause I've had ... quite the day." Petra smiled as he laid down, rolling the lock between his fingers. Joss burrowed himself into the boy's side.

Abner nodded to Cantus. "You can sleep. I won't be drifting off again."

"It's fine," Cantus said, pulling a knee up to rest his elbow on. His eyes narrowed.

Abner studied the ash heap by his feet. "You actually think I'm different from who I was at the castle?"

"Well, you haven't gotten drunk and demanded I lick your boot, so yes, I'd say you're behaving differently. Tessa's still unspoiled, which is—" Cantus massaged his thumb into his hand, staring at that rather than Abner. "Why is that?"

Abner drew in a quick breath. "So Elena…"

Cantus groaned.

"Did you leave her 'unspoiled'?"

Cantus chuckled, shaking his head, "I'm not talking about Elena with you, Abner."

"Well, I at least deserve some credit for remembering her name."

"It shouldn't be, but for you, yes," Cantus nodded, "well done." The silence deepened until Cantus yawned. He watched Petra breathe deep and slow. "Wake me if you need to," he said, laying down and letting himself drift off.

Abner studied his hands. No flash of blood dripping from his fingers, no weight of guilt dragging him by the throat. *Different.*

They set off early the next morning, the camp taking very little time to pack together with five of them doing the work.

"I've been meaning to ask," Petra said, leaning around Abner's shoulder after a long while of riding in silence. "Why are we only going at a walk?"

"Tessa is still learning how to ride, so we have to go slow."

"Alright ... but I know how to ride. Can't the girls ride behind us? Abner and Tessa, me and—"

"No," Cantus said, pulling his elbow back to cover Ava.

"Fine, fine." Petra raised both hands. "But the point still stands."

"What about Joss?" Ava asked. "He can't ride with us."

"Oh, Joss can keep up to these old nags, trust me."

"Old nags?" Abner scoffed. "You honestly think that dog could outpace a horse?"

Petra slipped off the horse's back, walking beside it. "I think he could run circles around this one."

"That's not a challenge," said Tessa, leaning forward to fix Abner in a hardened stare.

"It kind of is," Petra said.

"Tessa, climb on." Abner pulled his reins short, Tessa's horse stopping with him.

"I am not going to race the dog with you," Tessa said, shaking her head.

"I'll let you ride alone." Petra nodded. "I think that's only fair. A horse with two people and packs would be too easy of a victory. Hardly worth gloating over."

Abner tried to pull the grin down from his cheeks, but it hung like a banner across his face announcing his delight.

Petra mounted Tessa's horse and galloped across the plain. Ava slipped down to hold Joss back from following. The dog whined and tossed his head.

"Just a moment now, Joss." Ava said, rubbing his ear.

Petra rolled two large rocks into place as markers for the finish.

"Ready?" Petra called, his voice dimmed by distance.

Abner threw his chin.

Cantus' horse pranced as he pulled it to one side, the animal snorting and tossing its mane at the shifting energy.

A whistle cut through the air and Abner surged forward.

Ava let go of Joss.

The thudding hooves beating the grass made Abner draw his breath in rapid gasps. Energy singed his fingertips, and he couldn't stop the laugh dribbling over his lips.

Joss appeared at the horse's shoulder. The dog streaked through the grass like a bolt from a bow, ears flat to his skull.

Abner rose over the horse's neck, urging it forward with his ankles pressed to its sides. The rocks were close now, Abner just had to maintain his lead a little while longer.

Joss wasn't slowing. Petra used a steady trill of whistles to call him on.

"Yes Joss! That's my boy!" Petra gripped the dog hopping in his lap. "Fastest in the land!"

Abner pulled his horse back to slow him gently. He trotted to Petra with his smile intact. "Horses have better endurance, so with a longer track I think we'd—"

"Just accept the loss, Prince," laughed Petra, rubbing the fur around Joss' jaw. The dog panted and leaned into Petra's hands, smiling at the attention.

"I'm just saying we're not done with you. Or that mutt," Abner said, patting his horse's neck.

"Bring the next challenge whenever you want."

Abner turned back to the others, all cheering for the dog. For once, he didn't mind. When they were all together again, Abner held an arm out to Tessa.

"Come on."

"I thought I was—"

"The boy's right. We can go much faster this way." Her hand gripped his arm to swing herself up over the horse's hips. Ava was perched behind Cantus and Petra brought his horse next to Abner's.

"You'll need to wrap your legs around the horse," Cantus said over his shoulder.

"What?" Ava's cheeks bloomed pink, her eyes snapping wide.

"Sitting with knees together might be proper, but, untrained and riding fast, it'll get you killed." He extended his arm to help her adjust herself.

Petra's averted gaze was noticeable as she positioned her skirt into place over her knees.

Abner smiled at Tessa's feather-light touch on his shoulders. Reaching behind, he pulled her arm around his chest. Her other followed so she could grip her hands together. His thoughts raced to things that made his smile change its tone, but he worked to keep it from his face as the three horses began to move forward, gradually picking up speed.

The five companions crossed the plain to the last collection of buildings before the forest's edge during the morning ride. Abner's stomach began to plead for a pause to eat when a wooden building loomed above them, surrounded by a brick wall with a wide gate blocking off the entrance. Farms with their adjoining fields lay scattered about in no reasonable order behind them.

"What is this place?" Tessa asked as Petra pulled his horse to a snorting stop.

He slipped down the horse's side and ran a hand along the wooden gate. "This is home."

Petra banged his fist on the door, smiling at the call from within, "Just a moment, love! Oh, Darby, put that down!"

They all dismounted.

"I almost forgot," he said, whipping around to face them. "Spice trade, I—"

The heavy door creaked open, revealing a plump face, red with exertion. "Petra, my love!" She pulled him to her chest, smiling eyes closed as she ran a hand over his hair. "I wondered when you'd be coming back to us." She released him.

"I'm sorry, Mother," Petra said, "the *spice trade* keeps me busy this time of year."

"Ah, I've always known not to keep the leash on you too short, love. And, you brought friends?"

Two small faces peeked around the woman's skirt.

"Petra! Petra's home!" the little girl said, twin braids flopping against her back as she bounded to hug him around the middle.

"Come here, Joss!" the boy said, tapping his knees.

The dog stepped forward to lick his ears.

"Grrr," the boy growled playfully, ruffling the dog's fur.

Joss barked, dancing around him.

"Come on, boy!" he said, slipping around the large woman's skirt.

"Go on, Joss. Go play." Petra whistled and the dog darted through the door.

"Well, I hope your friends will tell me all about themselves at the midmark meal. Cooky and I were just finishing up."

"I'll give you a hand, if you'd like," Ava said, stepping forward.

"Well, that'd be just fine. Come on inside, love."

Ava smirked at Petra as his mother slung an arm around her shoulders and led her through the gate. Petra smiled as he gestured for Cantus, Tessa, and Abner to follow.

The building was tall, brick walls running out from its sides to circle a wide, garden-bordered lawn. Children chased each other across the short green grass. A crowd of eager little faces formed around Petra. The buzz of bees filled the air, a breeze carrying the scent of flowers past them, and Abner's shoulders slipped lower through a sigh as he tied up the horses with enough line to graze on the lush lawn.

"Tell us a story, Petra!" the girl with the braids said, pulling at his hand.

A clay pot smashed on the ground.

The mother's yell echoed from within the house. "Oh, not again! How many times do I have to buy—"

"Darby, come hear the story," Petra called, waving him forward. The boy pelted to Petra's side, putting as much distance between him and the remains of the pot as he could. "It's alright, Mother!" Petra waved to her standing in the doorway.

"Darby," she wagged a finger at him. "How many fortunes have I spent replacing what your curious little fingers break?"

"That's why you keep me around," Petra said.

The old woman threw up her hands and disappeared inside. Darby stuck himself to Petra's elbow as the thief plopped down on the grass, slipping the scabbard from his back.

"Now what shall it be? A passionate romance?"

The boys in the group grunted, one sticking out his tongue.

"No?" Petra smiled, fiddling with a piece of grass before plucking it from the ground. "How about, *The Demon From The Northern Waste?*"

Cantus held up his hands. "Anything but that one. Please."

Petra's grin stretched so wide his face looked in danger of cracking. "Now I have to tell it."

Cantus stomped away, covering his ears as Petra began:

> *No one knows when the demon comes,*
> *Or why he feasts on children's blood,*
> *How he slips through open windows,*
> *To steal their breath from their pillows.*

The familiar rhyme washed over Abner's ears, and he smirked at the memories it stirred.

Tessa left to join Cantus by the flowering trees.

Petra punctuated his words with jabs at the children, clawed hands tickling their bellies as they rolled in giggling fits. Before the rhyme was done, the food was ready.

It took some time to corral the children onto the blankets spread over the lawn, but with the revealing of the baked pastries they all found a place to sit and enjoy them.

"I made this one," Ava said, plucking the fruit-layered bread from the top of one pile. She put it in Petra's waiting hand.

"Hm," Petra said, examining it with an eyebrow raised. "I'm not sure."

"Go on and eat it." Ava nudged his arm.

Petra pinned a corner between his teeth, but couldn't stifle the small groan of pleasure as he popped the rest into his mouth.

"Don't choke on it," Ava laughed.

"Does it bother you," Cantus muttered to Tessa, too quiet to be heard by any beyond Abner, "that the thief has stolen your friend?"

Tessa looked at Ava, whose smile stretched wide despite her jaw working through a pastry. "She's not gone, just shared."

Cantus grunted.

"Who are you?" the girl with the braids said, coming to sit on her knees in front of Cantus. "You're big."

Cantus pushed his face into a smile. "You think so?"

"Mhm!" the girl nodded her chin vigorously. "As tall as a house. Well, not my house, cause mine is big."

"I don't..."

"Hannah, let the man eat in peace," said Petra.

"I once saw a house that was green!" Hannah giggled, her braid rolling over her shoulder.

"Really? Why was it green?"

"I don't know, I guess they really liked green. But I like..." her face twisted, the question of her favorite color of sudden vital importance, "red. I like red." She bounced happily.

"Red is ... good?"

"Blue's better!" said a boy behind her.

She thrust her chin out as she spun to face him. "Red!"

"Blue!"

"Red!"

"Elijah, Hannah, enough!" called Petra's mother. "Always bickering over something with you two. Eat your food so you can get back to playing."

Abner struggled to think up a story for why the five of them were together, the truth being unacceptable to share, but the old woman never got around to asking. Scolding the children into eating, breaking up little fights, or listening to a long rambling story with the attentive ear of a mother filled the whole span of her time. When they broke apart, Abner and Tessa found themselves sitting together while the others played with the children who now used Cantus as a wall to practice climbing.

"This is ... nice." Abner said, breaking the silence between them.

"It's peace," Tessa agreed.

Abner laughed as two boys screamed past, racing after a third who had a shiny rock held in his fist. "Despite the children."

"No arguing, Darby. You're going to help me with the washing up and give Cooky a break." The old woman planted her hands on her wide hips. "You need to learn to keep your fingers to yourself."

Darby, head hanging low, followed her inside.

"Is it really selfish, to want peace?" Abner asked.

"I know that you want to just," Tessa sighed, "I know you want to be Abner, the nobody from Lydia, but I don't know that the world is going to let you."

Abner's face twisted as he blew out a slow breath. "That's not what I wanted you to say."

Tessa nodded. "I know."

"I—"

Thud! Thud! Thud!

"Open!" the voice demanded from the other side of the door. "Open in the name of the king!"

XXIII

"Open in the name of the king!"

There was no time to plan. Esther sprang to her feet as the gate burst open.

Soldiers flooded into the threshold of grass, some with bows already half drawn, others gripping swords.

Abner shoved the hilt of his dagger into her hand.

"Go!" he said, pulling her shoulder behind him.

I wish I could. Her feet were frozen behind Abner, her eyes locked on the sword wielder's glinting armor. *Six swords, four bows.* A torch was passed near the archers, lighting the tips of their arrows to flame.

"To the back gate! Back gate!" called Petra. "Cantus! It's boarded up! You'll have to—"

"Come on children!" Ava tried to keep her voice calm, but it was one mark below a scream. "Come on!"

Petra sent Joss to guard the children's heels with a piercing whistle.

The commander of the soldiers, declared through the crimson cloak fastened to his shoulder, lifted his hand.

Petra reached Abner's side.

"Well, good sirs!" Petra cast his arms wide, working to calm his breathing and put on his mask of charisma. "We just had our midmark meal but there may be leftovers. Care for a bite?"

The commander's hand paused. "You have a traitor there, boy."

Petra's smirk grew as he tipped his chin. "And what an honored guest he—"

Abner pulled Petra down, smashing his face into the grass as the archers launched their arrows. They sailed through the air, all going high above the company's heads. Even Esther, still guarding her back, was able to drop to the ground in time.

"Has the aim of Alberon's army fallen that badly? Pathetic." Abner rose to his feet, Petra spitting grass beside him.

The commander smiled.

The horses screamed.

Abner kept his eyes on the soldiers, whipping his sword from its sheath, but Esther looked behind.

The garden was in flames. Passing the tongues of fire between them as if it was a dance, the flowering trees' budding branches became consumed. The spitting flames turned the lawn into a pit of smoke.

The animal part of Esther's brain darted for an escape, but the only path away from the blistering heat was blocked by swords as the archers pulled back to give the other soldiers room to advance. Two charged toward Abner, two ran at Petra, and one, with a flash of surprise clouding his eyes, set himself on her.

Esther couldn't do much to defend herself. The dagger was short, the man she faced much stronger, and each move of his blade boxed her in more against Abner's back. She whipped away from the sword slashing toward her neck.

It missed.

Abner cried out behind her. The prince thrust his opponents away, turning toward Esther's attacker. Eyes burning and shoulder dripping red, Abner knocked the soldier's blade aside and pummeled him in the nose with the hilt of his sword. The ruby on the pommel broke off and fell into the grass.

Sinking to the ground and clutching his broken nose, the soldier whimpered into his hand, spitting blood.

Abner reengaged with the two swords before him.

An archer sighted down the shaft of an arrow aimed at Abner's back.

He's—"Look out!" Esther hurled the dagger like a rock at the archer. It thunked off his forehead and he fell back unconscious.

"Flank!" Abner's eyes darted away from the vanquished threat.

"No idea—" Petra beat back one swordsman, "—what that—" he pushed his knife into the arm of another, "—means!"

"Watch your side!" Abner shouted, driving his sword through an opening in one man's armor. He kicked him off the blade.

Petra threw himself on the ground, the arrow meant for him knocking the soldier with the knife in his arm backward. The thief breathed into the dirt before getting hauled to his feet by the other soldier.

Esther darted to retrieve her dagger.

"We need to—"

"PETRA!" screamed a voice from above. The young boy's cry filled the air. "I want out! Petra, get me out!"

"Darby, get away from there! It's not safe!"

Darby's tear-streaked face, twisted in terror, leaned out through an upper window as flame-laced curtains burned around him.

A stone of dread settled in Esther's gut.

Petra's smirk melted away in the heat of the fire blazing up the sides of the wooden house. His rage-maddened eyes fell to the swordsman before him and the archer beyond. Moving with slashing limbs so furious that Esther's eyes couldn't keep track of them, Petra sliced open every bit of exposed skin the swordsman possessed until he fell back bleeding on the grass. The archer held his aim with a shaking fist. His shot went wide and before he could nock another, Petra buried his long sword into the archer's leather-clad chest.

"Wait! Petra!" Abner yanked his sword free from his last attacker.

Petra sprinted toward the flames, leaving his sword behind.

"Ow, ow, stop it! I don't—"

"Darby!" screamed Petra's mother, grabbing him out of sight. "Get back! It's going to—"

The building collapsed on itself. The lower level accepted the weight of the one above where Darby and Petra's mother were with a wave of sparks and heat that flung Petra onto his back.

Abner pushed Esther toward the back gate. "Let's go! Go!"

"Fire! Now!" barked the commander.

The last two archers aimed their bows. Their sight suffered from the smoke, both arrows going wide and sinking into the grass beside the prince and Esther. Abner pulled Petra up by the arm.

Petra stumbled toward the burning structure, his feet barely keeping his weight from collapsing back to the ground.

"They're gone!" Abner said, catching him by the shoulder. He dragged Petra back from the flames, roaring through the doorway. "They're gone!"

Petra rammed an elbow into Abner's gut and pushed the choking prince away. Esther darted forward, wincing at the stinging heat. Together, Abner and she dragged Petra around the side of the house.

"Get off! Darby! DARBY!"

❖ ❖ ❖

The back gate swung on one hinge. The nail-studded boards had been ripped off and were now a splintered mess scattered on the ground. Abner pushed Petra and Tessa through the gate as a roar from above announced wood falling loose from the upper story. His sleeve caught a tongue of flame as he flung himself through before the opening was buried beneath the load of burning boards. Beating his arm against his side to snuff it out before it charred his skin, Abner joined the others.

A wild neigh drew their eyes to the forest edge. Cantus waved at them as Ava stroked the horse's nose, trying to get it quiet.

"Around the side! Search for them, they can't be far now!"

Every muscle in Abner's body jumped, his eyes popping wide. He knew that voice. It was the only one in all of Alberon that robbed him of the will to fight, because he knew he would lose.

In a moment, he would come around the side of the wall and it would be over.

Snatching Tessa's hand, Abner plowed into Petra's shoulder, shoving him to the cover of the trees.

The prince ignored Cantus' nod of acknowledgment. "Where are the others?"

"Further back, with Cooky."

"And the horses?" Abner strode deeper beneath the trees.

"They bolted but I managed to get this one."

"That's a problem," Abner said. The terrain was already growing rough, boulders and trees crowding close.

"One among many. We have twenty and three children and one old cook to defend, and you're bleeding." Cantus glanced at Abner's shoulder as he shook out his arm. Blood droplets dripped to the ferns beneath their feet.

Tessa bent and ripped the fronds from the ground. "Let's not make it any easier for them to track us."

"How did they find us?" Cantus nodded toward the stream as he adjusted their course. "We were only stopped there for a mark or so."

"The king will have sent riders with my face to every town in the kingdom by now. Maybe someone saw us and found some soldiers, hoping information was enough for a reward. Ava already found us, he could do the same. To be honest ... I'm surprised we've lasted this long."

"So anywhere we go, wherever we run, you'll be marked. Bleeding—" Cantus shook his head. "He's thorough, I'll give your father that much."

Joss was stuck to Petra's hip, and the thief used his hand on the dog's head like the blind with a walking stick to navigate the forest floor as his own sightless eyes stared forward.

Ava walked slightly behind him, leading the horse. Her weak smile to Petra had been ignored.

The only thing that brought him back to life was the crowd of dirty-faced children who rushed to his side as soon as they slipped into view through the large boulders.

The horse tugged its reins out of Ava's grasp and turned to bolt at the sudden tide of little people surging forward. Abner caught hold of the animal's neck and calmed it before tying it on the far side of the narrow hollow.

A stream cut a path through the ground.

Cooky sat near it with a rag and a line of children, scrubbing at their cheeks until they shone red. At the sight of Petra, though, she dropped her rag and rushed over, bouncing in her haste. "I can't find Darby," she said, eyes wide. "Is he with you? All the rest are here."

Petra gave a barely perceptible shake of his head, his eyes shining with intention. "I'm sure he'll be along."

Cooky put a hand over her heart.

"Where is he, though?" asked a freckle-cheeked boy, tugging on Petra's cloak.

Petra paused. "He's lost. But he'll find his way home again."

"And Mother? Is she lost too?"

Cooky ran a hand over Hannah's braids, smoothing the flyaway strands flat. "Oh, dearie."

"Yes. I think she is."

"Well, you can find them, Petra!" said another boy, raising his fists. "Because you're the best hunter, brother, of all the kingdoms everywhere!"

Petra shook his head. "Alright, if Mother were here, what would she be telling you?"

"Uh," Hannah wrung her hands together as she looked up at the trees, "go play while I get some chores done?"

"Go on then," Petra nudged the freckled boy forward.

Abner and Cantus stood to one side.

"It's decent," Abner admitted, looking over the rocky terrain.

"I didn't have a map to pick a better spot from, this was the first that offered any real cover."

Abner pointed to each entrance of the rocky hollow. "Between those boulders is the way we came, then there's the river flowing in and out. I think those are few enough that we can defend them."

"Also," added Cantus, "if they find us, we'll have ways to run. Running is definitely something to consider."

Abner paused. "I've never known Dennison to leave options for running."

"Dennison?" Cantus' eyes lit, narrowing as they hardened. "Think we can win against him?"

Abner shook his head. "No. If he finds us, we're all dead."

He left Cantus to go clean his shoulder. Tessa met him at the stream. Abner allowed her to dab at the wound leaking red with the hem of her sleeve while he scrubbed out his fingers in silence.

"Are you..."

"I'm fine, it's—" Abner swallowed. "I told you that in a fair fight I've never been beaten. There's one exception to that, and that man now hunts us. I can't defeat Dennison. I had just started to hope—but, apparently too much has happened. You were right. For me, peace is something the world won't let me have. It doesn't matter—" his fingers scraped at the grime stuck beneath his nails, "I'll never be clean."

"If you don't want to be a rabbit, don't hop." Tessa bent down beside him, rinsing her sleeve.

Abner glared at her.

"What I mean is you aren't under some curse to always be a part of horrific things. Maybe you'll never get to just—I don't know—groom horses and have a quiet life in some village somewhere, but you don't ever have to go back to who you were."

Abner didn't know what to say, so he scooped a handful of biting cold water and splashed Tessa in the face.

She turned to him with half her hair dripping wet and sticking to her forehead, her eyes shining with mirthful rage over smiling lips.

Berries gathered and approved by Tessa and small slices of cheese from the packs on the horse served as their meal.

"Now, what story tonight?" Petra's smile strained to lift his cheeks. The children were gathered around him, one sitting on his lap, all eager eyes watching. "How about The Mountain Song?"

"That one's boring," complained a boy, tugging at his ear.

"Nuh-uh!" said Hannah. "It has dragons! And magic!"

"Bor-ring!" insisted the boy.

"You know, it's late. Let's all get some sleep now and have a story in the morning," Petra said, knocking Hannah gently on the cheek with his knuckle.

"Shouldn't we stay up and wait for Mother?" yawned the freckle-cheeked boy.

"I miss Mother!" said one girl, crossing her arms over her chest.

"Hush now, dearie." Cooky pulled the girl onto her lap.

Petra's eyes fell. Penny winked at him in the grass through the grime of battle still crusted across her blade. "I forgot to clean this," he said, standing. Cooky and he shared a shining-eyed stare before he sucked in a breath and turned away.

Abner shifted, remembering how it felt standing over the water barrel after Shiloh trying to scrape his own shaking hands clean.

Ava rose and drifted to where Petra sat scrubbing the blade at the narrow channel the river cut as it entered the hollow.

Abner strained to hear through the children's chatter.

"Are you alright?" Ava knelt next to him, gently touching his arm to still his hands.

Petra's breath rattled through his shoulders. He nodded, turning to her with a smile.

"I'm so sorry."

His smile faltered, and, after a moment, was too much effort to prop up as tears leaked out of his eyes.

Ava took his face into her hands as it crumpled.

He shook his head. "I couldn't do anything," he whispered against her palms.

Ava pulled him forward, clutching him to her chest. Her breath shook. "You're alright."

"I tried. I just—"

"You're alright," she said into his hair.

His shoulders trembled, and she wrapped them in a fierce grip.

Abner turned away.

He met Tessa's stare.

XXIV

Abner shook his head. "Why wouldn't they just stay here? We can lead the soldiers away."

"Children," Tessa said, throwing her hands toward the assembled mass of bodies behind her, all chomping through their meager meal of cheese, "cannot live in the woods."

"You did," Cantus said.

"And I almost starved before I found help! There are poisonous snakes, bears, mountain lions, berries that look safe but aren't—"

"Lions?" Abner jolted, checking over his shoulder. "There are lions here?"

"Mountain lions. They are smaller, no manes, they're just different!" She threw a hand out to silence him. "Not to mention an army is hunting us down and children leave a lot of tracks!"

"I didn't notice any," Cantus said.

"You both were thinking tactics but I know hunting. We need to start paying attention to what we leave behind."

"Is that where you were this morning?" Abner folded his arms. "I was wondering where you had snuck off to."

"I needed to have a look around and make sure we weren't easily followed. It took a very long time to cover our path."

Cantus' brow furrowed. "And? What did you see?"

"Your giant footprints for one," Tessa snapped. "Apparently you filled all your time waiting for us by pacing back and forth at the edge of the forest. I could track every footstep."

"What about soldiers, did you see any of them?" Abner asked.

Tessa nodded. "They camped on the border of the forest, but as far as I could tell weren't venturing very far in yet. I had covered over most of what was easy to see as we passed through yesterday, so I don't think they know what direction we went." She paused. "That won't last, so we need to make a decision on what to do with them." She threw her head toward the group behind.

Petra stomped across their path, yawning as he scratched up his side.

"Then we have to—"

"As much as I can appreciate—" Petra covered over another excessive yawn, "all of you wanting to snatch the weight of the world from each other's shoulders, these are my orphans, my problem." Petra cut off Abner's reply with a hand. "My problem. Besides, I already have the safe house to the south, we'll just take them there."

"Oh," Tessa's brow rose. "I suppose that could work."

Petra nodded. "Mhm." He sat down next to Ava.

Tessa, Cantus, and Abner glanced at each other before breaking apart. Abner kept Tessa in his sight as he brushed their horse's coat. She bent to scoop a handful of water from the stream, splashing some over her eyes.

"What's her name?" asked a little girl, pink spilling into her cheeks as Abner looked down at her.

"I'm not sure. Why don't you pick one?"

The girl smiled. "Princess—uh—Tabby. Princess Tabby."

Abner winced.

"Can I pet her?"

He nodded, bringing her to the horse's shoulder so she could run her fingers down the animal's side.

Behind the girl, Tessa rose and stretched.

The little girl wanted to know all about the horse. While Abner groomed up her coat and cleaned out her hooves, he gave a detailed explanation of why he was doing it. She probably would have lost interest quickly if she hadn't been allowed to move to the horse's head and stroke the soft nose.

A loud giggle filled the air.

Abner glanced at Ava, who was listening to a little boy with absolute attention as he twisted his fingers and told about the time he found a rock and threw it all the way over the garden wall. Nearby, Petra was reciting the mountain song and Cantus stood watching him.

The giggle came again, and Abner's eyes roved over the camp.

Tessa.

Tessa?

She sat in the middle of a wide group of children, her shoulders shuddering with laughter. The children ran restlessly around her or rolled on their sides in giggling fits, reacting to her mirthful energy.

"Remember though, children," she donned a mask of grave attention, "remember!" A giggle spilled into her palm.

"What? You can't say it?" a little boy asked, grabbing her hands.

"I will—I will! Alright," she sucked in a deep breath. "Water can be wet, but is it?"

"What? That doesn't make sense!" laughed the boy, falling into her lap.

"Yes it does! Because it—okay, okay, okay. How about this one?"

The children leaned forward.

"Strings are used to fasten clothing made from ... other ... strings!" She spread her hands as if the comment spoke for itself.

Something was very wrong.

Abner left the girl petting the horse's nose and strode to Tessa. He knelt behind her. "Tessa?"

She turned to look at him. "Oh, it's you."

"It *is* me. What are you doing?"

Tessa reached up, running a finger along his jaw. "I like your face."

Abner smiled, brows raising.

"I like it when you do that the best."

"You mean smile?"

Tessa nodded, turning away from the children to study his face. The little boy tumbled out of her lap, giggling. "Your eyes get like honey."

Abner squinted at her. "Did we eat some berries that looked okay but weren't?"

Tessa shook her head. She leaned in.

Abner's breath pulled into his chest.

"My head's a cloud," she whispered against his cheek.

"Your head's a cloud." He sighed, chin dropping. "Alright, wait here. Don't float away, little cloud."

The laughing children reclaimed her attention.

Abner called Cantus over as he stood. "The only thing I've seen her take in is water." He gestured to Tessa rolling on the ground beneath a mass of children.

"Think she could've gotten something in the forest?"

"With how much she's been yelling at us to be careful and not touch anything? She wouldn't eat anything she didn't know was safe."

"So ... the water."

"I think it's the water. But," Abner's brows shot up, "if we need to test it, you know to be sure, I mean—she looks like she is having a marvelous time."

"You're not drinking the water," Cantus said, furrowed brow heavy.

Abner spread his hands.

After explaining the situation to Petra, he agreed they should not leave camp to go to the safe house until she recovered since they were sure to leave tracks behind.

Ava helped Tessa to settle onto a mat. Soon she was asleep.

Waiting until Cantus' back was turned, Abner dipped a flask into the water.

Cooky cobbled together a quick meal while the children laid out for a mid-morning nap.

Ava fell against Petra's side, curling into his shoulder.

Petra's wide eyes stared at the curly hair brushing his chin. "Well, hello there."

Ava tipped her chin up to smile at him. "Hello."

His eyes flit across her face, grinning as he tried to read her expression.

Pulling him forward with her fingers twisting into his hair, Ava planted a firm, smooth kiss on his lips.

He drew back, laughing. "Okay, I think we should wait for that water to wear off." He raised his brows, unable to wipe away his grin. "See how you feel then."

Ava shook her head, one corner of her mouth raised. "I didn't drink the water."

"Oh, so this is—" Petra laughed, "This is you? That makes it so much better."

He wrapped an arm around her shoulders, gripping her side as he drew her up to cover her mouth with his kiss.

Abner cleared his throat.

Ava bit her lip.

Petra leaned away, his cheeks slowly seeping red.

"I think I feel like taking a walk," Ava declared into the tense silence, slipping to her feet. She lifted a shoulder at Petra.

"I don't think that's a good idea," Cantus said, staring at Petra while he choked the stick clutched between his hands, grinding it into the dirt at his feet.

"Then you can stay here." Ava tossed the words over her shoulder. "Petra?"

Petra's mouth tightened. "Please don't murder me in my sleep," he said, rising to follow her.

"I make no promise," Cantus muttered, watching the two of them disappear through the trees.

Joss was told to stay at the camp, and he sat near the water waiting for them.

"Well," Abner said, stretching his feet in front of him, "he's about to have a fun time."

Cantus threw the stick at Abner's head, the prince knocking it aside.

"You should tell her how you feel."

"Sorry?"

"Rather than just brood. I know you're a man who likes to show and never tell, but sometimes women need to be told they have options."

Cantus sighed. "I didn't like Tessa and I don't feel that for Ava."

"Then why are you so opposed to her enjoying herself?"

"It's not proper, or good for her." Cantus slapped dust from the toe of his boot. "With her brother at the castle, she needs someone to protect her. I was his friend. Watching her throw herself at a dirty thief would drive Nathaniel mad."

"As it does you?"

Cantus nodded.

"Well, Elena is either the most fascinating creature in the world to endear herself so uncompromisingly to you, or you are the most boring man to ever breathe to stick to one woman who you don't even get to enjoy."

Cantus raised an eyebrow at Abner.

The prince's eyes drifted to Tessa's shoulder rising and falling in sleep. Warmth settled in his gut.

As if drawn awake by his stare, Tessa's eyes shot open. She sprang to her feet, gaze darting over the clearing. Her shoulders dropped in relief at the sight of Abner and Cantus.

"What happened? Why was I?" She gestured to the mat.

"I'm not sure, but aren't you thirsty?" Abner smirked, nodding to the water.

"Don't," Cantus said, glaring at Abner. "There's something wrong with the stream. It made you all ... giggly."

"I giggled?" Tessa's face pinched in disgust. "I thought that was a dream. Where's Ava?"

"On a walk," Abner said with a lopsided grin.

"She's doing what?" Tessa threw out her hands, forgetting to lower her voice. The children jumped, some sitting up to rub their eyes. "Which way did she—never mind, I can track her myself. Leaving giant footprints—I just cleaned up after—" Tessa stomped after them.

"We should have probably warned her of the mood she'll be interrupting," Abner said.

Cantus raised his brow.

It apparently did not take long to find them. Tessa shoved Petra and Ava through the boulders a few moments later.

"Am I allowed to talk now?" Ava asked, turning to Tessa. "I'm sorry, we were just—"

"I don't care if you spend every moment you are here kissing each other. But you do it *in the camp*!" Tessa threw her hands into a wide circle.

Ava sighed, nodding.

"Now I need to go clean up the mess of tracks. Again!"

Cantus met Ava as her cheeks filled with red. "After the children are settled at the safe house, you and I need to talk."

"I don't think I want to." Ava glared at him.

"I didn't ask you," Cantus folded his arms, "I'm telling you what is going to happen."

Ava's teeth ground together as Cantus turned away to begin packing supplies onto the horse.

"Well, this has been a morning." Petra wrapped an arm around her shoulders.

She pulled her mouth into a smile.

"What made you..."

"I didn't see the point in waiting. Who knows what—" she shrugged.

"Hm." Petra's brow folded as he took her meaning, his mask shifting to reveal the pain underneath for a brief moment. He covered it over as he gave her a quick kiss before slipping away to help Cooky corral the children.

They walked in a two abreast line and held hands with their partner to keep the footprints manageable as they left the camp.

The forest shifted. The evergreens spreading their heavy-needled branches above the traveler's heads were replaced by a rainbow of colors announcing the change in seasons. Petra, Ava, and Cooky struggled to keep the children's feet moving forward and not darting to grab fistfuls of little leaves from the ground to hurl at one another. Abner let himself fall behind to where Tessa, with a broom of ferns in her hand, was masking their progress.

"It's beautiful," Abner said, gesturing to the trees. "I can see why you wanted to stay here as a child."

"I didn't live in the forest because of the pretty leaves."

"Why did you then?"

She looked at him.

"The story Lady Hildren told us of you finding her and being the long-lost niece of Hildren House is obviously false. I just keep calling you Lady Tessa because that's who you are to me. But you didn't come from there, so where did you come from?"

Tessa sighed, hesitated, then shook her head.

"What?" Abner jabbed her with his elbow. "What could you possibly have to tell me that's worse than where I came from?"

"You don't need an answer, so you aren't getting one," Tessa said with a one-sided shrug.

"Alright, let's change subjects. Should we discuss my face or my smile?"

"What?"

"You declared certain things while you were under the water's influence."

Tessa stopped walking. "What things?"

"Your head is apparently a cloud," Abner laughed, ticking the list off on his fingers, "water can be wet, but not always, and that my smile turns my eyes to ... honey, I think it was?"

"That wasn't me." Her blushing cheeks seemed to speak otherwise.

Abner dropped his voice low. "Maybe that water did you a favor. Spoke the words you couldn't."

"Maybe you want to move your hand off my shoulder before it gets broken."

Abner stared at his fingers. "I think my hand is finally getting better. You know, I haven't thought about it in a while. It went through battle and it feels better."

"So happy for you," Tessa said, pushing his shoulder forward so she could sweep over his boot prints. She stretched her back, looking over the path they had already walked. "Does it seem odd that they're staying out of the forest?"

"The soldiers?" Abner nodded. "I'm not sure why they haven't caught us yet, but I'm glad for whatever is keeping them back."

"Maybe they're suddenly afraid of trees?"

Abner shook his head, ignoring her attempt at humor. "Dennison is leading them. He's not afraid of anything and the men would follow him anywhere."

"Then why?"

"I'm not sure. It is a big forest, maybe you covered the tracks well enough that they lost us? I don't know."

The children began complaining of sore feet.

"Almost there," Petra called back.

"How will Mother find us, since we left?" said a girl.

"Hush now, dearie," said Cooky, puffing as she struggled to keep up with the tide of children. "They'll be along."

"But how?"

"Hush."

Petra directed the group toward the forest edge to sneak along the tree line. The hill, crowned by the small town, made the procession come to a sudden halt. The buildings crowded together, their placement above the steep incline adding natural defenses to the otherwise open, unwalled layout. Petra called back to Abner and Tessa. They edged around the children to join him, Cantus close behind.

"I'll go out with Cooky and the children five or six at a time."

"We'll watch the rest until you come back," Tessa nodded.

"Be careful," Ava said.

Petra winked at her, leaving with a group of six and Cooky as Joss bounded next to them. As soon as he was gone, Cantus turned to Ava.

"Now," he began. Ava walked away, arms crossed.

"Stay—" Tessa called.

"I know! In the camp."

Petra returned a while later, alone save for Joss, out of breath from his run down the hill. "Should go faster now," he said. "I had to take some time to explain things." He left with the next group of six.

Cantus walked to Ava. "Have you calmed down yet?"

"If I wasn't certain I'd break my hand and you wouldn't even flinch, I would knock you in the mouth," Ava said.

"So ... no. Fine. You need to start thinking—"

Ava groaned, her forehead falling into her hands.

"How is your husband going to feel someday with you having every available man that crosses your path? That is assuming you don't intend to marry the thief."

"I would hardly call kissing Petra the same as having every available man. Besides, who says I plan on getting married at all?"

"Of course you're going to get married," Cantus said.

Ava shrugged. "Just because you're willing to be ever miserable in the hope of a future that'll never happen, doesn't mean the rest of us are. Some of us actually like to be happy."

"I don't—what are you talking about?"

"Lady Elena. Everyone on the staff knew the story. You were fifteen, found your love, and now you'll go to your grave only ever loving her, but never getting to actually be with her. That's not me, and it's not the life I'm willing to live." She turned away. "Maybe if you had done something—instead of being such an honorable coward—you'd actually be happy now."

There was a long pause.

"Two weeks."

"What?"

"I spent two weeks befriending the kitchen staff, helping their families. It got me access to the tunnel in the kitchen. From there it is two lefts, one right, over a beam, and down the hole to get out of the castle the only way one won't be seen. Thomas in the stables was keeping horses for us. Everything was in place for us to run, but when I asked her ... she said no."

Ava turned back to him. "Why?"

"I can't blame her. I offered her a life of possible danger and certain poverty. She had other prospects, I'm sure."

Ava shook her head.

"My point is, sometimes you risk everything and it still doesn't work. It's not about the risk. It's about knowing why it's worth it."

"I don't need to defend myself to you."

Ava brushed past Cantus.

A muscle popped to the surface in his jaw.

Petra's third trip took six more children, leaving only five sitting around Abner and the horse.

Ava touched Tessa's elbow. "I'm sorry about earlier," she said. "I've been a little—"

"It's fine," Tessa shook her head, and Ava wrapped her arms around her shoulders.

"How's your back?"

"The new string has been working well, but I think it got a little loose in the fight."

"Do you want me to adjust it?"

Tessa nodded and the two of them walked just out of sight of the men.

When Petra returned from leaving the final group at his safe house, the five companions stared at one another. The loss of the children's frolicking energy hit like a punch to the gut. Not knowing what else to do, they made their way deeper into the forest. They stopped in a wide clearing, Ava digging out some bread for them to nibble on.

"Cantus, I feel we should talk."

Cantus chewed through a moment of silence. "Why?"

Petra's face pinched. "I wasn't entirely joking with the 'don't kill me' thing."

"Relax, Thief." He took another bite. "I could beat you to a bleeding muck and it wouldn't change anything. You're not the problem."

"I'm ... not?"

Cantus glanced to where the girls sat, Ava twisting Tessa's hair into little spirals. "She keeps making decisions that are unwise. I don't know why she's decided to throw her life away but if she won't guard it, I will."

"But you're okay with me, as a person?"

"Besides the obvious hatred for thieves and criminals like yourself?" Cantus shrugged. "You talk too much."

Petra nodded. "Fair, but did you know, I also am fond of poetry?"

"So?"

"It just rounds me out as a person. Makes it harder to hate me, I think."

Cantus grunted.

"Well, good talk then." Petra slapped his thighs as he stood, striding to settle into a seat beside Ava.

Abner raised his brow at Cantus, tossing his eyes to the sky with a shake of his head.

The soldier froze mid-bite, eyes narrowing on the thief. Springing to his feet, Cantus pelted to Petra, hauling him up by the front of his tunic. "Poetry!"

"I'm sorry?"

"Poetry. Recite the—the mountain song!" He released Petra's clothes.

With eyes pulled wide, Petra began stuttering through the verse.

> *Out of the void, dark and grim,*
> *A lone mountain rose within,*
> *A spark, a breath, in the hollow womb,*
> *Burst light to dispel the gloom.*
>
> *First to emerge, armored scales,*
> *Bent the neck, swept the tail,*
> *From their breath a spark arose,*
> *Lighting Heavens, Above, and Below.*
>
> *Man was made and quickly left,*
> *Safety at the mountain's breast,*
> *Power they sought, Death they won—*

"Shut it—shut it—don't you see?" Cantus swept his arms in an arc around him.

Tessa met Abner's stare.

"The mountain! They never left the mountain!"

"Who?"

Cantus pulled the tooth from where it now hung around his neck. "The dragons."

"It's a story," Tessa shook her head. "The mountain, the dragons, it's all—"

"And which mountain? Alberon is bordered by a line of them, so do you suggest we climb each one?" Abner shrugged.

"I think we've already found our path," Cantus said, his chin rising in triumph. "Water flows downhill." Silence. "How do you not understand? The water! The stream! It's magic. All magic flows from the mountain!"

Ava nodded. "So we follow the stream and…"

"We find the dragons!" Cantus smiled, triumphant.

Tessa met Abner's eyes. "No, don't…"

Abner lifted a shoulder. "I guess we are now hunting dragons."

Tessa groaned, dropping her head into her palms.

XXV

Finding the stream again took some time, and as they rejoined the babbling water Esther would've liked nothing more than to dunk Abner's face into it.

"What about this?" he began again.

She groaned into her hands.

"Say a fish drinks the water, does it giggle? Could a fish giggle?"

"Take it a step further, Abner," Petra grinned. "We eat the fish that drank. Have we drunk?"

"Good point," Abner said, raising his brow as he turned around to face her. "Tessa? What do you say? Fish tonight and you and I can ... giggle together?"

"Can we please stop using that word!" Esther's fingers drew heavy lines down her cheeks.

Ava frowned. "Poor Lady Tessa. Stop teasing her, boys."

"Yes, Mother." Petra flinched as soon as the words passed his lips.

Ava touched his arm.

"It is great, the loss you suffered," Cantus offered the rare nugget of sympathy with a heavy nod. "I hope you find peace."

Petra stared at him. He cleared his throat. "So, fish tonight?"

Ava chuckled.

"Well if I'm being truthful," Abner said, "I've always despised the taste of fish."

The company stopped as the sunlight began to lessen at the first decent spot along the stream and settled quickly into sleep. With the tent on one of the horses that ran, Ava and Esther slept in the open. Cantus was sure to put himself as a buffer body between Petra and the girls. The thief didn't seem to mind as he slung an arm around Joss' back, pushing his face into the dog's fur, and fell asleep. Abner agreed to keep watch. Esther drifted as Cantus and Ava's hushed voices discussed everything they missed at the castle and what they would do for a meal made hot from the kitchens.

It was cold and dark when she woke again.

The night noises of the forest had grown quiet. It was the first sign to Esther that something was wrong. She sat up on her mat, blinking at the shadows. Her ears strained out the sound of the stream babbling next to her.

Abner leaned against a wide tree trunk, chin to his chest as his body rose and fell with each deep breath.

Is that?

A shadow leaned against a trunk at an odd angle, but it was so still. No, it must be something beyond the tree that would make sense if she were closer. She rubbed the crust of sleep from her eyes and laid back, resisting the urge to kick Abner into doing his job of keeping watch.

Snap.

The twig breaking sent her eyes popping open as she sprang to her feet. The shadow against the tree was gone.

"Up!" she kicked Cantus in the leg, before dragging Ava up by the arm. "We need to go!"

"What is it?" Cantus said, struggling to blink himself awake.

"A shadow. There was a shadow and now there isn't. Someone was watching us."

Abner and Cantus shared a look before jumping off the ground. They swept the area with their eyes.

"Awfully dark for morning, isn't it?" yawned Petra, rubbing his neck.

"Shut it," snapped Esther.

"Behind," said a deep voice, the scrape of a sword sending her off balance and crashing away from the sound.

Petra dragged Ava back as he flung himself forward in a crouch. He was properly awake now as he reached toward the empty sheath on his shoulder. He cursed.

It was dark save for the attacker's blade reflecting a small shine of light. The whitened scar threading through one eyebrow and running down his cheek drew Esther's eye. The scarred man cocked his chin at Petra, rolled his cloak off his arm, and turned his sword point to him.

Ripping two long-bladed daggers from sheaths at his hip, Petra sprang forward. It took five strikes for him to be disarmed of both weapons, a sixth blow from the enemy's hilt sending him smacking into the trunk of a tree.

Joss took his opening, sinking his teeth into the attacker's arm. A few hard blows to the dog's head rid the attacking man of its bite. When Petra regained himself, his attention was consumed with the dog's weeping eyes.

Cantus roared forward, his blade singing through the air as it clashed with the scarred man's weapon.

Esther grabbed Ava out of the way and stood defending her, pinning her back to an oak's wide trunk at the side of the clearing. If the two combatants weren't so close maybe she could throw her dagger or a rock.

Cantus lasted longer than Petra but was also disarmed, pushed into the dirt with a kick to the chest.

The scarred man looked at her next, the dagger shaking in her fist, and scoffed, passing by.

Abner seemed to be frozen. He had his back pressed to the tree behind him, sword held in a limp grip, not breathing as he watched the scarred face come forward. He was going to die if he didn't move.

The man raised his sword.

Why isn't he moving?

Esther drew back the dagger as she sprang forward, aiming for a strike into the scarred man's shoulder.

Her hand was caught a breath from his back as he twisted to face her. Keeping his grip on her hand, he kicked her knees from beneath her, sending her thudding to the ground.

Her back roared, stings of pain echoing down her legs.

Abner came back to life. Leaping in front of Esther, he launched into a series of hard quick strikes on the opposing sword. Even against the soldiers at the orphanage, Esther had never seen him fight like that. Power poured into every movement, and Abner held the ground in front of her with furious skill.

Cantus appeared at the attacker's back.

Surprise slowed the scarred hand only a moment before he forced the two men to crash together. They fell in a tangle of limbs near Esther.

The scarred man raised his sword above them.

Abner's hand found hers.

"That's match." A sword slid back into its sheath.

Abner swallowed, blinking the speckles of sweat from his eyes. "You're not going to kill me, Dennison?"

"I've come to help you take your place as King, Abner." He reached for the prince's arm, allowing Cantus to push himself to his feet on his own.

As Abner rose, he pulled Dennison into a firm embrace.

Dennison drew back. "And not a moment too soon," he said, glancing over Abner and Cantus. "Your technique is sloppy at best."

"I was injured," Abner said, working to breathe normally again. "Still healing."

"And the army?"

Abner looked at Cantus as the soldier offered a hand to Esther.

The string is holding, thank the stars. I'm sore, but alright.

"You have raised an army, have you not? The people, a neighboring kingdom? You did have a plan before running from the castle and showing your father your intentions. Please tell me you have a plan."

"We ... do." Abner muttered something imperceptible.

"What?"

"We're going to find dragons."

Dennison closed his eyes.

"The stream, we think it's magic and if we follow it we should be able to find the mountain from the ancient song and—"

"Ridiculous. Abner, your father is desperate enough to believe in anything that will save him. I taught you more sense than that." Dennison shook his head. "Do you have any proof? Anything that might—"

Cantus pulled the dragon tooth from around his neck, handing it to Dennison.

He rolled it over his palm before tossing it back to the soldier. "So, nothing." Dennison sighed. "Well, it's late to raise anything, since your father has already flooded the countryside with soldiers and the towns with your portrait. We'll have to think of a way around that." Dennison looked between the three faces, eyes glancing quickly over Petra and Ava kneeling beside Joss. "Why don't you get some rest? I'll watch for you. Not that any soldiers will be around."

"Why are you alone?" Abner asked.

Dennison smiled. "Go rest, Sire. I'll explain things when it's properly morning."

Esther drew close to Cantus' side as Abner and Dennison sat together. "So, that's Dennison. Think the prince will slip back to being his old, charming self?"

Cantus scraped a bit of dirt from the inside of his lip. "I hope not." He laid down on his mat, keeping his eyes fixed on Dennison until they slipped closed.

"And everyone is fine with the person who just attacked us?" Petra's mouth wore an incredulous smile. "We're all just going to close our eyes and drift off to sleep?"

He was ignored.

Esther woke before it was light as her open mouth dripped water onto her wrist. The sizzle of cooking meat crackled in her ears. Her nose drew her to her knees, sniffing the scent off the air.

Dennison stared at her through the smoke.

Everyone else still breathed heavy and slow, Petra adjusting his sleeping grip on Joss under his arm.

"Have you trained?" Dennison asked her, turning the rounds of salted meat speared by a long thin piece of metal to cook the other side.

Esther swallowed, eyes on the meat. "Some, but I'm not very good."

"True," Dennison nodded, "but I think that's because you've been trying to fight like them." He tossed his head to Abner. "There's a skill one needs to excel at doing something, and a different skill to be able to teach it." He smiled. "He is a talented swordsman, but a bleeding awful tutor I would wager."

"It's been mainly Cantus actually," Esther said, moving closer to the fire, so she could fill her lungs with the vapor of hot food.

"Really?" Dennison flipped the meat, sighing as he replaced the under-cooked side. "Surprised you're doing as well as you are then."

"He's strong," Esther said doubtfully, glancing at Cantus.

"There's a lot more to a fight than strength. Reach, speed, footwork, equipment, training." He nodded toward Cantus. "The stronger man doesn't always win."

Esther watched the fire's curling fingers. When the last bit of pink dripped away from the meat and he pulled it from the metal, she had to clasp her fingers in her lap to stop them from reaching for it.

Glancing at her with a smile, he tossed one over the fire.

Esther snatched it out of the air, passing it between her hands and blowing on it. She bit into it when it was cooled enough to hold, but the juice inside still scalded her tongue. She didn't mind, eyes rolling closed as the flavor burst along the sides of her mouth. It was an effort to leave any for the rest as she waited for them to stir.

After their meal, during which Dennison filled their time with his own ideas of useful strategies for them to employ and a detailed explanation of how he had misdirected the soldiers searching for them until he could find a moment to pursue them alone, the captain told them his plan for the day.

Cantus rolled his tongue over his teeth.

Dennison wanted to see the extent of their skills. It began with stick sparring like they had been doing. Ava hastily explained she had no interest in learning, and so they were paired off easily. Cantus and Esther traded polite blows, to the frustration of Dennison, while Petra delighted

Abner with tricky footwork that he had to think quickly to compensate for.

Dennison raised his chin. "That's match."

Abner lowered his stick, Petra following suit.

"Interesting form." Dennison nodded to Petra.

Petra smiled at him, his eyes shining. "Do you think so? I was so worried you wouldn't approve!"

The company froze to stare at Petra as his glaring smile slipped away.

"Have I offended you, boy?" Dennison's tone was confused but unbothered.

Petra scoffed. "Why would I mind that the man who last night attacked us, and hit my dog, is now critiquing my fighting?"

Dennison shrugged. "I needed to see the skill level of those surrounding the prince."

"Well you accomplished that goal already, so what's the point now?"

"I don't think an encounter with someone of my skill is a fair assessment. Obviously none of you would come close to my level. So I put you against each other."

Petra spread his hands. "All of you are hearing him, yes? Why is he here? Any man who would strike a dog is—"

"Apologies, but you are offended about the dog? Still? The mutt bit me."

"That's right, I'd forgotten." Petra turned to the black and white patched face laying on Ava's lap. "Good boy, Joss! I hope you got a nice big mouthful of the villainous wretch!"

Joss lifted his head, blinking at Petra with a panting smile.

He stomped to the dog and scratched him behind his ears. "A walk?"

Ava nodded, rising with him.

"In the camp!" Esther called.

Petra made a rude hand gesture back to her, sending a blush to her cheeks, as Joss trotted after them.

"Just as well. No sticks now. Abner, Tessa. Fight." Dennison nodded to the two of them. Abner threw his stick aside, hesitantly raising his hands. "Come on, son, move your feet. Put her on the ground."

Abner moved forward.

Esther slipped out of his grasp.

He spun, trying to snatch her in his grip, but she was faster. His breath quickened, mouth pulling into a heavy frown.

Esther smirked as she hopped out of his reach. It was a mistake. She couldn't move. Her back stiffened into a stooped posture, her breath caged in pain high in her chest.

Abner's shoulder barreled into her, knocking her to the ground. His hands softened as they pinned her down, something flickering through his expression that made Esther's face heat. She thrust her neck to one side, biting into the stretch of skin between his thumb and his palm. He ripped away from her jaw. She dragged herself out of reach.

"That shouldn't be allowed," he said, examining the small cuts her teeth had made into his skin.

"He only said no sticks," Esther forced out, finally able to draw a full breath, wiping her mouth as she spit out the taste. *Thank the stars for this stronger string.*

His eyes narrowed over his smirk. "Some lady of the royal court."

Abner insisted that the decision of where to go from here was one that the entire company should have a voice in.

Cantus and Esther went to find Ava and Petra.

As they walked, the soldier asked about tracking to fill the time.

Esther pointed out different animal prints, droppings, and other useful information about plants they passed. She saved him from a nasty rash when his hand almost drifted through a tangled vine running up the side of a tree. She had discovered the properties of that four-pronged leaf the hard way.

"They've gone farther than I thought they would." Cantus glanced back at the camp already well out of sight through the trees.

"Have you thought about how to convince Dennison of your plan?" Esther asked, eyes treading over the path. "Not that I believe in it, but I agree that wandering around the kingdom hoping we're not caught and killed is going to eventually lead to us being caught and killed. It'll be a waste of time but at least it will put us out of sight and not endangering others for a while."

"I don't have to convince him," Cantus said, kicking aside a fern that stretched across their path. "I just need to keep Abner believing in it. Though, knowing him, that'll end up being the same thing."

"Dennison doesn't seem to like you much."

Cantus shook his head. "His proudest achievement is Abner. Because he's the prince, he's had a lot of attention and resources poured into him, and his failings have been mostly overlooked. I have no power or status. I could be the best soldier in the kingdom and it would only ever register as mediocre service to Dennison. I would be doing my job, nothing more."

"How is anyone supposed to advance that way?"

"The point of the work isn't to advance. It's to defend and enforce the laws."

"And when the maker of the laws or the enforcers are unjust?"

Cantus raised his brow. "We end up with a soldier, a prince, a thief, a servant, and a demon hiking through the woods to search for dragons."

Esther laughed.

They found Ava and Petra sitting together under a tree. His tools picked at the unpickable while Ava leaned into his shoulder, shredding a crimson leaf into tidy bits. They both jumped when Cantus called to them.

❖ ❖ ❖

"I hope you and I are of one mind about this," Dennison began.

Abner nodded before he had heard what Dennison wanted to say.

"Lady Tessa cannot be kept. At least, not after everything is settled."

"I'm sorry?" Abner's brows drew together.

"I just wanted it to be clear between us. She makes a competent companion but would be unacceptable as Queen."

"Not that I was thinking—I wasn't—but what makes her unworthy?"

Dennison spread his hands with a laugh. "Where should I start? She chomped through a hunk of meat this morning like a dog—"

"I always thought it was kind of adorable the way she eats."

Dennison grimaced, shaking his head. "Your own fancies aside, it wouldn't do for the lady of the throne. You and your house will be representing the strength and interests of the kingdom abroad. It's very important what image you choose to present. And what I saw a moment ago with her biting you to get the upper hand was," he paused, "certainly spirited, but not the image of a lady. If you must have her as a diversion, keep it discreet. Meanwhile—"

Cantus and Tessa returned, Petra, Ava, and Joss trailing behind.

Dennison changed his tone. "And I would have come to aid you sooner, but the king demanded my presence at Lady Hildren's execution. Of course this was the one he chose to make an example of, and it went on for days."

The ground disappeared from beneath Abner as he met Cantus' stare.

Dennison continued, oblivious to the change. "They brought out some device from the homeland and it made slow work of her. I think the king quite enjoyed having her set up in the courtyard as a constant spectacle. He wouldn't allow anyone to leave until it was done. Not even to hunt you."

"Cantus, let me ex—"

Cantus' knuckles smashed into Abner's jaw. The soldier didn't bother drawing his sword, instead pummeling every bit of Abner he could reach.

Dennison pulled him off.

Tessa met Abner's stare as he spit blood from the fresh cut on his lip. She followed Cantus back into the forest, calling for him to wait.

"Tessa, don't—"

Dennison caught Abner's arm. "It would be best to let that work itself out. Unless you would like me to go handle it?" Dennison's hand rested on the hilt of his sword.

"You mean?" Abner shook his head. "No, no."

"He struck you, Sire. He drew royal blood. That's—"

"That's something I've earned. I—maybe you've forgotten what house Cantus is from?"

Dennison's brow drew a hard line. A light dawned on the captain's features. "Ah, the old woman."

"Lady Hildren was his great aunt. He tried to free her from her cell as we escaped, but it was taking too long—we left her. What happened … it's my fault." Abner ran a hand along his jaw.

Joss' panting breath paused as he lapped loudly from the stream.

"Her life," Dennison said, putting a heavy emphasis on his words, "is not equal to yours. You did right by saving yourself. What would you have done with her out here?"

"All the same," Abner said. "I'll take whatever blows he decides to send."

Dennison seemed as if he wanted to say more, but let it pass with a tight smile. "As you wish it, Highness."

Petra glared at Dennison, only breaking the look when Ava touched his arm.

Oh, itchy, itches everywhere. Who can I get to give me scratches or—ah—a belly rub?

Joss pushed his wet nose into Petra's hand.

Locking stares with the dog, Petra dropped to one knee in front of him. "J–Joss?"

Yes?

"How did you—how can you talk?"

How can you talk? asked the dog, tipping his head to one side. *You didn't use to.*

Ava dropped next to him. They locked eyes before both turning back to the dog.

"You're not mad," Abner assured him. "I heard him too."

Now, about that belly rub…

XXVI

"Cantus! Wait, please!"

Esther pelted through the forest undergrowth after him, not bothering to be careful with her footprints as she followed the soldier plowing over branches and vines without pause. She caught his arm, yanking him to a stop. Her back sent a stab of pain in warning.

He knocked her aside with his shoulder. "Get out of here, Tessa!"

She grabbed at him again.

Heavy cords of muscle sprang within his neck.

"Listen to me!" she said.

"What?" He stopped at last, facing her. "What could you possibly say to excuse yourself for leaving an old woman to be tortured to death for your mistake?"

"I'm sorry. I—"

"Sorry?" Cantus nodded, eyes shining as his voice dropped low. "Your apology is a little hollow considering what you've done." He began to turn away, but paused. A cold light dawned in his eyes. "The soldiers didn't breach the room, did they? You—or Abner—knocked me in the head."

"We would all have died if—"

Cantus tried to pull away, sending her backward by planting an elbow into her gut.

Esther's breath flew from her lungs and she lost her grip. As she fell back, her face scraped against a rough rock.

Pitiless eyes stared down at her. Cantus spoke through his teeth, "You're a coward."

She kept her hand from checking the stinging patch on her cheek for blood.

"No better than the king." He turned away. "You follow me, I will hurt you. And before you ask, no. I forgave you for leaving her body behind, but this—this will likely be a stain between us never washed clean."

Cantus strode out of sight as she struggled to lift herself off the ground. He left a trail of broken branches in his wake as he stomped through the trees.

Esther's pulse beat in her ears and down her sides as she pushed her legs into motion, returning to camp.

Abner met her, eyes running across the red marks on her face. "What did he—" His fingers reached to touch them, but she knocked his hand away.

"Only what I deserve."

Abner looked after Cantus, mouth twisting into a scowl. "I'm sorry. I didn't think he'd—I never would have let you follow him if I thought he would actually hurt you."

Esther scoffed, leaving him to sit alone.

They waited for Cantus to return. Dennison thought it a waste of time but Abner insisted, and the captain acquiesced. When he came back into view, Cantus directed his words to Petra and Ava, who sat with Joss under a pine tree's spreading branches.

They paused in their conversation as Cantus folded his arms.

"I'm leaving." He huffed. "I think my life and feelings are less important than the goal of ending the king's reign, so I will still be serving the cause. But I can't be near ... anyway, whether you find dragons or not, the support of the people is necessary. So I will be going to gather those willing to fight against the king. If you find any help on the mountain, bring it to Shiloh." He nodded.

"Cantus, you can't just—" He strode away, and Esther's voice faded.

"On a brighter note, Joss can talk!" Petra lifted his shoulders. "In our heads anyway."

"I wonder why though?" Ava chased an itch over Joss' neck.

Left, a little left—just—ahh.

"Maybe the stream does more than make women giggle?" Petra offered.

"In the forest I lived with a talking fox. It's just something animals do here," Esther said.

Petra raised his brow. "Well that's ... different." He frowned, shaking his head. "I need to—Joss, stay here."

"You had a talking fox, but dragons are outside the realm of believable to you?" Abner asked.

"Fox always talked," Esther snapped, waving him away. "Dragons only exist in stories. There's a difference in believing your own eyes as you see strange things and believing everything unseen. Talking dogs do not make dragons any more likely."

Joss barked.

"I think the water's worn off," Ava said, running a hand over his ears. She turned to call to Petra, but her voice died as her brows tightened.

Petra slung his cloak around his shoulders. Beside him, Cantus belted on his sword. As Petra popped his chin up to secure the cloak, his eyes met Ava's.

She rose as he made his way over to her.

"We should probably..."

"You're leaving," Ava said.

Petra grimaced. "Yes."

"Why?"

"I ... think I'd be more use out there? Cantus has all the tact of a battering ram." He smirked. "He'll need help. I've been thinking about it all day. How useless I feel wandering the forest. It's not running away from you or ... I just need to be doing something."

"Alright." She extended a hand and Petra flinched back. "It was a pleasure getting to know you, Petra."

Petra took her hand. "The pleasure was ... mine?"

She shrugged a shoulder. "That's all we need to say."

"I'll miss you?"

Ava sighed. "I'll miss your dog."

A laugh burst past his lips. "Is that what all this was about?"

"The whole time."

"I was used ... for the dog. Should have known. Joss, how could you?"

The fur-lined amber eyes blinked as Joss' panting tongue rolled over his jaw.

"The face of betrayal."

Ava popped onto her toes, giving Petra's cheek a quick kiss. "Good fortune," she said. "I hope you don't die."

"Likewise," Petra nodded.

She smiled.

"And, if we should meet again?" Petra asked before she could slip away.

Ava shrugged her shoulders.

"Ava!" Cantus waved her over.

Petra watched her go.

Esther moved to the horse, pretending to tidy its mane as Cantus took Ava's elbow and led her out of sight of the others. She closed her eyes, straining to listen to their words. *What if he takes her with them? Why would she stay?*

"You should come with us," he said, his voice low. "I won't be able to protect you if you stay here."

"They're still my friends."

There was a pause. Esther let out her breath.

"I don't need your protection from them."

"They left her to die!" Cantus said, the vehemence behind his words turning his tone to gravel. "They lied to me all this time. I don't trust them and neither should you."

"I'm sorry about your aunt, really I am. I don't know what happened that day but I'm sure they had their reasons."

"Cowardice. That was the reason. I could have gone back for her. Instead she was alone and at the mercy of an evil power, all because they were too afraid to tell me the truth."

"I'm sure you would have died in some very heroic way trying to save her," Ava said. "Besides, wouldn't going with you put me around Petra, the greatest evil in the land?"

"An acceptable risk."

"It's not your job to protect me, and I'm tired of being treated like the next task for you to take on. I'm not your responsibility."

"I'm not just looking for a way to fill my idle time, Ava. You need to be taken care of. You're not like the rest of us. I'd like to stop you from having to make decisions that turn you into something else." The words came like a load that he strained to lift.

The pause before she answered drew Esther forward against the horse's neck, her heels tipping up as she waited.

"Goodbye Cantus. I wish you all the good fortune in the world."

A heavy sigh. "Goodbye Ava."

She crossed out of the tree line and met Esther's eyes. Giving a nod, Ava strode to Joss, kneeling to cover his wet nose with kisses.

"It's for the best, Sire," said Dennison, standing at Abner's side.

Cantus and Petra pulled packs on their shoulders, the horse's reins held tight in the soldier's fist. Abner had reluctantly offered the horse to Cantus as it would have a hard time navigating mountains and there were too many in the company staying behind to make it anything more than a pack animal.

"We'll meet you in Shiloh with any help we find," Cantus said again.

"Till then, dear travelers!" Petra called, sweeping into a bow. Joss licked his forehead before he popped up.

Cantus shook his head, squeezing the bridge of his nose between his fingertips. He turned away.

They're gone.

The children leaving had been a loss, but this was devastating. When had Cantus and Petra become important? Abner raised his chin.

"Now, about this plan of yours," Dennison began, "I think you'll find it of more value to search a neighboring kingdom for allies as opposed to..." He waved a dismissive hand.

"We're at least going to follow the stream," Abner said. "Cantus wasn't wrong. There's something special about this water. Its source may not have dragons but it might have help of some kind. We owe it to the people to see."

Dennison narrowed his eyes, pursing his lips so his breath came at a trickle. "I would caution you, Abner."

"I know what I'm doing, Dennison," Abner said, striding toward Tessa.

"Do you?" Dennison challenged.

Abner followed her eyes to the spot the men had disappeared. "Ready to leave?"

Ava was the last to turn away.

As the four of them left the camp, Abner's footsteps stomped heavier through the mud along the bank of the stream. Their heads all hung a little lower. He tried to think of something to say to draw their spirits up, but no words came. The forest began to grow thicker around the water's edge, pushing them deeper into the muddy banks as they followed the path the stream had carved itself through the invading greenery.

"This mud is—" Ava paused to rip her foot out of a deep pocket she had sunk into, "—impossible!"

Dennison offered to carry the girls' packs for them, and Ava gratefully gave it up. Before long they were forced to move with their backs bent against the twisted branches and vines entwined above them. Soon they were practically crawling through the thicket. Tessa tried to mask her discomfort in a scowl of concentration, but Abner saw her pause more than once, hand to her back, her body rigid.

"Imagine Cantus trying to squeeze through here," Abner said.

Ava laughed behind him.

When the plants crowded to the very edge of the stream's banks, Abner paused.

"Let's keep moving," Tessa said.

Abner gestured to the green shoots blocking his path.

"Into the water then. It'll do good to leave no footprints for a while anyway." Tessa's feet splashed into the stream. Ava followed, lifting her skirt to keep the water from dragging it down.

Abner unstrapped his sword and held it in his fist, in case the water grew deeper. *This would be so much easier with that sheath.*

Dennison, bringing up the rear, grunted as he followed them into the biting cold brook.

By the time the path opened up again, their feet had warmed to the water. The soggy, dragging weight of his shoes pushing through the tugging current gave way to the squelching march through the mud. Abner grimaced.

The day ebbed away, drawing Abner's thoughts to a hot meal and rest for his feet that still felt soggy despite the outside of his boots looking dry.

"Far enough for one day?" he asked the others.

Ava sank immediately down on the grass, slipping her shoes off to rub at her toes.

Dennison stretched his back, grimacing at the water. "How do you know this magic is from the stream?"

Tessa smiled at Ava. "Why don't you have a drink to test it?"

"Dennison does not giggle," Abner said.

Ava and Tessa laughed against each other's shoulders.

"What is it? I feel I have missed some vital information."

"The stream makes people very ... happy," Abner explained. "Tessa had some very interesting things to say about—"

Tessa aimed a kick at his leg, her mouth stretched into a tight smile. "We are never going to speak of that again."

Abner picked a golden leaf from the branch above his head, studying it against his fingers. "No, I can't promise you that." He winked at her.

Her mouth twisted. "Then I can't promise you that I—"

Ava groaned. "Do you two need to take a walk to sort this out?"

Tessa's face pinched in confusion.

"I don't have the patience without Petra here to listen to your little nips at one another so, Lady Tessa, you know I love you, but either walk it out or learn to get along."

Tessa couldn't meet Abner's stare as an uncomfortable moment of silence pulled out between them.

"So should we…" Abner lifted one shoulder with a smile.

"No!" Tessa said, drawing back.

Abner chuckled. "Calm yourself, Lady Tessa. It was a joke, obviously."

Ava sighed. "Obviously."

Dennison had used all the meat he had packed with him for their first meal.

Tessa, unable to bear the thought of cold food after such a grueling day, went hunting.

Abner insisted on lending a hand for protection.

"So what're we eating?" Abner asked after they had freed themselves from the thicket and the babble of the stream had faded behind them.

"Whatever we find," Tessa answered, waving at him to be quiet.

"Well, what are we looking for?" Abner asked.

"Didn't they teach hunting in your years of military training," her voice was a frustrated whisper, "and its need for silence?"

Abner wrinkled his nose. "A little, but we had servants for that. Besides, we planned ahead and brought our own food."

"What about for your idiotic little mission to find the dragons? You didn't carry weeks worth of food with you then, did you?"

Abner pointed to his empty belt. "We didn't need to. We were looking for news in towns, not journeying through the woods."

"What a waste of training. So all you know how to do is swing a sword?" She moved away from him, shaking her head.

"No, no. I also know axes, shields, not as good with a pike to be honest, horseback riding, strategy, and … I'm sure there are others I'm forgetting." Abner fell into step beside her. Tessa caught him before his foot landed, his abdomen jumping to tension at the touch of her hand. "I was joking before, but if you—"

She pulled her arm back, eyes going wide. "I wasn't—you were about to step on those."

Abner looked at his feet. Ahead of him were little scratches in the dirt between the clumps of clover. He raised an eyebrow at Tessa.

She placed a finger to her mouth before bending to examine the trail. Holding up a hand to keep Abner back, Tessa took measured silent breaths, drawing her limbs forward one at a time before placing them with absolute precision. Four paces from Abner, she darted forward, thrusting her arm into a mound of earth and leaves.

A frenzied squeaking filled the air as Tessa pulled out a fistful of forest mice. Their small fluffy gray bodies struggled to twist away. Closing a hand around each head, she gave a sharp twist, and the resulting *thok* sent their bodies limp.

Abner jumped with each mouse, staring at her.

The little gray bodies lay cradled in her palms. "Sorry little ones," she said.

"That was ... horrible."

She stomped past him. "I lived in the woods. What did you expect me to live off of? Berries and tree roots?"

"Honestly, yes." Abner followed her. "They're so little and furry, I thought you would have animal friends and—"

"I had Fox. We had to eat. So," she held up the mice, "do you want to eat or not?"

Abner stared at the fistful of tiny dead animals. He swallowed. "How do we make these little furry things into food?"

"Skin, clean, and cook them."

"And that'll be enough for all of us, or should we try to find more?"

"That's where the berries and roots come in."

"Mice?" said Dennison after they returned, his mouth twisting. "Of course you would hunt mice."

Tessa's eyes narrowed. "Bigger game means more to carry, and stronger tools needed to hunt. If you weren't so busy teaching soldiers how to lop off innocent heads and instead gave them some useful skills, maybe you would know that."

"You challenge my skill, Lady?" Dennison said, scoffing. "Without Abner and Cantus protecting you, you would have burned at the old woman's side. You have only lived through the last few weeks because of *my* soldiers' ability to 'lop off heads.'"

"Aren't they the king's soldiers?" Tessa challenged.

Abner stood between them.

Dennison sighed. "I would hardly expect you to understand the complexities. And Abner, if you needed proof to convince you of what I said before," he tossed a hand at Tessa, "she proves herself with every moment."

"What?" Tessa crossed her arms.

"Nothing, it's nothing," Abner said.

Tessa leaned back. "It doesn't seem like noth—"

Ava smacked her hands together. Three hard strikes. The others turned to her. "I am not cleaning these nasty little mice by myself. Everyone needs to help. So shut it, and get to work."

Tessa sat next to her and began cutting up a mouse's middle to its jaw with the dagger, severing the clinging fat to peel the skin away like a coat.

Abner leaned forward.

Tessa's jaw locked. "Are you men going to stand there watching and useless or are you going to help?"

"I don't—"

"Sit," Tessa nodded to her side. "I'll teach you."

Esther knelt by the stream, rubbing the dagger clean in the water as Ava roasted the mice behind her. Bootsteps announced his approach before he reached her, and Esther blew a huff of air past tight lips.

"What, Abner? I—"

Dennison raised his chin at her. "I feel we may have lost our footing."

Esther turned back to scrub at the blade.

"I don't always make the best first impression. Things are different here than I expected to find. Regardless, I see you are important to Prince Abner, and that lends you importance."

Her jaw tightened, hands scrubbing harder.

"I will train you into a competent fighter, if you would like. Though I warn you, your various limitations will make you unlikely to be able to pick up a sword and defeat most anyone you come across, like Abner. You will probably only ever be mediocre at best."

"How inspiring," Esther said, voice dead and flat as the stretching expanse of The Northern Waste.

"Would you rather be coddled?" Dennison asked, folding his arms.

"No."

"Good. Rise a little earlier than the others tomorrow, and we can get in some practice without distractions."

Esther nodded at the ground, the current tugging against her icy fingers. Her eyes followed him as he walked away.

After a silent meal, save for the babbling of the stream over stones and the crackle of the fire, they fell asleep watching the great stars dancing through the branches above.

Esther was kicked awake what seemed like a moment later.

Dennison stood over her. The sky stretched dark behind his head with only a hint of gray to betray the sun's coming rise. He tossed his chin, calling her to her feet, before putting some distance between them and the sleepers.

Esther shivered against the cold. Her back was sore, and the chill of the morning before the sun made her muscles tighten.

"You seemed like an early riser." Dennison flexed the selected stick at the middle. "Should we wait till the lady has completed her morning care routine?"

Esther spat the stale water from her mouth, collected by sleep. "I'm used to waking myself."

Dennison grunted. He passed her a stick and folded his arms, eyes slowly rolling over her from hair to heel. "This," he paused, mouth twisting to one side, "will be an interesting challenge. Alright, set your feet."

Esther complied, turning her heel to create the arrow to her enemy as Cantus had taught her, while her weight sat on the heel behind.

Dennison smiled. "Is that it?"

Esther held up her stick, tipping her chin to one side.

The sky wheeled across her vision. Her jaw bit the dirt. Pain burst through her knee.

"Don't lean into your back heel. It leaves you vulnerable in front and slow." Dennison helped her up. "Set your feet."

Esther obeyed, keeping her weight off her back heel.

"Is that it?" Dennison asked again.

Gritting her teeth, Esther nodded.

Dennison charged forward, flipping his stick at her head. She crashed to one side, her feet tangling beneath her.

"Weight doesn't go on your toes either. You have no balance to react to anything that way. Set your feet."

Esther pulled her body into alignment and then stopped, her mouth a hard line. "Apparently I keep doing it wrong. Are you going to teach me the right way or are you just here to enjoy watching me trip?"

Dennison smiled. "I read you as the type that needs to be shown why something is wrong—to be knocked down a few times before you'd listen. Was I in error?"

Esther rolled the stick in her hand, her jaw locked tight.

"Very well. Let's begin with your feet."

They worked on balance that morning, standing side by side to practice shifting the weight in even, measured movements through different stances, blocks, and strikes.

"It's about control," Dennison said, as they went through a slow chain of lower blocks and slashes. "Giving jerky starts of motion in reaction to your opponent will leave you off balance and vulnerable."

"And everyone practices these same patterns, then?" Esther echoed his every movement, holding her back in a stiff line. "Till one person gets tired and gives up the fight? How accommodating of them."

Dennison thoughtfully stabbed through an imaginary opponent's gut with his stick. "Our minds remember patterns better, and muscle seems to carry memory. Do a motion long enough, it becomes natural, easier. You won't have to think, '*I need to block.*' You will just do it."

"How long does that take?"

"Longer than we have this morning," Dennison said, pulling himself to stand and glancing at the blue sky between the crowding branches.

The sun was hidden, but Esther guessed it couldn't be much past first mark.

"You've done better than I expected. I think you've made progress today."

"Should we work again tomorrow?" Esther dug into the dirt with her stick.

"If you'd like."

XXVII

Crack! Abner's brow rose. He was only allowed a moment of surprise before—*crack*—another blow knocked against his grip. He glanced at Dennison. The captain tossed his chin, refixing Abner's attention onto his opponent.

"When did you—"

A three-strike series sent him back a step, Tessa's face set.

I can have a bit more fun with this. Abner pushed forward, testing her footwork. He nicked her.

She wrung out her knuckles with a hiss. Her eyes pinched as she reset herself.

When he disarmed her, it took effort to drive the point of her stick to the ground and break her grip. He knocked her back with his shoulder.

She kept her feet but lost ground, breathing hard through her nose.

"You've improved," Abner said as he returned the weapon to her.

"I lost." Tessa scraped a few loose strands back from her forehead.

"Obviously, but it was a lot closer of a fight than usual."

She pulled a drink of lake water from the pouch, cringing at the taste. "If you have the time to talk, I'm still terrible."

Abner folded his arms. "But improved. Greatly. And to what do we owe this miraculous burst of new skill?"

Dennison passed by and Tessa's face colored.

Abner's eyes narrowed.

At midmark, Dennison bit through the skin of the yellow fruit Tessa assured them was safe with a grimace. Spitting it to the side, he rubbed the sticky juice from his hands.

"Let's talk about this morning, Lady," he began.

Tessa's mouth tightened.

"What happened?"

"My back hurt," she said, biting into the fruit and crunching it noisily through her jaw.

"You don't have to block every one of his blows. You can move out of the way. Meeting a stronger opponent strike for strike is a waste of energy. Don't fight the blade. Always fight the man."

Abner looked between them. "I knew it!" He nodded at Dennison's stare. "I knew you were helping her. How long?"

"The past eight days," Dennison lifted his shoulders.

Abner's stare narrowed, one side pinching more than the other. "When? We've all been together."

"While you snored the morning away," Tessa said, taking another bite.

He looked at Ava.

She shrugged back at him.

"I will give you one compliment however," Dennison said.

Abner's eyes widened. *When was the last time he complimented me?*

"You didn't flail around like you normally do. But you're still holding your back stiff, it'll knock you off your balance if you—"

"Letting my back go loose will drop me faster than any sword would." Tessa swallowed heavily. "I just need to learn to move faster. But not flail."

Dennison's chin tipped.

Abner cut in. "I thought we'd make faster progress following the stream. How much farther do you think it's going to run?"

"It's winding quite a bit," Dennison agreed, "We've been climbing for the last few days. Should reach something soon."

"We have?" Ava asked. "I've wondered why my legs have been hurting."

Tessa nodded. "I think we're getting closer."

What the company would find when they reached the source of the stream was something that had been growing on Abner's mind more as each day passed. The likelihood of there being absolutely nothing seemed to grow with it. What would they do if all this time had been wasted?

Dennison didn't allow them to sit at their midmark meal for long. His orders sending his company of soldiers to search the northern parts of the forest were, by this time, either discarded as fruitless or completed. The soldiers likely had begun working their way south. He didn't take any confidantes into his plan before executing it, having not known the state of Abner's resources before he found them, so as far as the soldiers knew they were to hunt down their quarry whatever the cost.

Though the travelers had a vast lead ahead of any pursuit, the stream often crossed back near their previous path as the water worked its way down the gradual slope.

It was a jarring sight when the last layer of foliage was pulled aside by Dennison to reveal a rocky mountain giant rising up ahead of them. The barrenness of the stone face, after the long trek through lush green growth, brought Abner's spirits plummeting to his gut.

"That's it then? The mountain?" Abner's face wrinkled as he stared up the incline through the glaring sunlight. He sneezed.

The stream beckoned them through its babble as it skirted the mountain slope, crossing it like a snake slithering over the giant's foot. The path led around the mountain, not up it. Abner's limbs filled with new vigor as his eyes dropped from the near vertical climb that began at the giant's ankle and rose to the sky.

"Shall we?" Ava stepped from the cover of the tree line, picking her way along the pebbled banks of the stream as it cut its path through the rock.

They plunged into the shadow of the mountain, the water drawing them between two opposing slopes that it splashed between. As the incline steepened, Abner would have offered Tessa a hand, but she linked arms with Ava and the two struggled up the path together.

Even in the shadow of the rocky giants the stream carried the seeds of life. As if the forest had taken a breath but then resumed growing along this new ground like an army conquering the desert to wilderness. The water changed as they rounded the mountain as well, white boats of foam floating past them as the river spilled with greater speed.

There's something strange about this place. Abner could feel it in the quickening breeze that slipped chilly fingers round his neck, lifting his hair as he shivered. And the sound. It had built so gradually, Abner couldn't place when he had first noticed it. But the steady roar of some heavy, powerful thing thundered to them, carried by the water. *Shouldn't I be afraid?*

Instead of a shock of fear, a spray of mist stung their eyes as the group arrived at the source of the noise. The water thundered, cascading over a high rock wall, stones barring their way in almost too perfect a placement as to be natural. The roar came from the churning of the pooling water beneath the wall. The surrounding rocks were made ever-slick with the spray and the green moss clinging tight to the crevices between them.

Without a word, Abner and Tessa moved forward to climb. Their feet dug into the moss for a better grip and Abner raised his weight onto the mist-splattered rock.

Yellow eyes.

Abner fell back, pulling Tessa with him.

A heavy golden body crouched at the top of the wall. The hanging mane dripped collected mist from the pool. A deeper, wilder roar than the churning of the water ripped the air around his ears apart.

Abner drew his sword. "I thought you said there weren't any lions here."

"There aren't," Tessa's voice was nearly lost in the water's noise and his own thudding heartbeat.

The great lion's head shifted, its long barbed tail whipping into sight before flashing behind its wide body again.

"Well, Beast!" Dennison was at Abner's side, sword drawn.

That is your choice? Very well. I could eat.

The voice in Abner's mind was quickly overwhelmed by a deep growl as the lion launched from the wall with claws stretching toward them. The first strike of its paw on Abner's sword nearly knocked it from his grip.

He twisted his blade to slash along the padded underside of the lion's paw.

It didn't seem to notice, launching toward his shoulder, jaw open.

Dennison grunted beside him as blow after blow missed the beast or was knocked aside. Any attempt to edge around the lion was beaten back.

The creature used every claw and tooth to its advantage, striking at them with the cruel barb on its tail.

When it ducked low, Abner lunged forward, ready to cleave through its heavy wrinkled forehead. Dennison had to knock aside the stinging barb that flew at the prince's chest. The claws ripped the air a breath from his pounding heart as Abner pulled himself out of reach.

Abner's limbs jolted. His foot slipped on the wet rock, the ground beating the breath from his lungs.

The captain moved in to defend him, his sword entangling with its claws as it tried to bite into his shoulder. The lion's barbed tail speared Dennison through the side. He fell to his knees, holding just beneath his lowest rib before collapsing onto the rocky bank, shoulders shuddering in convulsions.

"Dennison!" *Up! I need to—*

A slippered foot crushed Abner's newly-healed fingers. Ava slid in front of the two men. She tripped back on her dress beneath the dripping fur and wild yellow eyes. Her shoulders trembled, hugging her neck. "Is there another way?"

The fire in the beast's eyes dampened as its great mane tipped to one side to better study her empty hands.

"You said we made a choice. Is there another way?"

Always, growled the voice. The lion's eyes narrowed.

"Take me then, and let them pass?"

"Ava, get back!" Tessa yelled. Abner had forgotten about her, glad she had stayed out of the way with only a borrowed dagger to defend herself.

That is your choice? To be a meal so others may pass beyond you? Curious.

Ava swallowed, ignoring Tessa's cries for her to move. "What I have, I give."

The lion struck with one heavy paw, the clawed blades pinning Ava's face onto the rocky bank as hot huffs of breath hit her hair. It leaned down over her, black lips raised high over its teeth. Ava's eyes met Tessa's, heavy tears leaking from the corners.

Tessa swung at the lion's back. She was knocked aside by the length of its tail only to crash against the rock wall and slip into the rushing water.

Abner threw himself out to catch her as she flailed for something to grip. He caught her hand before the current could pull her downstream. Tugging her to the bank, Abner rose.

The lion's attention had never left Ava, its tail lashing the air. *You have been found worthy. Pass on, dear one.*

Ava's face pinched tight, her throat letting out a sob, as the lion leaned down. Instead of the bite of teeth, the brush of heavy yellow fur covered her. The lion ran its jaw along her curls, a deep rumble grating its voice as it rubbed its cheek against her.

It's ... nuzzling? Abner and Tessa glanced at each other, lowering their weapons.

The lion removed its claws from Ava's cheek, allowing her to rise, as small bubbles of blood marked her skin. *Now, about the rest of you.* The barbed tail cut through the air.

Dennison lay crumpled on the ground and Abner stood guarding him and Tessa.

Ava's quiet plea was lost to the noise of the water.

An ear flicked to her and then rolled away. The beast's heavy stare fixed on Dennison. *That one. Turn him over.*

Ava nodded to Abner.

Mouth held tight in a grimace, he turned Dennison belly up, keeping ready to leap in front of the captain and defend him. The shuddering had slowed and Abner stared, terrified, at Dennison's sweat-lined brow.

Back away. The growl grated through the lion's throat.

Tessa pulled his shoulder.

The lion padded forward, its mouth opened to pant heavily past its massive jaw. Dennison grimaced through whatever sleep he was caught in as the hot animal breath hit the wound piercing his side. The lion's tongue rolled along the skin.

One. Two. Three. Four. Abner wasn't sure why he counted the licks the lion gave in the eternity before Dennison's eyes opened.

Nostrils flared, the captain stared at the great beast as it turned its back to him.

Abner's shoulders dropped as he let go of the stinging tension in his chest. *Everything is fine. Somehow. Everything is fine.*

The lion's tail curled over its back, poised to strike. *Why are you here?* It took root at the base of the wall where the water pummeled the air the loudest.

"We—" Abner's voice was swallowed up in the noise of the fall.

The lion yawned, lips pulling high over its long spear-like teeth. Its gaze drifted over the water.

It wants me to drink? Abner grimaced at the churning pool. Scooping a handful, he hesitated before pouring it into his mouth.

We—he thought as hard as he could, forehead gaining a thousand wrinkles as he struggled to push the message through the air to the lion. *We've come to seek ... after the dragons. The stream is magic ... we have followed it through the forest to find help.*

The lion blinked at them.

Abner was certain his thoughts were echoing only in his own mind.

The beast gathered itself, launching up the wall with a single bound. Its barbed tail lashed through the air a final time before the lion was gone.

He was a fool to think he could—

Then enter. If you dare.

Abner's eyes met Tessa's as she gently wiped the blood spots from Ava's cheek.

Beware the dark.

Esther's heartbeat thudded through her neck.

"What does that mean?" Abner yelled over the roar of the waterfall. "Beware the dark?"

"I assume we don't want to be here at nightfall," Dennison said. His eyes blinked heavily as he checked the area. Already the mountain's shadow seemed deeper.

Esther nodded to the rock wall, Abner joining her to stand at the base once again. The slimy moss was slick between her fingers as she pulled herself up the first few handholds. Her back ached beneath the pack, and her limbs shook as she fell over the top of the wall. She tumbled onto solid ground as the pulsing pain reached the point that she couldn't hide it from her face.

Abner pulled himself up beside her, taking in the grassy bank stretching ahead. The sound of the water was suddenly less.

The lion was nowhere to be seen.

"Those roots," Esther pushed the words past the strain of keeping herself held together. "We can rip them down and make a rope." The long hairy tangles hung from the trees growing out from the mountain's near-vertical, rocky side. Esther's feet were only barely able to stand. Her back quivered after a few shuffling steps, and she fell into a heap on the ground.

Abner's footsteps thumped toward her.

"I thought that new corset string was supposed to fix you," he said, moving her hair out of her eyes as he turned her to lay on her side.

Esther coughed, drawing up packed wetness from her chest. "Don't think that's possible now. Besides, I've taken a few hits with it."

"Stay here," Abner said, stepping over her to rip a fistful of thin roots from a flowering bush sending a cascade of dried petals over his head. He strode out of sight. "You terrify me when you do that."

Esther blinked against the grass, listening to Ava scramble up the wall.

"Lady Tessa?" Ava said, slipping down to her side. Her eyes stumbled over Esther's limp frame. "What happened? Did *it* come back? Are you alright?"

"She's had one of her fits," Abner grunted through a heavy strain as Dennison scaled the wall.

Ava studied Esther's face.

"I'm fine." Esther swallowed. "Just need my corset tightened."

Ava helped her rise to her knees. "Oh no."

Esther turned her chin. "What is it?"

"The string's gotten frayed. I can't tighten it or it's sure to snap."

"Can you do something with this?" Abner dropped a tightly wound roll of bandages in Ava's hand.

Esther's eyes pinched.

He shrugged. "I bought them in Naamah. I thought they might help, like they helped my hand. The salve broke, but maybe these can do something."

Ava twisted Esther back around to measure the fabric against the hole. "This won't work ... but maybe if I ... give me a moment." Ava sat down with the roll of fabric. *Rrrrrip.*

The wave of weakness grew, sending Esther's back swaying on the rising tide. Abner caught her arm before her torso could fall. Esther pinned herself in place with her elbows, bracing her palms against the ground.

His hand hadn't moved.

Esther's face heated. "What?"

"I—"Abner swallowed.

Ava returned to her side, holding a long rope of stripped bandage twisted into a thin tight cord, which she threaded through the holes.

Esther sighed in relief as the corset tightened to hug her waist. She could breathe again.

"Shouldn't we be getting on?" Dennison glanced pointedly at the darkening sky growing heavy with clouds.

Esther nodded, allowing a moment for the weakness to recede as the crushing pressure lessened. When it was bearable, she stood.

Abner walked beside Esther, her pack slung over his shoulder. He smirked at her.

"Stop," she groaned, her eyes heavy.

"I'm a little disappointed, you know. I drank the water and my head has yet to turn into a cloud." Abner's gaze narrowed as he stared ahead. "I do feel ... odd, though. Like I was a boy again and just ... happy. No great cause, just happy to be..." He chuckled. "Maybe the water only works on you. You should take a drink. If nothing else, you could keep me entertained by telling me how lovely you find my elbows or my teeth."

Night bugs began to spark along the greenery. The little lights winked around them. Clouds continued to roll in from the east and collect overhead. When the rain started, Esther grimaced as the heavy drops *plinked* against her nose. She missed her cloak, her gloves, her mask. It was hot to keep on in the summer months, but as the weather turned cold, she was always grateful for the coverage.

Abner smiled at the sky dripping water on his cheeks. "I just love that smell," he said, pulling a deep breath through his chest. He shook out his sopping hair at Esther. She shrank away, unable to stop the smile before he saw it.

Dennison's face soured. "Cursed weather. I knew our luck would turn."

Abner grinned, reaching for Esther as the rain began to pelt harder.

She slipped around Ava, pinning herself to her friend's side. Esther raised her brow.

"You think I won't," Abner said, laughing. But he didn't.

Esther was left to plod through the soggy ground in peace.

The banks of the stream were now thoroughly muddy, the islands of grass anchored between the little channels rushing to join the great river as it wound to the waterfall and the world beyond.

When the mouth of a cave came into view, Dennison stretched his stride and angled toward it. The stream flowed out from the dark entrance. The captain shook out his shoulders, rubbing together stiff fingers, as he stomped his wet feet just out of reach from the rain's splattering blows. It was as good a place as any to take shelter from the deepening dark. The stream flowed between the cave's disjointed stony teeth, filling most of the cavern save for a narrow path threading along one side.

"So," Ava said, rubbing warmth back into her arms. "This is it? The source?"

"No." Abner swept his dripping hair from his forehead, spraying the rock behind him with flecks of water. "It can't be."

Esther crept along the edge of the cave river now flowing wide and deep to fill the room. She shivered as the air turned chilly against her dripping clothes and hair. Reaching the back wall, her eyes strained wide against the growing dark. In vain, she hunted for any break in the cave's stone. Pressing an ear to the rock, she closed her eyes, silencing her breath to listen.

"No," she called to them, waving as she made her way back. "I can hear splashing beyond the wall, there must be a way through."

"Likely to lead to us being buried alive," said Dennison, keeping toward the front of the cave. What little light the world had left shrouded him in shadow as he folded heavy arms. "Sire, I think now we must be honest with ourselves. This is a foolish waste of your time."

Abner was already wading into the water to cross to the other side, holding his packs and sheath above his shoulders to keep them dry. "What are you talking about? Dennison, did you see that thing at the waterfall? It was a lion with a stinger for its tail. Such a thing isn't natural and—"

"Exactly why we should turn back now. I admit, I thought we would find nothing at your so-called magic stream, but since there is something it should be left alone until we have the power to come back and conquer it. What you're doing is reckless. I mean it, boy. You need to think!"

Esther plunged into the cold water after Abner, ignoring the fierce shiver that shook her shoulders. The current dragged at her weary muscles, but also tugged away the weight from her legs and back. She could bear it. Relief eclipsed even the biting cold.

Ava and Dennison followed, the captain's face set in a scowl as he surged through the water. Abner reset his sheath at his side and Esther took back her pack with a nod of thanks.

"A wise king listens to advice from more experienced—"

"Good thing I'm not a king then, Dennison. We go on."

The captain's face tightened in anger, his eyes narrowing to slits. "Your decisions are becoming more erratic, Prince."

"This way, there's a path!" exclaimed Ava, pushing her hand through a deep shadow along the rock wall.

Abner looked back at the captain, raising an eyebrow. "There's a path," he said, moving to where Ava had disappeared into the shadow. He must have knocked into her by accident. Ava's sudden piercing scream echoed and Esther and the captain raced toward the darkness. They slid to a stop on the edge of an empty black hole.

"*Thsss.*"

XXVIII

"We're going to die," Ava said, thrashing to keep her chin above water.

Abner lent her his shoulder, towing her as he pushed through the little waves to reach the wall of the wide cavern. He spit aside water and blinked his eyes clear to stare around the dark lake they had landed in. His ears still rang with her wild scream as she had fallen.

Ava's white-tipped fingers bit into the rock, her face lit by the strange glow from the water as she stared at him. "We're going to die."

"We are not going to die." Abner found a handhold in the rock, swinging his gaze over the cavern in search of a way out. There was no break in the water from one end of the wall to the other. No rock or sandy shore. Nothing but water between the barren faces of stone. A nagging fear opened in his chest. *What do I do? What if—*

"There's no way out," Ava whispered. "We're going to die."

Abner forced his throat to swallow. He shivered as little waves knocked against his collarbone. "Where is this water coming from?"

Ava's eyes pulled wide, reflecting the lake's shine. "It's getting deeper."

"Right, it's deeper." Abner smiled. "The water has to be fed from somewhere. Maybe there's a hole in the wall beneath the surface. We could use it to get out." Abner stretched his fingers beneath the water to feel over the wet stone.

Ava watched him, each of their huffing breaths echoing against the murky rock. "We'll never find it just pawing over the whole wall." She tried to stare through the water, keeping one hand on the rock wall and using the other to sweep her billowing dress out of the way. "Oh."

"Oh?" Abner met her eyes.

"Can you help me out of this dress? I have an idea."

Jusst another sstep, Sstrangersss.

Esther jumped away from the wall as something cold and muscled rolled over her knuckles. Dennison gripped her shoulder to steady her beside the hole Abner and Ava had disappeared down. She shivered.

"Who are you?" Dennison asked into the dark.

The night had deepened and the turn of the tunnel cut out what little light there was left. The black wall of air before them was so complete, Esther couldn't see the far side of the hole blocking their path or any shape of the form that hissed at them from its depths.

Who are you? That'sss far more interessting to me.

"We are travelers who just lost friends. They fell. Do you know how to find them?" Esther's voice bounced off the walls, echoing back to her.

"*Thsss.*" The hiss faded into a stretched silence. *If they fell down then down isss where they'll be.*

"That's the only way? To fall down after them?" Doubt colored Dennison's tone.

It'sss the quickesst way.

There was some strange quality about the voice, a tilt in tone that made Esther pause over the hole. As if it were laughing at some secret joke with every word. She glared into the black. "You're lying."

I never lie. The undercurrent of mirth flowed deeper than ever. *Honesstly.*

"*Thsss, thsss, thsss,*" chorused several voices.

The scratching of claws across rock around and above them sent Esther tripping back onto the soaked folds of her dress.

"There's more of them," Dennison said in disgust, helping her by feel to her feet.

Go ahead now, into the darknesss, the first voice spoke through the scratches.

"There has to be another way," Esther said, stomping her heel onto the ground to scatter the unseen hissing voices.

Dennison shuffled along the wall. "It's narrow, but I think we can edge around. The hole doesn't cover the entire path. Can you manage?"

Esther nodded.

"Lady?"

"Oh, sorry. Yes, I'll be fine." She was glad of the dark as her pale cheeks grew warm.

No, no, no, no. Don't do that. We're ssso hungry.

A cold something fell against her neck, sending Esther into a wild swatting dance. A small prick of teeth bit into her throat.

Dennison sounded as if he suffered similarly.

Esther tripped backward into the moonlight as more of the cold little bodies dropped onto her, the creatures weighing on her hair, her dress, her shoulders. They were black with red spots running up their sides, like smooth-skinned lizards a little longer than her hand. *I can't get free! I can't—*

Without thought of how much pain it would cause, Esther ran toward the dark tunnel and, gathering her weight, launched off the edge of the hole. She arced through darkness for a moment before her ankles were struck by sudden ground on the far side.

The blow rolled through every limb with jarring force shaking her free of all biting teeth and clinging claws. Save one that bit her hand with furious need.

Esther ripped herself free, throwing it down the hole, the hiss fading away.

"Little devils—get—be gone!"

"Jump!" Esther called to him across the hole.

"Are you mad?"

"Just—jump!"

Esther threw herself out of his way as Dennison landed heavily, his feet scraping the stone to stop his weight. "They're gone," he said.

"Probably don't like coming on this side of the hole, for some reason." Esther used the wall to climb to her feet. The new bandage threading through her corset had held her back rigid, despite the fall. Esther's limbs quaked with gratitude. The pain was bearable.

Dennison spit down the hole. He sniffed.

"Whatever they'd scatter from is probably bad for us," Esther said, staring into the dark but seeing nothing. Her breath shook. "Do we risk a light?"

"We cannot leave Abner."

"No," Esther agreed. "Nor Ava. But there has to be another way to reach them besides falling down after them."

"We could pass a hundred branching paths without knowing it in this pitch. Let's have some light."

Esther dug through her pack by feel. Her fingers brushed the smooth side of her fire stone, and she smirked into the black. She struck it against the wall, satisfied by the arc of sparks cast.

Dennison tore a strip of fabric from his tunic. He muttered, "I'll be in rags by the time we return to Lydia."

"We'll need something to catch the sparks," Esther said, groping along the floor. Her smirk grew wider still as her hands closed on a smooth stick a little longer than her forearm. "Here!"

Her ears marked his footsteps coming closer, moving to one side so they didn't collide in the black. His feet stomped the stone in front of her.

"I found something." She sent out an arc of sparks from the wall, lighting up his face and the cloth in his hand.

"Cast the light again, Lady?" Dennison said, quietly.

Esther stared at it until the last spark faded. *Oh. Not a stick.*

A long bone lay clutched in her grip, cut into a jagged shard as if broken by some massive jaw. Her thudding heart made her fingers clumsy. *Light. Now.* It took a few tries to coordinate where to send the sparks in the dark and for the cloth to catch, but when the torch at last blazed to life it cast a quivering glow around them.

Piles of bones pocked the path, all broken and sucked dry. She tried to keep her mind from wandering over imaginings of what unseen predator might lurk in the dark that would gather such a collection. Esther selected another long broken bone to have in hand in case something happened to their first.

"Beware the dark." Dennison's jaw tightened. "The lion's warning was not for nightfall, but for this cave. And whatever beast lies hidden in this darkness."

Esther rolled her wrist, testing the bone's weight in her hand. "Then let's get moving."

He studied her tense features.

"Abner and Ava will need our help."

He nodded, drawing out his sword.

As they walked, Esther listened. Beyond the *plink* of distant water drops hitting stone and their own scraping footsteps, her ears stretched but found nothing. No bird calls, no wind; just a damp, cold nothing inside the mountain's gut.

Dennison cleared his throat.

Esther jumped.

"I don't know if Abner has made his intentions known," he began.

"Intentions?" Esther hoped the fire's flickering yellow light disguised the heat prickling her cheeks. "He has none."

"I assure you, he does." Dennison stared ahead, his mouth twisting. "I've known that boy a long time. I've never seen him act the way he does around you. Defiant. Illogical."

"Because he's normally such a wealth of wisdom," Esther muttered.

"Normally he is teachable, not—" Dennison pushed out a breath. "Just be aware of what your encouragement does to him. What it might cost him."

"I don't want anything from him," Esther said.

"For now."

She would have argued but a change in the air pulled her feet to a stop. Some instinct from her years as both prey and hunter tightened the hand holding the bone shard. The heavy smell of rot and sweat rolled to them like an invading fog.

Dennison stopped walking as well, turning to look behind. His eyes stretched, reflecting the flash of yellow fangs. The wide toothy maw strained toward him, a desperate moan rattling its throat.

Esther drove the bone shard into the roof of the monster's open mouth. She cut her arm on one of its teeth.

Its black-slitted eyes trembled as they ticked toward her. A low, croaking groan rattled from its throat. Its strength gave out. The clawed arms fell.

The sudden weight sent Esther to the ground with it. Dennison's breath huffed behind her as Esther planted a foot on its wide gray forehead to pull the shard of bone from the creature's skull. It broke as it came out and she grimaced, dropping her fragment.

Dennison lifted the light high above the creature, squinting. Esther leaned against the wall, kicking aside the bones as she worked to slow her pulse. She prodded at the shallow scrape on her arm. *Barely broke the skin. Poisoned?* She glanced over the massive gray body, collapsed in a heap. *I guess I'll find out.*

"You, ah, were leading with the wrong foot," Dennison said, turning his back to the tunnel already traveled.

"I was leading with the—I saved your face from becoming a meal for that monster. A thank you would suffice."

"Just because the job was done, doesn't mean it couldn't have been done better."

Esther sighed, stomping to keep up with the light.

"But ... thank you."

She glared ahead into the dark.

"There's a kind of clasp at the back."

Abner's fingers hesitated over her shoulders as Ava pulled her wet curls to one side. A hiss from above and a splash in the water drew his eyes, but seeing nothing through the waves he went back to working at the fabric.

"You have to slip it loose. And don't tear it. This is my only one."

His hand pinched at the cloth, searching for something to loosen the infernal thing, so he could stop treading water feeling like a fool for being unable to undo a woman's dress.

"The idea would probably amuse you," Ava muttered. "A woman having to run around in her undergarments because she didn't have anything else. Probably would do it on purpose just to see me blush."

Abner's relief was audible as he found the silver metal piece that was clipped between the two sides. "Bleeding—" his fingers stumbled over it.

"Lift—lift it!"

Kicking his feet furiously to keep his chin above the water, Abner yanked the dress clasp up and down with both hands. It slipped loose. He helped Ava free her arms from the soaked fabric. An underwater wave gently knocked his feet toward the wall. Abner studied the rising deep. The lights had grown dimmer as the water crept higher up the stone and forced them to find new handholds.

Ava passed the heavy fabric to Abner, clutching her slip to her chest and dropping her chin to the water.

"Right. Stay here." Abner turned from her.

Her idea wasn't bad, he admitted only to himself. Using the billowing fabric to watch for changes in the water's direction beneath the surface could help them find a way out. The cloth being sucked to the wall would mean water was flowing out of the lake to somewhere else and pulling the fabric with it. It billowing wide told of water flowing into the lake. He kicked the dress down, one hand on the wall and the other knotted into the pink cloth. It swayed gently as he began his slow search of the stone beneath the water.

Ava clung to the rock, marking where he'd started. "Anything?"

"If there was, I would tell you." Abner coughed out the wave that broke against his lips. "Aha! Here's something! Like that."

Her sigh carried across the water.

Halfway through his crawl around the room, Abner's nails bit into the rock, frustration hardening his grip. He was running out of wall to search and had found nothing except the slight billowing his own motion caused. *She's safe. She's with Dennison, so she's safe. I just have to find her.* Then there was only a quarter of the wall left to search. He sneezed into the water splashing at his nose. *There has to be—*

"Ab—Abner, look!" Ava pointed over the water at him.

The dress unfurled slowly beneath the waves, the blue light tracing patterns over the pink fabric.

He returned Ava's smile. "Here's something."

She nodded at the dress. "Now give it back."

Abner slapped a wet hand on the stone, marking the dull gray to shiny black before he pushed off the wall and swam back to Ava. "Can you swim?" he asked, holding her arm above the water so she could maneuver herself into the dress.

"Not really," she grunted, struggling with the wet, clingy fabric. She eyed the water.

"Can you hold your breath?"

She pulled in air slowly through her nose, as if testing it. "I guess we'll find out."

"Maybe I should try first," Abner said. "I could come back for you."

Her skin reflected the shifting lights of the water. "I don't..." Her smile faded, eyes forming twin moons. Her face split into a scream.

What—Abner's head smacked the stone behind, blinding him. His ears rang. He blinked, vision returning through a white haze as the long tail whipped across the surface.

The thing swam back down below the waves.

Ava yelled something he couldn't understand, plastering herself to the wall.

He sent a splash of water over his face to try to shock his body into working again. "Get to the hole!" Abner pulled Ava along as he edged to where his handprint marked the wall. The ringing faded, and he swayed with the waves, watching the pulsing blue light twist and dim as the layers of water between them grew.

"I can't—I can't move," Ava said, shaking behind his shoulder.

The thing rounded on itself, the light illuminating the head as it shifted from side to side, climbing through the water. A long silver snake with blue sparks embedded through its thick, strangely-ridged body swam toward them, its eyes pinning Abner's in a cold gray stare.

His sword would be impossible to wield in the water, any thrust below the surface losing all its force before it got to the creature. *I need to think. What can I do?*

As the snake reached striking distance it turned in a wide arc, as if studying for a point of attack.

Abner's breath hit the water as his chin dropped low.

A cape of arms unfurled from the creature's body as if the snake had ten extra tails, lit up by a thousand sparks of blue light.

Abner tugged Ava to one side as the snake darted forward, propelled by its long arms.

Its fanged mouth slipped wide. The fangs struck stone while the arms found purchase around Abner's legs. Rolling its wounded head through the water, the snake pulled itself to Abner.

He fought against the curling muscle of the arms as they pinned down his hands.

Ava struggled behind him.

There wasn't much time left. *Think. Think.* Abner couldn't move. *Think!*

The snake rose out of the water, their noses almost touching.

Don't fight the blade. Always fight the man. Dennison's voice echoed in memory.

Abner couldn't free his hands. There was no way he could—*oh.*

The snake tasted the air, its grip around Abner's limbs tightening.

Tipping his chin back, Abner set his jaw and threw his forehead to crack the snake's nose. It hissed, coils loosening on his arms, lessening its binding tension in its shock of pain. Wrenching his hands free, Abner caught the snake's answering strike, wrapping his grip around its most prominent fangs. With a pull of force that drew a yell from his chest, Abner broke the teeth of the creature, and his legs were released. It twisted over itself, churning the water into a boil with its frenzied coiling.

"Let's go!" Abner yelled.

Ava gulped a large breath of air, shutting her eyes tight as Abner pulled her below the waves.

The hole was large enough for him to work his way through, brushing his shoulders on the worn-smooth stone. He pushed Ava in first, guarding their passage.

She began to crawl up the tunnel, bubbles spilling over her shoulder.

If they didn't reach an outlet with air in time…

Abner cast a last look back, locking with the gray eyes of the snake as it coiled at the floor of the cavern. Before it could move, he turned from the deformed creature and worked his way up the water-filled slope. His muscles were held taut with sparks of energy as he was sure of feeling a strike on his back at any moment. Just as the burn in Abner's lungs became unbearable—the relentless crush of need on his chest threatening to turn his vision black—the rock gave way and open water greeted them. Kicking off the floor of the newly-discovered cavern with an arm around Ava to pull her along, Abner's face broke free.

Air…sweet air. His lungs drank greedily, as he scrambled to the rocky shore. *We made it out, Tessa.* "I don't understand," Abner said at last, as they sat together on the rock to let the water out of their shoes. "It could fit through the hole, so why didn't it keep pursuing us?"

"Maybe it decided we just weren't worth the trouble?" Ava said, knocking her shoe against the ground with three hard strikes.

The quiet steady lapping of water against rock filled the air between them. Abner's pulse eventually slowed to match. Left behind, now that the panic of escape had ebbed, was a weight of exhaustion. He dragged in one slow breath after another, too tired to do more than be.

"If someone had told me a year ago that Prince Abner would have removed my dress and saved me from a giant snake monster all in—I assume—one night, I would've called them mad." Ava sniffed through a wet nose. "How did I end up here?"

Abner was glad of the dark, not wanting Ava to see the small smile her words brought unbidden to his mouth. He flexed his hands. *Different.*

The two crept through the black, searching for a stone wall to guide them. There was a passage, and, beyond that, another. With nothing but cool rock beneath their fingertips they shuffled on, straining for a light, until, at last, they found the cloud-covered moon.

The light went out.

Dennison's footsteps halted beside Esther. A stutter of a spark lit the long scar furrowing his cheek as they both stared at the expiring torch.

"Quick!" Esther said, sweeping her hands across the rocky floor. A moist smooth something squished beneath her palm. Esther explored the cold thing with her fingers, breath held in her chest.

A thin stalk beneath a narrow, flat top embedded into dirt piled in a corner.

Esther smiled, ripping it free. "Push this into the hollow part of the bone."

"Lady?" Distaste soured his tone as she thrust the squished mushroom into his hand.

"Just don't eat them. I don't know if they're poisonous. But they're dry enough to burn."

Dennison grunted, crushing the fungus into the hollow canal and wrapping a new length of torn fabric at the top. When she struck the torch to life with a spray of sparks, Esther met Dennison's relieved smile with one of her own. The bone piles had ended several passages ago, and they had rejoined the stream as it cut through the rock. So far the water had not left their side.

When a patch of gray illuminated a square of rock ahead of them, Dennison pulled to a stop.

Esther closed her eyes to listen, straining through the noise of the stream.

"We cannot go that way," Dennison said. "Abner is somewhere behind. We have to find him and get him safely out of this infernal dark. Go ahead if you want. I have—"

"Quiet!" Esther whispered, gesturing to the light.

"I won't tell you again! Stay here!" Abner's voice echoed down the tunnel, rising over the babble of the stream.

"Is that an order from the prince?"

"If it'll make you listen, fine. I order you."

Dennison and Esther scrambled through the narrow cave opening.

Abner and Ava glared at eachother, standing next to another chink in the mountainside a little farther down the slope.

Ava shook her head. "She's my friend—"

"Thank the stars you're both okay!" Esther waved at them, her chest bursting with relief.

Ava screeched, gathering her skirt to climb up the slope.

Abner's eyes danced between the two new arrivals. His shoulders relaxed over his tired smile. "Still alive then?"

Esther reached down to pull Ava up the slope, turning to avoid a mouthful of messy curls as she was tugged into a tight embrace.

The companions looked back at the cavernous mouth of the mountain, ready to swallow them again into darkness. The stream was gone, left behind in the cave.

"So," Abner hesitated, "Do we go back in?"

"Not on your life, Abner," Dennison's voice was stern. "That danger in the dark we were warned of was in that cave, and there was probably more we didn't meet. This curiosity quest of yours isn't worth it."

Esther edged around Ava to put her ear to the rock wall. "I can't tell where it goes, the rock is too thick."

Ava bit her lip, her eyes skipping from the cave, across the mountain face, and over the side. "What if, in the morning, we went on but marked our way in case we needed to come back and try going through the cave? The stream led us here and water goes downhill. So if we go up we might run into it again."

Esther returned Abner's shrug. A bush grew off the side of the mountain, large red berries crowning its narrow black branches. Esther smeared a berry across the gray stone, making their first mark as the company moved away from the cave to get some rest.

When Esther volunteered herself to keep watch, Abner picked a particularly jagged rock to sit against and leaned into it. She tried not to notice, but heat prickled at her cheeks as she avoided his stare. When Dennison's breath deepened at last, Abner rose and picked his way to her.

"Can we speak?" he asked.

"Alright," Esther said, unease tightening her gut.

Abner led her away from the others. He wasted a long moment digging up a small rock embedded in packed dirt with the toe of his boot.

"Are you—"

"Give me a moment, alright?" Abner snapped. He sighed. "Wait, come back. Please?"

Esther turned her shoulders toward him, her mouth twisting.

"I don't want to have you somewhere else, again."

"What?"

"I mean, I didn't like not knowing where you were in the cave. Despite us facing terrible danger, I wanted you with me."

Esther raised her brow. "You wanted me in danger?"

"No, obviously not, you're twisting what I'm saying."

"I'm just trying to understand."

"Right." Abner pushed out a heavy breath. "I hate talking like this. I wish I could just—" he threw his hands forward, "—show you."

"Show me?"

Abner's eyes tightened as they skipped across her expression. "That almost sounded like an invitation. Just, stay close to me from now on, alright?"

She became aware of her blood pounding through every limb as he turned away. She hardly recognized him as the prince. He was just Abner. Her skin prickled. The moment was getting carried farther out of her reach. In a breath it could slip out of sight forever.

"Abner," she said, pausing his foot midstep.

He turned back to her.

Breathe, you idiot. "Show me."

XXIX

It took two strides for him to reach her. A small noise of uncertainty escaped his throat as he slipped a hand beneath her hair. His eyes studied her.

Esther's lips twitched into a smile. She leaned into his palm to soak in the warmth through her cheek.

That was all the encouragement he needed to pull her forward and place a feather-light kiss on her lips that almost tickled. He leaned away, the effort of restraint obvious in the tight set of his mouth.

It created a knot of tension in Esther's chest. With an irritated sigh, she gripped his tunic and pulled his body to hers, spilling the tension through her lips and giving him the opportunity to relieve his own. It didn't matter that she had no idea what she was doing with her hands or her mouth as they poured their energy into one another. Everything just felt so good. Showering sparks of light, as if someone was striking a fire stone behind her closed lids, filled Esther's vision as her waist was drawn into a tight grip.

Hollow black eyes, a bleeding chest, ticking movements. Fox's image sent a burst of energy through her, and she pulled away from it in fright.

"Agh!" Abner grimaced, rubbing his lip with his thumb. "Stars above, that hurt."

"I'm sorry," Esther said, clutching the rocky mountainside and trying to blink away the image. "I'm sorry. I can't."

Abner was breathing hard. "I don't—I don't understand. You asked me to, didn't you? I'm not insane, you asked?"

Esther pushed a breath through shaking lips. "I just can't. I'm sorry."

"Why? Why not? Obviously you wanted to, unless—"

She looked at him.

His brow shot high above his eyes. "My kiss apparently is that terrible that you've changed your mind. That's bleeding wonderful, I'm really glad you were able to sort that out for yourself!" He picked up a rock and hurled it off the side of the mountain.

"It's ... Fox."

He clamped his eyes shut, shaking his head. "What?"

"I saw him," Esther swallowed.

Abner cast his eyes along the bare rock. "And do you see him now?"

"Obviously not."

"Well you might, you just said you were seeing things."

"Of all people you should—Fox died at Shiloh. When I'm asleep I see him. Now I'm seeing him when I'm awake. I can't just—"

A hollow laugh shook through Abner's shoulders. "So, the world won't let me be just Abner? Or is it you? I can never be any different in your eyes. Always the evil prince. You'll never see me as anything else. You just ... can't."

"That's not true," Esther said, but Abner shook his head, stomping away.

She waited a moment before following him back to the others. The heat died from Esther's gut and her eyes prickled as she resumed her seat.

Abner's shoulder rose and fell with each angry breath.

Morning came too soon. Abner's eyes stung at the glare of early sunlight.

Wordlessly they began to pick their way along the mountainside. They now had no stream to follow and a very long drop if they should slip. The wind picked up. They were forced into a narrow line, hugging the rock wall as they edged across the giant.

Ava and Tessa kicked their ankles free of the tangled mess the air made of their dresses. Just as Tessa looked ready to rip the dress off and hurl it down the mountainside they were greeted by the sound of water splattering against stone. Ava nudged her arm, smiling, and the two of them picked up their pace as the path widened.

"Looks like we'll have to climb." Tessa stood beside the waterfall, squinting up the giant.

The stream had made a narrow chasm for itself into the hard rock, surging out in a heavy spray. The waterfall struck the stone, the path broken beneath its relentless pouring.

Abner tested the rock along the falls against his grip. Sandy pieces broke off onto his fingers. He held them up as evidence to the others. Even a goat wouldn't be able to climb up this slope that crumbled away against the slightest pressure.

The water pummeled the air.

Below the rock cradling the pooling water, Abner could see nothing as white clouds hugged the giant's knees. They had already climbed into the heavens apparently. Abner squinted at the sky, checking that the sun was as unreachable as ever. High above them another layer of clouds marched across the blue expanse.

Abner cleaned his hand in the spray. "The rock isn't fit to hold us. We'll have to find another path."

"Do you mean go back?" Ava glanced down the mountain path, a shiver passing through her shoulders. "I didn't see any other way to follow the stream."

Dennison crossed his arms. "Probably best to find a way back down the mountain while our necks are still whole, put this venture behind us until more important matters are settled."

"What are you doing?" Abner caught Tessa's waist as her foot skidded through the hold she was testing her weight against.

Her lips parted, a gasp raising her chest.

Abner's eyes narrowed as he dropped his grip and let her catch her own footing. "Might need to go wash at the water now, since you've been touched by something so unclean."

He turned his back before she could answer.

"Abner," Dennison's voice was stern, "I think this is enough nonsense. It's time to put away this idea that there is anything other than broken bones and disappointment waiting for us where this stream begins."

"You didn't see what we saw, Dennison. There was another of them in the cave. A snake with—"

"Either there is nothing, or else nothing of use to us since it will look on us as a meal more likely than anything else."

"If we just—"

Dennison shook his head.

"There's a path through," Tessa said from behind Abner.

He turned, eyes darting over her dripping hair and wet, clinging clothes. *She actually washed? Really?*

Tessa broke through the rushing water with her arm, soaking her side and pelting Abner with the spray. Abner squinted, struggling to see anything beyond the water's sting. He used his sword to elongate the tunnel, bracing it with both hands as the blade was pummeled from above, and revealed a wide flat rock on the other side of the waterfall.

"Easy to miss." Tessa's voice was a breath away from his shoulder. His skin could feel her presence, tingling in response to it. "The force of the waterfall makes jumping to the other side risky. We might be able to put something together—"

"With what?" Abner looked at her, raising his brow in challenge.

Ava glanced between them.

Dennison kicked a pebble off the mountain side, not bothering to look at the path.

"Can we speak?" Tessa said through tight lips.

"Because last time that went so well."

Ava's brows rose.

Tessa's cheeks reddened. She looked ready to push him off the mountain as she tipped her chin at Ava with a glare that told Abner to watch his words.

"I'll give you two a moment," Ava said, turning with a barely concealed look back.

Tessa ticked her hip to one side as if he were a tiresome toddler that drew on her patience. "Enough of this. I don't understand why you're so hurt—"

"Hurt? I'm not hurt."

"But I only told you so you'd understand—"

"Angry. Angry is a much better description."

"Would you rather I didn't explain? I was trying to do the right thing for once."

"That's the hard part about trying to be better, isn't it, Lady Tessa?" Abner's face stretched into a bitter smile. "Sometimes you do all the right things and people still don't see any change in you. So it doesn't really matter whether you hop or not, does it? You'll never be anything other than what you were. For you, that's a person pretending, always holding back a bit of the truth. Always looking out for yourself when it comes to the moment. For me, the son of the evil king, a murderer. Never anything more, at least not to you."

"That's not true. I just—it's more complicated than turning a corner and you're a new person. And we have more pressing issues to deal with right now. Your father, for one. How to get up this last leg of the mountain. Rejoining Cantus. Our list of legitimate things to worry over is quite long, and we're wasting time."

"So what's the point of talking now?" Abner tossed his shoulders into a shrug.

Tessa sighed. "I want us to be at least neutral. That way we can stop wasting effort snapping at each other."

"Neutral? That's what you want?"

She swallowed, eyes drifting down before she forced her gaze back to his. "Yes."

"Fine," Abner said, taking a step back from her. "We'll see how that works out."

"So ideas? Plans? Anything?"

"About what?"

She threw her hand toward the waterfall.

"Oh." Abner took a quick assessment of the area with his eyes. "We have no rope, there's no vegetation to cut. No, it's impossible." He shrugged at her glare.

"What about—" Ava picked her way hesitantly back. "The bandage in your corset, it's thicker than string, it could hold our weight all wrapped together, couldn't it? We can help each other across one by one."

"But if it breaks—" Tessa's brow creased.

"We could catch the person's hand before they fell," Abner said. "The waterfall doesn't actually look that wide now that we've found the other side."

Tessa rubbed the toe of her shoe across the slick brown stone. "Right, that's what I meant."

"I like that idea much better than trying to claw my way up a mountain with a full dress and the rocks crumbling beneath my weight," Ava said.

"The real trouble is the first and the last to cross. They won't have others to brace them."

"I'll go first," Tessa said. "Try my best to jump it."

"That's foolish, Lady." Dennison's brow wrinkled, at last rejoining the discussion.

"There's no way I can make it across without the corset holding me up. So I should go first. I can undo the bandage and then pass it back to you from the other side." She paused, folding her arms. "Someone has to be first. Might as well be me."

"And you think you'd be able to brace someone else crossing? Won't you be too weak?" Abner didn't mean it as an insult, but Tessa's eyes flashed anyway.

"I'll sit on it if I have to." Tessa dropped her pack. She moved farther from the edge to take a running start. Her body jerked forward. She stopped, breathing hard.

"Are you sure about this?" Abner said as Tessa cut two long slits into her dress and the slip beneath with the dagger. *What if she doesn't clear it?*

The thought punched him in the gut. He reached for her arm but it was too late.

She sprang forward, gathering speed to leap over the waterfall.

She'll be fine. She's—

Her feet left their side of the falls, wavering for balance on the mist-splattered rock. She was sinking too fast, her hands gripping at nothing. She dropped out of sight.

—gone.

Abner raced to the edge, followed by Dennison and Ava. "Tessa! Tessa!"

"There!" Ava shouted, pointing down the water line. "I can see her!"

Abner cut a tunnel through the water, holding the sword to split the spray. He planted his boot on the slick rock to brace himself.

Dennison caught his shoulder. "Careful, Abner," he said quietly. "She's not worth your death."

"Come on, Tessa! You need to climb!" Abner grunted, straining to keep the tunnel open.

She edged deeper under the water.

"What are you doing? Climb up!" He moved the sword to follow her, twisting it to keep the water from falling on her shoulders as much as possible. His own arm was soon drenched for his effort. His teeth shivered against each other as the wind drove the chill deep into his bones. Abner's muscles shook, the pounding weight of water a steady battering ram against his grip.

"I'm alright!" The mere sound of her voice sent a river of warm relief washing through Abner from hair to heel, but he didn't let his hand relax with it.

Ava touched his shoulder, smiling. "She's alright," she breathed, eyes on the water. "She'll find a way up."

She did. It took a long time of careful placement as the water-slicked rock was unforgiving of any false step. Her slow effort was rewarded as her hand gripped the far ledge.

"Be careful!" Abner yelled through the water.

Her fingers bit at the rock, straining white against the gray stone. At last, she collapsed onto the flat outcropping of the mountain's far side.

Ava's shrill cheer cut through all other noise and Abner fell against the rock wall, arms burning as he wiped speckles of moisture from his face.

Tessa crawled away from the deadly drop.

Dennison grunted behind him, gathering the packs. He didn't return Abner's smile.

Now for the next task. "Send it over!" Abner called, catching glimpses of her through the spray.

She thrust a rude hand gesture back at him, still breathing heavily.

Abner laughed.

Ava pulled him away as Tessa worked on the bandage lacing. "She wouldn't want you to watch," she said, firmly.

"I wasn't—never mind." Abner pushed his shoulder into the wall. He waited for the relief to dissipate and his limbs to feel real again.

"Prince," Dennison acknowledged Abner with a nod, pausing in his task of repacking one of the bags. "May we speak?"

Abner ignored the sting of irritation that phrase now provoked. *She's safe, she made it.* All he had to do now was get to her. He nodded at Dennison to continue.

"I think more than ever, this is a point we won't be able to return from. Crossing this waterfall is dangerous, and you should—"

"I've never seen you turn from something because of danger, Dennison. Why are you asking me to be a coward, when you aren't?"

"It's unnecessary. Risks should be weighed against the benefit they will yield. Anything else is foolish." Dennison pulled his chin high. "I don't know how many other ways I can say this. You are being reckless, wasting time and risking your life on things that will yield no benefit. Stop this. Be done with it, so we can get on to more important things, like the throne waiting for you to take."

"I can't abandon this, Dennison. Not when we're so close. Every obstacle, there's been a way through. I see that as meaning that this is all leading somewhere."

"And the path down the mountain to the main road will lead you to Lydia. So? You choose where you are led by what path you take. And the one you are on now," he looked over Abner's shoulder toward Tessa and the mountain, shaking his head.

"Here!" Ava called, drawing Abner's attention just in time to see the corded bandage be pushed down by the water's force.

He clapped Dennison's arm, moving past him. *There's always a way.*

Tessa leaned into the stone wall, her knees poking through the slits in her dress as she worked to draw up the line. The stained, soaked corset lay in the dirt beside her.

As predicted, Tessa was weakened. Her next attempt to throw the cord to them was a little closer than the first but was also pushed almost immediately down by the waterfall. Tessa paused before her third attempt, twisting the end into a large knot and holding it under the water.

"What is she doing?" Ava asked.

Looking up toward the sun, Tessa drew her arm back past her ear. She launched the dripping knot with a yell that carried over the noise of the spray slapping the rock. She clutched her end of the cord to her chest, catching herself on the mountain wall before she could fall to her knees. The weighted ball of bandage arced up and out.

Abner snatched it from the air with a spray of water.

Handing the cord to Ava, Abner looked around, wiping his blade dry against a corner of his tunic before slipping it into his sheath. *Tessa can barely hold her own weight, let alone mine. Her running leap nearly killed her.* He needed something to help him launch cleanly off the edge. Rubbing a pinch of sand from the mountain side, Abner looked back at the slick rock. Smiling, he grabbed fistfuls of sediment. Abner spread the light dirt over the path like a farmer with seed in the field. He tested his feet against the grip of the sand.

"Dennison!" he called, gesturing to the cord. "Hold it steady. I might need it."

"Abner." Dennison came reluctantly forward. Ava handed him the dripping knot. "Don't—"

Abner's boots pounded against the sand, gathering speed before launching from the edge. Every limb felt disjointed from his core as he began to fall forward, the spray of water washing over his shoulder. The far edge of the path punched him through the gut, rattling his bones.

Tessa dropped against the wall breathing hard.

Abner's mouth twisted, grunting as he pushed his weight onto the mountain path. He took the cord from Tessa.

"I can—" she gestured weakly.

"Shut it." Abner positioned himself closer to the rock wall, gaining slack in the line to sling it across his back. He spread sand beneath his feet. "You'll have to cross through the water!" he called out. "Ava next."

A tug on the rope made Abner's teeth grit together as he ground an anchor for his feet against the rock. He tugged back. *Ready.*

Ava edged with arms and legs folded over the rope across the deadly drop.

Abner's chest pinched tight as he pulled in quick breaths, catching the moments of air between the falling water. He blinked to clear his eyes only for them to fill again. Once she was safe on their side, there was a long pause.

Abner squinted as he tugged on the cord. He waited.

Dennison's weight dropped against the fabric, swinging to their side. He worked to climb one handed up to the ledge, as Abner braced him from above. The strain was a knife cutting into Abner's back. His teeth bared, his breath stopped as every muscle clenched. *Just. Hold. On.* When the cord tore apart in his hand, Dennison caught the edge. Abner pulled him up by the back of his tunic, letting the torn bandage fall with the water. Both men knelt, fighting for their breath.

"I thought," Abner coughed as his limbs pulsed with freedom from the crushing pressure, "you might just leave."

Dennison pushed himself to his feet, offering Abner a hand. "If I were going to leave you, Abner, I would have done so already." He handed out packs, hesitating in front of Tessa.

She nodded. "I'll manage." Her legs slipped out from under her, and Abner caught her before her jaw bit the dirt.

"I didn't think about what would happen to you if the cord tore," he said, picking up her legs so she was cradled in his arms.

"I did," she sighed, her weight falling against his chest. "I just didn't want to seem … it was the only way across."

"Next time, speak your mind," Abner said. His anger at her was still there, but overshadowed in the moment by the feeling of her held close and the responding strength of his arms.

She closed her eyes, leaning against him as her breathing slowed.

Heat spread through his chest. This was something he could do, a load he knew he could carry, as they began to climb up the side of the mountain. The feeling of competence lessened as their path became narrower, the climb steeper, and Abner's boots slowed him down with the weight of water retained from their morning trial.

It was an utter surprise when the group rounded a curve and the large slope of the mountain, which had risen above their heads for so long, fell away. A massive lake capped the summit, the head of the mountain having broken off at some point long ago, with a few small islands dotting the bowl of water. Lush heavy forests grew along the rim to block the horizon.

"It's," Ava breathed, "beautiful."

Tessa smiled.

"There's nothing here but a lake." Dennison cast his hand out encompassing the clouds gathering in the sky. "Spot any dragons, Abner? Help of any kind?"

"We—we haven't gone around the lake yet," Abner floundered. "Let's see if there's anyone here."

Dennison followed behind them with stomping feet and a heavy scowl. Directly opposite of where they had started and hidden from their sight till then by a many-spired island, was a little hut with smoke curling out of a chute in the middle of a thatched roof. Beside the hut were neat rows of vegetables, their green tops spilling over the rich brown dirt. Dennison and Abner pulled to a halt.

"Put me down," Tessa whispered. "You might need your sword hand free."

Abner laid her at the base of a wide trunk.

She pushed herself deeper into the shadows against the gray bark and nodded.

Abner drew his sword as quietly as he could.

Dennison followed suit.

Ava stepped in front of them. "We don't know, they could be friendly. Let's see if we can talk before we go chopping, shall we?"

Abner brushed past her.

The door pushed open at his hand. The wood-floored room held two cots, a heavy black box tucked beneath a carved wooden table, and a chute for the fire from the brick hearth to rise through. Abner's eyes narrowed. *Empty*.

"Stars above! Visitors! Oh, at last!"

There was something deeply unsettling about the little face that greeted Abner as he turned his back to the empty house. Perhaps it was the unexpectedness that made Abner's mouth twist. The small boy had shocking red hair that sprang from his head in every direction. Or possibly it was the wide grin he wore, the pointed teeth akin more to the snake from the cave than any child Abner had ever seen. *No, it's the eyes.* Their rims were yellowed slightly. They lacked any color except a black vertical slit which pulsed with the boy's smile.

"When the manticore told us you were coming, I didn't dare believe it!" chirped the boy through a slight lisp. His eyes pulsed with some unknown joy. "Visitors!"

"What are you?" Dennison said, gripping his sword tighter.

"Is that a riddle? I love riddles. Let's have a game." The grin slipped away as the boy thought. "Me, one, all things become, pulled by both moon and sun, without me all life fails, no, not a one prevails. Any guesses?"

"No games right now, unless it's the catch?" Abner dropped his sword point toward the ground.

"Catch?"

"For your help. You are some master of the mountain, are you not? A great magician or something?"

"Oh," the boy's brows shot up in surprise. "Oh, you think I'm—yes, yes I suppose I am!"

"Abner, he's obviously a child." Dennison shook his head.

"I don't think it would be the strangest thing we've seen," Abner muttered. Louder, to the boy, he said, "And this riddle is a part of it? We have to guess."

The boy smiled, tilting his head so the light danced off the green scales along his neck.

"Can you repeat it, please?" Ava leaned forward listening.

"Me, one all—"

"Come, Klessen, on with your chores!" came a voice.

"Oh, no." Klessen said, turning slowly.

When the older, similar-featured man strode into view, he dropped the woven basket under his arm at the sight of the travelers. The load of fungus and weeds spilled onto the grass.

"What is the meaning of this?" demanded the man in a lisp like the boy's but with a much deeper tone.

Abner shifted forward, swallowing hard. *Why didn't I plan out something to say?* "We've traveled to ask for your help. Alberon is in danger."

"I'm sorry, is that a place or a person? Why—why would we care if Albion is in danger? Come away from them, Klessen."

Klessen moved to the man's side, crossing his arms at the interruption to his fun.

"I will deal with you in a moment. Of all the—"

"*Alberon*, it's the country just beyond the mountains. Technically the mountain itself is in our borders, but—"

"Oh, no," laughed the man, smoothing over his long beige robe that reached to the grass at his feet. "No kingdom of man has a claim on this mountain. And no kingdom of man is its concern. Off with you now."

"But—" Ava drew back as the man's slitted eyes twitched to her.

Abner's grip tightened. "We have traveled here through many dangers. Please, won't you consider—"

"No."

"At least a rest then. Perhaps a meal? One of our group is injured and cannot travel. We'll have to wait for tomorrow's light to leave anyway."

The man dropped his shoulders with a sigh. He ran a black nailed hand over his clean-sheared head. "Very well. Go wash."

"Wash?"

"Before we eat. I'm not having your dirty little pink fingers picking through my food. No idea where you've been." He turned away, muttering to himself as he gathered his spilled basket and marched past them into the house. "KLESSEN!"

The red hair bobbed after him, and Dennison and Ava looked to Abner.

He nodded with more assurance than he felt. "Give it time. He'll come around."

Retrieving Tessa and washing up to their elbows at the lake, Abner tried to think of persuasions he could put to the man during their meal. He hadn't yet thought of anything compelling as Klessen and the man pulled fistfuls of vegetables from the garden. His mind still clutched at nothing as they were called to sit down inside the hut.

"By the stars," the man said, reverence deepening his tone as he bowed his head and lifted his hands.

Klessen nudged Ava who sat closest to him, copying the man's motion.

"The first lights still burn as we wait. May the truth worth all shine on us as the light now does, when the True One returns." Opening his eyes, the man raised a hairless brow at them. "May His glory never fade."

Abner dropped his hands slowly. "True One?" he asked.

The man tossed a hand to move his sleeve away from his fingers as he selected a red shiny-skinned fruit. "The true king. You've heard the story of the beginning, yes? The spark, the light? He's the spark. The first light." The man bit into the fruit, pointed teeth ripping away a chunk as he pulled up the corners of his mouth to grin at Abner.

Tessa poked at a pink scrape on her arm. "Not poisoned. Huh."

"Where's the meat?" Dennison hadn't moved toward the food.

"Animals talk, you know. You can only listen to their sad little pleas so many times before it turns your stomach. This form you have is a rather inefficient killer. So we live on greens, mostly." The man took another bite, Klessen beside him mirroring the motion. The others hesitantly selected food for themselves. "Now the teeth make it difficult, a leftover from our pasts, but we have firm guts. With teeth like yours, I'm sure you never have to eat meat."

"Where we are from, very few animals talk," Tessa said, sniffing at the thin orange fruit.

"How nice it must be to have no prickles of conscience about your diet." He squinted at her. "You're the sick one, yes?"

"I'm not sick," Tessa let the fruit drift away from her mouth. Her chin rose against the slit-eyed scrutiny. "I fell."

"So you're here for, what? Magic to heal you?"

"Is there?" Tessa's eyes narrowed at his silence. "Then no. I'm just here to help."

The man tipped his chin, green scales flashing in the light dancing from the fire. "Hm."

Klessen watched Ava chew slowly.

She forced a breath to lower her shoulders as she pushed her mouth to smile. "Can we have the answer?"

Klessen's brow dropped. "The—what?"

"To your riddle."

Klessen's eyes widened with his fanged smile. "Can't you figure it out? Have a listen again." He repeated it.

Ava shook her head. "I have no idea."

"About what you said before," Abner began, drawing the man's eyes back to him. "We just need—"

"Why?"

Abner's irritation rose in a ripple of tension through his shoulders. *Why what?*

The man licked his lips before continuing. "Why do you need anything? Why should I give it to you? Why should it be my task to clean up your home?"

"Because it's the right thing to do. Everyone has a responsibility to make things better in the world if they have the ability to. You may claim there's no magic here, but your very existence speaks otherwise."

The man leaned against the cushion propped behind him by a wooden beam. "Let us imagine I can and do help you. What would you do with my help?"

"We would defeat my father, the king."

"And what would that change?"

"Everything!"

"Would it though? Or would the world just take a little longer to sink back down into rot? You being King of ... what was it?"

"Alberon."

"Whatever you call yourselves—or another man, you're still men. Men are corrupted. Unable to keep to a task or hold fast to any ideal beyond what is convenient or strikes them as important at the time. Blown by the wind. What really makes you different from your father?"

"I suppose that's the point." Abner swallowed. "I'm not. But because I know my tendency toward evil, I know to fight against it."

Surprise raised the man's brow line high up his bald forehead. "And you would all vouch for him?"

Dennison and Ava offered their nods quickly, but Tessa gave him a thoughtful, prolonged stare.

"Yes," she said at last.

"How touching. Well, I would not. I don't know you or your troubles, and frankly have offered more than I wished to already. You may sleep outside and in the morning you will leave the way you came. As for the rest of the day, do as you wish, just stay out of the way. Klessen, there are still chores to be done."

Klessen sighed.

"We never asked your name, Sir." Abner's words pulled the man's feet to a shuffling stop, a bowl of leftovers in each hand.

"No, you didn't." He walked away, setting the bowls down and cutting the vegetables into smaller chunks that he tossed into a heavy black cauldron beside him on the carved wooden table.

Dennison cleared his throat, narrowed eyes fixed on the man's back.

"Want to help me feed the chickens?" Klessen asked, grabbing Ava's hand.

"Oh, I—of course."

"Dennison." Abner nodded at the pair and the captain followed Ava as she was pulled away by her strange little friend. Abner offered a hand to Tessa. She allowed herself to be pulled to her feet, hugging an arm around her gut as she stumbled against Abner's shoulder. He made sure they were out of easy hearing from the house before he set her back against a tree.

"What are you going to do? He seems determined to be as little help as possible."

Abner picked up a gray stone, embedded with rippling curves worn smooth from its years riding the lake. He tossed it at the water, and it thunked as it hit a small wave. "I don't know. I have to think of something to say that will change his mind."

"And if you can't, what happens tomorrow?"

Abner picked up another rock. He launched this one with more strength, enjoying the snap of his muscles as the stone left his grip.

"Well?"

"I don't know!"

The silence between them was only broken by the gentle lake waves spilling against the dirt.

"What if we went further in?" Tessa dropped her eyes as Abner turned to face her. "If he won't help, maybe there's someone else who will."

"The stream ends here. This is the source."

"We were following the stream to get to the mountain. Who's to say that he is the only one here?"

Abner was thoughtful, quiet for a moment. "I don't think going on is an option. You can't travel. Whatever this is, it's getting worse. I have no idea what would be waiting for us and I wouldn't be able to carry you indefinitely."

"Then leave me behind."

Abner laughed.

Tessa didn't.

His smile slipped away. "You're serious? Have I not, at least, made my feelings perfectly clear? You think I'd leave you?"

"I think you know as well as I do that I'm not going to be able to get back across that waterfall, let alone through the cave, over a wall. Any of it. I need to be half-carried every step that I take. And Cantus is waiting at Shiloh for you."

Abner blinked heavily. "What if we both stayed?"

"That's not an option." Tessa shook her head.

Abner knelt down in front of her. "It could be."

She shook her head harder, a shiver rifling through her shoulders as she pulled in a sharp breath. "I'm not going to be the one to turn you into a coward, Abner. You are the only one with a claim to stop this."

He let his head drop, already heavy with the weight of a crown so far away. "I don't want it," he muttered. Her hand, cool against his cheek, drew his eyes to meet hers.

"I know. But I also now know ... that won't stop you."

Warmth filled him and—before he knew what he was doing—he moved forward, hand threading through her hair. Abner stopped a breath from her lips. "Sorry," he said, leaning back.

Her chest rose noticeably with each breath.

He was the first to look away. "I could come back for you, when everything is done." His eyes skimmed over the water, stomach sinking at the thought of leaving her behind.

"After everything settles you'll have a kingdom to run. You won't be able to just ride off on your own."

"I'll think of something," Abner promised, sucking in a breath as he met her stare. "I'm not leaving you alone."

"We'll see."

The food that evening was a stew comprised of chopped bits from the previous meal and heated in a broth that seemed to be one part lake mud, one part muck. Abner had trouble keeping the taste from echoing through his features. Dennison seemed to agree as, after a small bite, he set the wooden bowl away from him, opting to stare at the firelight and let his stomach growl.

Klessen licked his bowl clean. He whispered something in the man's ear, who gave him a nod. Klessen gripped Ava's hand. "Come play with me!"

Ava abandoned her bowl and followed him to the corner where the cots were. He produced a many sided block and tossed it in the air to let it fall on the floor.

"Thank you for hosting us," Abner volunteered after he forced his throat to swallow.

The man grunted, pouring a second helping for himself.

"Are there any others here, like you?"

The man's black-slitted stare met Abner's as his lip pulled high over sharp teeth. "Why does that concern you?"

"Curiosity."

The man hissed a laugh. "Curious how strong we are so when you're done with your little quest of murder you can get to the real work of men. Looking to conquer the mountains for your own?"

There was a pause as the two assessed each other.

"Without your help, or someone with power, we've already failed."

"Then why are you still trying to save this Albarren?" The man shrugged. "Nature has spoken, accept your fate and have done with it. It's more peaceful that way."

Dennison shook his head.

Once more. Try. "I have watched people slaughtered at his hand, innocents sacrificed to him, for years and done nothing but help him—"

"Oh, excellent recommendation for your bid for a crown and army."

"I will not turn my back on the people now. Not while there is strength left in it. Things will have to change, but Alberon is worth saving." He turned to Tessa, who nodded him on with the ghost of a smile. "What about one more day? To allow our companion to rest. Her injury stops her from being able to descend the mountain safely and I need time to think of a way to get her down."

"Abner," Dennison shook his head at him.

The man's throat rumbled with indecision. "I will think on it."

"Let us speak. Outside." Dennison's stare burned him with its intensity.

Abner's mouth tightened.

"Now, Prince!"

Stinging heat rose up the back of his neck as Abner pushed himself to stand. Rarely had Dennison used that tone with him, as Abner's respect for the older captain was absolute. The few times he had disobeyed had brought Dennison's hand to the back of his neck and Abner had learned that resistance was pointless.

Tessa moved to rise and Dennison stopped her with a raised palm.

"We talk alone. You've meddled enough in his head."

Abner gave her a reassuring nod as he followed Dennison.

Outside, the night sky was lit with a spectacular display of stars.

Dennison coughed. "We are done playing games, Abner. It's over, time to leave."

"We have nothing to show for our time yet, if we—"

"Exactly. Stop wasting what little time we have and do what needs to be done."

"I can't. Not without help."

"There is none, Abner. You can depend on me, you know this, but beyond that—even your friends here are useless at best, and at worst will destroy any chance you have."

Abner pulled his chin high. "Tessa can't travel. What am I supposed to do? Leave her behind?"

Dennison's brow raised. "All the better. Honestly it may have been cleaner for her to fall down the waterfall and show you how reckless your decisions have become, but she was somehow able to claw herself back up. And you! You jumped right after her. I don't think there's a clearer picture of what this has done to you. I've had enough of watching you almost destroy yourself for something that doesn't matter. Your eyes are off the point. All this talk about the people and what you owe them. Your father owes you the throne, it is your right. It's time to take your place that I have spent the last twenty and one years preparing you for."

"I don't feel prepared. Dennison, I don't see how we can win on our own. We need others."

"If you're bent on making deals with beasts and monsters for your salvation, you do so without me. That is your choice, Abner. To trust these things who care nothing for you, who should be put down like the beasts of other lands, or to listen to reason. Prove to me I didn't waste my time."

The admiration Dennison reserved for Abner dissolved from his eyes like mist at the prince's silence. Each man's breathing hit heavily on Abner's ears.

"So be it." Dennison turned his back, casting his voice over his shoulder. "I had expected so much more for you."

"Wait!" Abner called, halting Dennison's step. "I need more time. Help me. Just a little more time." He ignored the heat rising up his neck, the desperation seeping into his tone.

Dennison snatched a pack from their pile at the base of a large tree, and began to pick his way through the dark around the lake.

"Wait!" Abner cast a stone to thunk into the water, hoping the splash would draw the captain's eyes back to him. Would make him pause. Anything. His eyes stung as Dennison stomped through the trees.

He's gone.

Esther picked at a wooden pockmark on the side of her empty bowl, trying to pretend she hadn't been listening as Abner returned.

His hair dripped wet as he sank onto the floor close to the fire, the rim of his eyes red.

Ava met her glance with a sigh.

"One less mouth to feed, then?" asked the man, peeking through the open door.

"It's hopeless," Abner muttered to the flames.

"We're okay." Esther shrugged. "We're—we'll just—"

Abner pinned Esther with a glare. "No, we're not. We have no help, nothing. And now Dennison has gone, likely to rejoin my father and the army. I'm only as good at anything as he taught me to be. With him, maybe we could have had a chance, but Dennison against us—"

The man grunted. "Your courage has left with him, then? Rather a harsh turn in character. I thought you were to be the people's champion. Probably just as well. I'm sure you'll find a nice hole somewhere to hide in."

"We're still going to face them." Abner glared at the man.

"And then you—what?" The man paused over the bucket of water he had pulled from under the table to scrub the dishes.

Esther leaned forward.

"At least I am. I don't think there's a way I can win, but just because it's hopeless doesn't excuse me to do nothing." Abner turned back to the fire.

"Hm." The man's eyes assessed the prince through a narrowed stare.

"This place is special to your kind, isn't it?" Esther forced herself to stare unmoved as the slitted eyes flicked over her. The air in the room seemed to thin. She forced a calm, casual air to her tone. "It would be a tragedy if the king were to come to the mountain. I've seen what he does to his enemies. He would destroy this place, make you into some kind of spectacle to his glory in his arena. It would serve your interests to help us stop him before it came to that."

The fanged teeth broke apart as the man laughed. "Oh, I'd love to see him try, Sick One. Forgive me for not carrying fear of an army that would have to climb a mountain one behind the other only to reach the top and face a being they are woefully unmatched to." He laughed again. "Maybe I'd make an exception and eat meat that day."

Ava's shocked gasp was turned into a cough.

"You underestimate Dennison and the king."

"No, little prince. You underestimate me."

Abner sighed heavily. "Is there anything you can do for us? We'll need supplies, rope. The climb down will be nearly impossible for Tessa."

"About that." The scaled man hissed a sigh. "I wasn't entirely forthright, before. There is some magic here."

Abner scoffed. "I'm shocked."

"It won't help you with your little war. But you, Sick One, I can do something for."

Abner met her eyes as heat rose to Esther's cheeks. *What?*

"There is a cost. It isn't something to be done lightly. But it will help you." The man stared through the door into the growing night. "The stars are almost to the proper shine. Discuss if you need to and then meet me outside with your decision."

"What's the cost?" Abner said, pausing the man's step.

"It doesn't matter," Esther answered before the man could. "I don't need time. I'll do it."

"Lady Tessa, shouldn't you at least—"

Esther threw up a hand, cutting off Ava's words. "No, I'll do it." She tried to ignore Abner's stare burning into her cheek. "If it'll stop me from being useless, I'll pay whatever price."

The man's mouth drew to one side. "Hm."

"Tessa," Abner whispered as he caught her arm, her legs quaking as she forced them to move. "You have no idea what he means by 'help you'. He might consider killing you as helping release you from pain. He might mean anything."

"No, that's not it," volunteered the man.

"I'm done being useless. Whatever happens, I'm not going to be a weight for everyone else to carry anymore."

"No one ever said you were useless." Abner dragged her up as her knees gave out beneath her.

"You did," she panted. Her hips pulsed as if they might burst apart, her head swam. The man's face appeared at Abner's shoulder and Esther reached for his offered arm.

Abner forced himself between them. "I'll bring her." He pushed his jaw out, as if daring the man to challenge him.

The man led the way out of the hut and into the dark. Ava and Klessen followed behind Abner as he carried Esther into the deepening shadow.

Abner's boots struck the ground, rattling Esther's bones. He scowled at her and the request for him to smooth his gait died from her lips.

"I never called you useless," he muttered.

"In Naamah," Esther said. "Right before we were thrown in jail."

"That was ... I didn't mean *useless* useless, just not useful in that situation."

"Not useful," Esther said, "so useless."

"Why does it even matter? What I think of you?" Abner's ankle rolled and his grip bit into her leg as he struggled to keep her upright.

Esther was grateful for the disturbance despite the jarring force rattling through her hips. Her hiss of pain saved her from having to answer.

A boat lay tipped to one side, bound to a stake driven through the muddy bank. The floor was a mess of rotting leaves, dried brown pine needles, and old hollow acorns that Abner had to brush aside. He placed Esther gingerly on the one seat.

"Now this isn't built to hold much weight at once. I'll have to make two trips to ferry you across."

Abner took a seat at the prow of the boat, leaning against the large beam at the very front. The man stood behind Esther and used a long-handled oar to push them into the water and begin their slow voyage to the many-spired island at the heart of the lake.

Esther's eyes were drawn over the side, the starlight from above dancing on the waves. She wished she could lean out to brush her hand over the lake's rippling surface.

"I crossed the Merdian Sea as a boy." Abner said, head swaying with the lapping cadence. "Always liked being on the water."

"And you, Sick One? Ever set sail?"

"No."

"Shame. There's nothing quite so wild and lovely as the ocean." The oar stroked the water aside.

"I'll keep that in mind if I don't end up dead in the next few days."

The man's smile pulled his tone to a higher note. "I'm sure it will take at least a week for you to fail. Give your prince some credit."

They reached the island, its rocky chutes rising from the ground like spikes adorning the lake's crown. Between the spikes, the man wove until he arrived at the center of the island, which stood at the center of the lake, the center of the mountain, the center of the world.

Esther could feel it in the air. There was something about this place that called her to drop to the ground, to not dare another step, but Abner carried her forward. She wondered if he felt it too. At the heart of the island there was a stone table, small, with a large book locked and bound with strips of cloth. The leather cover was faded and cracked from years beneath the sun, the spine splintering from long use.

"This," the man said, indicating the table and the book, "is what we came here for. I will get your friend now, but you must wait for my return and not open that book. It is sacred and not to be touched."

"Is it powerful?" Abner asked, setting Esther down. His eyes betrayed his doubt as he studied the beaten cover.

"Well, yes," the man said. "Obviously." He was gone.

Esther avoided Abner's eye.

"Don't do this because of some comment I made offhandedly when I was annoyed," Abner said, irritation putting a bite to his tone.

"Never mind that now, what about what the man said? About the book."

Abner glanced at it, a shrug popping his shoulders up. "What of it?"

"It could help us."

Abner shook his head. "It's sacred to them. We don't even know how to use it. I'll find another way." He broke the silence between them before it grew too wide. "I mean it though. You're not useless, and even if you were temporarily less useful what does that matter? Your value isn't in what you can do. I don't ... admire you because of the odd collection of skills you have. Frankly, your 'usefulness' often puts you into trouble. I'd almost rather you were less useful."

"Well I can't stand it, this feeling of being carted around like a pack."

Abner stared at Esther as if he had never truly seen her before. The look in his eyes made her mouth twist as she turned away.

"Whatever happens, that feeling is going to end."

The man's return brought Esther to her feet with Abner's help. He looked at the bound book, surprise raising his bald brow high. "How much information do you want before we start?"

"What do I need to do?"

"Just stand near the book, I'll do the rest."

Esther nodded, shuffling forward on weak legs that tingled with nipping energy through any weight she tried to move.

"And," Abner said, pulling her back, "the cost. What is it?"

"Ah, yes. Put simply, it will weaken you."

"How?" Esther froze. *Wasn't this supposed to make me strong again?*

"It will be—how can I explain so you understand? It will be borrowing strength from one part of you and giving it to another. It leaves both weaker than if you hadn't been hurt or had let yourself heal naturally. Though, at this point I don't think that will happen for you."

"You can't just fix what's wrong?" Abner pushed out a scoff. "Seems your magic is weaker than Healers in Alberon."

"Ah, well, if I were to 'just fix it' as you say, pour pure magic into her to remake her, instead of using magic to pass through and redirect what is already there, it would be like trying to pour an ocean into an old clay pot. Human bodies were not built to contain that energy. She'd burst apart into nothing."

"And you're certain your way won't kill her?" Abner asked.

The man's shoulder lifted into a one-sided shrug, and he nodded vaguely.

Abner's words were a whisper against her ear. "I can find another way. Don't do this."

"Of course I'm doing it." Esther wished she could push away from him and march forward to face the man with her chin high and dignity intact, but Abner had to help her to the edge of the stone table. She expected the man's touch to be cold, but warmth spread through her back as he traced patterns across it. Occasional pressure sent her forward into the edge of the table, her hands almost brushing the leather of the book as she braced herself.

"Yes, there it is. And, another. My, you have made a mess of this."

Her teeth gritted together, the force of pressure steadily more.

"You will have to be very careful with yourself," the man said quietly, his hands disappearing from her back.

"So any fall on her backside would—"

"It would take a harder hit than that, but yes. A significant hit to your legs or back and you would likely never be able to use either again. There's a chance, if you were able to somehow keep your legs strong while you waited for your body to heal, that we could repeat this, but I don't think that's likely." He unbound the book.

Esther pulled in a breath, hugging it in her chest before releasing the slow trickle of air. *Another.* She focused on her own steady breathing while the man took an age to undo and put aside each layer of protection over the book.

What will it feel like? Her mind struggled against this silly worry. In the face of all she could gain, what did it matter if having strength moved through her hurt or felt odd and out of her control? Even if her body became a stranger to her, she would have a body again. *If only he'd get on with it.*

At last he looked to the stars, his chest puffing with a monstrous breath.

The chant was low, the words unfamiliar, and although his fingers traced along the lines of the book his eyes never glanced at the page. The words rattled from his bones. His hand moved over her back.

Esther's breath pulled at her chest as cinching pressure began to tighten its vice grip around her waist. She itched, as if a bucket of stinging insects was spilled over her back and nipped at her skin while a thousand

barbed legs trotted across. Her nails bit into the stone with a force that cracked them to the pink skin they protected. The man's yellow eyes rolled up into his head. His image seemed to shiver, as if it were about to fade away, before the world was swallowed whole.
    White.

Abner blinked at the forest bathed in morning light. He sat up, brushing dried yellow leaves out of his hair. *What happened? Where— he's gone!* His eyes raked over the unfamiliar wood, desperately searching between the gray trunks crowding around him. *Barrels?* Nine of them sat in a huddle, utterly out of place. The sight was put aside in his panic. The barrels weren't her and so didn't matter.

"Tessa!"

Breaking free of a cluster of leaves, using the trunk of a heavy-limbed tree for support, Tessa rose into view. "I'm here," she grunted.

The anchor of dread weighing on his gut fell away. He was already running forward, not thinking as he caught her waist and pulled her to his chest. Her hand pushed him away, and he bent to the gentle pressure. "You're okay?" he asked, blinking to clear his vision.

"I'm..." Tessa hesitated, running a hand down her back. She bounced on her heels, eyes shadowed under her furrowed brow. Her chest broke with her sudden breath, throat grating through a sob.

Abner caught her as she crumpled forward. "What? What is it? I thought—"

"I'm okay," Tessa's voice shook. Her fingers clung to him as her limbs trembled.

He cradled her to his chest.

"I can't believe it. I'm okay."

His chin moved over her hair, stirring the smell of the changing seasons. "You're okay," he said, pressing his mouth to her forehead.

"Um..." a voice interrupted from behind.

Ava.

Tessa was already breaking away, still shaking but grinning at the ability to stand on her own strength. She worked to slow her breathing.

"Sorry, take your time. It's just—where are we?"

"And what happened?" Tessa's brow creased. "The last I remember, the man was chanting."

Abner nodded. "A burst of light from his hand dropped you like a stone. After that, the man turned to me. I knew something had changed when he raised his hand, so I tried to draw my sword but there was just a flash of white, and I was here."

"Right, just a blinding light and I woke up on the ground." Ava nodded. "I didn't see where it came from."

"So once again, he had more magic than he let on." Abner sighed, kicking away a stick from his boot. "Now the question is where did he send us?"

Tessa's eyes stretched wide. "Home. He sent me home."

"What?" Ava looked just as confused as Abner felt.

"I know this place, come on!" Tessa strode forward. The trees fell away to reveal an open grassy slope, a barren strip of cracked dirt running up the side. "The water trail." She nodded. "We're close."

"We're near Shiloh?" Abner asked, drawing Tessa's feet to slow their quick trot. Ava panted as she struggled with her dress through long grassy weeds.

"We should see it in a moment," Tessa said. Each step was slower than the last as her eyes fixed on a point somewhere ahead and her mouth twisted.

Abner touched her arm. "Are you worried about Cantus? I won't let him hurt you. You'll be safe, or, as safe as any of us are. He needs us and he knows it."

"I just…"

Ava whispered a curse as her dress tore on a thorn behind them.

"I never thought I'd see it again. All the—" she swallowed.

I hadn't thought of that. Half-eaten eyes and rotted flesh filled his mind. What would the corpse garden the king's army had left in its wake look like now? *Not him. Me. I did this.* His nerves tightened his jaw as Tessa hesitated to break through the last layer of foliage.

The bowled valley of Shiloh stretched to the main road. It was empty save for some new mounds of dirt near the wall of the outpost. Abner's eyes brushed over the ground several times before he was satisfied that there were no decaying bodies hiding in the weeds. Cantus had apparently cleaned up while they had been gone.

Beside him, Tessa shook.

Ava slipped a hand through her arm.

"Ready, Lady Tessa?"

"No." She moved forward anyway.

Abner stepped carefully. The thought of gray hands reaching toward his turned back sent tingling energy down his spine. It was childish, this fear that those who had died forsook the stars and waited to break through the dirt, dragging him into oblivion as repayment for what Abner had brought to Shiloh. He stepped carefully all the same.

"From the tree line!" called a voice on the outpost wall. "At the ready!"

The gates of Shiloh remained shut as a group of archers took aim at them over the wall. Abner opened empty hands toward them.

"We are friends!" he called. "Get Cantus!"

"Who are you?" The point of every arrow shifted toward the prince. *I'll have to correct that later.* "Just get Cantus! He is expecting us."

Tessa was lost in her own thoughts, misty eyes studying Shiloh.

One bow disappeared. The others drew back slightly. The wait before the gates rolled open felt eternal, but when Cantus at last emerged, he greeted Abner with a nod.

Coming forward with the others, Abner opened his mouth to explain why they had no help, how they had tried, and to ask about the state of things in Shiloh.

Cantus' mouth twisted, looking over Abner's shoulder at the emptiness behind him. "So, a boy is all the help you could find?"

"What?" Abner turned, staring at the red, springing hair. "Klessen!" *How? He wasn't there a moment ago. Was he?*

The boy turned from the valley. Every one of his sharp teeth was displayed as he stretched his smile, fixing them with his pulsing black-slitted eyes.

Cantus pulled back, gripping his sword. "What is it?"

"I'm Klessen!" he said, cheer pulling his cheeks up high like twin apples. "And your name?"

"Can ... tus?"

"And we are in, what did you call it again?" Klessen strained his words through a wrinkled brow. "Alibram?"

"Alberon," Abner said.

"Klessen, what are you doing here?" Ava asked.

Cantus nodded with a sigh at the sight of her.

"I thought I could help."

"And your master? What will he think of you coming to help?" Ava's hip ticked to one side.

Her brow raised as he squirmed instead of answering. He adjusted something bulky beneath his heavy black cloak.

Abner's gaze narrowed. "Never mind that now. We can't take him back." He shrugged at Ava's glare. "We have a war to win. We'll keep him safe away from the fight and when all is done figure out some way to get him home."

Klessen's smile reignited.

"Very well. Any other surprises?" Cantus asked, raking the valley with his eyes.

"You'll want to collect those barrels," Klessen said, wrinkling his nose at the sky. "And probably soon, it smells like rain."

"Right, there were barrels in the wood. Are they from you?"

Klessen nodded, eyes still on the sky. "It's water from the lake of the mountain. You'll need it."

"I'll send some men and a cart horse," Cantus nodded. "Before anything else though, here," Cantus moved forward and carefully pulled the hood over Klessen's hair, partially obscuring his eyes. "It will spook the men otherwise."

Klessen's black slits watched him closely.

"I assume you would like to come in?" Cantus leaned back.

"A moment before we do?" Abner nodded to one side.

Cantus flashed a hand signal to the wall before following Abner a few paces away from the others.

"I know we didn't leave things on the best of terms before—"

"Abner—"

"I wish I'd made several different choices, but what's happened—I can't change it. So, I just—I'm—"

"Abner!" Cantus gripped his arm, cutting off his words. "It's already forgiven."

Abner held his breath, somehow more tense than he'd been before. Was this some trick?

"Because, Abner, forgiveness is the one luxury I *can* afford." He paused, scanning the horizon before continuing. "I don't know that I trust you, yet. But I don't wish you ill and will do good for you if I can. After all, I just spent the last however long committing treason to secure your throne."

Abner let out his breath, arms going loose at his sides. "And how did that go?"

"Well enough. Two hundred men, there're some women and children we're sheltering in case the king decides to draw us out by attacking villages."

"And weapons? Equipment?"

"Not much to speak of besides axes for trees and kitchen knives, but we do have a few smiths and other tradesmen who have been working to fix that. I'll show you when we get inside. Where's..." Cantus' brow creased.

"Dennison left on the mountain, I assume to rejoin my father."

"Really?" Cantus scoffed. "Never thought him a coward."

"He's not," Abner snapped. "He just thought I was wasting time. Maybe he could see I wasn't in a hurry to reclaim a position I don't—" Abner's voice faded and he scuffed the ground with his boot.

"You'd better get over that quick." Cantus met his glance with a hardened expression. "We're here ready to die so you can ascend the throne and fix this. If it's all for nothing because you decide to go run off and have babies with Tessa and shovel horse muck in some—"

"I know. I'm here, aren't I? I'm ready to do what needs to be done."

Cantus nodded, his features loosening. "Then come, your army is waiting."

Cantus had been busy. Shiloh was refitted from a walled-in outpost with a smattering of dirty little homes and dusty streets, to a wooden fortress bursting with those busy at work. At the sight of the prince, many people jumped, gripping their weapons. Cantus settled them with a word and the men went back to their tasks, wary eyes watching Abner as he passed. The soldier gave orders for a team to gather the water barrels, supplied with directions from Tessa of an alternate route to drive the cart, avoiding the water trail.

"What did you tell people to get them here?" Abner ignored the prickle on his neck as he turned from the glaring youth gripping a large farming sickle.

"Mainly that we had a chance to overthrow a great evil, the chance may not come again if we didn't act now." Cantus' glance at the youth sent his eyes ducking away. "That seemed enough for most."

"And after the great evil is overthrown? What do they expect to happen?"

"That didn't come up much."

"They're in for a surprise then," Abner muttered. He tried to roll his shoulders free of the nerves tightening his muscles. His peace was so short-lived. Now every glancing eye could be a helper or a deadly enemy. He had no way of telling which.

Tessa's foot tripped on the back of Abner's boot. "Apologies," she said, pulling back as if brushing against him had stung.

He pushed away the answering sting that brought.

"Here's the tavern, you'll remember. We're using it now as a kind of meeting room."

Tessa's feet skidded to a stop.

Abner paused. "You don't have to go in if you'd rather not."

Tessa struggled to speak, gave up, and turned away.

Ava followed her without a word, looping an arm around her side.

Klessen's hood bobbed between the two directions. Choosing his friend, the boy trotted after Ava and Tessa. Abner watched them turn the corner near the ruined seamstress shop before following Cantus into the darkened tavern.

❖ ❖ ❖

"I don't understand, Lady Tessa." Ava sat down next to her. "Why does this empty town affect you so much?"

Esther pushed a breath through her stinging throat. "I'm not Lady Tessa. That was a lie. It's all a lie."

"What is?"

Klessen joined them on the ground, pulling a block from his belt. "Want to play, Ava?"

"Not now, Klessen. What are you trying to say?"

"I am not nobility. I didn't escape during the king's taking power. I lied about all of it. Everything you know about me is a lie!"

"I already knew you weren't born a noblewoman. But you're still Lady Tessa to me." Ava gently pulled Esther's hands away from her eyes. "It doesn't matter who you were before."

"It does! Of course it does. Being here—I'd forgotten. After what happened, how could I even think—" Esther swallowed. "I failed them all."

"Well..." Ava chewed her lip.

Klessen's block rolled across the ground with a muted thud.

"Maybe you could have done better. I don't know. But you're here now and working like the rest of us to make this right. It's all you can do, and it's enough."

Esther answered her friend's smile with a small one of her own. "I don't know how, through all this mess, I ended up with you."

Ava knocked her knuckles against Esther's shoulder. "Good fortune."

"The best." Esther sighed. "We should get back. Make sure Abner's okay."

"What's happening between you two, by the way?"

"Nothing."

Ava's eyes narrowed, her lips raising in a smile of disbelief.

Esther's jaw stiffened. "Nothing."

Ava shrugged, but the clever slant of her eyes didn't lessen. "Shame."

"Well, what have I found here? Two damsels from a distant land in need of manly protection?"

Both girls jumped at the sudden loud voice. They squinted up at the shadow blocking the sun.

"Now, ladies, how can I service you?" The figure knelt in front of them, the light glancing off his oiled black hair and the single thin blade hanging from his hip.

"Hello Death," Esther sighed.

His eyes shot wider, running over her features in a rush to place her. "Have we? Oh. Oh now I remember. Didn't recognize you with your clothes on, dear." He winked.

Ava's mouth fell open. "Um ... what?"

"What are you doing here?"

"I'm here to help. And where's your princely protector?"

Esther's eyes narrowed. "Probably protecting something. How much coin did Cantus promise you, or are you helping out of the goodness of your cowardly, sputtering spark?"

Death chuckled.

"I'm sorry but—who are you?"

"Death." He smiled at Ava, glancing over her with a quick flicker of interest. "But you can call me anything you please."

Ava snorted quietly, raising her brow.

Klessen squinted at him. "No, you're not. She doesn't look like that, Ava, don't worry."

Death's mouth tipped. "What have we here?" he asked, reaching for Klessen's hood.

"Trying to convince another maiden to lower her standards, eh, *Death?*"

Ava popped to her feet to look around him. "Petra!"

A delighted grin sprang across Petra's mouth at the sight of her. "I—you're here!"

"Petra, m'boy." Death smiled, turning slowly to face him.

Petra raised his chin, eyes narrowing. His grin slipped to one side.

"I was only just about to start unloading supplies when I thought I heard someone in need of help. So I came over but all is well. I'll just be..." Death slipped away.

Petra sighed, tossing his eyes to the sky. He turned to Ava. "Have you eaten? I know the best—and only—place for a meal in town."

"I—" Ava's shining eyes met Esther's.

"Go on. I'm not hungry."

With a grateful nod, Ava threaded a hand through Petra's offered arm. He smiled, turning back. "Oh, it's good to see you too, Tessa."

Esther nodded.

"Where's Joss?" Ava searched the ground.

Petra's mouth twisted. "I let him stay with the children. Figured they could use the company of a good dog, and war isn't a place for him."

Esther rose, brushing herself off. "Come on Klessen, let's go find the others."

"But I want to go with them!" said Klessen, shoulders drooping.

"Alright Klessen, come on!" called Ava.

Esther put out a hand to block him. "Just keep that hood up, understand? You'll be safer that way. People might be frightened, they've never seen anything like you before." *Like Jathan taught me. The hood stays up.*

"Hm," Klessen grunted, slipping around her arm to dart after Petra and Ava.

"And who is this?" Petra asked, smiling at the hood brushing his elbow.

"I'm Klessen," said Klessen, looking up to fix him with a sharp smile.

Petra's eyes widened and he tripped a half step backward. He smiled at Ava. "Nice to meet you, Klessen."

Esther waited until they had rounded a corner to let her face crumple again. Her breath shook. *Abner isn't the problem. It's me. I failed to protect them. My idiotic attempt at revenge was just trying to move the weight of guilt off of me, but it's useless. There is no getting clean from this. How dare I even try? As if I could be happy now that they're gone.*

Outside Jathan's bar, Esther hesitated. Her eyes skimmed over the knotted wood, the smooth carved handle, the two swaying signs, everything just as she remembered. As if nothing had changed, except her. But the voice that drew her to pull open the door and enter was not Jathan's or the many he serviced. Abner was shouting. Esther rushed inside.

"We tried! There's nothing left on that mountain for us. You've done a well-enough job raising the people. That'll have to do."

"Maybe if I—"

"Cantus, it's up to us! That's it!" Abner caught Esther's eye as he threw out his hand. He let go of a heavy breath. "We'll have to handle this carefully. Every loss for my father is also a loss for us."

"What does that mean?"

"Every soldier killed is one less to defend us when this is all over. He's not the only threat in this world. My uncle's still coming and we, somehow, have to be ready. That's the issue of war within a kingdom. Every victory weakens the crown you are trying to win."

Cantus sighed. "So how do we proceed? To win but not win?"

Abner sat on a stool at the bar, threading his fingers together into a net to catch his forehead. "I don't know. Give me a day with all the lists and I'll think of something."

Cantus shuffled the papers strewn with numbers and letters into a messy pile. "Have you eaten?"

Esther met Cantus' eyes, surprised at being addressed. "Petra and Ava went to eat but I said I wasn't hungry."

"Right." His gaze strayed to the door. "He's a decent sort, once you get to know him. And the thing, it's with him?"

"Yes, *Klessen* went with them."

"You're sure we can't use it in some way, Abner?"

Abner groaned. "He's a boy, Cantus. I won't let him anywhere near the battle."

"Normally I would agree, but since he's all we have by way of surprising the king, between using him or us all being killed, I would at least give him the option to be a help." Cantus strode to the door and Abner glared over the counter, irritation rising from both like heat off the ground on a high summer day.

"Cantus," Esther said, pausing his step. His eyes met hers. "Thank you for taking care of the bodies. I—it was well done."

"Everyone deserves dignity in death." The door snapped closed behind him.

The morning was spent by Abner pouring over every scrap of paper several times, making notes with the bottle of ink and quill, scribbling them out moments later, and giving little groans of frustration with every idea cast aside.

Esther sat across from him, slipping the edge of a thick parchment beneath her fingernail and tapping her heel. At last, she asked, "Can I help somehow?"

Abner's brows furrowed, the light catching his eyes just right.

Esther looked down.

"Read me the inventory page. How many horses?"

"I can't—ah—"

Abner met her eyes. "You can't read?" He sighed. "Then no, just … go."

"What are you thinking?"

His eyes skimmed over his list of failed ideas. "We need to show enough power to get the king to leave Lydia. We have no equipment and not enough supplies for a siege, so we have to get him in the open. But, there's a balance we have to strike. Too little force, he sends Dennison, we die without a chance to get rid of the king. We fail. Too much and it only pushes him to fortify himself in the castle, using the surrounding peasants as human shields. We won't be able to breach Lydia. We fail."

Esther shifted in her chair. "And if we were to make Lydia less desirable?"

Abner squinted at her. "Meaning?"

"Like pushing smoke into a burrow to draw out prey. It's vulnerable to lack of water, isn't it? That's what the nobleman told me, that Lydia wouldn't last long in a siege without water."

"And the common people the king lets die of thirst as he hoards what little there is for himself? Even if we could somehow spoil the supply, I don't want to give the capital city so many reasons to hate us." Abner paused. "Good thought though. We'll need to find some clever..."

"About before," Esther began, but Abner's eyes had already gone back to the papers in front of him.

The quill spotted ink as he tapped the tip on the heavy parchment with a wrinkled brow.

"Never mind. There's more important things to think about. I'll let you focus."

"Thank you," he said, not looking up as he dashed a quick line on one page.

She left the tavern, the fourth mark sun glaring through her squinting eyes. *What to do now?* No one seemed to notice her as she wandered through the streets. Walking with her back straight and a relaxed pace through Shiloh, instead of sweating under a heavy cloak pulled forward so she could hardly see beyond the ground at her feet, was a new experience for Esther. Her back and hips were not pulsing under crushing pressure and that was almost enough to make her weep. She found Cantus, Ava, Petra, and Klessen all sitting around empty plates.

"We're back for the next meal already and haven't seen you all day," Petra said, raising his brow. He lifted a hand to signal someone to bring a plate for her.

"Where's Abner?" Cantus asked.

Klessen leaned around Ava to look at her.

"He'll likely be locked in with those papers you left him till dark." Esther hesitantly slipped into a chair next to Cantus. A gray frock brushed her arm as a plate clapped onto the table. Esther picked at the cold food, nibbling some bread.

"Anything yet?"

Esther forced herself to meet Cantus' eye. "He'll think of something."

Cantus brushed a hand over his mouth as he rose. "I should go then. See if I can't lend a hand."

"Be along in a moment," Petra said, nodding to him. He shrugged to Ava. "Since I'm so important now."

"Lady Tessa? Is it—it's really you?" The old peasant woman shuffled into view, clasping her hands together over her dirty frock as the wrinkles around her eyes deepened with her smile. "And the two of you there, oh what a lovely picture!"

Esther's eyes turned to Cantus.

The soldier shook his head with a sigh.

"To think that we would all be here together again!" She tapped her nose. "Of course you may not remember your visit to our Little Brennon town. I had quite the fright when you had your ... accident in our storeroom. But now you seem perfectly healthy and lovely as ever."

Esther's cheeks reddened. Petra's tight smile echoed the awkwardness she felt before he escaped to follow Cantus.

"Now," the woman slipped into Cantus' vacated chair next to Esther, and scratched at her chin with one long nail. "When your young Cantus turned up in Riverton without you, I will admit I was quite vexed with him. Of course I stayed in the city with my son Ezra after what happened to—well, I just couldn't bear to go far ... and when he said you were away with that Abner fellow, I'll admit I was even more so. But here you are and that's all done with, I suppose. If he can forgive you, so can I."

"I'm sorry?" Esther managed.

"That prince, humph, if he can still be called so, has no business with Your Ladyship. Lord Cantus, now, he will do much better. He is such a good man. He works night and day for the people, he has given us hope. And that is worth much more than some near-moldy, leftover bread the king passes out at the Event. And that prince has done nothing for us since his first breath! We are the people who work his fields, gather his crops, press his wine." The woman smiled at Ava, eyes glazing quickly over Klessen's stooped hood as his hands picked at his block. "And he's such a nice man. Just," her smile returned to Esther, "make sure you show your appreciation to him, Your Ladyship. Men like that kind of thing."

Ava's mouth pinched, trying to stifle the mirth shining in her eyes. "We should probably be—"

"Yes," Esther nodded gratefully. "Good day."

The woman smiled as the two girls linked arms and Klessen trotted at Ava's side holding her hand.

"I'm surprised," Ava said, glancing back at the old peasant woman, her smile fading away. "I heard about what happened as I passed through to find you, and was warned to stay far away from Little Brennon. Everyone was saying—I'm impressed she still finds a reason to smile."

"What happened?" Dread settled into Esther's gut.

Ava paused. "They're all dead."

The rain hit the roof above Abner's head in a steady drumming rhythm. Cantus sat across from him, idly flipping through papers. Tessa, Ava, Petra, and Klessen were sitting together at a corner table, whispering quietly. He couldn't think about what they had shared with him, about the few dozen new lives to hang on his conscience that had been sacrificed for his play at peace. He was on the verge of spending even more.

"Remind me why we can't just send him a note saying we're in Shiloh and shoot him full of arrows from the wall?" Tessa's fingers drummed on the table.

Petra smirked from his corner near Ava.

"None of our archers could hit that mark." Abner tossed his quill down, rubbing at his tired eyes. "They'd have to hit a perfect shot in the armor gap at the neck in both the king and Dennison at the same moment. Even then, it would leave a score of high-ranking commanders to rally the men and become a new problem. Also, he's not going to move in range of arrows unless he has a good reason."

Tessa leaned back against the wall, returning to her study of the grainy wooden table.

Abner couldn't help sighing as he looked back at the ink-splattered pages. *At least the rain makes a pleasant noise to listen to as I'm working through the impossible. Rain. Water.* "Klessen," Abner's head snapped up to meet the slit-eyed stare, "why did you say we would need the water barrels?"

"Don't you know what water from the mountain does?" Klessen asked, tipping his head to one side.

Petra leaned forward. "It makes animals talk."

Klessen's face pinched. "Sort of."

"And it makes people..." Abner's eyes met Tessa's threatening stare, "happy."

"Sometimes."

"You'll have to help us with this riddle, Klessen," Ava said. "We don't understand."

"The water brings back the natural way of things. The *vade mecum* breathes magic into the air, which is brought to the water, and carried over the ground. There's a wall humans have built around themselves and brought to everything on this side of the mountain ring. The water strips you of it and lets what is underneath out into the light. Things were made to be in the light, in relationship to one another, and so you get to know the real thing. Animals can talk, humans are honest, and the weight of hiding the truth is gone. It only lasts for so long though. I made sure to bring a lot of water, just in case."

"So with this water we would be able to…" Cantus trailed off.

"I know what I would do with it." Klessen nodded with a smile. "I would get some animals, give them the water, and set them on the army. Nothing frightens man more than uncontrollable nature, yes?" He sniffed, wiping his nose with the back of his hand. "Probably have the soldiers running for higher ground at the sight of them."

Abner stared at Klessen, eyes prickling before he remembered to blink. "That … could actually work."

"How would we get wild animals, Abner? And force-feed them water?" Cantus shook his head. "They'd be more likely to turn on us than anything else."

"What if they were already partly trained?" Tessa drew Abner's eye. A muscle in her neck strained as she pulled in a breath. "There's a tiger, two bears, and a lion that Death has access to. It's a start at least."

"I don't want to ask more of him," Cantus' brow furrowed. "He's already giving us trained fighters. The price for them was high but nothing that a trip to the castle treasury won't compensate for. He'll only triple his price for helping if he realizes we need more than he's already giving."

"I like it." Abner drew a few quick arrows on the parchment nearest his hand. "They're fast. They could—we'd need to draw the king here and buy time for the animals to be retrieved. Does anyone know that we've set up in Shiloh?"

"Would Shiloh still be standing if they did?"

Abner smiled. "Perfect."

XXXII

I should speak to him. Abner stifled a yawn.

Klessen sat on the roof. His heels lightly kicked the clay pots hanging from the jutting awning, causing the long brown vines to sway in a slow mourning song of their lost vibrancy. The boy's eyes arced between horizons, greeting the stars as if they were old friends. His shoulders jumped when Abner pulled himself up the trellis to sit next to him on the mossy, rotting shingles.

"Do you mind company?" Abner asked.

Klessen's shoulders loosened. "I don't."

Abner blew out a slow breath, the chill of the changing air turning it to smoke. "Isn't it uncomfortable," he asked quietly, joining in Klessen's perusal of the night sky, "to sit here with the sacred text of your people belted to your back?"

Klessen's gaze narrowed.

"Should we expect trouble from your master for your thieving?"

Klessen lifted his chin. "You should expect trouble regardless." The boy's noticeably absent smile left an unsettling void in his wide-slitted eyes.

"You seem different tonight, Klessen. You slip away from the group after the meal and sit by yourself in the dark on a rooftop? What's bothering you?"

"I read your story."

Abner didn't know what that meant, but a cold rush of dread flowed down his back.

"About your father. Your mother." Klessen paused. "You." The boy tipped his chin, studying Abner through slanted eyes. "You aren't a very good man."

Abner's face filled with heat. "No. I'm not."

"But you're becoming a better one." Klessen's eyes turned back to the sky. "Is that enough, do you think? To just be better?"

"It's all one can hope for," Abner said through a strained brow.

Klessen let out a shuddering breath.

"The past can't be changed. There's no way back. We've all fallen short, but there has to be a way ... up, to be different. You just focus on making the next better choice, every chance you can."

"That sounds exhausting."

Abner nodded, one corner of his mouth pulling into a near-invisible smile.

"I shouldn't have let him bind the book," Klessen said, pulling his knees to his chin. His heel knocked against a clay pot, sending it clapping against its neighbor. "It just kept hurting. You get your hopes wound up in their story. Maybe this one will work, this nation seems nice, this man seems good. But it always turns bad. Always." Klessen lowered his eyes to the ground. "After centuries of disappointment, things become hopeless. I don't know why I think now is different. But you are the first to come to the mountain and you haven't even tried to take the book to use it for yourself." Klessen turned to Abner. "Tell me, if you did have magic that could kill kings, what would you do with it?"

Abner leaned away from Klessen's sudden intensity. "I'd stop my father from doing any more harm."

"And then?"

"I—" Abner hesitated. "I might use it to defend us against attacks."

"What about other lands? You could conquer the world with this power!"

"That's not what I want."

Klessen's mouth twisted. "Hm."

"You even talk like him, you know," Abner said, smiling.

"Well, two bodies, one spark."

Abner's brow shot high. "What?"

"I wonder if words sink deep enough to make an impression on the spark or is it just being around one another for so long?"

"You—and the man on the mountain—share a spark?"

"Yes. These forms weren't meant to hold one like ours, so we were split."

Abner took a moment to digest the idea. *To split oneself in two?* The reality of Abner's spark leaving his body when he died already hollowed him out with fear. But to break oneself apart intentionally? He shivered. "Why?"

The boy blinked at him.

"Why would you do that to yourself?"

"We were chosen."

"By who?"

"The True One."

"The—he's real?"

"Of course." The boy paused. "I was given the *vade mecum* as a help to watch humanity's progress after the great betrayal. It only took a few hundred years and many thousands of failed hopes to get me to abandon my post. I wonder what He'll say when He returns and sees."

"So you were supposed to help humanity—"

"To watch humanity, to judge when they were worthy of help."

"—and the book—"

"*Vade mecum.*"

"—allowed you to watch from the mountain before you closed it." Abner tried to make the ideas fit in with what he already knew. *I have been watched, judged all this time?* "But why only tell us about this now? If I had known—"

"Your father, what would he have done? Knowing a treasure of magic he didn't understand was hidden on his doorstep?"

Abner's chin tipped. "He would have taken it."

"He would have *tried*," Klessen's brow rose. "Destroy himself and the rest of the world along with him. But he'd try."

Surprised by a yawn, Abner let his jaw stretch till it popped. Despite himself, it had been a very long day.

"Go to sleep, Prince," Klessen said, himself showing no signs of weariness as his eyes raised to the stars.

"Will you be alright?"

"I'll be my normal self again in the morning when the weight of the stars is covered over by the sun." Klessen's breath hissed through his teeth in a long sigh. "I feel it now but it won't last forever."

Abner's mind was consumed with thoughts of the mountain and the weight of the stars as he laid on the cot set up for him in the upper loft of the old bar. The comfort of not sleeping on bare dirt was lost on him until he opened his eyes to the streaming sunlight of morning. Abner obeyed the call to hush his grumbling stomach with food.

"I don't believe it," Tessa said, drawing Abner's eyes from the steaming hunks of potatoes wafting delicious heavy smells to his nose. She stared past him and Abner turned from his food to look. "It's him."

"Who?" His eyes shifted through the faces of the crowded square. "Death?"

"Not him. *Next* to him. No, don't look, don't look." She ducked her eyes down.

Abner turned from the black stare. "Him?"

"He was at the Event. He fights amazingly!" Tessa's voice was a reverent whisper.

Abner shrugged. "I've seen him in previous years. He's alright, rather boring to watch."

"How can you—" She turned hot eyes to him. "He couldn't be touched, he was so fast. Easily the best fighter of the day."

"Hardly. Against one opponent he does fine, but wastes so much energy flipping around. It's rather cowardly fighting when it comes down to it. And if he has multiple opponents, he takes too long to dispatch each." Abner chewed through a potato hunk on his plate, relishing the warmth over his tongue as a chill wind blew against the back of his neck.

Above, the sky spoke of another wet day which would turn the streets into a squelching, muddy mess.

"I think you're jealous."

Abner scoffed. "His fighting skill isn't something that would earn jealousy from me. Your attention might."

Her face colored.

"Are you planning to go talk to him or just sit and stare?"

"I couldn't—"

"You should."

Tessa pushed out a breath. "No."

"Well, I have business with Death, so you can come along or be a coward stuck to your seat."

Tessa met his challenge with the expected flashing eyes and angry scowl. He grinned as she planted her hands and pushed herself to her feet.

"It's too easy," he chuckled.

Death's eyes met him as he approached. "Ah," said Death, mouth full of chunks of potato, "if it isn't my patron!" He swallowed forcefully.

Abner folded his arms. "I'm surprised to see you, Death."

"I tend to come unexpectedly. Keeps things interesting." He winked at Tessa. "I assume Cantus has shared the conditions of our—"

"Quiet," Abner warned, arm tensing.

Death lowered his voice, eyes dropping to slits. "Don't want the people to know you are paying some and not others, eh?"

Abner leaned forward, his voice almost indecipherable. "Finish your meal and meet me at the old tavern." He straightened and turned away.

"And what should I expect at this meeting of ours, Prince?"

Abner paused. "A new deal." He didn't need to turn to know Death was interested. Abner glanced at Tessa's blushing cheeks. "Why didn't you say anything?"

She shook her head.

"You are more nervous to meet some low-level fighter than me, the prince. I'll admit, it stings."

Tessa answered his smirk with a tired sigh.

❖ ❖ ❖

Esther followed Abner into Jathan's bar, skimming the door frame with her finger.

Death waited for them, lounging with his feet propped on a table. "Ah, at last the man arrives. If I had known you were planning to take time for a morning excursion, I would have gotten a second round." He met Cantus' glare. "Only joking."

"Have you told him anything?" Abner asked. He tossed the coils of rope fibers Ava had promised to twist into cords on a chair by the door.

Cantus shook his head. "Thought it best to wait for you."

"Alright." Abner pulled out a chair across from Death, leaning back with practiced carelessness. "Where do you keep your beasts, Death?"

His brow rose. "You mean Esmeralda?"

"All of them."

"They're kept in locked cages beneath the arena."

"But we saw the tiger on the road," Esther said, eyes narrowing. "Don't waste our time with lies."

"She sometimes comes with us for a traveling performance we run to the north. Trade brings in bored merchants with money to spend on thrills. When the weather turns she goes back underground though."

Abner nodded, satisfied.

"Why the interest?" Death leaned forward, displaying his own.

"We have means to use them to our advantage. If you could lend them to us, it would greatly increase our odds of victory."

"And what do you offer for this additional investment of mine?"

Abner's head tipped to one side. "Consider, if we lose, you receive nothing. It is in your best interest to help us in any way you can."

Death smirked, raising an eyebrow at Esther.

"Fine, we'll double your price."

Death picked at a loose thread on his sleeve.

Abner's brow rose. "You want triple?"

Death met Abner's eyes. "If I understand right, you have some plan in which my help is the cornerstone to hope of success. That makes me the most valuable person in this room. How much is your throne and your life worth to you, Prince? That is my price."

"Why take one sum when you can be guaranteed a lifetime of wealth?" Abner said, not showing any signs of stress, but Esther's gut twisted.

Death's eyes flickered to Esther and then returned to study the prince. "I'm listening."

"A contract for the Event held once every two years, three hundred crowns per performance, guaranteed by written word and stamped signet."

"And?"

"As well as what Cantus promised for your help originally."

"How do I know you won't go back on your word as your father did?"

"You will carry the document with you. The written word is binding, even for a king."

Death licked his lips, eyes glinting. "I see the evidence of your training, Sire. Your offer is ... tempting. But there's one problem. I don't have access to the animals in the off-season. They're under guard."

"Why didn't you say that before?" Esther demanded. "Stars above, you can't even—"

"We'll get them out." Abner held up a hand, cutting off Esther's words. "But we'll need one of your trainers to come along to handle the beasts."

Death tapped a pale finger to his lip. "I have a man for the job."

"And—this will be in the contract—when all is over the Event will change. No more human sacrifices. The animals, the fights, all are fine, but we are done burning up people's sparks to the king's glory." Abner met Cantus' stare with a heavy nod. "Never again."

"That," Death blinked at the table, eyes shining, "is the best idea you've had all day."

Esther fumed silently, having left the men to get some fresh air and feel the sun on her skin only to find it covered by a heavy gray curtain. *Why do we even need him? I could get us in, now that my back is better. With the water to tame the beasts and Petra to pick the locks, I could be back with them in four days. Rather than waiting on this scavenger.* Her feet clipped beneath her at a furious pace. *Abner is promising too much to this treacherous, weak-sparked—*

Her shoulder smashed into an unexpected corner, her eyes snapping wide in shock. Clutching the dust-coated wall with shaking hands, she waited. The jarring pain quieted, the pulse of unbearable pressure on her hips and legs noticeably absent, and Esther shut her eyes to force a slow breath through trembling lips. *I'm alright. I'm alright. I'm not broken. I'm alright.* The threat of returning weakness hung like a terrifying shadow with every bump or bruise. *How am I going to find courage to fight in a battle if I shake every time I'm touched? How am I still useless?*

Apparently, her courage would not be needed. When Esther returned to the bar sometime after midmark, Abner was in the middle of compiling a list of two groups to leave Shiloh. Esther was not in either.

"Of course I'm going! I snuck into your castle right under your nose, Prince. I have the best chance of getting us in!"

"You had help. If Lady Hildren hadn't—" Abner's voice died away. The air in the room felt stiff. Abner cast an apologetic look at Cantus. "Regardless, I'm not letting you risk your strength on something someone else can accomplish just as well."

"It's okay, Tessa. Maybe if you just—"

"No, Ava!" snapped Esther, her face flooding with heat. "I'm not like you! I'm not content to just sit and be useless while others—" Her eyes met Ava's as the large brown orbs swam in quick tears. "Oh, no. I'm—I'm sorry. Ava—I didn't—"

Ava was already gone, the door of the bar smacking against its frame behind her.

"That…"

"I know, Abner," Esther groaned, the snap creeping back into her tone. "You don't need to say it."

"What is wrong with you? Ava is—"

"I know!" Esther threw her hands toward the ceiling. "But you keep treating me as if I'm still broken. Did you forget that I was healed?"

"Have you forgotten the cost? The man on the mountain said you'd be vulnerable. One significant hit and—"

"Or have you forgotten that I bested you when we first met?" She continued, throat closing over the fresh wound his words prodded to widen. "I'm not incompetent, I'm not weak! Stop treating me like some … just some girl!"

Abner leaned back, studying her. "So what is it you want, exactly?"

She sucked in a heavy, steadying breath. "I want to be in one of the groups being sent out. I'd prefer the one to get the tiger, but if you need me to fight, I'll do that too."

"Fine."

Cantus stood. "Abner, I thought you said—"

"Of the two it's the safer option. If I don't put you on one, you'll likely just show up wherever I am not, won't you, Tessa?"

Esther raised her chin.

"So, go get yourself a tiger. But, by the stars, you had better be careful." Abner spent a long moment studying her, his features held in tension. "Please. Now, go find your friend."

The heat died from her belly, her insides twisting within her. As the drizzle from the sky hit her brow with a thousand pattering blows, Esther's eyes squinted through the falling water. Ava could be anywhere, but, thank the stars it was another wet day. They were light, but Esther could trace Ava's hurried step through the imprints her slipper shoes made through the mud. The ground had only just dried in rolling hills and canyons of footprints from yesterday's soaking in time to be filled up with little muddy lakes of today's water. She followed cautiously, bending an ear toward Ava's quiet sniffles. Rounding the corner into the alleyway, Esther hesitated.

Everything from Ava's shaking shoulders to her bent posture as she leaned against the wall, told Esther to leave. Even crying Ava was unwilling to sit on her dress in the mud.

More of a lady than I ever was. She won't want to talk to me. How could she? Esther crept forward. "I'm sorry."

Ava jumped, yipping in fright. Clutching her chest, she forced a deep breath in through her nose. "Don't surprise me like that."

"I'm sorry."

Ava fixed her with a red-rimmed glare. "What are you sorry for? You were just being honest."

"No, I wasn't," Esther said, moving tentatively to Ava's side and staring out at the rain.

Ava dragged a heavy breath through a thickly packed nose.

"I was being angry. Not even with you. I didn't mean to lash at you. If only Abner would—"

"It's not Abner's fault. He cares about you." Ava's eyes didn't hold any warmth, but at least her tone was losing some of its bite. "Honestly, you should be taking better care of the gift you were given. Who becomes crippled and then gets a second chance? You want to risk it all just to feel better about yourself? To not be someone like me?"

"Ava, I wish I was someone like you."

"I'm not weak."

"I know."

"Do you? Because it seems like the only people you give your respect to, when it really gets to the point, are the people who can pick up a sword and hack someone apart. That's not me. It never will be." Ava paused. "There are different kinds of strength."

"I know. I'm sorry."

Ava raised her brow, not meeting Esther's eyes.

After several long moments of thrumming water filling the space between them, Ava straightened and pulled Esther into a sidelong hug. "Should we get back to the others?" she asked quietly.

"Probably," Esther nodded but neither girl moved and the rain sounds reclaimed their attention.

❖ ❖ ❖

Petra—Abner wrote quickly, filling in the easy gaps first as he remade his lists—*Locks*
Clive – Animals
Tessa –

The quill hesitated over the parchment. Doubt echoed to his fingertips. He moved on.
Abner – Lead force to Little Brennon
Cantus – Second

Petra settled into a chair at the bar, brushing wet hair from his forehead and using some oil to make Penny wink in the lantern glow. Abner tried to ignore the sporadic flickers of light and the unsteady rhythm of water dripping from Petra's cloak, which amplified the tension binding his temple.

"You really should get a breath of air, Prince. All this stooping over parchment can't be good for you."

Abner read over his list. "The locks on the animal cages shouldn't be a problem for you, correct? How long do you need to open them?"

Petra sniffed. "Depends on the lock." He pulled out the unpickable lock from a pocket in his cloak. "There's this one I still haven't gotten to crack, but others I can have open in a few moments."

"If only we knew what kind of locks they used, you could practice and have it measured out. We'd know exactly how long you'd need for each cage."

"Has anyone seen the locks?"

"Death has, they're his animals."

Petra smirked.

The night before the two groups were due to leave, Abner put aside his parchment and opened the bar's cabinets to share its contents with the people. He had spent too much time sequestered in the dark tavern, making plans for other people's lives in order to save as many of them as he could. Now it was time to be seen.

Musicians were found and Shiloh's homes were searched for instruments to play. The people all gathered in the square for a dance and a drink as the stars began to spark to life.

Tessa was at a table by herself, watching Ava and Petra spin Klessen around in a twirling mess of feet, oblivious to the prescribed steps.

Abner smiled at their red, laughing faces as he sat next to Tessa. His voice broke through the thickened air between them, loud enough for only Tessa to hear above the thrumming music. "I'm only trying to protect you because—"

"Because you care about me?" Tessa mocked.

"Yes."

She turned away. "I know."

A cheer from across the wide circle of dancers drew Abner's eyes. Someone had set up a game of darts.

Abner nodded toward them. "I challenge you."

"I'm not in the mood."

"Oh, you're afraid? What if I promise not to mock you too harshly when you lose?"

Tessa knew what he was doing, she must have, but she shook her head with a smile and followed him.

The men recognized Abner, moving aside as he approached. Glaring, they abandoned their game, dropping the small darts on a table before stomping away.

His back stiffened as spit hit the dirt behind his boot. When Abner turned back to Tessa, her brow wore a deep crease. *No, Tessa. Save that compassion for someone who deserves it.*

"No matter," he said brightly, "this game only requires two." He handed her a dart and counted paces from the board to take his first shot.

A blade whistled past his ear, piercing the centermost circle on the parchment nailed to the wooden wall. Whipping around, Abner met the black-eyed stare with a glare of his own. *Not him again.*

The man held up three fingers and Abner gave a nod.

"Next time you can just ask, friend."

He strode past Abner to retrieve his blade and exchange it for some darts.

"He can't actually," said Death, strolling by with an obviously drunk peasant woman under his arm. "Marvelous party you've thrown, by the way." He gave a grunt of pleasure as he pulled a gulp from his mug.

The girl fell against his chest, cheeks red as she cackled.

"But he doesn't speak a word of our tongue. Bought him off a ship from the north. Very expensive, but talented."

The dark-eyed man gestured at Tessa to step up for a throw, but she shook her head. He lifted a shoulder as he turned and landed another perfect mark. He raised a dark brow at Abner.

Abner had never been very good at darts. It wasn't a game Dennison thought offered any strategic benefit, and his father was not the type to play. He did his best, but his dart sank into the third circle, drawing a groan from his chest and a smirk from Tessa.

"Well then," Abner gestured to her. "Your turn, Lady."

Her hand shook with nerves as she raised it to her eye line, sighting down the length of the dart. She took a breath, the tremors gradually growing still. The dart sailed through the air, ripping a hole through the parchment just on the edge of the center circle.

The man smirked at Abner, nodding at Tessa. He gestured for the prince to move aside so he could take another shot.

Tessa got better with every throw, creeping closer to the center, though never quite right.

Abner allowed himself to be edged out of the game.

The man grew in excitement as Tessa practiced. At one point he stopped, gesturing for her to stand straighter, to pull in a deeper breath, drawing a line from his eye to the board. At least, that is what Abner assumed he meant. When she did so, he nodded.

Her dart sang through the air and struck a hair off center. She smiled.

He frowned. Wiggling a hand, he retrieved her dart and prompted her to try again.

Abner went to get a drink, trying not to be bothered by her smile. He met Petra as he sat with Ava, laughing and red-faced together, Klessen perched on the table between them. "I meant to ask you. Why's that sheath on your back empty?"

The shine of mirth died from Petra's eyes. He swallowed. "I lost the sword when the soldiers attacked the orphanage. I could get a new one, I suppose. But we don't have many to go around, and I've grown fond of the shorter twin blades anyway. And there's always Penny."

"Well, since it's just sitting empty—"

"No." Petra's smile reignited. "You get the crown and the gold, Prince. I'm keeping my empty sheath."

Abner laughed with him. "Fair enough."

"Another dance!" Klessen said, throwing up his palms. The sides of his hands flickered green in the dim light. Ava gripped both and pulled him into the twirling mess. Abner left them to their fun.

Cantus nursed a mug as he leaned against a table, a stooped man muttering to him at his elbow. The old man's gray eyes glared at Abner before the elder ducked away.

"Who was that?" Abner asked, joining Cantus' perusal of the dance.

"He's from a village to the north, I don't remember which one. He thinks we should be storming Lydia by now, not having a party. That we're wasting time dancing and drinking when the kingdom is waiting for us to take it."

Abner raised a brow.

The old man's shoulders were held taut with a rolling anger as he stomped away.

"Is that what you think?" he asked, turning back to Cantus.

"No," the soldier answered quickly. "We don't have the numbers, Abner." His voice dropped low so Abner had to study his mouth to discern what he was saying over the strumming melody of the dance. "We can't be stronger. We have to be more clever. Even then, I'm not sure it's enough. Maybe I shouldn't have started this. Maybe I should have let Tessa die, let you stay prince. Then these villagers would still be in their homes. Little Brennon wouldn't be dead. All could be well."

Abner scoffed. "Talking nonsense doesn't become you, Cantus. Neither does doubt. A world where I wait in selfishness to carry on my father's bloody legacy and Tessa's dead? Where these people suffer in fear? All would not be well. But we will change it."

Cantus answered by taking a drink.

"Whatever happens," Abner said, feeling a hot glare on his back, "I am glad we started this."

The dark-eyed man tapped his chest. "Hideo," he said, his voice shockingly deep. His hands moved as if he were offering Esther something.

"Hih-day-oh?" Esther repeated the sounds carefully.

He nodded, gesturing again.

"Is that your name? Hideo?" Esther matched his smile. "Tessa," she said, tapping her chest.

"Tess-ah," Hideo said slowly, as if weighing the name against the girl. He dropped into a sudden bow. It was a deep, powerful gesture; his back held stiff with none of the side-leaning indolence common in the courts of Alberon. A fierce spark of pride lit his dark eyes as he rose.

Esther wished she knew how to speak his tongue. She wanted to learn how he moved so fast, how he was able to keep such power and purpose in his muscles. How she could be like him; untouchable and deadly.

Hideo led her to an open table and gestured for her to sit. "Please," he said. Esther's brow shot high, and a small cunning smile crept up one corner of his bearded cheek. He held up a hand.

"I'll wait here," she promised.

With a firm nod, Hideo disappeared through the crowd of dancers.

Esther caught Abner's eyes. She broke away from his stare, surprise bringing a flush to her cheeks. On the corner of her vision, Abner left Cantus and made his way toward her.

"Dance with me," he said, leaning on the wood table.

"No."

"What good is a magically healed back if you don't use it?"

Esther smiled coldly. "My point exactly."

Abner smirked. "Then show me how well you've healed." He tipped his head toward the spinning couples. "This may be our last night for frivolous feelings."

"I can't. I promised Hideo I'd wait for his return."

Abner tossed his eyes to the sky. He leaned close enough for Esther to catch the sting of drink on his breath. "He looks old enough to be your father. Honestly, it's beginning to get a bit odd, this devotion to him."

"Now, Prince, if everything goes according to your parchment, you'll be King in a few days. Jealousy of a man—"

Hideo appeared suddenly, giving Abner a wary glance.

Esther swallowed her words, hoping the heat stinging through her cheeks was invisible to everyone else. *He understands more than Death thinks. What did he hear?*

Abner slowly shifted aside.

Hideo resumed his seat across from Esther. His dark eyes reflected the warm glow of the torchlight as he set a wooden box carefully on the table between them.

"For me?" Esther hesitated.

He gave a single firm nod.

Abner chuckled coldly, shaking his head.

She tried to ignore him as she unclasped the metal latch. *Blades.* Twenty small gleaming knives the size of her palm were arranged in the box. They were identical to the one Hideo had pierced the target with earlier. She ran a fingertip over the thin sharp point of several before looking up.

"For me?" she said again.

Hideo tipped his head subtly toward Abner.

He won't speak in front of him. She nodded, and pulled the box closer, tracing the blades' edges. *They're so elegant. Smooth. Beautiful.*

"You both should probably get some rest. Your group leaves at first mark."

Esther looked at Abner. His eyes were hard as he stared at her gift.

"I'll arrange it with Death. Your friend here is going along to be your guard. He'll keep you safe and out of trouble."

Esther scoffed. "Why didn't you just assign Petra to be a babysitter for me?"

"Petra has other things to focus on." Abner said with a smile stretched by tension. "Believe me, if it wasn't for needing to be seen in Little Brennon with our men, I'd be the one stuck to your side. For now, it's him. Just ... make sure he keeps his hands to himself."

Esther's face swam in heat as Hideo's dark eyes narrowed in confusion.

Shut it, Abner.

XXXIII

Ezra had better stick to the plan. Abner glared at the broad ox shoulders, his jaw glued together with tension.

Beside him, Cantus rolled his arm with a grunt. He shrugged at Abner's look. "I'm fine. Just didn't expect to have to fight before we fought."

Abner nodded, returning to his glaring study of Ezra's shoulder as it bent to pick up a bundle of branches. *Neither did I.* His knuckles still ached from beating the men back into line. Twenty and five bodies milled around the bend that widened into Little Brennon's central lane. Three of those wore large, fresh bruises along their jaws. The farmhouse where Tessa had insisted on leaving the ten copper bits was as eerily silent as it had been the last time Abner had passed by. *If she were here now, at least I'd know she was safe. What would she say about all of this?*

The scene from the night before re-echoed through his mind.

Abner had finished explaining the basics of the plan to the forty assembled men, their faces lit by two lanterns casting a pale, muted light. No one spoke. "Questions?"

"I have," the giant said, standing tall. "Why are we listening to you?"

Abner paused, noting the murmur of agreement.

"I have a new plan. We take him in, turn him over for the thousand crown reward, take our families and live rich lives somewhere else." Ezra looked at the young man seated beside him. "I like my plan better."

"And the families you'll leave behind?" Cantus moved to Abner's side. "Who will stop what happened here in Little Brennon from happening again?"

The giant's chest puffed. "Most of my family and every friend are gone, because of that snake you let slither into our ranks. Brennon did nothing but help you, and you let them die. Now you use our necks as stepping stones in your climb to a stolen throne." The giant moved to stand in front of Cantus, tucking his chin to fix the soldier with a cold stare. "Other families are not my problem." He turned his back.

"That's a coward's view." Spit struck the dirt at the giant's heel.

Ezra answered Cantus by plowing a fist into his gut.

Three younger men hurled themselves at Abner. Cantus faced the giant alone as Abner beat them off. It only took a few moments for Abner to be standing over them, massaging the sting from his red knuckles, as the three boys held their scruffy jaws with misty eyes at his feet. Cantus had Ezra forcibly kneeling, his large meaty hand held at an odd angle.

"Enough," Abner said, knocking Cantus' arm. "Let him up."

Cantus let go and Ezra rose, glaring at Abner with twin coals burning hatred. "What's your name, soldier?" Cantus asked, rolling his shoulder.

He spit to one side, "Ezra."

"Ezra." Abner swallowed. "You joined with Cantus of your own will. I could recite some speech about duty and honor to try to convince you to fight, but you had your own reasons for coming. I am trying to stop what happened to you from happening to anyone else in Alberon again. Can I count on your help?" Abner paused, allowing Ezra to consider. "Tomorrow, what will you do?"

Ezra rubbed at his wrist, jaw tight.

Forty pairs of eyes waited to see if the giant would bend.

Ezra turned his back to the group gathered in the lantern's circle, stomping off to stare into the dark.

Abner sighed, waving at Cantus to leave it alone before going to brush down the horses.

Now, Little Brennon was lit by mid-morning daylight. The monstrous fire spewed more smoke than warmth as it spread its wide gray column to the sky. It was the second day they had raised the signal, the smoke carrying the challenge to Lydia.

Here I am.

The wind changed, the ash-laden air burning Abner's eyes.

"Are you sure they'll come?" Cantus asked.

Abner rubbed the smoke from his eyes before answering. "Someone from Lydia will. They can't ignore a potential chance to capture me and squash us before we've gained ground."

"And you're sure we're ready for them?" Cantus' back was straight, the grip on his sword unshakable, but there was an energy to his tension that made him seem uncertain.

"You want to run?" Abner asked, turning his gaze away.

"I don't want us to lose," Cantus said. "These people have waited ten years for this chance. Who knows if it will ever come again?"

A whistle pierced the air.

Abner sucked in a deep breath. A few men cast uncertain glances around them. Abner's head dropped into a heavy nod that he hoped was reassuring and confident as the five, including Ezra, split away. Anxiety spread his limbs as he waited. When the first four-abreast line of soldiers rounded the bend, weapons gripped in tight hands, Abner feigned a look of shock.

"At the ready!" he called.

The men formed a clumsy line. They gripped single-bladed axes, little heavier than hatchets, against rough wooden shields. Matched against the army's metal, it seemed a pitiful pairing.

"Abner!" called the commander lazily, hidden in the unit's center.

The soldiers set their feet, forming a wall of metal.

"Enough of this nonsense, boy. Come back to Lydia with me. Your father is waiting anxiously for your return. I am not interested in whatever war games you are trying to play."

"Shields up men," Abner called out. "Conquer, no compromise." His brow pulled tight, casting his eyes into shadow.

The king's soldiers moved first, closing the distance toward the under-equipped citizen army without fear of the ax wielders. The lines met and Abner's surprise—as the men held their ground—stirred a well of pride at their clumsy spirit. Strike after strike, his men took the beating of metal on their shield with shoulders used to crushing weight.

But they would not win. They couldn't. The tide turned as two men were cut—one slashed across the gut, the other taking a nasty cut on his leg. The man with the open gut stared in shock at his own spilling blood.

Abner's stomach sank. "Back!" he called. "Fall back to Shiloh!"

The men fled behind Abner, their feet pounding the dirt road.

The clanging metal stomp of thirty armed warriors pursued them. The soldiers did not rush, confident in their numbers to finish the job.

Abner cast a look back.

A young man mishandled his ax and it clattered between his ankles, tangling his feet and sending his bruised jaw smacking into the dirt.

"Keep going!" Abner said to Cantus. "Give the signal." He rushed back between his fleeing men to the one struggling to rise. "On your feet, boy!" Abner pulled him up by the shoulder.

A splash of red wet the boy's brown tunic. The edge of the ax lay stained at his feet. The boy's shaking fingers pressed into his wound, spilling the pool of blood that had gathered there.

The metal stomp was getting closer.

There was no time to debate what the better decision would be. Flinging his arm around the boy's side, Abner hugged him to his own. "I'm going to get you out of here."

A promise easier said than kept.

"Run the rabbit down, men! Conquer, no compromise!" the commander's voice rang out.

Cantus hasn't given the signal! Abner whistled, stumbling with the boy's awkward weight. He had to lick his lips to whistle again, making the note shrill, piercing.

"Abner!" Cantus called from ahead. The others formed another line of defense behind him.

"Fall back!" Abner yelled, pushing his step into a wild gait. "Fall back to Shiloh!"

He was listening for it, the snap of braided rope, the rumbling rolling chaos that it would unleash, but there was nothing. *Bleeding glory, Ezra! What are you doing?*

The boy and the prince would reach the square in a moment, followed by thirty armored soldiers.

Cantus was waiting for him.

Ezra was apparently sleeping at his station.

It's not going to work. Abner's lungs burned.

"Always knew Dennison had raised a coward with you, Prince!" the commander called out. "Bleeding soft!"

With a final gust of breath, Abner let loose a shrill whistle.

Snap! Snap! Snap! Snap!

The cords came loose. Abner cast a glance up, blinking away the stinging sweat from his eyes, to the hill bordering Little Brennon's town square.

The trees began to roll. Ezra and four others helped the felled logs pick up speed by pushing them along with their axes.

"Keep moving!" Abner yelled over the cascade of noise.

The boy choked, coughing a sudden spill of red over the dirt.

"Don't stop!"

The ground shook as the logs crashed onto the road, splintering the space around Abner's ears into shards. The startled cries from the horses hidden ahead, the screams from the first lines of armored soldiers overwhelmed by the avalanche behind, and the commander's harsh, barking orders helped to ground Abner's mind as he stumbled to where Cantus waited.

The horses were being collected from the shadows of houses lining the square. The boy was taken and belted to someone's back, while another man held Abner's horse for him to mount. Surprised, Abner planted a boot on the man's offered knee and swung himself into the saddle.

The twang of arrows drew Abner's eyes to the wall of logs. He counted death cries, standing in his stirrups to watch the progress. His archers in the trees took down three with the first volley, a few bolts clanging off the heavy armor plating the soldiers. The second volley laid flat two more, one of the arrows sinking through the neck of the cloaked commander. There was only one way out for the surviving men. Abner had seen to that. The soldiers broke ranks, holding armor-plated arms over their heads and sprinting down the road toward Lydia.

I'll wait for you in Shiloh, Father.

Petra pulled in a sharp breath as Esther appeared beside him. "Quite the sneaky little thing, aren't you?"

"Sorry," Esther said. "What are you looking at?"

"Nothing, just trying to see if I could catch a glimpse. I've…" he paused, Penny winking against his thumb in the midmark sun, "I've always wanted to see Lydia."

"You haven't been to Lydia?"

Petra glanced at her. "Why the surprise?"

"You just seem like the type who's been everywhere."

Petra grinned. "Not everywhere. It would not go well for me if I were caught in Lydia. Too much risk, not enough reward. I've been as close as Riverton. You get enough Lydians there to make checking belts worth your while. But I've never been to the place itself. I've always been … curious."

Esther sniffed, the chilled air stinging her nose. "Maybe Death will hire you as a performer? You can be a part of his troupe."

Petra laughed.

"I can still smell smoke," Esther said, turning back to the south. She pulled in a deep breath, trying to clear her lungs.

"It's been going for two days," Petra agreed. His shoulders jumped through a cough. He shook his head at her look, coughing again into his palm. "I've always had a weak chest. Every spring I can hardly breathe."

Petra nodded past Esther's shoulder. "That'll be Abner sending up his signal. We'll be making our move tonight."

Esther nodded, her pink, freshly scrubbed hands brushing over her soft-as-a-flower-petal dress stitched by the women gathered at Shiloh. They owed Death, yet again, for the silky material. "At least I'll be able to take these braids out soon. Ava seemed to get some cruel pleasure in making them tight."

Petra's eyes swept over her hair, the crisscrossing locks pinned to her head in a fashionably uncomfortable way. "Well I think you look quite ... noble."

Esther's mouth twisted. "Yes, the only thing he'll allow me to do. Look noble. I guess I have a talent for it."

"But you aren't. Who are you? Where did you come from?"

"I ... I'm no one." Esther shook her head, picking apart a blade of grass. "I'm from nowhere. My parents were ... well—" The memories hit, her throat closed, and her voice died away.

"It's okay," Petra's eyes grew hard. "I understand. I cheered when my father fell ill. Even as a little boy I knew he was horrible, and he made my mother worse. Every time he'd—" Petra severed his thoughts before they could escape. He cleared his throat. "When she followed, I was alone. Until Cooky found me sneaking food off carts in the market. Took me home and I met Mother." He stared at the dirt between his feet, his eyes unfocused.

"I always thought the woman at the orphanage was your real mother."

"She is; well, closest I've had anyway. Now she's gone too." Petra forced a tight smile. "Somehow I always end up back alone. Cursed, I guess."

"If your story proves anything, it's that family can be anyone."

Petra stared at her.

Esther shook her head, looking out to the arena crowning the neighboring hill. "No, you're not alone."

"I understand his fascination now."

"What?" Heat warmed her gut, and she pinched her lips together to hide her smile.

"You're very easy to talk to, Tessa of Nowhere." Petra rose, offering her a hand. "Come, Hideo is probably looking for you to give another lesson in playing with knives, and we should meet with the others."

"Sleeping on the job, Ezra?" Abner scowled at the giant as he swung a leg over his horse's back.

The animal buckled a moment under the weight before tossing its head to gain some slack for its nose.

Ezra shrugged. "That was my nephew you had under your arm. Surprised you saved him, but I wasn't about to let you both be buried under a mess of logs for your trouble."

Abner kicked his horse forward to cut Ezra off. "That wasn't your decision to make. You had orders."

Ezra sneered. "I had the ax. I made a decision. If I were the prince, I'd be grateful." Ezra tried to push his horse to sidestep Abner's, but the prince reached out and yanked the reins back toward him.

"You put everyone else in danger! I'm not grateful. Next time, do as you are told!" Abner gathered his own reins through his fist, tightening his grip on the beast. "Otherwise this conversation will go differently."

"If I'd followed your order, Prince, you wouldn't be alive to have this conversation." Ezra glanced over him from hair to heel. "Why did you go back for the boy?"

"I thought I could help him."

"And when you saw you couldn't? Even from high above, I knew that cut would bring him down."

Abner hesitated.

"He's my nephew," Ezra continued, gaze narrowing. "He's nothing to you. So why?"

"He's my man. I take care of them ... when I can." Abner pulled his horse's nose around to where Cantus and his band waited to gallop back to Shiloh. "Next time do as you're told, Ezra, or I'll gut you myself!" he snapped over his shoulder, kicking his horse's side, pushing the beast into a surge of speed. "You, with me!" Abner yelled as his horse charged past Cantus to the front of the group.

Cantus dropped his shoulder before trotting after Abner, leaving the men to jostle into line behind them.

"Explain." Abner slowed to a walk as Cantus' bay drew to his side.

"Explain what?"

"You were supposed to signal to Ezra to send down the logs. You didn't. You put everyone in danger just as much as he did."

"It doesn't matter." Cantus raised a brow at the dark look Abner cast him. "Abner, none of this works without you. Out of all of us, you are the one person that needs to survive."

"What are you talking about?"

"You're heir to the throne. The old line is ended. If we defeat the king, Dennison, and all the rest, but we don't have you to put into power afterward, it would be chaos. We'd be overrun by a neighboring kingdom or collapse without structure." Cantus' brow gained a deep furrow. "I've had a lot of time to think over the shortsightedness of my past plans on how to deal with your father. If you die, Alberon dies with you."

"I'm not sacrificing forty of our men for my own skin!" Abner snapped.

"You may have to, and more besides. You should get used to that as a future king." Cantus shook his head. "What you should have done is sent someone else to get the boy, if you really were so determined. A body can't live without a head, and you are this rebellion's head. These men have no hope without you. So get beyond whatever you're trying to prove to yourself about your own morality and do your job!"

"You speak very candidly to your future king, if that's how you see me, Cantus." Abner's jaw knotted in anger.

"I speak to a friend who I would make King. We don't have time for flattery, so I'm going to tell you truth. Guard your neck, Abner. Yours is the only life we cannot lose."

Abner sighed. "Somehow I miss the doubt-ridden Cantus."

"Doubting is a waste of time now. There's no turning back. This storm of events we've started can't be stopped. We must weather it." Cantus paused, looking back over the men still too far behind to hear. "Hope we live long enough to see the sun rise on a new world."

Abner glared at the long, stone-cobbled road ahead. *A new world.*

Esther dropped her hood, careful not to snag any pins, as she approached the iron-grated trellis. Gathering all her loose-threaded memories of courtly manners, she met the guard's surprised stare with a smile. He moved to the grate.

"Lady?"

He was young with dark hair, and his shadowed eyes raked the area behind her, checking for accompaniment.

Her bald-headed companion stood a little straighter.

"I'm so sorry for the trouble. I was wondering, might I come in to take a peek at the animals? I was at the last Event and it was utterly thrilling. I'd love to see them up close."

His large black brow pulled tight over his eyes. "I'd lose a hand if I was caught letting you, Lady."

"Oh, how disappointing. And there's nothing I could say to convince you? No present I could give?" Esther held up the pouch of gold crowns and copper bits, gathered from the people to fuel her deception, clinking it lightly against the bars for emphasis.

The shadowed eyes flitted hungrily between Esther and the pouch. "For just a moment." He grabbed the pouch through the bars and then left the iron trellis.

Esther glanced at Clive.

The grated metal whined as it was raised and the guard reappeared, brushing his hands. "This way." As he turned, a zip near Esther's ear was the only sign of the passing dart that pierced the guard's unarmored neck.

Clive moved around her, pushing the long tube back into his leather belt beneath his cloak. They were joined by the others.

"Quite the performance," Petra smiled at her, digging to retrieve the coin pouch. "Maybe Death should hire you instead."

Her part was done and the others rushed forward to take their turn. The group formed a wall around her, as if Abner had instructed them to blockade her from any chance of usefulness besides being a momentary distraction. She scowled as their echoing steps marched through the tunnel beneath the hill. They followed the gradual bend of the tunnel, until they emerged into the torch-lit chamber housing cages of prowling animals.

Clive crept in, glancing wide-eyed around the room. "Normally there are more guards here. I was expecting to have to dart them all."

"Thank Abner's group for that, they're busy dealing with him," Petra said, striding to a cage. He whispered a curse. "They're different locks. Death, you rotten liar!"

"Can you open them?" Esther asked, nervously checking over the shadowed corners of the room.

"With a bit more time."

Esther had nothing to do that was helpful, so she wandered among the cages while Clive went from animal to animal, darting them to sleep. Petra worked on the locks. The five others Abner had assigned to move the animals went to fetch the cart and drag it down the tunnel to load up. Hideo stopped, letting Esther go ahead, to stare at the twin black bears as they breathed heavily in sleep.

There's more here than we thought. Two bears, some smaller wild cats, and five stocky doglike animals with heavy shoulders. *Where is—?*

The tiger paced in its narrow cage, almost brushing the bars with each sweep past the metal walling it from freedom. Its mouth hung open, huffs of breath rattling through its chest. Awake, it was more terrifying than she remembered. Its yellow eyes, locked with hers, were lit by an insatiable hunger.

Clive appeared at her elbow. "One side, Lady."

Esther felt an empathetic sting in her own neck as the beast was darted to the ground.

"Almost finished." Clive moved past her. "I'm shocked at how smooth this has gone."

Scanning the cages, Esther frowned. *So am I.* A tiger, two bears, smaller wild cats, five dogs. "Is there another room to this place?"

Clive shook his head as he rose from the last of the dog cages. "None that I've seen."

"Then where do they keep the lion?"

Petra paused on his last lock. "He isn't here?" He cast a look around.

Esther strode to the stone opening and put her ear to the wall. "There's ... something." As if the stone shivered. An echo of an echo. "Someone grab a light and come with me."

"Tessa," Petra's voice adopted Abner's tone, and she struggled with the urge to throw something at him. "That isn't part of the plan."

"We need him. You weren't at the Event, you didn't see how the people reacted to that lion. Hideo, will you come?"

"That's not how we're doing things," Petra said, eyes darkening. "We're not splitting with no idea what the other group is stirring up. Abner wants you safe. If anyone is going to have a look, I will."

"After you," Esther gestured for him to proceed.

Petra shook his head. "Now I understand his frustration." He nodded to Hideo, who followed. "We go silently," Petra whispered, then louder he said, "The rest of you finish loading up the animals. Three sharp whistles means we're in trouble and you are to leave. And Clive, let's have a few of your darts, just in case we do find a lion wandering around."

"What about the last cage?" demanded one of the men, a floppy-necked cat tucked under his arm.

"Already done, Master Tubbs. Tug on the lock, it'll open."

They went obediently back to work as Petra tucked the dart tube into his belt.

Muttering to himself, Petra slipped into the dark tunnel.

Esther followed at his shoulder, Hideo arriving like a shadow beside her. Creeping through the tunnel, Esther strained her ears for any noise. Her eyes drifted almost closed to focus more on the feel of the air, looking for a change. A remembered flash of teeth and claws, of gray rolls of skin, drew her eyes whipping over her shoulder to check her back.

No creature of the cave stalked the dark behind.

She shivered against the thought. Her foot struck a stone and Hideo caught her shoulder before she could fall.

"Let's try to be a bit more careful, eh, Tessa?" Petra said ahead of her.

Esther cleared her throat. "Shouldn't we have grabbed a torch from the room? We could see if there were any openings that way."

"And they could see us coming," Petra whispered back. "First rule of thieving: arrive with surprise."

The night had deepened, the darkness of the passageway with it. *I'm not afraid.* When Petra stopped in front of her, her yip of surprise at his boot suddenly underfoot sent a hand clapping over her mouth. *What is wrong with me?*

"This way," Petra whispered.

She felt it too, a slight ruffle on the hem of her dress. There was a door.

A wave of fresh night air greeted them as Petra pushed the door aside, crisper and colder than that of the tunnel behind. They crept forward for a few heartbeats before they heard voices. Esther's pace quickened, slipping around Petra.

"Forward you lot," said a gruff heavy voice.

One sharp turn of the tunnel brought her within view of the stars through the large grated gate marking the border of the arena. Esther ignored the tunnels branching to either side, rushing up the slight slope to look across the sand.

There it was, the golden muscled back lit by torchlight as the lion made its slow lumbering track along the inner wall of the arena. He had just passed the door across the sand marked by animal bones, and so Esther had time before he was anywhere near her.

We should have brought Clive to dart him through the grate. If we could find how to open this metal door, we could pull him out and load him up. Easy.

Petra appeared at her side.

"Thought you could sneak out of the king's conscription, did yeh?" The sneering voice came from the king's box above her, and Esther pressed her cheek to the cold metal, trying to see better as a family of peasants in stained clothes were pushed against the side of the box by several guards. Their armor flashed as they drew swords against the unarmed father, mother, and two children.

"Please," the father said, bracing himself against the wall, the girl pinned behind him. "Please, we can't. They're ... too young for war."

They weren't quite children, within that middle realm before adulthood that still made them ineffective in a fight. No, the king would use them as expendable pieces to swell his ranks. Human shields as Abner had called them. Esther's blood heated.

"Where'd yeh find them, Tabor?" The gruff voice asked.

"Skirting around the hill by the gate," he sneered, "No doubt to join in with the rabbit's band of rebels. High treason, that's what it is."

"Don't try to talk me out of it," Esther whispered, glancing at Petra. He was already gone.

Hideo was staring out at the arena, studying the sand as if reliving a memory. He shook himself free of the thought, following Esther as she raced after the thief, snatching her full skirt into her arms.

Petra's home-sewn cloak swirled out from his angry stride. A rough wooden ladder gave him a moment of pause. He met Hideo's eyes, a finger to his lips.

Hideo nodded.

"Stay here," Petra mouthed, spreading a hand at Esther as he adjusted the long tube in his belt to give his legs room to move.

Not a bleeding chance.

"What do yeh offer me?" The gruff voice echoed down the tunnel. "What, from your great hoard of nothing, will yeh give me for this favor? Yeh're only lucky your leg is so mangled, old man, yeh wouldn't be worth the cloth of your uniform, else we'd be taking yeh too."

She followed Hideo up the ladder as silently as her limbs shaking with rage would carry her. They climbed the worn rungs until they reached a closed trap door, which Petra eased open to let in some torchlight, both palms flat on the wood. Petra watched Esther extricate herself from the narrow opening with a tight smile and a quick shake of his head. He repeated his signal of finger to the lips before crouching forward and stepping slowly through the wood scaffolding surrounding the arena.

"Then take me instead. I'll go if yeh'll let my children be," said a woman's voice.

"Why not take all three? She could do a great service to the army, eh, Malchus?"

The gruff voice laughed.

Petra paused at the edge of the firelight, the guards just around the corner, checking the pocket of darts in his cloak and adjusting the points away from him so he wouldn't get accidentally stuck. With a breath, he drew out his twin long-handled knives.

Hideo handed Esther two small blades, taking one in each hand for himself from his crossed chest belt. *Curse this dress.* Esther wished she wore a belt like Hideo's to arm herself, but it could have sparked suspicion in the guard.

"We'll take yeh, not to worry little mother. But first we'll have to teach yeh the price of disobedience." The gruff voice, Malchus, paused. "Throw the girl over the side, let the lion have its way. The boy will be taken into the army as planned."

Petra sprang into the torchlight, the others following behind.

"What—who are yeh?"

Petra answered by cleaving open the nearest guard's throat. The other four stumbled back from the sudden spray of red on their tunics as their companion dropped with a gargled cry.

"Toss her," Malchus said, nodding to the soldier nearest to the peasant family.

The girl bit and kicked, but was no match for the heavy-muscled warrior.

Esther threw a blade. It sank into his shoulder, and he let the girl go with a groan of enraged pain. She toppled toward the sand, her terror-soaked shriek sending Esther's limbs into a burst of panic.

"Not my children, yeh bleedin' animal!" screamed the mother, launching herself at the guard.

Hideo sent a blade flying at Malchus which nearly cut Esther's throat as she surged forward through its path. It sliced the air a hair's-breadth in front of her.

The guard who threw the girl, surprised by the sudden assault of motherly fury, was knocked over the box wall. Esther reached the side just as his neck split into a mess on the sands below.

The girl is still alive. But the lion…

Behind, blades clashed as Petra knocked aside a sword with one knife, bringing the other to swipe at the soldier's underarm. His cloak swirled open with the motion.

Ah.

Esther darted, bending around a guard's jutting elbow as he struck at Hideo. A large dripping gash on one eye had the guard practically blinded, but he swung furiously anyway. The guard seemed more likely to behead one of his comrades than ever land a hit on his agile foe. Esther smirked as she pinched between the father huddled over his son and the complex, shifting blades. She grabbed Petra's cloak and dug a hand into a pocket, gathering the three darts into her fist.

"What are you doing?" Petra demanded. He hissed as the blade slipped past his guard and cut a red line across his knuckles.

Esther's hands clapped onto the wood railing, about to hurl herself off. Malchus, whom Hideo's blade had somehow missed, had the mother by her hair. The slap across her face echoed over the wooden boards. Her hands clawed at his fist. Esther had to make a choice, her thoughts on the lion below as another strike smacked across the woman's cheek.

Esther jumped off the rail.

Like the first time, the fall was over before fear could get a good grip on her throat. Esther rolled, absorbing the ground's blow to her legs in a spray of sand. It drew the yellow eyes of the lion away from the dead man, its mouth hanging open like a teeth-barred cage. She set her feet so she blocked the girl, whose cheeks were crusted in wet sand, and then realized her mistake.

I forgot Clive's tube! That's in Petra's belt and it's unreachable now. What good are darts if I have nothing to strike with?

"What's your name?" Esther called back to the girl.

The lion began to stalk forward, chest almost touching the sand.

"M–mara." Her voice shook with sobs.

"Stay behind me, Mara. You understand? No matter what happens." Esther pulled back her arm and launched a dart, her muscles snapping.

It flew through the air, hitting the lion square between the eyes before glancing off.

The lion's forehead gained a thousand wrinkles as it snarled.

Esther's breath shook. "Just stay behind me."

The lion launched forward.

She had one dart gripped in each hand and no real plan on how to use them.

With a great burst of strength, the lion stretched up on its hind legs, claws reaching for Esther. His spear-lined jaw opened to greet her neck.

Esther let one dart fall, using every bit of force she could muster on the one she had left to push it into the padded underside of the heavy paw. It broke the skin as they fell back onto the sand, Esther twisting to avoid the lion's weight landing on her. A pinch on her leg sent her eyes jumping open. Over her senses, a fog bank drifted as the lion slipped to one side, heavy in sleep.

Esther's breath shuddered through her tired lungs as oblivion took her gliding over a gentle sea.

XXXIV

Esther grimaced, shivering as water droplets dripped down her neck. "Tessa?"

"No?" Esther groaned, a smile tugging at her lips.

"Can you open your eyes?"

She did. Abner leaned over her, studying her face. She forced her chest to let in air.

"How do you feel? Can you walk?"

Esther's legs were sore but when she tried to move, her foot obeyed. "I think so." She swallowed, shutting her eyes. "What happened?"

"I was hoping you could tell me. More specifically, I'd like to know when you became a bleeding idiot." Abner's eyes hardened, his mouth set in a scowl.

Esther turned away, choosing to stare instead at the barren wood floor, the single window cut into the wall, and the clay cup near her head.

"No, no, Tessa. Now is your time to answer for your actions." He paused and Esther's jaw locked. "What about *be careful* was confusing to you? Hm?"

"I was careful."

"Really? So when you tried to split the group to go off—practically alone—after the lion, that was careful? Or when you jumped into the arena with said lion to rescue some girl and ended up getting stuck by your own dart? The men all think you were being brave. But that's not what it was about, was it, Tessa?" He moved around the cot, kneeling so he could stare into her eyes. "You were afraid. Afraid of being useless. So you got desperate. Stupid."

"Was I supposed to let her die?"

"There had to be a better way." He swallowed through a tight jaw. "I asked you to do one thing—"

"And I did it."

"I trusted you. I gave you what you asked for." Abner twisted the cloth in his hand, wringing out the water on the floor, his eyes glaring into a far corner of the room. "You didn't listen. You don't listen. I am trying to save you, I—why is it so hard for all of you to just listen?" He threw the rag to the floor, the sound echoing like a slap. "What am I supposed to do now? Hm? Should I—should I just lock you up? Is that the way to keep you safe?"

Anger twisted Esther's mouth into a sneer. "Go ahead and try it."

Abner's face hardened until it broke. He rubbed at his forehead as if he could mold himself back together. "This," he groaned through his hands. "This is why. I hate this." His knuckles knocked against the wooden floor, chest rising with a heavy sigh. "I don't want to rule over you, Tessa. Any soldier who doesn't follow orders is a danger, but you're not just any soldier. My reasons for protecting you are ... complicated."

"They're only complicated because you're making them that way."

"Meaning?"

"Stop trying to decide for me what I am allowed to do, and let me do what I can to help."

Abner's eyes dropped, growing misty as he studied the floor. He breathed deep through a heavy nose. "One thing. Can you promise me to do one thing? I'll choose to trust you again but I need your word."

"What is it?"

"In three days, Dennison and the king," he swallowed, "my father, will be here. You are to stay by Cantus, no matter what happens. You understand? Most importantly, you do not come anywhere near me."

The words punched through Esther's gut. "You don't want me near you?"

Abner's mouth twitched. "Dennison had ample time to observe my attachment to you. You are our side's greatest weakness. The king doesn't have to get to me. He just has to get to you." Abner's eyes ran over her face, as if committing it to memory. "I'm not sure what I wouldn't give for you."

Her breath stuck and she nodded.

Abner tipped gently forward, kissing her cheek. "Get some rest, Lady Tessa. You'll need to be ready for battle in three days' time."

❖ ❖ ❖

Abner straightened, Cantus at his side. Together they faced the crowd gathered outside the small wooden house Tessa was recovering in.

The men rested with weapons in hand, becoming used to the weight and feel of bearing arms. Abner tried to see them as he had during his studies, pieces to be moved and used for his own ends, but they were men. Their faces were lined and hardened by years of hard labor and a harsh hand, but softened at the embrace of their women and children. They were real men. Even if everything went to plan, many of them would lie dead in three days. How could Abner bear to move forward, knowing a father would be ripped from his son with every advance the enemy made?

"You will be split into scores of twenty." Abner swallowed, pushing his voice to echo louder down the dusty road. "I'll choose a man to captain each and meet with them to go over what your job will be."

"What was in that wagon that arrived today?" yelled a voice from somewhere in the middle.

Abner held up a hand. "I won't be telling anyone more than they need to know. It's a waste of precious time. We have tasks to complete. To prepare." Some faces soured at this, but no one spoke up again. Cantus and Petra split the men and Abner chose his ten captains.

"Go eat with your families. Afterward, meet me in the old tavern and we will begin."

The men jostled away, laughter echoing as they walked.

"Cantus?" Abner called him back with a nod.

"How did she take the news?"

"Tessa is going to be with you," Abner said, glancing back to the house where she rested.

"What? I thought—"

"She's been given instructions not to come near me."

"And you think she'll obey? She hasn't yet."

Abner scoffed. "Of all people, Cantus, you should not speak of obeying orders."

"That was different. I was doing it to save you, and the war."

"I'm sure she thinks she is doing her best for the cause as well. Regardless, she's coming. Keep her safe."

Cantus shook his head. "You're being a fool. But I'll do my best for her, just like any soldier."

"No, you are to defend her life as you would mine." He paused. "What good is a king without a queen?"

"You wouldn't."

"I will."

Cantus shook his head. "A bleeding fool."

"Your word, Cantus."

"Fine. I give it."

Abner smiled. "Wishing you found a different heir to the throne yet?"

"Don't tempt me. I still have three days."

Abner had just enough time before he met with the captains to dig outside the wall.

The boy had breathed his last the night before and Ezra had his time to mourn. Abner had never really taken seriously the danger of fire to a corpse. A person's spark being consumed and snuffing out with the flames when the embers died seemed too mystical for his liking. But, in case Ezra believed, the boy could not stay in Shiloh. Abner found a wide-bladed shovel and left through the gate, picking a shady spot of yellow grass at the forest edge. He struck the ground, loosening the tension of his mind through the grip of his muscles. He treasured the bite of wood against his palms, the good honest feeling of his body at work to achieve an honorable goal.

This. This is what I'll miss.

Cantus joined him. The two dug together in silence until a large hole was made out of the ground to hold the remains of the boy who had died. Cantus pushed his shovel into the dirt, wiping the sweat from his brow.

"Deep enough?"

Abner nodded, rubbing his sore palms.

"I'll tell the people, no lights tonight. Ezra can carry the boy out and lay him down in his time. We should go. The men will be waiting."

"Do you think any of them find it, Cantus? Their way to the stars?" Abner stared up at the stretching blue sky that had pushed them out of view.

"I do."

"Maybe we'll find out for ourselves soon enough."

Cantus joined Abner's study of the sky. "Maybe."

When the door opened as the sun dipped down in the sky, Esther turned from the window expecting to see Abner.

"Cantus." She paused, uncertain.

His eyes darkened in the shadow of his furrowed brow. "Abner says you are to be in the fight after all."

Esther swallowed. "He took some convincing, but yes."

"I thought you had grown some sense through all of this, but since your arrival at Shiloh ... things need to change." Cantus moved into the room, and set his feet, glaring at her. "Abner may choose to give you endless chances, but there's more at stake here than just you. How do I know I can trust you?"

"Don't expect me to fall in line and obey orders like a good little soldier. That's not me. Trust me to do what I can and you won't be disappointed."

Cantus took a breath. He unfastened the cloak from his shoulders. "Here."

"What is this for?" She took the warm cloak in her hands.

Cantus' mouth twitched into a smile. "I thought you'd appreciate wearing something you're used to."

Esther allowed herself a breathy chuckle, the tension fading from her shoulders as they were wrapped in the heavy black fabric.

"Maybe it's time for The Demon of Shiloh to have one last run." Cantus said as Esther pulled the hood up over her head. It slipped past her eyes and she sighed, comforted in obscurity.

"Why?" She pushed the hood off her head. "Why give me this?"

"Dennison won't recognize you. He may have soldiers looking. And we should use every advantage we can." Cantus paused. "I'd like to start seeing you as an advantage instead of a weakness."

"I'm grateful."

"Be ready tomorrow in the square by second mark. Oh, and no candle tonight. To aid the dead."

Esther nodded and he was gone. She turned back to the window.

Every candle, every lantern, every light stayed cold that night. Shiloh lay silent and dark beneath the full, vibrant weight of the stars. Esther leaned against the window, staring up at them. Sparks of light and clouds of rich deep color spread so vast that her eyes couldn't take it all in. Others stood in windows across from her, mouths slipping open as they stared silently up.

Below, the giant carried his kin through the town to lay him in the ground outside the city. The boy's spark would rise and find its way to the stars without any competing lights to confuse it. Or, at least, that was the story. Esther had to admit, staring at the vastness above, that there were things beyond her senses that she didn't understand. Maybe the boy would find a home among the stars. Maybe. She would keep the room dark to give him his best chance.

"May you make your way to peace."

XXXV

Abner glanced at Petra as he drew out his twin blades. "Not Penny?"

"I'm sure she'll have a chance to come out to play." Petra's smile faded as he ground his boot into the dirt. "You nervous?"

Abner kept his eyes pointed ahead to the gate, the wood trembling with the force of hundreds of marching, metal-clad feet. "I am."

Petra nodded, pulling in a loud breath. "So," he forced a smile, "what's the first thing you're going to do when we win you that castle?"

Abner smirked, shaking his head.

"Come, there has to be something you miss."

The marching stopped. The silence rang.

"Open!" bellowed a voice. "Open in the name of the king!"

Abner tried not to notice the fear gathering in Petra's eyes as he worked to keep his smile. The prince allowed himself one last full breath. He held the air in his chest a moment longer than needed to take stock of how it felt to breathe. He nodded to Petra. The gates of Shiloh opened.

The first lines of soldiers peered at them, confused. Petra smirked, shrugging at Abner's side in the empty, dust-blown street.

Ahead, the valley of Shiloh was filled with soldiers, outnumbering Abner's men three to one. There were no siege weapons. The king's confidence showed in that. Abner defended a wooden fort after all. His father likely saw it as a child standing before a sand castle. Most of the soldiers wore metal armor with a few lines of archers in leather. A ring of cloth-clad soldiers made Abner pause. Why have an obvious vulnerability at the center of the army? *These must be the conscripts Petra told me of. No armor, no training, vulnerable to slaughter. There was a time when I might have done the same, used anyone and everything I could to my advantage.* The king's standard flew, drawing Abner's eyes like a light on the vast ocean of metal.

"There's more of them than I thought there would be," Petra muttered at his side.

"Where's your army, Abner?" called the king from his horse. He pushed the beast forward until a single line of soldiers stood between them. "Come out of that pit of muck you've burrowed in and let's have a talk. As a proper father and son."

Together Petra and Abner moved forward.

Petra muttered, "I'll get them back. For Darby."

Each heartbeat became a painful reminder of what he risked losing as it drummed against his ribs. He didn't fear his father, not anymore. Abner feared what he'd be forced to do to him. What he would become when it was all over. The captain at the king's side was what sent his heart thudding with fear for himself.

The king dismounted—Dennison with him—and strode to plant himself just out of sword reach. Two soldiers took up positions on their flanks. No one drew weapons.

Abner's hand twitched, watching Dennison. *I've never beaten him. Why would this time be any different? I should have spent more effort training myself for this. Looking for dragons. What have I to show for it?*

"I assume, boy," began the king, picking a spare piece of food from his teeth. "You want terms?"

"What terms would you offer me, Father?"

"Your life. For all that's worth."

"In exchange for?"

"I don't have time for this nonsense. You will come back to Lydia with me, and do as you are told to strengthen our line. We will deal with your ... ambitions after things with that snake from across the sea are dealt with."

"And the people?"

The king grinned. "I'll let you choose which half we execute."

Abner's nails bit into his palm, but he kept his features smooth. "Shall we discuss it inside? The sun's growing hot, and we can sit together to have a civilized conversation."

"Didn't I tell you, Dennison?" The king laughed. "It's too easy. I knew you'd give in. One look at a *real* army and you would surrender to me." He spoke in a rush, the words spilling from his mouth like water off the mountain. His gleaming eyes betrayed the brokenness of his fear-ridden mind. "Of course you did. You've always been weak. Pathetic. But as my only heir, thanks to that witch of a mother of yours who couldn't even—"

There was no warning. Dennison threw an arm around the king, carving into his gut like a pig being slaughtered.

Abner's father cried out, unable to twist away. Dennison's arm was like an iron chain pinning him in place so the king could only writhe in panic.

Abner was frozen, staring into the wild eyes, driven mad by pain.

Wheeling the king around to face the army, Dennison withdrew his knife and carved across the king's throat. He let him drop to choke on the grass alone.

"Sorry, old friend," Dennison muttered. "Your end had come." He raised a fist to the air.

No one challenged him beyond the whisper that rolled through the ranks. Both the guards flanking the captain gave a nod of support.

Dennison turned to Abner. The knife dripped beads of scarlet on the long yellow grass.

"You—" Abner swallowed, eyes on his father's twitching form. "You've killed him." Behind, the army became a blur of confusion to Abner's eyes. *He's dead.*

"Abner..." Dennison paused. "I've realized, despite your potential, you're not ready to assume power. This man's leading was intolerable, his end long overdue. I took that burden. No boy should have to kill his own father until he can bear the weight of it. Now, for our future." He came forward a step. "I will take the throne as steward until you are ready." Another step forward.

Abner swallowed, a sick feeling turning his gut.

"It will be as it was always meant to. I've raised you as my own, and, at last, you will be. We were never meant to be on opposing sides."

Dennison's hand on Abner's shoulder sat as a heavy weight, sinking him back to the ground. To reality. *My father is dead.* "An intriguing idea." He pulled his stare from the still-twitching limbs to Dennison with difficulty. "Why don't we go inside to work out the details?"

Dennison's eyes narrowed, glancing behind Abner at the empty, dust-blown street. He chuckled. "Come, Abner. I taught you every tactic in your head. Think I'd fall for that trick?"

"Trick?"

Dennison scoffed. "You should teach your men to hide better. I count at least three bows peeking out from the hay on those rooftops. Archers!" A torchbearer passed in front of the rows of bow-wielding soldiers, setting their arrow tips to flame. Their leather armor stretched as they drew back their shot. "Traitors can't be merely beaten. They must be stopped. Let fly!"

"No!" Abner yelled, as the arrows arced into the sky only to fall amid the wooden homes of Shiloh.

The flames bit into the wood, eating through the hay-topped buildings with unnatural speed. A wave of heat rolled to them.

Abner stumbled back, pushing out a breath as his face tensed in pain.

"Consistency, Abner. That's what you've been missing. You can always know I will do what is best for you. No matter how cruel it may make me appear."

A yell went up from somewhere in the ranks of soldiers behind.

"No!" Petra dropped to his knees, coughing heavily. "By the stars, *why?*"

Abner's face pinched, looking sideways at Petra, voice hushed beneath the crackle of feasting flames, "A bit much, don't you think?"

Petra's shoulders shook. He pulled in a deep breath. "Tessa thinks I might have a future as a performer."

Abner smirked. "She's been wrong before."

"Now, that's settled," Dennison drank in the smoke as if it were the aroma of an aged, favorite wine.

The yell echoed louder.

Abner turned, still wearing his smirk. "That's match."

A golden blur streaked behind Dennison, ripping through his left guardsman's unplated neck.

Dennison turned.

The chaos caused by twelve wild animals forming several surprise flanks, darting into and through a formation, broke any semblance of order the soldiers had. They became a confused mass of flashing metal as all eyes turned to their feet.

Before the men could recover, eight scores of Abner's fighters burst from the trees like water flooding the valley. There was no line to break as the commanders screamed to be heard.

It's working.

"How?" Dennison watched the lion bound forward, cutting through another soldier's neck with its heavy paw.

"I found what I was looking for."

Dennison turned, eyes dark.

"You and I," Abner said, drawing his blade. "For the kingdom."

"You can't beat me, boy."

Abner's breath shook as he set his feet. "But still I must try."

Esther leaned against a tree, her boot stirring the scent of pine needles coating the ground to perfume the air.

She had been waiting two days to move. Her nerves the first day were knotted around her gut, but they gradually loosened as time wore on and nothing happened. Now, at the muffled sound of the soldier's heavy metal feet stomping through *her* valley, her anger was stirred.

The wildflowers that sprang to life on the border of the road brought splashes of color to the neglected grasses.

The soldiers seemed to go out of their way to crush the bright buds as they left the road to flood into the bowl of Shiloh. *Can this ground soak up any more blood?* She would find out soon enough.

A citizen soldier, one of Cantus' score, gestured to her while keeping far back from the tree line.

Esther sighed and crept away, returning to the others hidden just out of sight of the flashing metal march.

A black cloak like her own but half her height nearly trampled her toes as it darted around the trees in some kind of game. Esther scowled. She stomped to Cantus, pulling down her mask. "I thought Abner wanted Klessen to stay with Ava."

Cantus nodded to the man who whispered news to him.

The man departed, casting a nervous glance at the tree line.

"What?" Cantus whispered to her.

"Klessen is supposed to be with the women and children. He isn't supposed to fight."

"He came to us," Cantus shrugged. "Said he was sent."

"Sent by who? Abner?"

Cantus shook his head. "I don't think so, but does it matter?" He lowered his voice below the hushed tone everyone used as they waited to move. "We need every advantage we can. You've seen what we're up against."

"Yes, I've seen them." Esther ground her teeth.

"Remember," Cantus brought her eyes back from the tree line, "No killing unless it's necessary. Every soldier we don't kill is one we can use to defend ourselves later. Abner's orders."

Esther scowled, resecuring her mask. "He's making this more difficult than it needs to be."

"Think of Ava's brother. Many of these soldiers could be conscripted, here under threat to their families, or just trying to survive. It wouldn't be in the interest of victory or justice to end those lives."

"I'll see how kind you are when they are 'just trying to survive' by swinging a sword at your throat."

"I'm not saying don't kill, just be sparing. Careful."

"But the red cloaks are still fine to gut?"

"Yes, any commanders you see need to be put down by any means necessary."

"Well, at least I'll get something out of this," Esther muttered.

"And Tessa?" Cantus studied her through the shadow cast by the black hood. "You gave your word. Stay by my side, no matter what happens."

The marching stopped.

She nodded.

Cantus called the men into line with a gesture. They had been watching for it and quickly formed their score around him and Esther as point. He led the way to the tree line.

Esther winced at the rustle caused by their shuffling feet across the forest floor.

They paused beneath the heavy-needled branches, weapons in hand. Now was the moment. At least the wait would be over.

Finally.

Cantus grabbed her shoulder, stopping her as her muscles twitched forward. He shook his head, nodding toward Shiloh.

She had forgotten the animals. They stalked through the high grass toward the soldiers, and Esther cursed the stars that Cantus was her watchdog. She stretched her thoughts, trying somehow to catch what the great striped cat was thinking in its water-enriched mind.

Darting across the road on silent paws, the animals were lost in the sea of grass.

"The king," soldiers spoke to one another and Esther strained forward to listen. "The king is dead."

Cantus met Esther's stare.

"How?"

"The captain's in command now."

"What do we do?"

"Has he given the order? I can't see."

Flames flashed to life, transforming Shiloh into a pillar of heavy black smoke with a foundation of raging fire.

It hurt more than she thought it would, watching everything from the beloved dead consumed.

The animals pounced, the flames their signal to attack. They did not care who went down beneath their claws. Their one goal was to cause chaos, and they achieved it with a reckless, wild ferocity that Esther envied.

She grinned.

Men were pulled to the ground, their cries cutting suddenly, and those around them jumped away in terror. They couldn't strike properly at the animals without hitting each other and by the time they caught sight of a flash of fur in the grass, it was too late. Some soldiers on the outer edge fled the battle, everyone else too overwhelmed by chaos to notice.

She was only able to watch for a few moments before Cantus gave the signal and behind her men were pushing forward, calling with loud voices for bravery and strength. Her feet pounded the ground beneath her, launching her toward the enemy.

For Shiloh. For Abner.

Petra threw himself forward, engaging with the few brave enough to charge past the lion to the captain's side.

Between the beast driving the men wild with fear, and Petra's skill at keeping multiple opponents busy, Abner was able to focus solely on Dennison. The goal was simple. *Keep his attention.* If the captain gained the chance to rally, Abner would be hard-pressed to end this. He didn't have to last forever, just long enough for others to arrive. Even Dennison could not take down a score of men without injury. Abner hoped Ezra and the others would not take too long to break through the line.

Dennison drew his sword. "A final lesson for you, boy?" He swiped the air a few times, warming up his muscles. "Don't start a fight you can't end." He lunged.

Abner pulled out of the way by a breath.

Dennison's forehead wrinkled. "Coward."

Abner continued to dodge, only using his blade in defense, delaying as long as he could. *Once I engage with his attack, it will all be over. I cannot win.* His foot nearly slipped on a stone. Abner caught himself, pulling away from the heat still burning behind him.

Out of the corner of his vision, Petra let his knives lock with the swords of his three attackers. He thrust them away with a great heave of force to regain some ground further from the flames.

"Enough of this, Abner. Set your feet like a man. Don't dart about like a ... like a rabbit."

At one time, that would have been enough. Abner's fury would have ignited, his jaw would have clenched, and he would have wildly struck out at anything near him. Now, Abner brushed the insult aside like a bug buzzing at his ear, his mind only clinging tighter to his task. *Keep his attention.*

But Abner was running out of room. The fire burned behind, the heat making his shoulders tense as his body warned him away.

The prince's sword clashed against the captain's.

"Finally."

He followed Dennison's combinations, blocking his strikes with feverish energy. *Any moment now.*

But the moment did not come.

Abner was left whole.

"Are you toying with me, Dennison?" Abner grunted as their blades locked.

"I'm giving you time. Reconsider. Your friends here will die, my soldiers will see to that."

Abner thrust him away.

"And that girl, if she somehow survives, will be dealt with. You will be free to go back to life as it was meant to be. No more of her poison corrupting you."

He wasn't even winded, while Abner huffed like a horse working a field in high summer. The promise of Tessa dead by the captain's hand was enough to shift Abner's focus. Dennison—the one who had raised, taught, and believed in him—faded in the scar-lined face. He was a monster and he must be slain. Abner's blade sang through the air. He twisted, driving through a complex improvised chain, forcing Dennison to face the billowing black smoke as the wind shifted.

The captain struggled to keep his eyes from closing against the ash.

Abner used the irritant's distraction to swing at Dennison's head, only to nick him above the eye.

Dennison's blade answered with a swipe to Abner's side.

Abner didn't feel it touch, but he pulled out of reach to regain his breath. His eyes flickered over the captain's shoulders. "I think you have more confidence in your army than you should."

The chaos continued.

Dennison smiled, ignoring the blood beginning to drip down his brow. "I'll get to that."

Abner needed to draw his attention back. He put all the force he could muster into his next strike.

Red.

Esther's eyes followed the bright cloak as it swirled out from the commander's broad shoulders.

He grabbed an armored soldier who was trying to crawl away from a bloody-muzzled dog, shoving him back toward the beast. "Defend me!" the commander screamed. "On your feet! Cowards! Men of Alb—"

A silver blade stuck out from his temple as he fell.

"Hideo would be proud," Cantus said, glancing at her shot. He defended her side before the pit of flashing, mangled armor. Even if Esther had the desire to slip away, the tumult of bodies, animals, and swords made it impossible. Still, Cantus kept a close eye on her in case things changed.

For now, Abner could take care of himself while she hunted. Esther pulled another blade from the belt slung across her chest, a last gift from Hideo before his score left to assume their positions.

Next target.

Whenever a soldier was foolish enough to lunge at the mysterious black figure, Cantus was quick to push them back. Mostly he used the flat of his sword to club them to sleep, but a few he had to kick away for others to deal with. Cantus kept edging them along the front line of the battle, seeking more red cloaks and always keeping his distance from Shiloh.

He doesn't trust me. Esther's fingers crawled over several empty pockets in the belt before she found another blade.

"How many do you have left?" Cantus shouted, breaking a soldier's nose with his palm.

The man fell back with a cry and a citizen soldier sliced open his throat with an ax.

"Watch it!" Cantus snapped as the air between them was washed in red. "Only take life when needed."

The man's eyes burned with furious hunger.

Cantus struck him across the jaw, breaking the trance. "He is no different than you. Remember who you are. That is strength." He pulled the ax from the dead man's neck, handing it back to the fighter. "Be braver. Go."

He ran from Cantus, rejoining the fight.

"Bold words, friend."

Cantus spun, raising his sword. It almost slipped from his hand. "Nathaniel?"

"I don't want to kill you, boy," Dennison warned, pushing Abner back as he wiped the line of blood from his brow. "Don't make me do something I'll regret."

Abner swung his sword again, hoping his instincts trained since childhood by the man who now tested them would somehow be enough.

Dennison's blade became a blur of silver motion.

Abner's head cracked against the ground, his ankles stinging, and he tried to blink away the white flooding his vision.

"Stay down. Let me fix this mess you've made."

Where are they? He couldn't draw a proper breath, his chest sending tremors through his limbs. *It's not enough. I can't beat him.*

Dennison's shadow blocked the sun as he moved to face the army.

I've tried. It's impossible.

The captain's chest swelled with a massive breath as he bashed his metal-cased arm against his armor, a driving beat Abner had learned to feel in his bones.

Years of training echoed with that call to unity, and Abner's muscles tensed.

The soldiers were rallying, answering through the clamor with an echo of the rhythm Dennison struck.

It's too late. I've already failed. I can't.

Abner sighed, hope leaking from several wounds. He swallowed, setting his jaw. The prince dug his sword into the dirt and pulled himself to his knees.

Dennison turned. "Stay down, boy. I've hurt you enough you should know your lesson by now. Don't make me—"

Abner rose with the sword's help, his legs swaying beneath him. The point of the blade wavered through the air as he set his feet.

Dennison's jaw was tight as he matched the prince's posture.

Abner managed to block one strike before he was smashed into the ground again. His sword clattered out of reach.

Again.

He dragged himself, swaying, to his feet as he lifted empty fists.

The ground punched his sight to black. He blinked at the sky as he came back to himself, struggling to make sense of the colors. His throat grated.

Again.

He rose.

He couldn't see Dennison's blow coming, he only felt it collide with the side of his head. A heavy solid *thunk* that dropped him like a sack.

The captain pinned him down with his knee, accenting his words with blows to Abner's jaw. "Why—can't—you—just—listen?" He gripped Abner's tunic, pulling the prince's blood-speckled face toward his own. "I am trying to help you."

Abner groaned, every bone aching and longing for quiet. "And I'm ... trying to save ... them."

"Them?" Dennison scoffed, dropping him to the ground. "When did you get so foolish? I've taught you better. *They* are not worth *you*. As if any of them wouldn't murder you themselves if they had the chance." Dennison turned away.

Still I must try.

Abner spit to one side, spraying the ground in blood.

Dennison resumed the beat against his chest.

Abner needed to move. To somehow rise up. Again. To stop this.

The beat came from behind, but Cantus and Nathaniel ignored it.

Nathaniel wore a bitter smile. "What, Cantus? Why are you surprised? The king drew out peasant boys and gave them swords. Of course I'd be brought to put you down."

"I want you to know ... I've looked after Ava. She's safe."

Esther studied his face. His dark hair held a waviness reminiscent of his sister's curls. The resemblance might have been stronger if he didn't have a large scar dragging from the corner of his eye to his jawline.

"Safe? With you?" Nathaniel's brow rose, his jaw locking behind his pasted-on smile. "That's a comfort. Well, put your sword up. I don't want to kill a man without a weapon."

"I don't want to kill you, Nathaniel."

"But alas, we must."

The soldiers began to answer the beat, pounding the rhythm on their metal-cased chests. Nathaniel backed to join a group gathering as the line reformed.

"Cantus?" Esther could only watch as the expressions hardened on the men's faces, the clashing fists on their chests seeming to strike the fear from their eyes.

The animals ducked low at the sudden change of noise, and Esther couldn't blame them. A part of her wanted to run and hide from it as well.

"What happened to you?" Cantus hadn't raised his sword. He wasn't pulling the people back or leading them forward. He seemed stuck.

"You mean this?" Nathaniel's fingers brushed the scar. "That was my reward for letting you escape. Maybe when this is all over we'll match again."

"Cantus!" Esther grabbed his shoulder. "We need to do something."

Cantus blinked forcefully. "There's nothing we can do. The battle's turned. Fall back to the trees with the others. It's your job to keep them hidden now."

"What are you saying?"

The animals fled past them, darting through the grass.

"We've failed!" Cantus pushed her away. "Abner's as good as dead, if he isn't already. I need to get to him."

He was right. In other areas where the soldiers pushed forward, men were being cut down. Their lack of training and inferior equipment cost several lives with every repetition of the rallying cry.

"Keep holding the line, Cantus," said a voice at his elbow.

Cantus jumped away from the boy peeking out beneath a black hood. "Where have you been?"

"You need to hold the line. It's almost time. Be ready."

The metal beat railed on, so powerful it rattled Esther's bones.

"Time? Time for what?" Esther reached for Klessen as he darted around the enemy line.

He paused, sucking in a deep breath of smoke. "Time to be whole again."

Do what you can.

Abner ached with exhaustion, his muscles long since spent. Around him, the smoke from the fire billowed toward the men, as if their fight was remaking the world into ash. His vision swam, hazy at the corners. Slowly, painfully, Abner dragged himself to his feet. A flash of motion drew Abner's eye. He resettled his stare on the captain's back. His legs shook with weakness beneath him as he raised empty fists.

Keep his attention. One more time.

"Dennison!" Abner's voice barked through the smoke, grated raw by pain.

The captain turned, wincing as the stained air struck his eyes.

That moment of distraction was all Petra needed. The thief launched himself, spitting into a strip of cloth as he landed on Dennison's back. Penny fell from his hand. The captain tried to twist away, but Petra gripped him with his legs, throwing the cloth over his face like a bridle on a wild horse.

Dennison screamed, dropping to his knees. Abner had never heard the captain utter a noise like that. Unchecked anguish echoed, as a hiss from beneath the rag told of the burn it delivered.

Petra twisted the cloth so it bit tighter into the captain's skin.

A flash of metal in Dennison's hand—

"Petra!"

Too late.

Dennison's knife sank into the boy's side.

Abner stumbled forward, but there was nothing he could do.

Petra's face tightened, strengthening the vice grip of his hands until they shook.

Dennison stabbed him again, burying the knife to the hilt.

Still the boy held on, his breath kept captive by the tension of his hands.

Dennison was just a man after all, his cry weakening as he fell to the ground, unconscious.

Petra let the rag drop and tried to stand. His legs gave out beneath him and he collapsed, the knife still buried in his flesh.

Dennison is down. Petra actually did it.

Abner retrieved his sword, using it like a cane to support his weight. His eyes grazed over the two armies, still fighting. Several scores of peasants-turned-soldiers lay mangled with scattered armored bodies dotting the field. That must be where the help he had been waiting for was lost.

The soldiers still fought for Dennison, unaware of the battle Petra had just won.

How do I stop this?

Klessen's hood flew off his wild red hair as he jumped over Dennison.

"Wait! Stop!"

The small boy pelted past Abner toward the flaming remains of Shiloh. The inferno accepted him with a roar of heat that sent Abner stumbling backward. He was lost to the flames and Abner's gut took another blow.

Why did he—"Klessen!"

A new noise began beneath the roar of the fire and the clang of metal from behind. A deep hum, like a call the ground quaked to answer.

Abner dug his sword into the dirt to help his balance as his bones trembled with it. When the light came from the east, streaking through the sky like a star brought to break the world, Abner didn't have time to run. It crashed into Shiloh, throwing a blast of charred wood out from the impact site. Abner was thrown to the ground with it. His ears rang, his vision blurred, and he struggled to think past the pain throbbing through his head. Half-burnt boards, put out by the collision, sent curling spires of smoke to the sky.

The light faded. Klessen was nowhere to be seen in the smoldering ruin.

A monster rose in his place.

It was green, a dark murky green, with rows of scales and a great arching neck. Talons, curved to cruelty, dug into the ground to launch its massive weight.

Abner would have scrambled away if he could move.

The dragon flared its wings, stretching wider than the full breadth of Shiloh, before striking at the ground to launch on a burst of air to the sky.

Abner pushed himself to rise as the dragon flew around the valley. Even from its great height, he measured its vastness and felt his own minuscule power as laughable. Pathetic. A boy playing with a wooden stick. He glanced at the metal still clutched in his hand, the sword he had kept since the beginning, and noticed for the first time the setting where the supposedly enchanted ruby had sat now lay empty. It didn't matter. One glimpse of the real thing told him that any thought of controlling the beast was insane. Idiotic.

They were all at its mercy now.

Abner.

Esther had to believe he was alive, that somehow the light which pummeled Shiloh to pieces had left him whole. It took Cantus' hand on her arm, holding her back, to stop her from running to him.

No one advanced now, the rallying beat abandoned, as the dragon filled the air with a roar and a spout of red flame.

"Is that?"

Esther tipped her chin in a slow nod. "Klessen." *It must be.*

"We found a dragon after all."

"I guess we did."

The beast turned, stretching its snout and folding its wings to dive toward the ground.

Nathaniel and the other soldiers threw themselves backward. Cantus grabbed Esther's hood, pushing her down at his side as the wings burst open and a wall of air shoved Esther's face into the dirt. She spit grass, unable to see beyond her hood. Great waves of pressure beat against her back until the massive creature dug four taloned feet into the ground. A growl echoed from deep in its armored chest and Esther pushed her face up to stare at the black slit eyes and rows of sharp, yellow-lined teeth. Mesmerizing. Deadly.

Cantus pushed to his knees, straightening slowly with hands extended toward the beast.

The dragon growled, blinking a double eyelid, as its snout rose with Cantus. It turned its smoking nostrils to the terrified men, its breath rumbling.

Speak.

Cantus twitched away as the breath hit his shoulder. He turned his back to the dragon, raising both fists above his head. The men before him couldn't see the tremor in his rigid posture, but the hem of his tunic shivered against his knees.

"Enough!" His voice grated, rough with pain and fear, but echoing unnaturally loud in the silence of the dragon's wake. "There is no enemy here to fight. Not anymore. You are one people. One! You, men of Alberon, have not lost today. We have all gained. We are one people, whole again. I," he shook his head, furrowed brow deepening, "I am not a man of speeches, I'm a soldier like all of you. Every man on this field today has earned his place among the stars. But no more. No more spilling our blood. Brothers, let us see what world we make when duty to country and virtue to self are one and the same. Bravery. Strength. Honor!" He beat his chest.

The silence rang.

After a pause, weapons clattered to the ground. Some, but not all. Many men seemed consumed by the dragon baring its teeth, frozen into place where they stood.

The beast woke them with a roar that shattered the air, its long snakelike neck jutting forward as if it would snap them up.

The men fell to the grass, covering their heads with trembling fingers.

Some took up Cantus' words as their own, joining in a chant of "Bravery! Strength! Honor!"

We've done it. Justice. Peace. At last. Esther's throat tightened, her eyes misting.

"Bunch of cowards!" yelled a soldier, ripping his red cloak back from his neck.

I missed one.

He began to run at Cantus, raising his sword with a mighty yell.

Cantus thrust him back.

He charged forward again and Cantus used the point of his sword to put him down.

A soldier darted in from the other side, apparently not noticing Esther. She rose, surprising him like a demon in the night, and dropped him with a single blade. She met Cantus' eyes with a nod.

The next soldier was bolder, quicker. He drove his metal-clad heel into Esther's leg, sending her stumbling. Snatching her arm, the soldier dragged her toward him and brought the hilt of his sword down on her back.

Esther not only felt her bone snap, she heard it echo in her ears. She fell forward, her mind slipping away, as all pain in her leg died.

But ... we'd won.

The men laid down their weapons. The few foolish enough to challenge a dragon were no match for the beast. Not all at once, but in gradual pockets, the air was filled with a new chant. A new ideal for the soldiers to aspire to.

"Bravery! Strength! Honor!"

Abner could have wept with relief. *It's done. There's no one left to fight. It's ... done.* His legs crumpled beneath him. He allowed the grief and pain, before dimmed by urgency, to claim his focus. A cough sharpened his attention.

He turned to the two bodies, piled together beneath smoldering planks cast off by the fire.

Petra's shoulders shook beneath the rubble.

The prince tripped forward to pull him out of the wreckage.

"I thought you were dead," Abner said, pushing the young man's hair back from his eyes. The blood seeping through Petra's tunic and Abner's own helplessness gave him enough nervous energy to keep moving.

"Not quite," Petra answered, trying to smile through his grimace. "Give it a moment." His eyes flickered down toward his wound.

"What—" Abner pulled a breath through his nose. "What can I do?"

Petra cried out as Abner's fingers touched the handle of the blade stuck in his side.

"I'm sorry, I'm sorry. I'm not ... not a Healer. I don't know how to help."

"Just a favor, Prince? Agh—" Muscles sprang to view throughout Petra's neck as he struggled to speak through a clenched jaw. "Think of something poetic—maybe heroic—to tell her I said in the end. I can't think. It—" he swallowed. "It hurts."

"No, you'll be fine." Abner nodded. "You'll spend the next hundred years thinking of something."

Petra laughed, drawing a ragged cough from his chest. He bent forward until the fit ended. "Not even a babe born yesterday has that much time." He let his eyes linger in a slow blink. "At least I'm ... not alone."

A white band fluttered at Abner's elbow.

"Who—where did you come from?"

"I'm one of the king's Healers. The bloodletting's stopped, time for me to clean up what I can of the mess you've all made."

Abner tipped back, allowing him more room. The man was older, just past his prime with gray sneaking in at his temples. He tutted quietly as he peered around the knife in Petra's side.

"How can I help?"

"Water."

"Of course." Abner stumbled, pushing himself to run. The trough lay on the forest side of the outpost, probably used for livestock during the hot months. He only hoped it hadn't all baked away in the days since the last rain, or been blown to bits with the rest of the town. He raced back to them with the dripping cloth sack holding all the water he could scoop. "I got it from an animal trough," Abner explained, handing it to the Healer. "Is that alright?"

"Yes, it's fine. Water just needs to be wet to wash the wound." His fingers flicked away a bug from the liquid.

"Right, of course."

Petra screamed as the knife was drawn out of his side, falling back unconscious. His wound was splashed clean, the blood quickly filling the space again.

Abner shook his shoulder. "Petra!"

"Calm yourself, he'll be fine." The Healer threaded a needle faster than Alberon's best seamstress and began to stitch Petra's flesh as if it were cloth.

"He will?"

"Of course," the Healer said, pulling the thread tighter so the two sides of skin met. "I'm here."

Abner stared at his hands as they worked. The Healer moved on to the next wound. "How did you learn to do this?"

"There's an academy to the south. Master Byron teaches this technique, I studied under him for two years." He tied it off, cutting the thread with a knife.

"Wait, but—" Abner held out a hand as the Healer stood, gesturing to Petra.

"He's had all the help I can give him. Others need me." He went to look at Dennison, assuring himself of the steady breath from the captain before moving on, muttering about burn care.

The dragon launched into the air again, startling Abner with its sudden departure. It angled over the forests to the east. The battle was done. The dragon was gone. It was over.

What do I do now?

XXXVI

Lydia.

It shone like a blinding beacon as Abner and his company marched toward it. The soldiers were in their units again, most of the captains dead. The people went home. The city greeted them as glorified conquerors. Abner let the ribbons cast from the women leaning from windows above flutter past him, his mind set on a wagon which thundered behind.

At the castle, an area for the injured was organized in the throne room for those well enough to travel but still needing care. Abner's side was seen to. He had a gash that he hadn't noticed in the mess of the battle but every bump in the road on the journey from Shiloh had sent his teeth gritting together. He ignored the other cuts and bruises lining his body, pushing away the Healer's dabbing cloths. *I've had worse. Probably.*

Tessa mumbled in her sleep.

Abner spent a day by her cot, waving off the requests of the nobles to meet with him as he waited for her to wake.

Finally, Cantus himself came to get him. "They're hounding me now." He faced Abner with folded arms. "You've won your throne. Now it's time to rule."

Abner sighed.

He left instructions with a servant to find him if Tessa stirred and followed Cantus through the halls to the old meeting room coated with dust and blocked by a black, silver-studded door.

Abner took the available seat, surrounded by old, white beards. A few he recognized, but he hadn't paid enough attention growing up to remember their names. Cantus took his place at Abner's shoulder.

"Abner," an old beard rose. "We can appreciate the service you have done for Alberon. Your father was becoming a difficult man to predict. His weak will sent us in a direction of vulnerability that we could not—"

"Do you have a point?" Abner interrupted. The old noble's words stirred his anger as the man not worth grieving still hung heavy on his mind. "I suggest you find it."

"We have conferred and agreed. As the noble houses of Alberon, we deem a change is necessary."

Abner spread his hands with a scoff.

"You will not be king, Abner."

"I'm sorry?" Abner sat back in his chair. "Who then? Or do you plan to set up some new way among yourselves? No king? That would invite chaos."

"Agreed. There should be a king. Just not one of your line."

"Who?"

Their eyes drifted above Abner and he turned.

Cantus blinked at them. "What are you saying?"

"It is time the noble houses had power. Enough of these foreigners dictating to us. You, my Lord Cantus, are heir to Hildren House. The last male heir of the nobility young enough to marry and secure succession. You shall be crowned king." His age-grayed eyes fell back to Abner. He allowed his wrinkle-lined mouth to curve into a cold smile. "You may leave here as Abner, free to disappear, or the doomed prince in chains. The choice is yours."

Abner's mind buzzed. The wood table beneath his fingertips did not feel real. He dug his nail into the grain. "I know exactly how much power you and your house guards hold. Let's not waste time with empty threats." Abner stood and faced Cantus.

The soldier's brow was deeply furrowed, as if he had trouble comprehending the moment. "Abner I," he swallowed, eyes to the ground. "You have to believe ... I had no idea."

"Of course you didn't."

"I can step aside."

"You shouldn't."

Cantus met his eyes.

"I've never met a man more willing to do whatever is needed to protect those he cares for. You will be a good king." Abner smiled, clapping him on the shoulder. "A better one than me. The people rallied to you. You drove us to the mountain. This is the way it should be." Abner dropped his voice. "Just watch your flank. These men aren't doing this out of kindness to you. They seek advantage."

Cantus nodded. "Where will you go?"

Abner paused at the door.

"Probably going to shovel horse muck somewhere?" Cantus' mouth twitched into a grin.

Abner's eyes sparked, a new future forming in his mind. "I've got some ideas."

"All hail King Cantus!" chorused the voices behind, "All hail Hildren House!"

He left Cantus in the snake nest, knowing the soldier could handle them.

I can't move my legs. Esther kept her eyes closed, trying to understand the statement. *I can't move.* In a way she was relieved, no longer waiting for the bump or bruise that would end her life. It did not lurk in the shadows, watching for its moment to pounce. It was here. She found it strangely easier to deal with this new reality rather than continue to be driven mad by uncertainty.

"You have such long hair," Ava's voice said and Esther peeked open her eyes. Ava's fingers twisted a quick braid to lie against Petra's ear. "Almost like a girl's."

"Oh?" Petra murmured, his mouth pulling into a one-sided smile as he twisted the tool in the unpickable lock. "Is that your way of saying I should cut it?"

"Not on your life," Ava said, grinning. "Just a warning. Expect to wake up some mornings with it pinned and curled to perfection."

Petra's smile widened, his brow rose.

A comfortable, companionable silence resumed.

His side was wrapped in a bandage. Brown blankets and a white sheet spilled from his raised cot to brush the stone beneath. Under his head was a sack of grain to prop him up.

Esther's eyes skipped across the room and over the columns. A passing Healer's footsteps echoed off the cold stone. She knew this place. The throne room of the castle.

Petra bit his lower lip as his tool bent, slipping deeper into the lock.

Ava's hand froze. "Is that—"

The tool broke. He cursed.

"It's okay," Ava put a hand on his shoulder. "You'll get it eventually. My master lock picker." She kissed him and he smiled. "Your lips are so warm."

His chuckle as she leaned away was overtaken by a deep, wet cough. He turned from Ava, pushing himself over the side of his cot. Petra pulled the air from his chest as if it were being dragged through mud.

"Are you okay? H–Healer!" Ava's fingers pressed white into Petra's shoulder.

The fit ended, Petra's hand moving to cover the red and yellow stain with a length of clean brown blanket. "Fine, I'm fine," Petra said, meeting Esther's eyes as he surreptitiously wiped his mouth.

Ava's brow gained a dozen wrinkles.

Petra smiled at her. "Look who decided to rejoin the land of the living. Finally."

Esther's eyes widened as they both turned to her.

"Tessa!" Ava said, rising from Petra's side and rushing to her. "Thank the stars! You're awake!"

A servant glanced at them, tossing the stack of blankets she carried on an empty cot before trotting out of the hall.

Petra gave Esther a subtle nod, sinking back against the sack of grain. He let the weight of his smile go, exhaustion pulling his face slack, his limbs drooping behind Ava's back.

"Where…" Esther's voice rasped. *What if he's gone?*

"We're in the castle, in Lydia. You were given something to sleep until we got here since we couldn't do much for the injured in Shiloh. But don't worry, we won. It's a long story, the king is dead, Dennison is in prison, and the soldiers surrendered."

"The dragon?"

Ava nodded. "Klessen's gone back to the mountain."

"And Ab—" she swallowed.

"Abner's alive," Petra said.

"What happened?"

"A slash to his side. He, at least, is able to move while he heals."

Ava shot him a look. "Maybe they would let you if you didn't keep trying to sneak off."

"Well until you got here I was just so bored," Petra smiled at her, and Esther had to study his profile to see the strain. "Had to make a little bit of trouble."

"And now that I am here?" Ava perched on the side of Petra's cot.

"Have I tried to leave?"

Ava narrowed her eyes. "We'll see."

Abner chose this moment to arrive, bursting through the door so suddenly that Esther's arms gripped the side of her cot. His eyes found hers. He smiled. Sinking to a knee beside her, he touched her hand. "Will you come with me?"

"I can't walk."

"I'll carry you. I would have been back sooner, but I had some preparations to make."

Right. King Abner. Probably shouldn't let him carry me. Abner gently lifted the blankets off of her, ignoring her mumbled protests, and Esther's eyes followed the trail of pink sores from the back of her knee to the side of her ankle as he slowly raised her to sit. Ava adjusted Esther's clothes.

She bit back a scream as he lifted her. The dead weight hanging from her hips felt as if her legs were stretched stiff, extended and locked. They were going to break. It was worse than being carried before. She would rather the throb of pain down her legs than this terror of shattering at the wrong touch.

A carriage waited in the courtyard. Abner settled himself onto the seat next to her, an arm around her shoulders to keep her tucked into his side, as the carriage began its jolting descent through the city of Lydia. The sun was warm. The steady drum of Abner's heart beneath her ear comforted her to doze.

She didn't open her eyes again until salty air stung her throat and the carriage lurched to a stop.

"Where are we?" Esther blinked as waves hit with a spray of white foam against the warm, golden shore. Birds overhead called to one another, and the waves stirred up more of the salty smell.

It's so wild. Beautiful.

"That," Abner said, exiting the carriage and reaching in for her. "Is the Merdian Sea. We're just outside of Lydia. You can even see the castle from the shore."

The roar of the water rolling up to kiss the land made Esther forget to breathe.

Abner winced as he settled her weight into his arms.

Esther frowned. "Are you alright? Maybe you shouldn't—"

"I've never been better," Abner said, tightening his grip on her back. "Come on. We're going for a swim."

"What?" Esther screeched as Abner began to jog toward the water. "But—Abner!"

His booted feet crashed into the white foam as he strode forward. He let her legs slip down into the water but kept a tight grip on her waist as it grew deeper around them. Esther at first clung with both hands to his shoulder, but her fingers gradually relaxed as Abner stopped charging forward and let them sway together in the chilly, waist high water. One hand slipped down to sail across the surface, and Esther smiled as it rose and fell over a little wave that worked to gain enough force to break. It felt good to feel, even though her legs swayed as mere weighted flesh beneath her, the biting cold hitting the middle of her back.

"I ... how to begin?" Abner hesitated. Swallowing, he turned to study her. "I'm leaving. I'd like you to come with me."

"Leaving?" Esther's brow creased. "Where?"

"There's an academy to the south. A place that trains Healers. Master Byron teaches there and I intend to study under him."

Esther leaned away. "You ... want to be a Healer?"

Abner nodded.

"But you can't. Abner, you can't just—" she paused, forcing deep breaths through her chest. "You're the king."

"No," he said, "I'm not. It's not been announced yet, but the nobles are supporting Cantus for king. It would be safer for all involved if I didn't stay to skulk around."

"But..." Esther's voice died away.

"And thank the stars they did!" Abner grinned, drawing Esther's stare. "What? I'm relieved." He laughed, forehead dipping toward hers. "I am not King. I never have to be King. I'm free to be Abner, just Abner. I'll be able to do something, to actually help. I've decided to be a Healer. Will you come with me?"

Esther opened her mouth, unsure what she was going to say before her voice spoke. "No."

Abner's smile died, his brow creasing. "No?"

Esther nodded, more firmly. "No."

He swallowed hard through a knotted jaw. "Am I allowed to know why?"

"If you're not going to be King," she hesitated, "then you have your whole life open to you. You can go anywhere. Be anything. You shouldn't start by strapping a useless anvil of weight to your neck."

"You're not useless." He took her cheek in his hand.

She closed her eyes, warmth spilling from his palm.

"You're hurt, and that's okay. I know there's other things we'll have to overcome, and I'm not expecting—we can figure out how to live with it, together."

Esther shook her head.

"Why don't you let me decide what I am willing to do for you, rather than telling me how much I'm allowed to care?"

"Because you're not thinking straight. You're happy about the news and that's making you—"

"If I were crowned king, I would be asking you to be my queen."

Esther blinked. "That's ridiculous."

"I don't care." Abner shook his head. "I don't care that it would miss me an opportunity to gain an ally or strengthen my position with the nobility here. I don't care who they'd pick for me. It's you. I think I've developed a taste that won't be satisfied by anyone else. You come with me or I go alone. I won't force you, choose what you want, but don't base it on what you think I should do."

A gull called above, drawing Esther's eyes to the sky as it glided on the wind. The waves broke warm against her back as she returned Abner's gaze.

"When do we leave?"

He kissed her.

Over the land of Alberon a crisp wind blew. It carried a gull away from the two who clung to one another, up along the cliffside in a great swell of air. The bird alighted to rest on the single window of a tower which stretched to touch the setting sun. From between the bars of a cage inside came a heavy, slow breath. Ragged. Pained. A key dragged through the rusty lock.

"My Lord Captain Dennison," said the young man from behind his stooped form on the floor.

The captain did not turn, squinting his one working eye at the wall.

"We are ready. Everything's been prepared, just as you said. We can set sail for Keldeema as soon as the sun sets. And I've just heard the prince is not taking the throne. It's to be King Cantus instead."

He sighed, a dark eye flickering to the window as the clouds became streaked with red. "That's match, son."

FIN

THE MOUNTAIN SONG

Out of the void, dark and grim,
A lone mountain rose within,
A spark, a breath, in the hollow womb,
Burst light to dispel the gloom.

First to emerge, armored scales,
Bent the neck, swept the tail,
From their breath a spark arose,
Lighting Heavens, Above, and Below.

Man was made and quickly left,
Safety at the mountain's breast,
Power they sought, Death they won
Glory—the highest—to become.

Now the barred cage rises high,
Stone giants to greet the sky,
Seekers sent though none return,
The mountain's mysteries set to learn.

Guard thy heart, thy eyes, thy mind,
There are things not meant to find,
Sparks of fire, pages dire,
Then nothing more to transpire.

About the Author

K. M. Evans is a writer of character-driven epic fantasy from her home in North Dakota, where she lives with her husband, two children, and two dogs.

Like Our Enemies is her debut novel.

Connect with her online:
Instagram: @k.m.evans_author

www.ingramcontent.com/pod-product-compliance
Lightning Source LLC
LaVergne TN
LVHW040037080526
838202LV00045B/3370